**A half hour later, Nicki and Julian returned to their suite. Tired yet exhilarated after the whirlwind day, she hopped over to the bed and fell back on it.**

"Julian!"

"Yes, baby."

"Get over here."

He walked over and sat on the bed, reached down and untied his shoes before crawling on the bed beside her. "Yes, my love."

"Have I told you lately that I love you?"

"I don't remember hearing that lately, no."

"Well, I do. You are amazing. I don't know how you pulled this trip together so quickly, but I can't thank you enough. I've never had an experience like this in my entire life. You made me feel like a princess in a fairy tale."

She wrapped her arms around his neck, pulled his lips toward hers. "Thank you." The first kiss was light, wispy, cushy lips brushing against each other like a whispered promise.

Dear Reader,

This letter is bittersweet, as it's for the last story in the Drakes of California series. As you've gotten to know them, you've gotten to know me better, as well. Many of the career choices, locations and story lines were inspired by experiences in my life. Living in Temecula sparked my love for wine country and the southern Drakes' vineyard and spa. Having grandparents who lived on a large farm in the South made it easy for me to hear the elder Drake voices and convey their love for the land. Griff, the old codger and horse lover in *Solid Gold Seduction*, was patterned after my grandfather, my dear Papa Nash. All of those years spent visiting him and my grandmother Amanda—whom he affectionately called "Pot'na," his partner for life—gave me an appreciation for country living.

I equally love bright lights, big city and New York is one of my favorites. Like London, I dabbled in the world of fashion. Like Nicki, I once had my sights set on Broadway. Like the women in this series, I dreamed of life with a man who embodied the kinds of qualities that make the Drake men so desirable. It is fitting that while bringing you Julian's story, my dream came true. Life imitated art. I got my real-life hero and am headed for my own happily-ever-after. In a sense, it all feels like Divine Order. I couldn't have written a better ending.

*Zuri Day*

# DECADENT
*Desire*

# ZURI DAY

**H**ARLEQUIN® KIMANI™ ROMANCE

Recycling programs
for this product may
not exist in your area.

ISBN-13: 978-0-373-86523-9

Decadent Desire

For questions and comments about the quality of this book please contact us
at CustomerService@Harlequin.com.

Printed in U.S.A.

**Zuri Day** is the national bestselling author of almost two dozen novels, including the popular Drakes of California series. Her books have earned her a coveted *Publishers Weekly* starred review and a Top Ten Pick out of all the romances featured in *PW* Spring 2014. Day is a winner of EMMA and AALAS (African American Literary Awards Show) Best Romance Awards, among others, and a multiple *RT Book Reviews* Best Multicultural Fiction finalist. Drakes of California book six, *Crystal Caress*, was voted Book of the Year and garnered her yet another EMMA Award in 2016. Her work has been featured in several national publications including *RT Book Reviews*, *Publishers Weekly*, *Sheen*, *Juicy* and *USA TODAY*. She loves interacting with her fans, the DayDreamers, and when she sees them in person gives out free hugs! Contact her and find out more at zuriday.com.

### Books by Zuri Day

#### Harlequin Kimani Romance

*Diamond Dreams*
*Champagne Kisses*
*Platinum Promises*
*Solid Gold Seduction*
*Secret Silver Linings*
*Crystal Caress*
*Silken Embrace*
*Sapphire Attraction*
*Lavish Loving*
*Decadent Desire*

Visit the Author Profile page
at Harlequin.com for more titles.

For Gabriel Ken Robinson, my real-life hero.

## Acknowledgments

I am blessed to work with Glenda Howard, who has made bringing the Drakes of California to life a total joy. Love you! The ever-supportive, classy Shannon Criss. You rock! Keyla Hernandez, amid a slew of story lines and schedules, you help keep me organized. Thanks bunches! The devil is in the details and copy editors edit the hell out of a manuscript. LOL. Thanks for being great at what you do. To the Kimani family, especially Nicki Night, Sheryl Lister, Wayne Jordan, A.C. Arthur, Deborah Mello, Cheris Hodges, Patricia Sargeant, Sherelle Green and Martha Kennerson. Y'all make my heart happy. Write on! To the romance queens, the BJs: Brenda Jackson and Beverly Jenkins. Thank you…for everything. To the DayDreamers, my wonderful readers, who have grown to love the Drake family as much as I do. I'll love you forever and appreciate your support. Remember…don't quit your daydream!

# Chapter 1

Anyone passing by Walter and Claire Drake's vast farm property in the Louisiana countryside just east of New Orleans would have thought a public festival was in full swing. Or maybe that a mini carnival had been set up for the Fourth of July holiday. A few excited would-be patrons had, in fact, been turned away from the private event by security manning the gated entrance.

Only those related to or invited by a Drake family member could attend the family's twenty-fifth biennial reunion, where descendants of former slaves and the owners who held them came together to honor their shared heritage and the enduring legacy of friendship between the slave Nicodemus Drake and his owner, Pierre. The story that forever bonded them had been passed down for generations.

The two men had grown up together, more like brothers than anything else. While making the journey to relocate from New Orleans to California, Pierre had fallen ill. Nicodemus's knowledge of herbal remedies and holistic healing had saved his life. Pierre was forever indebted to Nicodemus. In his will, Pierre deeded over to his lifelong friend more than a hundred acres of pristine land in tony Temecula, California—Southern California's wine country. He'd also stipulated that upon his death, Nicodemus and his immediate family would be given their freedom. This indeed occurred, and while the families dispersed across the United States—including Nicodemus's son who settled in Northern California—the ties that bound them, black and white alike, remained strong. In 1967, amid social unrest and war protests, Walter's grandparents had joined with Pierre's side of the family and held the first Drake reunion. Fifty years later, they still reunited every two years—bigger and stronger than ever.

Julian Drake, the youngest son of the fourth-generation Northern California clan, sat among a group of his relatives in the large, cool tent that was centered among colorful bounce houses, carnival rides and games. They were being entertained by a group of brothers and cousins going up against wives and girlfriends in a friendly yet competitive game of *Family Feud*. As often was the case, Julian sat quiet, contemplative, taking in everything going on around him. He'd been this way since childhood—his brothers loud and boisterous, Julian observant. Saying nothing, and missing nothing, either. So much so that during a visit to Louisiana his mother, Jennifer, had voiced her concern to his grandmother Claire.

"Almost eighteen months and still not talking," Jennifer had whispered, afraid to say the words out loud.

Claire had given Jennifer's hand a reassuring pat. "Don't worry none about that child. He's a special one. Not in that way," she'd quickly added when Jennifer's eyes grew wide. "Not that we would love him any less if that's the case. But I mean special as in gifted, maybe even like Nicodemus, as I am told, able to see into the future. Don't worry. He'll talk when he's ready, and when he does, he'll have something meaningful to say."

Claire had been right. Two months later Julian uttered his first words, a complete sentence, to his next-oldest brother, Terrell. Julian had been reading a book. Terrell wanted to play a game. Julian had looked up and pointedly demanded, "Leave me alone."

Jennifer had breathed a sigh of relief. His interactions with siblings and friends gradually increased. But to this day, he was still mostly a man of few words. Although when spoken, his statements usually had value.

Terrell was the exact opposite. He was a talkative extrovert who commanded attention everywhere he went and was the perfect host for these rounds of family fun.

"Next question," Terrell said, holding up a card while standing between his cousin Diamond and her husband, Jackson, whose hands were poised below bright red cowbells that served as buzzers.

"Name a side—"

Jackson clanged his bell. "Patricia!"

Men groaned. Women laughed. Julian smiled.

Terrell placed a hand on Jackson's shoulder. "The question is about a side dish, dude, not a side piece."

Jackson feigned shock. "What kind of man do you think I am? I thought you were going to say side*kick*." He winked at Julian.

"Who's Patricia?" Diamond crossed her arms in mock anger.

"Who cares?" Faye, the wife of Julian's cousin Dexter, asked. "Finish the question so Diamond can answer and we can win the game!"

Julian studied Faye's serious expression. She looked as if she were preparing to treat a patient rather than watch the ladies take a round of *Family Feud*. He hadn't gotten the chance to know her well but felt a shared camaraderie with the doctor, even though her title was MD instead of PsyD. In their last conversation, he'd discovered her heart for the less fortunate and had promised that once his internship ended and he started up his private practice, he'd offer monthly free counseling sessions at her clinic in San Diego. Since then he'd talked with his mother and decided to do the same on a more regular basis at the community center his family had built in their hometown. Every member of the family contributed in some way, including Terrell's twin sister, Teresa, who along with Faye and two women from Pierre's side of the family were now laughing and high-fiving at the women having beaten the men.

All of the couples were well matched, he reasoned, observing their effortless interactions. Even those with opposite personalities, like Faye and Dexter, who was as easygoing and extroverted as she was serious and subdued. Their dynamics reminded him of his own relationship. Nicki Long, his on-again, off-again girlfriend since college, was a private but sociable butterfly and professional dancer who fluttered seamlessly and graciously throughout life both on and off the stage. Watching the other couples made him miss her even more than he had since moving back to Paradise Cove three months ago.

Dexter walked by Julian and bopped him on the head. "Thanks a lot, genius!"

A nickname, but also the truth. Julian's IQ was near genius level—part of the being special his grandmother Claire had alluded to when he was a babe.

"For what? I wasn't even playing."

"That's his point," Terrell deadpanned, taking a seat beside Julian. "We needed that sharp mind of yours to best those conniving women. Now we're going to have to endure their endless ribbing for the next two years. All because of you!"

"No, because of Jackson and his sidekicks."

"Don't put all the blame on me." Jackson was more than ready to defend himself. He looked pointedly at Terrell. "I'm not the one who named sparrow as a bird that people eat."

"Hey." Terrell shrugged. "Chicken, turkey and duck had already been mentioned. Those are the only ones I…" His voice trailed off as he looked beyond Julian. "Is that who I think it is?"

Jackson looked up. "Who do you think it is?"

"Julian, isn't that your girl?"

Julian turned his head in the direction Terrell and Jackson were focused.

Nicki? He slowly rose from the chair as a tall, fit woman wearing a bright yellow maxi and a devilish smile walked toward him. She was with his youngest sister, London, who, given the look on her face, had obviously been in on the surprise.

He held out his arms to wrap her in a hug. "What are you doing here?"

"Milo decided to let us enjoy the holiday after all."

"The same director who works y'all for twelve hours a day, the one you questioned had a heart?"

"Yep. Guess there's something beating in there besides a drum after all. I texted London to surprise you and caught the first plane out."

"Surprised?" London asked, her smile widening.

"Delighted." His eyes drank in Nicki like a parched man guzzling water. "Let me take you around to meet everybody. Are you hungry? Can I get you a drink?"

Nicki laughed. "Okay, yes and yes."

"Hey, Nicki!"

"Hello, Terrell." She accepted his hug.

"You remember Atka, Teresa's husband."

"Of course. My mom still raves about your company's salmon that I had shipped to her house."

"And my cousin Jackson."

Nicki waved. "Hello."

Both were actually in-laws, but the Drakes disregarded that fact. Family was family. After going around to those nearby, Julian reached for Nicki's hand and headed toward the food tent. "We'll say hi to my parents and then get something to eat. You look beautiful, by the way."

"Thank you."

"You feel good, too. In fact—" he pulled her closer "—why don't we make our plates to go and find a more private place to…enjoy the meal?"

"Are we still talking about food?" she teased.

"Definitely not."

"Ha!"

Exactly thirty-nine minutes later, Julian and Nicki had successfully and surreptitiously left the farm, driven to a four-star hotel and checked in. Here, within the confines of a single room with a king bed, the quiet, studious doctor showed the wilder, passionate side that few would imagine. The door had barely closed when he reached for the hem of Nicki's maxi and backed her up to the bed.

"Julian, wait!"

"Shh. No talking."

They collapsed on the bed. Julian planted several kisses across Nicki's face before plunging his tongue into her mouth, his hungry, scalding kiss outmatched only by an ever-hardening shaft grinding against her thigh for proof of his ardent desire. He broke the kiss and tugged at her dress. She lifted her hips enough to free the unwanted material from beneath her body, then pulled the dress up and over her head and tossed it to the floor. His shirt quickly followed. Then pants, bra and undies. Julian groaned and delivered another hot kiss before his mouth left hers and went on a journey along the skin he'd missed immensely since Nicki's last visit to Paradise Cove over a month ago. He nibbled the sensitive area by her collarbone before inching down to modest breasts, pulling a hardened nipple into his mouth even as his hand traveled lower to Nicki's shaved treasure. He slid a finger along lips already creamy and teased her pearl with his fingertip even as his tongue caressed her other nipple.

"Ah!"

Her cry of pleasure made him smile as he continued to cherish every inch of her body with the same focus and attention to detail that he applied in professional life. Positioning himself between her legs, he scooted farther down, planted kisses on her pelvis, down her inner thighs, his tongue on a languid journey down the length of a leg solid and defined from years of lessons in tap, modern and jazz. She pulled her legs up and away from him, parted them in a perfect inverted split in the air. Her exposed, rock-hard pearl sent a clear message of what she wanted next.

He got the memo and without hesitation drew the nub into his mouth and then plunged his tongue inside her. Swirling, tickling, licking her joy trail as though it were chocolate ice cream. She ground herself against him. Short bursts of breath hinting of her impending climax. Just as she erupted, he replaced his tongue with several inches of hard passion and continued loving her.

Julian wasn't a dancer, but one couldn't tell. A disciplined workout regimen and martial arts training kept his six-foot-one-inch frame in shape, ready for several rounds of lovemaking. Finally, after Nicki's third orgasm, he gave in to his own shuddering release. A thin sheen of perspiration covered them both as he folded back the flowered spread, pulled away the cool white top sheet and covered them.

"See how much I missed you?" he asked, using his finger to smooth strands of dampened hair behind Nicki's ear.

"I felt how much." Her face was turned away from him, but Julian heard the smile in her voice.

"You sure I can't talk you into leaving New York, moving to the West Coast and ending this notion of a long-distance relationship? I can't see not having you, not having this—" he caressed her booty "—on a regular basis. Can you?"

Nicki turned to face him. "I almost died this month without having you around to do what you do, and very well, I might add. Of course I want to be with you. But you know I can't. I'm not the lead in this show, but it is Broadway. When are you coming to see the show?"

"I don't know, but I'd love to be there opening night. When does it start?"

"Next month."

"August? Isn't that unusual?"

"It's rare. Most shows open during the fall. We're hoping that being one of the few new shows next month will translate into a strong box office showing. What about you? Ready to open for business?"

"I already have a few clients. The office will open in two to three weeks, depending on how quickly I can hire an assistant. Mom worked with an interior designer friend to create the type of environment I want—professional and relaxing at the same time. It'll be finished by the time I get back in town."

"From here?"

"No, from Chicago. I fly there for a conference that begins on Wednesday."

"Office up and running, clients on the schedule. Sounds like the transition from intern to private practice was easy."

"There were challenges."

"Obviously none you couldn't handle."

He smiled, swiped the tip of her nose. "What's your point?"

"The point is that you can make opening night, maybe even bring some of your family along. It's going to be a great show. The Rapunzel fairy tale has been done before, but never like this."

"With Rapunzel rapping her lines? I think not. Bet those DJs in the '70s talking over beats had no idea what a revolution in music they were creating, a style that would end up on Broadway and take over the music world."

"The genre has definitely outlasted its critics. The show involves hip-hop, jazz, even country. It will appeal to a wide audience, which is why I think the chances of *A Hair's Tale* succeeding on Broadway are very good. It's a limited run right now. Only sixteen weeks. But if it remains as popular as it is now, the show can get extended indefinitely. Have an unbelievable run, like *The Lion King*, *Phantom* and *Cats*. As long as it's on Broadway, I want to be playing my role!"

"You're dramatic." A caress suggested it was a part of her that he enjoyed. "I'll tell them about it, see if they want to join me."

Nicki turned, her gaze loving as she took a finger and outlined Julian's thick brows, his aquiline nose and Cupid's bow lips. "Thank you, Doctor," she whispered.

"You're welcome, my private dancer," he cooed, brushing his hand across her long, silky tresses before pulling her into his arms, kissing her deeply and silently vowing to find a way to permanently shorten the distance between them.

# Chapter 2

*Julian Drake, PsyD.* A bit pretentious, Julian thought as he stopped and observed the gold-and-platinum name plaque on the door of his practice. His mother had purchased and mounted it as a welcome-home surprise, along with the office suite they'd given him for earning his psychology doctorate earlier than most and breezing through an eighteen-month internship with ease.

He appreciated the gesture, even though the nameplate wasn't his style at all. A plain black plastic slider with white lettering would have been fine with him, and the office suite had a few more rooms than he needed. Especially now while just getting started. His parents, Ike and Jennifer, were understandably proud, and ecstatic that he'd decided to open his practice in Paradise Cove instead of on the East Coast as Nicki had wanted. That she hadn't joined him was a disappointment for his family and devastating for him. His family loved Nicki. Her tomboyish ways with his brothers helped her fit right in, and her knack for style with a bohemian edge, along with being a professional dancer, made for a lot in common with his sisters. Jennifer had even approached Nicki with the idea of periodic dance workshops at the Drake Community Center. As much as he'd wanted it, Julian knew the chances of Nicki relocating with him was a long shot. After she got a major role in a Broadway show, he knew there was no shot at all. The entertainment world was all abuzz about the talented young writer who'd created the show and the composer who'd scored the work. His sister had even heard about it. When Julian told London about Nicki's invitation, she'd excitedly asked to join him, but the preview shows were sold out.

Julian was eager to get his practice up and running. The busier he was, the less time he'd have to think about how much he missed Nicki.

His cell phone vibrated. Had he thought her up? Retrieving it from his jacket pocket, he unlocked the door while answering the call.

"Dr. Drake." He hit the speaker button and continued through the reception area to the spacious corner office he occupied.

"Yes, Doctor. This is Natalie Moore from Superior Staffing. You left a message with our service last night requesting a call."

Julian immediately recognized the voice. "Natalie as in the Nat Pack?"

A short pause and then, "Do I know you?"

"Yes, you do. It's Julian."

"The Julian Drake I picked on all through grade school?"

"I think it lasted through junior high, and yes, it's me."

"No way! And you're a doctor now? Not surprising, since you left all your classmates behind in the dust. You skipped, what, one or two years?"

"More like doubled up on some and tested out of others. They didn't really skip me."

"However it happened, you graduated at sixteen. You'd already been gone a couple months when I found out. I can't believe you remember me."

"Didn't at first. Your married name threw me. But I'll never forget that high-pitched voice."

"And I'll never forget you had no voice at all. Always so quiet. And I'm divorced, by the way. Would have reverted to Johnson, but I have a son. The boy genius Julian, a doctor. That fits you. Will you be working at the urgent-care center that just opened up?"

"I'm a psychologist, not a medical doctor. I'm opening a private practice."

Another pause, this one a bit longer. "Come to give my dad some competition, huh? He's the go-to shrink in this town. Has treated patients here for over thirty years. So good luck with that."

"I have no desire to compete with Dr. Johnson or anyone else. Mental illnesses and behavioral disorders have steadily increased through the years that he's practiced and are still on the rise, which means, unfortunately, there are likely to be enough clients for both of us."

"That's what a couple other doctors thought. One still has an office here, though I heard she teaches at a community college to supplement her income. Guess the one or two people who slipped past my father weren't enough for her to pay the bills."

"Thanks for the encouragement."

"You're welcome."

Julian pondered Natalie's words as he gazed out the window. It was a beautiful day. During the festivities in Louisiana, the mercury had climbed to ninety degrees and above. Too hot for Julian, even for July. Or any other month. He much preferred the seventies experienced during Northern California summers. The office's location on the building's fifteenth floor offered unobstructed views of the town's tony square and the sprawling fields and ranches of Paradise Valley beyond it. His brother Warren owned one of those ranches. He thought how good a horse ride would feel but knew that with the work ahead of him, today wouldn't be when he got to do it.

"Where'd you graduate and do your internship?"

"Graduated from Columbia." Julian walked back to his desk and sat. "Interned in New York."

"Impressive, Doctor. Why'd you decide to come back here?"

Julian looked at his watch. Time to focus on the matter at hand—hiring an assistant. If she was as nosy now as she had been in high school, the Natalie he remembered could keep him on the phone all afternoon.

"Probably the same reason you did, to do business in my hometown. Speaking of which, I assume your call is regarding the information I filled out online?"

"Yes, Superior Staffing is my company, and yes, PC is still a very small town."

They shared a laugh. "Indeed. Will you be able to assist me, considering I'm viewed as your dad's competition?"

"Ha! Dad has probably forgotten more than you'll learn."

"Ouch!"

"Just calling it like I see it. You're no competition for him. As for an assistant, I do have a couple qualified recruits in mind who, based on what I know so far, would be good matches. At least from the online questionnaire that you filled out."

"So how do we proceed? I'd like to get someone hired as quickly as possible."

"Normally I'd set up the first appointment and send them over at your earliest convenience. But since it's you, a friend I've known since grade school, I think a follow-up interview is in order, one done in person so I can be sure to select the most appropriate candidates for the position. What about dinner tomorrow night at Acquired Taste?"

"I'm busy most evenings. How about lunch, around noon?"

"Perfect. See you then."

"And Natalie, no practical jokes, okay? The little kid is all grown up."

"You sure have, and quite nicely. I pulled up your profile online."

"Good. Then I'll be easy to recognize. See you tomorrow."

Julian dodged Natalie's flirty comment. He remembered her popularity in high school and had known several of the guys she'd dated. Pretty girl. Funny, too. He wanted her assistance in finding a competent assistant, but nothing more.

"Another great show, Nicki!"

"Thanks, hon." Nicki hugged Paige, her friend and cast mate. "Had to take it to the next level to shine beside you!"

"That's right, girl! Razzle!"

"Dazzle!" They high-fived. "If these previews are any indication, opening night is going to be huge."

"Is Julian coming?"

"That's the plan. What about Mike?"

"I don't know. He's always working."

"Hmm, the detective sounds like someone else I know."

The two laughed, locking arms as they walked down the dark and narrow backstage hallway to the exit just off Forty-Ninth Street. As usual, a group of theatergoers circled the exit, waiting for a chance to get a snapshot. Maybe even an autograph or a selfie. Most were there for Paige, the famous pop celebrity playing Rapunzel. But a lot of fans loved the best friend added in the modern retelling of the classic fairy tale and waited for Nicki, who played her. Though tired, Nicki obliged them. Countless times, she'd been that fan, waiting for her favorite star. Dying for an autograph. She'd dreamed of being that star since she was ten. And here she was.

Paige turned to her. "Hey, my car's here. Want a ride?"

"Seriously? Of course!"

The driver stood next to the rear car door he'd just

opened. "Good evening, ladies." A nod and smile accompanied the formal greeting.

"Joe, this is Nicki. Nicki, Joe."

"Hello, Joe."

They slid into the back seat of a roomy town car. Nicki rubbed her hand across the soft leather seat. "Is this one of the perks of being the star?"

"Thanks to my agent. I wouldn't have thought to request it on my own."

Nicki settled against the seat and sighed. "Lifestyles of the rich and famous."

Paige leaned forward toward a panel of buttons and raised the privacy partition.

"Ooh, fancy! Just like in the movies."

"I thought you'd like it. But I put it up because you had something to tell me."

The reminder sat Nicki straight up. "Oh my gosh, girl, you won't believe it. And I'm telling you right now. This can't be repeated. If I hear it back, I'll know where to come."

"Don't you know you can trust me by now?"

Nicki did. The entertainment business was cutthroat. Jobs on Broadway were limited. Competition was fierce and few made friends, Nicki included. Paige had been the exception. The two had met while doing regional theater, ironically both having boy troubles at the time. They commiserated and eventually met each other's boyfriends—Julian and Mike. Shortly after the play ended, Paige moved to New York. They'd been besties ever since.

"Remember a couple years ago when Julian and I broke up?"

"Like the for-real breakup, because you turned down his marriage proposal and broke the guy's heart? Yep, I remember."

"Dang, Paige, did you have to say it like that?"

"To clarify which off-and-on we were talking about? Yes, I did. Besides, isn't that what happened?"

"Anyway…remember my rebound guy, the pro basketball player?" Nicki placed air quotes around his title.

"Told you that he played pro ball, left out that he hadn't had a contract in years?"

"I still can't believe I didn't google his ass."

Nicki paused and looked out the window. A mental replay of meeting Vince Edwards played in her mind.

Late-night party uptown. Private. Rooftop. Being beautiful seemed the price of admission. A stranger approached while she sipped a drink. Introduced himself as Vince Edwards, a pro basketball player. He'd sure looked the part. Tall, attractive. Muscles and dimples in all the right places, with enough raw manly swagger to bottle and sell. When they hugged she got goose bumps, but along with the excitement came a foreboding feeling. She ignored it and gave him her number.

A couple of weeks into the romantic whirlwind, behaviors began to surface that had reminded Nicki of her earlier apprehensiveness. The first was declaring his love for her a week after they met. The second was falling in love with her brownstone that—number three—he wanted to move into after the second week. Nicki saw more red flags after this request than those waved in Arrowhead Stadium at a Chiefs football game. But she'd continued to date him. Until the fourth reason—a woman named Brittany. The woman with whom he currently lived. The woman who'd threatened to kick him out for cheating, and not just with Nicki. In a calm, almost pleasant voice, the astute stranger had passed along a few pertinent details Vince had not shared. Multiple children. Gambling habit. No new sports contract or endorsement deals. Nicki thanked the woman and meant it. Got back with Julian a short time later, thankful she'd dodged a bullet.

"I thought you blocked his number."

"I did. A call came up private. I answered it without a second thought."

"What did he want?"

"Nothing much. Just wondered if I had twenty thousand dollars to loan him."

Paige screeched. "WTF?"

"Oh, and he needs it by Friday. Can you believe it?"

"How'd he figure you had that kind of money?"

"I guess because I'm on a Broadway stage."

"Even so, why'd he think you'd loan it to him?"

"That's where it really gets crazy. He's taking credit for the show I did in Atlanta shortly after we broke up. Says he pulled the strings that got me the job."

"Ooh, right! And he showed up backstage claiming y'all were a couple. Wasn't the director his sister or something?"

"Cousin, and it turned out only a distant one at that. He had nothing to do with me getting that job. I auditioned like everyone else. What a liar."

"You guys didn't even date that long. What was it, a month?"

"Barely."

"Jeez. So what did you say when he asked you?"

"What do you think I said? No! Then he had the nerve to ask me out!"

"What was your answer?" Paige asked, laughing.

"Hell no!"

Nicki tried not to laugh but was soon cracking up. Paige always made her feel better.

"Do you think he'll call again?"

"With the size of his ego? I don't doubt it."

They reached Paige's apartment building in trendy

SoHo. The driver dropped Paige off, headed toward the Brooklyn Bridge and twenty minutes later was at Nicki's place, a three-story brownstone that had been converted into two apartments. Hers was the larger one and occupied the two upper floors. It was spacious and airy, with tall ceilings and big windows to let in lots of natural light. Her respite from the grind of the theater district, where she practically lived six days a week.

"Bye, Joe." She blew a kiss to the driver, then opened the gate and hurried up the steps to the second-floor entrance. Within seconds she'd kicked off her shoes and walked to the kitchen in search of something sparkling with a kick. She wasn't much of a drinker, but a wine spritzer after two shows helped her wind down.

"Nothing," she mumbled, looking in the fridge. "Great."

Bypassing the heels she'd just kicked off, Nicki grabbed a pair of sandals from the hallway shoe rack and headed to the corner store that, luckily for her, stayed open until eleven. After picking out her favorite chardonnay and a liter of sparkling water, she headed back home. The street was sparsely populated and quiet, typical for this time on a Wednesday night. As she neared her walk-up, two men got out of a car parked in front. Ever the New Yorker, she was on instant alert but didn't pick up any negative vibes. They talked casually, even laughed as the driver tapped the key fob to lock the car. Nicki relaxed, stepped to the right to walk by them. The driver, to his left. She looked up, expecting a come-on. The man was not laughing. At all.

She took a step in the other direction. The passenger had come from the other side of the car and stood in front of her.

A frustrated sigh gave her the chance to quickly scan the areas behind and beside her. Suddenly the streets were empty. Not another person in sight. *Why didn't I buy groceries on Monday, instead of spending the day on Long*

*Island catching up with friends?* Instead of fifteen dollars and some change, her desire for a sparkling libation could cost a lot more. Her brownstone was only two doors down. If she could just get around them…

Summoning her Brooklyn-born-and-bred attitude, she raised to her full height of five foot eight and looked the man standing in front of her directly in the eye. At the same time, she positioned her house key between her index and middle fingers, ready to puncture a cheek or gouge out an eye.

"Let me by."

"Nicki Long, right?"

Caught entirely off guard, she couldn't hide her surprise. "Who are you?"

"Friends of Vince. Come to get the money you owe him."

Seriously? Vince's ego was bigger than she realized. But if he thought this Brooklyn babe could be intimated, he had another thought coming.

"You have the wrong Nicki. I don't owe Vince a thing." She took a step to go around the guy talking, the one on the right. He stepped, too, in front of her.

"Move," she commanded, now truly more annoyed than angry. "Vince has obviously lied to you, just like he did to me. I hope the promise of money wasn't one of them."

The tall, lanky driver studied his nails, wearing dark shades at almost midnight. "Vince did promise us money, as a matter of fact. From the money you owe him. So now instead of one problem—" he looked at his partner "—you have three."

"Look, I don't owe Vince. And I don't even know you, let alone owe you. You've got the wrong woman." Nicki pushed past him. A steely hand clamped onto her arm. Stopped her in her tracks. She whirled around.

"Let go of me." The driver increased the pressure. It hurt like heck. Her heart thudded erratically. But Nicki forced her features to remain relaxed. She pointedly looked at his hand on her arm and then into his eyes. "I said let. Me. Go."

"Hey, neighbor!"

Nicki's body almost sagged in relief. Miss Frances was an elaborative gossip and a constant snoop, but at this very moment Nicki could have kissed her on the mouth.

"Good evening!" She pushed past the men and walked toward the gate where Miss Frances stood wearing a flowered robe and a sleeping cap over pink foam rollers, her squinted eyes trained on the men now walking toward the car.

"We'll be at the show," the driver said, fake friendly. "Rapunzel," he added, making sure she knew he knew which one.

"We'll be sure to look for you." Nicki turned and watched the passenger taunt her as he opened his car door. "Break a leg."

A shiver ran down Nicki's spine. She turned away. Miss Frances continued to stare at the car as it started up and eased away from the curb.

"QZZ, zero, zero, zero, four."

"Ma'am?"

"The license plate number. Hurry up and write it down."

Nicki repeated the number, impressed that her neighbor had thought to get it. "I'll remember it. Thank you so much, Miss Frances. I don't know what would have happened if you hadn't come out when you did."

"I saw you trying to get past them. When the second one came over and blocked the walk, I figured it was trouble." Miss Frances turned keen eyes on Nicki. "You don't know those men?"

Nicki shook her head. "No."

"They obviously know you, came right to your doorstep. What did they want?"

"They had me confused with somebody else."

"How could that be when they're coming to your show?" Miss Frances's gaze was unflinching. Clearly she was unconvinced.

Nicki was equally convinced that what the two men wanted from her was not only something she wouldn't give, but also something her nosy, overly talkative neighbor didn't need to know.

"Thanks again for coming out to check on me. You more than likely prevented a crime."

"Watching out for each other is what neighbors do."

Nicki gave Miss Frances a quick hug and headed toward her gate.

"Watch yourself," Miss Frances yelled behind her. "Remember, those men said they'd see you tomorrow."

Nicki gave a final wave as she hurried up the steps and into her apartment. There was no need for Miss Frances's reminder. What the men had said—and even more so how they'd said it—was something that Nicki knew she'd never forget.

Once inside she opened the wine, poured a liberal amount into a goblet and took a long drink. She added some sparkling water and climbed the stairs to her bedroom. With each step her heart slowed and her hands shook less. The past several minutes replayed like a video in her mind. Even as it happened, it had felt like a movie. As if it were someone else. After recording the license number on a pad by her bed, she dialed Vince's number. It went to voice mail.

"If what happened tonight happens again, I'm going to the police. I will not be harassed, and I certainly will not be threatened by the likes of you or those fools you sent over tonight. Their actions were recorded. So is this phone call. Leave me alone, Vince Edwards. Goodbye."

She hung up, exhausted. Massaged her tense neck and shoulders. Despite the bravado in her message to Vince, the sinister-looking bullies had left Nicki shaken. She wondered if by chance the store's surveillance camera had picked up those guys accosting her tonight. She made a mental note to check with the owner tomorrow. For now, she wanted to go to sleep and escape a nightmare named Vince.

# Chapter 3

She'd planned to tell no one what happened last night. Especially Paige, because Nicki knew she would worry. But a few days later, while Nicki waited with Paige for the pop star's car to arrive, the words tumbled out.

"If my neighbor hadn't come out when she did," she finished, "I don't know what might have happened. A part of me wants to believe this was just a scare tactic to see if I could be frightened into sending the cash."

Paige's look was doubtful. "And the other part?"

"Really wishes those store cameras could have captured their images so that I'd have concrete evidence of how they harassed me."

"But their car was on the tape?" Nicki nodded. "Then take that along with a statement from your neighbor and file a police report. You can't ignore this, Nicki, or wish it away. I hope that night was the end of it, but if not, you'll want to have everything that happened documented. Do you still have the messages Vince left on your phone?"

"I think so."

"You need to keep all of that, and if he ever calls again, record it. And you need to tell Julian."

"Why would I do that?"

"Because the more people who are aware of what's happening, the better any future case might be. And because he's the man who loves you."

Joe waved as he pulled the car to the curb.

Nicki waved back and turned to walk away.

Paige called after her, "Where are you going? Joe will take you home."

"And get used to such lavish star treatment? I'm fine on the subway."

Paige waved off the comment and walked toward her. "Marry Julian and you'll have your own driver." She lowered her voice. "I know your real reason for preferring the train. To get off the subject of telling Julian what's going on. This business with Vince is out of control. He needs to know about it."

"I'll think about it." Nicki started walking again. Tossed a parting line over her shoulder. "See you mañana."

She headed to the downtown trains, jumping on the Brooklyn-bound number three. Passing a couple empty seats as the car swayed and wove its way through the underground tunnels, she placed a shoulder against a pole with the practiced ease of a native New Yorker, checking emails and reading texts. One was from Julian. He'd wished her *merde*, a dancer's good luck, as he did most nights. Made her think of Paige and the proposal that had happened months before Julian began his internship.

It had been lovely. Lit up on the marquee in the heart of Times Square. He'd gone to one knee, pulled out a telltale blue box and everything. A crowd had gathered, oohed and ahhed. He'd looked so hopeful. But she couldn't say yes. She'd smiled and hugged him excitedly, making the crowd think she accepted so he wouldn't be embarrassed. But later on she broke the truth. New York was her soul, Broadway her goal. That's when he decided they needed a break.

And then Vince happened. She'd heard there'd been no shortage of women vying to claim the spot as Julian's girlfriend that she'd vacated. A couple of them she knew. Word was he hadn't dated, had focused on work. Once they got back together, she found out why and felt even worse about her rebound fling. Her rejection had hurt him as deeply as he loved her, a love so strong that when she reached out to him several months later, he took her back, no problem.

The train reached her stop. It was late. Only one other person got off with her. She walked to the stairs and climbed up them, trying to ignore the fearful thought that the duo she'd started calling Bert and Ernie might be waiting for her. Time for a diversion. It was either that or a panic attack. Pulling out her phone, she called Julian. Contrary to Paige's advice, she would not tell him about what was going on. Julian didn't know about that ill-fated tryst. She intended to keep it that way.

"Hey, babe. Thanks for the encouraging text. Didn't read it until after, but the show was—" Nicki drew in a sharp breath as she watched a dark-colored sedan race toward her. Instinct took over. She ran against the light, chancing a look back as she crossed the street. Caught the first two letters on the license plate as the car zoomed through the intersection and continued on its way. Not after her. Just in a hurry. She remembered the license number Miss Frances had given her. The one she'd just seen wasn't it.

She eased out of the storefront entryway, feeling silly. Paranoid much? She felt someone's gaze and looked up to see an old man watching her intently. Could only imagine how she must have looked, running when no one was chasing her. Hiding from someone that he couldn't see. She looked down and realized the call to Julian was still live. God, no. Had she made a sound? Nicki quickly pushed the end button, praying that somehow in the frenzy a message that would sound weird at best, maybe even frightening, wouldn't go through. Minutes later a text came through. Her prayer had not been answered.

Babe, what's going on? Where are you?

She continued the short distance to her house, formulating an answer on the way. Just inside her home, she dropped her bag and texted back.

Sorry about that. Just wanted to beat the light, that's all.

Nicki continued up the stairs to her bedroom, hoping the casual answer would suffice. After several minutes had passed, she thought it had. She took a shower, washed her hair and slipped into a pair of comfy cotton pj's. Grabbing her phone, she continued downstairs for a cup of chamomile. Julian had called. Left a message and a text. Not only did he not buy her lie, he told her he'd see her on opening night, in person, to find out the truth. Damn, damn, damn!

One week after that text exchange and ten minutes before curtain, the Drake entourage entered the theater and were ushered to the third row in the orchestra's center section. They'd flown in for opening night on a company plane. A limo service met them at the private airstrip, with premium champagne and appetizers for the thirty-minute ride into the theater district. The men debonair, the women beautiful, they commanded the attention of the entire audience. Julian took the center seat. To his right was his oldest brother, Ike Jr., with his wife, Quinn. No question whose decision it was to accept his invitation. Ike, ten years older than his pretty wife, detested hip-hop or any similar sounding music. Or he had, until Quinn came into the picture. Of all Julian's brothers, Ike's temperament most closely matched his own. That the conservative executive who almost slept in a business suit tonight sported a matching shirt and slacks set from their fashion designer brother-in-law Ace Montgomery's collection was proof of how Quinn had relaxed him.

Julian loved observing the laid-back Ike, almost as much as the fact that California's next senator sat on his other side. After serving as mayor of Paradise Cove for several years, another brother, Niko, two years younger than Ike, was on a tireless campaign to represent the Golden State in the next election. He and attorney wife Monique crisscrossed the state tirelessly, so much so that the family staged a mock intervention to force a weekend of rest. The bribe? Tickets to Nicki's sold-out show. A Monday morning meeting with a political think tank had been thrown in also, but Julian chose not to focus on that. His brother was here, relaxed, laughing with Terrell, Julian's next oldest brother, in town with his wife, Aliyah. All in attendance to support his girl.

Their gesture was much appreciated. For almost a decade, his focus had been on getting his PsyD and completing his internship. Everything else had taken a back seat, including Nicki and his family. He blamed that fact on why Nicki turned down his marriage proposal. As for the people around him who shared his name? He hadn't realized how much he'd missed them until just now.

He nudged Ike. "Ready to get the party started?"

"What I'd start would more likely be a mass exit."

"Honey!" Quinn smacked his forearm. "That didn't sound very supportive."

"Hey, I'm here, aren't I?"

"Yes, with a pair of earplugs in your pocket."

Julian leaned forward toward Quinn. "You're kidding, right?" She shook her head. "Bro, really?"

"Guilty as charged."

Julian and Quinn shared a sigh of exasperation. She watched him idly tapping the chair arm with his fingers. "Nervous?"

"Excited."

"When's the last time you saw her perform?"

*New Orleans*, Julian thought with a smile, remembering their secret family reunion getaway. "It's been a while."

"London's going to hate that she missed it."

Niko's wife, Monique, sat next to Quinn. "All London is thinking about is fashion week. She and Ace are busy tightening up next week's show-stopping finale."

Julian's youngest sister, London, was a superstar model, her husband, Ace, a model turned fashion mogul.

"Fashion week is impressive," Quinn said, her eyes sparkling as she eyed the stage. "But this is Broadway."

As if on cue, the lights dimmed.

The stage went completely black. A single drumbeat burst out of the darkness. *Boom cha. Boom cha.* Then several more percussion instruments along with a sequencer delivering an old-school scratch over syncopated beats, building with every note. Lights, like stars, began to flicker everywhere. On stage and off.

A group of dancers appeared, Nicki among them, lithe, graceful, beautiful, twirling and gyrating and skipping across the stage. Julian watched. Focused. Entranced. Her body seemed a mass of barely contained energy mixed with soulful joy and childlike timidity, personifying the young character she portrayed. A bodysuit clung to her like a second skin, the crystals covering it catching the light, mixing with the twinkling orbs around her that made her a star as well. His heart swelled with pride and, but for strong discipline, another body part would have also grown in size. She was beautiful and talented, amazing and perfect. And she was his girl.

The dance ended. For a second no one moved, then as one, the theater erupted in a round of earsplitting applause mixed with whistles and yells. The second song in the act began, a solo by Rapunzel, and ninety minutes later the

audience had to catch their breaths from the wild, exhila-
rating ride on which they'd been taken. Shortly after the
show ended, an assistant came to escort the Drake family backstage.

Behind the door was a crush of sponsors, reporters, ac-
tors and their family members, all vying for space in the
close, humid quarters. Julian spotted Nicki across the room.
She posed with the actor who'd played Rapunzel. Camera
flashes temporarily brightened their drab surroundings.
A dozen conversations happened at once, a din that made
talking at length impossible. He motioned for the others
to follow him. Nicki saw his gesture. She whispered to
Rapunzel, who looked their way and joined Nicki as she
walked over.

Nicki hugged Julian before turning to Paige. "You remember Julian."

"Of course. Hey, handsome!"

"Hey, Paige. Excellent show." They shared a brief hug
and air-kisses.

"And this is part of the Drake family."

"My pleasure to meet everybody." Paige smiled as she
took in the beautiful tableau. "I've heard so much about
all of you."

"All good, I hope," Niko said.

"No, she told me the truth."

Amid the laughter, Nicki introduced Paige to the rest of
the family before leading the way through a narrow, dimly
lit hallway to the door with a star that bore her name. Once
inside, Julian allowed the others to offer their congrats
before once again pulling Nicki into his arms. "You were
amazing, baby."

"You liked it?"

"I loved it."

She pulled away to look at him. "Thanks for the flowers and the champagne. They're wonderful."

"So are you."

Niko stepped up to the couple. "I hate to break up this lovefest, but it's hot as heck in this shoe box. A star like you can't command a larger dressing room?"

"This is a larger one," Nicki deadpanned. "And I'm not a star yet, but thank you. Now get out of here. Give me a few minutes to change, and I'll meet you by the side exit. Except you," she finished, reaching for Julian's hand as the others exited. "You can help me undress."

"I haven't seen you in a month, girl," Julian whispered, running a hand down her back and cupping her butt. "Seeing all that loveliness and not getting a taste will be a pretty tall order."

She wrapped her arms around his neck. Gave him a peck on the lips. "It'll be worth the wait."

He kissed her back, deepened it with a swipe of his tongue to part her lips as he reached behind her and undid her zipper. Her last costume, a long, frilly number of sequins and lace, fell to the floor as Julian ran his hands along her torso, searching for and finding pert nipples ready to tweak. He lowered his mouth and pulled one in between his teeth, walked them toward the dressing table.

"Julian!"

"Just a little bit…"

He lifted her with the finesse of a dancing partner, set her on the table and positioned himself between her legs. The belt buckle was unfastened. Pants came unzipped. He reached for his ever-hardening shaft, rubbed the tip along her leg as he eased it toward her quivering folds and…

*Knock!* "Nicki? You in there?"

"Don't answer it," Julian whispered.

"It's not locked." Nicki shimmied off the table and reached for her robe. "Yeah, I'm in here." She cracked the door.

An assistant peeked her head in. "A reporter from *Variety* is here for you. A bunch of fans, too."

"Out in five minutes."

Shortly afterward, Nicki emerged from the dressing room looking fresh and effervescent, as though she'd emerged from a nap, not just performed a nonstop, high-energy show. Hair pulled into a topknot, face nearly devoid of makeup and eyes glowing, she wore a long, loose maxi with bold geometric prints, clunky jewelry and sandals. One could have easily mistaken her for a model instead of a dancer, and many had. Julian walked beside her, a strong but quiet presence amid the crowd.

"Nicki! Nicki!" Fans and the press clamored for her attention. She spent a moment with the reporters, then walked over to where dozens of fans held out programs and other memorabilia for her to sign. While she posed for a couple selfies, Julian texted Niko and requested the limo be brought around to the side entrance. When he turned back, she was rushing toward him.

"Let's go," she muttered, not stopping. "Where's the car?"

Julian quickly spotted Niko standing beside a white stretch limo and waving. He reached for her hand. "Come on."

He helped her into the limo. She fell back against the seat, clearly relieved.

"Looks like they didn't want to let you go back there," Niko teased.

"Yeah." Nicki glanced out the window, then turned to Julian. "Where are we eating? I'm starved."

"I've handled that," Terrell said. "Driver, we're ready."

The limo pulled away from the curb. Julian put an arm around Nicki. "What was that about?"

"What?"

"You left as though you were running away from someone."

Quinn overheard him. "What, someone freaked her out?"

All other conversation halted. Eyes turned toward her. "Julian is overexamining my hasty exit. I was simply ready to go."

He leaned over and spoke softly in her ear. "Ready to go, or trying to beat another light?"

She laughed off the remark, and in the familiar surroundings of New York City interacted more confidently with Julian's powerful family. She regaled them with stories of life in the city that never slept, including some memorable college moments with Julian before she'd dropped out to pursue dancing. Anyone looking on would see a beautiful, carefree woman out on the town. But Julian wasn't fooled. He was not only a doctor of behavioral study who'd graduated with honors, but a highly observant man who'd seen every side of Nicki. Something was going on with her. Something she obviously didn't want to share. They were in the city to celebrate her opening night, so he wouldn't push. But he wouldn't forget, either. It looked like he now had two problems—how to get Nicki to leave New York and move to California, and how to find out what was behind the urgency in his gut that made him want to hasten that move.

# Chapter 4

"Are you sure it was him?"

Though she hadn't gotten much sleep due to the Drakes' late departure from New York City, Nicki was up before seven o'clock. It was either that or keep lying in bed thinking through a continuous replay of what happened last night. Instead, she'd been shimmying into a pair of running shorts when Paige called with the critics' glowing reviews. The conversation had quickly shifted to less optimistic news.

"Paige, I'm positive. It was Vince. I don't think he saw the show, but he was there waiting on the sidewalk by the stage door. I saw him as soon as we walked outside."

"Maybe he did see it and came back there to congratulate you."

"Then why didn't he? Why is it that he started toward me, but when he saw Julian he quickly turned around and went the other way? I swear I don't know what's up with that guy, but his stalker-like ways are starting to freak me out."

"Did he call you?"

"Nope. But I tried calling him. Went to voice mail again."

"Did you leave a message?"

"Same as last time. Said I didn't have money to lend him and to leave me alone or I'd call the police." Nicki rubbed away the goose bumps that had suddenly popped up on her arms. "I want to believe he'll do as I asked, but there was something about him when I saw him last night. A desperate kind of look in his eyes..."

"I think you should go to the police."

"And say what? That a guy asked me for a loan and then came to my show?"

"That's not how you told it to me."

"It's how the police will see it."

"What about the black sedan?"

"What about it? Other than the license plate number, I don't have anything to prove that story. Even that isn't concrete proof those guys threatened me or were even by my house. They could deny it and the police would deduce that I could have written that number down from anywhere." Nicki's phone beeped. "Oh my God, Paige. I think this is him. See you tonight."

"Be careful. Record the call!"

Nicki clicked over. "Hello?" She opened her settings, looking for a record button.

"Hey, Nicki."

"Vince. What's going on? Why are you stalking me?"

"Stalking you? What are you talking about?"

She scrolled through her settings, pushed the call icon. Scrolled. Where was the record feature and why hadn't she tried finding it before now?

"The other night at the show."

"Yeah, I was there. So were hundreds of other people."

"You saw the show?"

"Of course. Why else would I be there?"

"Um, let's see, I can think of about twenty thousand reasons, unless you found someone else to give you the loan."

"Oh, that. No, I haven't found anyone, and the guys I owe are stepping up the pressure."

"Like you did to me by sending over your thuggish friends?"

She heard an anguished sigh. "I didn't send them over, Nicki. Not how you're thinking, anyway. I told them you owed me money. I didn't tell them to go over and collect it."

"Then how'd they know where I live?" Silence. "Exactly." Nicki gave up trying to find the record button. It was too hard to search, think and talk at the same time. "What you're doing is not cool, Vince. And while I'm sorry you've gotten yourself into a predicament, there's nothing I can do to help you."

"Not even with some of it—say, five thousand, or ten?"

"Why do you think I have that kind of money to loan out, or that I'd give it to you even if I did?"

"Because at one time you cared about me."

That much was true, Nicki secretly admitted. She'd fallen hard and fast for the tall charmer. Theirs had been a brief romance, but it also had been a whirlwind of intense fun and loving. Before it wasn't.

"Because even though I was a dog in the time that we hung out, my feelings for you were real. I wish I'd understood what a gift it was to have you in my life, but it took you leaving for me to find that out."

"I don't know what you want me to say. I don't hate you, and I can't loan you money."

"Is that guy the reason you won't go out, the one with you at the show last night?"

"Look, Vince, I've got to go."

"Just tell me. Is that your boyfriend? If so, I'll leave you alone, for real this time."

"You promise you won't call again?"

"Not even as friends? I like you, okay?"

"You don't even know me."

"I know what I like."

"Yes. That was my boyfriend. He and I have been together a very long time."

"How long?"

"More than five years." Nicki realized her mistake at once.

"So I'm not the only cheater on the phone."

"I didn't cheat. We'd broken up when you and I got together, and you and I only dated a month. New York is full of good women. Find one of them and treat her the way you should have treated me and all of the women who've been hurt by your actions. Okay?"

"Okay. Bye, Nicki."

Nicki hung up the phone, exhausted, depleted. Getting through that conversation without losing it had probably taken years off her life. What was that about? Declarations of love and sincere-sounding compliments?

She walked into her closet, mumbling, "Probably running the same kind of game that got me with him in the first place."

Minutes later, earbuds firmly in place, Nicki pushed past the gate to her brownstone and hit the sidewalk running. She'd done way too little of it lately, none since what happened the other night. The conversation with Vince had been taxing, but in a way it had also freed her. He'd said he would leave her alone. She believed it.

Running in place, she looked around her. How she loved the borough called Brooklyn. Bright, bustling, colorful, diverse. Nicki knew Julian wanted her to move west. He hadn't mentioned it on this trip but that didn't matter. California was beautiful, true enough. But who would ever want to leave all this energy and feel like they were on vacation forever?

The light turned. Nicki jogged across the street, down the block and around the corner. She saw the bike, heard a scream and felt a pain sharper than she'd ever experienced. One more step and she was on the ground. As she fell she screamed again, realizing that the first guttural wail had been wrenched from her own throat.

"I'm sorry. I couldn't stop. Are you all right?" Nicki couldn't speak past a jaw clenched against the pain shooting up from her right ankle. On her mind was a single thought—there'd be no dancing tonight.

Julian shook hands with his colleagues, tired but glad he'd agreed to the last-minute invite to join a San Francisco symposium on holistic alternatives to traditional remedies for mental illness. Most doctoral students couldn't wait until school was over. But Julian relished the classroom and missed the sometimes passionate discussions around another's point of view. He reached his car, slid inside and fired up the phone. After trying unsuccessfully to use it from several different locations inside during the day, he'd turned it off and placed it inside his briefcase. No hesitation in doing that. Julian lived a life that was consciously predictable. Which was why he was surprised to hear several pings as soon as his phone turned on that indicated missed calls.

He tapped and scrolled. Natalie? Couldn't imagine what she wanted. He'd hired a capable assistant, a forty-seven-year-old single mother named Katie. At their luncheon he'd made it clear to Natalie that he was not in competition with her father, and that she'd provided the only assistance he would ever need from her. There was a call from Katie and one from his mother. The other was from Nicki. He clicked on her number and was surprised to see she'd called multiple times. As he started his car and rolled out of the parking lot, he tapped the steering wheel to engage her number. Ready to leave a message, surprised when she answered the phone.

Confused, he glanced at the dashboard and then at his watch. "Babe, why are you answering the phone? You should be…what's wrong?"

It was after eight on the East Coast. She should be on stage. Something was definitely not right.

"Babe…"

Sniffles and then, "I'm hurt."

"What happened?"

In halting, pain-filled detail, she told him. "Tomorrow I'll see a specialist who'll determine exactly how long I'll be down. I pray that it's only a couple weeks. But it could be longer. Julian, I'm scared. If my ankle is broken, they'll replace me. What am I going to do?"

"You're going to be okay," he replied quickly, his voice calm and firm. "No matter what happens. And you'll come here, to Paradise Cove, so that I can make sure you get the very best care available. So that I can take care of you."

# Chapter 5

Julian had factored a good six months into getting his practice up and running with a stream of regular patients. Until that happened, he felt he'd have time on his hands. He'd hired an agent to book college talks and professional speaking engagements. Had set up a schedule with the Drake Community Center's director to offer free counseling to the troubled youth it served. The first month was understandably slow. In August, following an article featuring him in a national medical magazine, he began getting referrals from medical doctors in neighboring towns. Some from as far away as Sacramento and San Jose.

Last week, a former patient of Dr. Johnson had walked into his office. He'd been treated for ten years and felt it wasn't working. At first Julian refused outright, but after a thorough interview, he'd decided to treat the man. People regularly changed therapists. For the patient, the change proved beneficial. For Julian, it had been fateful. The satisfied patient had obviously been talking. Barely into September and a stream of Johnson's patients had called for appointments. He turned most of them down, but agreed to see the ones he felt would benefit from his counsel. One was in his office now, engaging in a pattern most likely developed in childhood and perfected throughout her adult life.

He stole a glance at the clock on the wall behind where his patient Vanessa sat. Nicki's plane would arrive in just over ninety minutes. To leave right now would be cutting it close, and Vanessa's time would be up in sixty seconds. But she was in crisis. He could not in good conscience end the session before her emotions stabilized.

He watched her twist a tissue to shreds as she recounted an incident from her abusive childhood. Tears for moments she'd probably relived thousands of times. It was neither healthy nor productive, but he knew why she did it. Why millions of people relived the very situations they'd most like to forget. How one could at first hate and then—after depression became the new normal and sadness felt sane—relish the pain.

In psychology it was called destiny neurosis, a form of repetition compulsion. The term was coined by Sigmund Freud in 1914 and expanded after further research. As she had during each previous session, Vanessa lamented over the beatings endured at the hands of her parents, and later a foster mom after the parents lost custody, yet was despondent that a physically abusive third marriage was ending. In the past, a cocktail of antianxiety and antidepressant medication had been prescribed as the cure for her chronic depression. Masking the pain, not fixing the problem. Prescription drug abuse was an epidemic in America. Seventy percent of the country was on some type of prescribed drug. A quarter of them were like Vanessa—depressed, abused, hurting. It's one of the reasons Julian had chosen psychology over psychiatry, to push himself toward holistic, drug-free healing and make prescribed medicine the absolute last resort.

"I just want to be loved without being beaten. You know?" She looked at him with red-rimmed eyes. "Is that too much to ask?"

"Not at all, Vanessa. Being beaten is not love. It is what you have come to associate with love, because the abuse you suffered was done by people who said they loved you, those who professed to care about you. Do you understand that?"

"What am I doing wrong, Doctor? How do I keep attracting the same type of man into my life?"

"By repeating the same thought patterns and the same actions that brought you to my office. But that's why I'm here. To help you replace toxic thoughts and actions with positive, productive ones." Julian looked at his watch and stood. "I have a couple things I'd like to give you." He continued talking as he walked over to a wall unit. He pulled a card from a drawer beneath the shelving and a blank journal from a stack on one of the shelves. On the front was a message in large, bold letters: Focus on Good Thoughts and Good Things Will Happen.

He walked back to Vanessa, who had stood as well. "I want you to begin keeping a journal. Every day, write at least one page of what you are thinking. It can be anything, any thought that comes to mind. How you're feeling. How you slept the night before. What you watched on TV or ate for dinner. Doesn't matter. The point is to get in touch with yourself and become conscious of the storyline that's playing in your head."

He held up the five-by-seven card. "Here is a list of questions to help get you started. Your first journal entry can be answering these questions. There are no wrong answers. Just write how you feel."

"But, Doctor—"

"No buts." He took her arm and gently guided her toward the door. "You can do this, Vanessa. It'll help you get better, okay? See you next week."

Traffic was light, and the gods were kind. Forty-five minutes at mostly ninety miles an hour helped him reach the airport within minutes of Nicki's arrival. Jennifer had suggested he send a car service. Much too impersonal for his queen, and for someone who'd experienced a career-threatening injury less than a week ago. He wanted to get her himself.

He parked the car and went inside, hoping she'd take his advice and use a wheelchair instead of trying to navigate the busy airport on crutches. So independent, his private dancer. A trait that over the years had often put them at odds. It had taken less coaxing than expected for her agreement to recuperate in Paradise Cove. And while he'd not promised that the specialist he'd lined up could cut her recovery from six weeks to four, it was a carrot he'd gladly dangled to bring her home.

Once inside he looked at the monitor for her flight number. The plane had landed. Most likely, she was on her way down. He checked his phone. There was a text from his mom.

Dinner with Nicki? Private room @ the club?

He quickly responded. Thanks, Mom. Not tonight.

Sunday brunch?

We'll see.

He looked up just as a set of elevator doors opened. A heavily wrapped ankle supported by an Aircast was the first body part through the doors. It was Nicki, busily texting while the wheelchair assistant pushed her toward baggage claim. Just as she looked up, his phone dinged.

He walked to her, smiling. "Is that a message telling me you've arrived?"

"Yep."

Reaching into his pocket, he pulled out a wad of bills,

peeled off a twenty and tipped the assistant. "Thanks, buddy. I'll take it from here."

"It's okay," Nicki protested. "I can walk."

"Perhaps. But what you will do is accept the generous offer to be ferried in your silver chariot from this building to my car." He leaned down and kissed her scowling lips. "You're welcome. How was the flight?"

"Fine, since I slept through most of it. Doctor gave me pain meds. Can't feel the throbbing ache in my ankle, which is great. But I end up not feeling much of anything else, either." She pointed out a large piece of hard plastic luggage with a colorful strip of material wrapped around the handle. "That's mine."

Julian retrieved it. "How many more?"

"That's it."

"You packed clothes for a four- to six-week stay in one suitcase?"

"You said I'd be treated by the best…what did you call him?"

"An orthopedic specialist."

"Yeah, him."

"Even the most gifted doctor cannot make the body heal faster. Here, you roll the suitcase and I'll roll you."

"If you insist."

"I do."

Julian quickly got Nicki settled into the front seat, and less than an hour from when he'd arrived at Oakland International Airport, they were headed back to PC. With rush-hour traffic waning, he set the cruise control to a law-abiding seventy miles per hour.

"You were supposed to call me last night."

Nicki spoke through a yawn. "Forgot."

"That was disobedient. When we get home, I'm going to have to spank you."

"Lucky me."

Said so sincerely and with such deadpan disinterest that Julian burst out laughing.

"So…what's the official verdict? Broken?"

"Technically, no, and did you know that an actual break or full tear of the ligament and tendons would have been better than the partial tears that I have?"

"I'd heard that before."

"I hadn't. Doesn't make sense that a more serious break would heal faster."

"Life doesn't always make sense."

Nicki fell silent. When they were together, she was usually the more talkative of the two. It was one of her traits that made them such a perfect couple. People didn't recognize how quiet Julian was when he and Nicki were together. The rare occasions when she was quieter than Julian were very obvious. Like now, when the only sound was the neo-soul on Julian's playlist.

He looked over. "You okay?"

She didn't answer right away. While staring out the window she finally replied, "Not really."

"I understand."

Nicki made a skeptical snort. "Please."

"I do, babe."

"You have no idea what I'm going through." Nicki's piercing look was only matched by the ever-increasing volume of her delivery. "How could you? You're not a dancer! You haven't been working toward a dream for well over ten years and then right when you are just about there, so close you can throw a rock and hit it, and thirty years old, something happens that takes it all away. Unless that exact thing has happened to you, there is no way you can relate."

Julian became silent, subconsciously and without thought interpreting the behavior from a professional perspective. Hurt. Fear. Disappointment. Misplaced anger. Nicki had lashed out at him, but her anger was actually toward the situation and the man on the bike who'd instigated it. Fear of the unknown and the unproductive projecting of a worst-case scenario upon an unpredictable situation. Understandable, considering the fickle nature of entertainment. In one day and out the next. That's why he knew better than to comment. There was no right answer for this type of reaction.

The silence lasted through two more songs.

Nicki repositioned her leg. "I hate when you do that."

"What?"

"Psychoanalyze me—and don't deny it. Over there all calm and quiet. I know what you're doing."

"Okay." Said low and drawn out, as if testing the word to see if any repercussions would come along with it.

"Stop!" Nicki punched his arm, but she was smiling. "Is there ever a moment when you're not trying to figure someone out?"

"I can't help being who I am, love."

"I know. I'm sorry."

"You're forgiven. This is a tough time. What did the director say?"

"I was supposed to call him after meeting with the specialist. I decided to wait until I see the doctor that was recommended to you. Do I have an appointment?"

"The earliest I could get you in was this Friday."

"Today is Tuesday." Nicki did a slow exhale. "I'll call tomorrow and ask Milo to wait until Friday to make any… permanent changes. Dammit!" Nicki used her good foot to stomp the floor.

They continued to talk intermittently between Nicki's quiet spells. Knowing she was in no mood to socialize, Julian waited until they were ten minutes outside Paradise

Cove and then called in an order to Acquired Taste for Nicki's favorite meal.

"I have some news that will make you feel a little better."

"What?"

"A place for us to stay."

"You bought a house?"

"I just closed on it. I hope you like it."

"What matters is if you like it. I'm only going to be here for a couple weeks."

"I know, but…you've always been uncomfortable staying at my parents'. So I had Terrell bring me a couple listings. I chose a town house that resembles a brownstone on the inside."

She gave him a look.

"On the inside, I said!" He reached over and took her hand. "I know that no place will ever come close to your beloved Brooklyn or Manhattan. But I want to make you as comfortable and happy as I can while you're here."

"Ah, that's sweet, babe."

"I do have to warn you about something."

"What?"

"I just got it, so it's pretty empty."

"I'm sure I can make it work."

"Just letting you know."

They arrived at the echoing town house a short time later. A sectional sofa was the living room's lone furniture. The master suite was also sparsely furnished, its major feature a king-size bed. Julian helped Nicki shower, tucked her in bed, then joined her there with two tray tables. They watched TV while enjoying burgers and fries. Once the trays were removed and they'd finished their drinks, Julian pulled back the covers and raised the short nightie that covered the shaved lips that he so adored. The good food, hot shower and crisp clean sheets had been arranged with the intention to make Nicki more comfortable. Now it was time to make both of them happy.

# *Chapter 6*

A steady throb served as her alarm clock. The ache forced her eyes open as she slowly floated up from a pain medication–induced fog. Her eyes flickered against bright sunlight and over to the digital clock on a nightstand. Ten o'clock? No way. She fell back against the pillows, but the cry for relief from the ache that went from the tear in her ankle to her shin would not be denied.

She threw back the covers and hobbled into the en suite bath. Her toiletry bag was set next to one of two brass-and-glass vessel sinks that contrasted beautifully against light-colored granite and ebony cabinets. A note was stuck on the mirror above it. Had he emptied her suitcase? What else had she slept through?

She read the extensive note, written in his neat, slanted penmanship.

> Morning, beautiful. You slept so peacefully as I prepared to leave I hadn't the heart to wake you. Breakfast is in the fridge, a credit card on the table. Please go online and order whatever you feel will make the town house a home. For ideas, call Mom. For company, call Quinn. Both cannot wait to see you. Or not—your choice. The main thing is to feel better. Restaurant choices don't compare to Times Square but all deliver. Call when you read this. Loving you…

She looked down and noticed that beside her toiletry bag was a bottle of water. So naturally thoughtful. Innately kind. Julian had always treated her wonderfully, with the sweetest adoration and the deepest respect. Hard to admit, but sometimes she took it for granted. It had taken a break and a few dates with Vince to remind her how good she had it, how special Julian was. And here he was showing her again.

She took a pain pill. After a quick shower during which she more than appreciated the double shower's built-in bench, Nicki wrapped a fresh bandage around her ankle, slipped on a loose mini and the Aircast and after a last-minute hop back to grab her cell, made her way downstairs with the aid of one crutch. She hadn't felt hungry, but a growling stomach let her know that nourishment was needed.

She opened the fridge and pulled out the lone white sack that sat next to bottles of water, orange and cranberry juices, and a variety of flavored coffees. She opened one of the coffees and drank almost half of it with the first swig. Inside the bag were pastries, a bagel and a breakfast sandwich. Forgetting Julian's warning, she opened a cabinet door to grab a plate. The cupboard was literally bare. She improvised a plate from the top of the paper container, scooped out the sandwich's insides and nuked them in the microwave.

While reassembling the sandwich it came to her. The reason she'd tossed and turned last night. The feeling of isolation she'd felt that morning. She slowly looked around the room and wondered if she'd ever before experienced life quite this way. No noise. Total silence. So quiet she felt she could hear herself think.

For a woman who'd grown up in the hustle and bustle of Prospect Heights, with traffic and trains, the conversation of close neighbors floating through her window, and a dozen other sounds, the quiet was strange, almost eerie. She rapped a line from the musical. Her voice bounced against the walls, evaporated into the eighteen-foot vaulted ceiling.

Last night she'd barely noticed, but against the bright

morning, the beauty of the home's architecture stood out. Tan-colored ceilings and Tasmanian oak floors were a nice and different accent against ivory walls and complemented an ultramodern, dual-stone fireplace that served both the living and dining rooms. Chandeliers, modern fixtures and recessed lighting all added to the home's warm yet sophisticated style.

Nice, she thought. Who was she kidding? The place was beyond nice. It was stunning. Like those she viewed in magazines and fantasized about owning. What was its value, she wondered. In Brooklyn such a home would go for two or three million. In Manhattan, five at least.

She reached the sofa, settled against the soft cashmere cushion and looked around her, thinking she could get used to a luxury lifestyle. Then she remembered why she was here. Not in New York. What the freak bicycle accident might cost her. The bright mood quickly faded.

Just as she was about to head to a pity party, her phone rang. She answered and put the call on speaker.

"Hey, babe."

"Good morning, love. How are you?"

"I'm okay."

"Did you get my note?"

"Uh-huh."

"Then why haven't you called me, as the note instructed?"

"Listen, Doctor…"

The sound of Julian's chuckle made her smile. "I knew that would rile you. My next appointment is due any minute, but I wanted to let you know that Quinn might be calling you. She asked and I gave her your number. Hope you don't mind."

"No, that's fine. I hadn't planned to get out, but after coming downstairs and seeing how empty this place really is, I might not have a choice. At the very least we need dishes and silverware."

"And towels. The two hanging in the bathroom are the only two in the house."

"Oh my God."

"Hey, I tried. It was either an empty house for just us or a fully furnished wing at my parents' house."

"I appreciate what you did for me, babe. This place is beautiful."

"Katie's calling. Appointment's here. Love you."

Nicki eased off the couch and took her now-empty containers into the kitchen to throw away. Not used to having downtime, she felt strangely out of sorts with so much of it now on her hands. A plan, that's it. A plan and a few projects. That's what she thought could help the time go quickly until her foot healed and she was back on stage in New York, where she belonged.

Back on the couch, she pressed the note icon on her phone and began to make a list. First: find a yoga studio. Nicki couldn't dance or put pressure on her ankle, but a yoga class, especially hot yoga, would help her stay limber and maybe even help her ankle heal, too. What else? Furnish Julian's house. That project alone could take four weeks. Four bedrooms—three unfurnished—three bathrooms, combined living/dining space and a patio, too? She'd keep it clean and simple, safe earth colors, Julian's style. But on what kind of budget? Sure, the black card on the table had no monetary limits, but did Julian? Did she? It had taken her almost a year to personalize her two-bedroom walkup. Just as a sense of anxiety began to creep in, her phone rang.

"Hello?"

"Nicki! It's Quinn. I'm so sorry for what happened to you!"

"Thanks, Quinn. I'm pretty bummed about it."

"I can't even imagine how you're feeling. You were so great in the show. Several scenes with the lead. Sold-out crowds."

"Hey, I don't need reminding."

"You're right. I'm…stupid and inconsiderate is what I am. Would you believe I was calling to cheer you up?"

"Ha! You meant well."

"How's the ankle?"

"Still swollen. Still throbbing."

"Is it broken?"

"Worse, the ligaments are torn and the tendons are ruptured. The doctor said a clean break would have healed faster."

"Tell you what. Why don't I come grab you, show you around our cosmopolitan…uh, town."

"I'm glad you didn't say city."

"I started to, but the lie wouldn't come out of my mouth. I don't know if you're up for it, but I knew you were here and wanted to offer."

"That's nice of you, Quinn. I didn't think I'd be up for much socializing, but I need to hear something besides my thoughts. I'm so used to having noise around me that the quiet feels claustrophobic."

"Totally understand. When I first moved from San Francisco, I thought I'd go small-town crazy! Is a half hour enough time for you to be ready?"

"Just casual, right?"

"Absolutely."

"Do you know where I am?"

"Yes, got the address from Julian."

"Okay, see you then."

Nicki checked the weather. Projection was high seventies. About the same as New York this time of year. Fall was her favorite month in the city. Perfect temps. Changing leaves. She ignored the stab of pain in her heart. Found where Julian had placed the clothes he'd unpacked from her luggage and threw on a pair of wide-legged pants—easiest to navigate around the heavy bandage and Aircast—and a fitted knit top that showed off her toned, flat stomach. A light jacket and bulky wooden jewelry completed the ensemble.

Quinn rang the doorbell moments after Nicki managed to get back downstairs. They walked outside to a sleek red Ferrari.

Nicki's mouth was agape. "This is you?"

Quinn smiled as she tapped the key fob. "Christmas present."

Nicki slid into the seat, folded the crutches and gingerly pulled her injured ankle inside. Seconds later they were out the driveway and zooming down the quiet residential street.

"Wow, this car is something!"

"You like it?"

"Not for me, but it fits you perfectly."

"I can see you behind the wheel."

"I barely even know how to drive, so that wouldn't be a good look."

"You're kidding!"

"I've got my license but not a car. You don't really need one in New York."

"I think not having a car would drive me crazy."

They reached one of the main thoroughfares of Paradise Cove, the one that ran north to south through the city.

"This tour is going to take all of ten minutes, so don't blink."

"I've been here before."

"Oh, really?"

"Yep."

"How long have you and Julian dated?"

"Almost six years, off and on."

"That's a long time, Nicki. Do you think you two will get married?"

"I don't know. He asked me once, but..."

"You turned him down?" Disbelief took Quinn's voice up a notch.

"I know. Sometimes I can't believe it, either." Nicki sighed. "I love Julian. He's a really good guy. But he's California, and I'm New York. I can't see myself living here, and I know this is where he wants to be."

"I said the same thing. Was only supposed to be here six months. But now? I love it. When I want a dose of the big city, I go to one. But I like coming back to the relative peace of a small town. Even more, I love being married to Ike. No city in the world can compare to having a Drake man love you."

"You're probably right. But after turning him down the first time, I doubt that he'll ask again."

They reached the town square.

"Ooh. What's that?"

"On the corner? That's London's store. Hang on." Quinn whipped around, barely slowing down. The car fishtailed, but she broke right hard and pulled into one of several empty parking spaces available on the quiet morning.

Nicki slowly released the death grip her fingers had on the dash. "I just saw my life pass in front of me."

"That scare you? Don't worry. I know what I'm doing."

"Maybe, but while I'm riding can we practice safety first so that my ankle remains the only thing broken?"

Quinn laughed. "Sure, come on."

"Where are we going?"

"You don't want to go inside?"

"Since getting here nearly cost me my life, I guess I could. Is this London as in—"

"Yes, that London. Oh, wait. Your foot. I forgot just that quickly. We can go another day."

"I'm hoping the specialist will tell me that my PC days are numbered. Let's go in. I won't be able to walk around much. But I'd like to see her shop."

"You can sit and I'll bring over stuff that I think you'll like."

"Okay."

A chime sounded as Quinn opened the door. Inside, the color of the walls grabbed Nicki's attention right away. She would have thought textured black wallpaper too dark for a retail establishment. But a white ceiling and bright lights everywhere gave the expansive room a runway vibe. Uniquely designed separates in bold prints, like the ones in the display that had caught Nicki's eye, adorned the walls and clothes racks. Mirrors abounded. Music with an alternative sound was a nice yet unobtrusive companion to one's shopping experience. Despite her plan to sit and be pampered, Nicki was drawn to minimally filled racks of clothing that were just her style. Of the garments she'd seen so far, she wanted them all.

A pretty young woman came from behind the retro counter made of stainless steel. The door chimed again. Two more women entered. One honed in on her target and made a beeline for Nicki.

"It is you?"

"Excuse me?"

"Nicki Long?"

"Yes," she said slowly, cautiously.

"I told my friend it was you! What happened to your foot? Is that why you're here and not on Broadway?"

It was the very thing Nicki knew she wouldn't like about small towns—everyone trying to be in her business.

"Just a sprain."

"Oh, thank goodness. So you'll be back in the show soon."

"That's the plan."

"My mom and I are trying to get tickets. We're thinking about going over the Thanksgiving holiday. Hey, is it possible for me to get a picture with you?"

"Sure."

The woman waved over her friend, who took the phone and snapped the picture.

"Thank you!"

"You're welcome. What's your name?"

"Ashley," Quinn interrupted. "The local gossip trying to break news like that celebrity news show, *XYZ*. Writes a blog gossiping about everything she thinks she knows. You're guaranteed to be on it tomorrow." Quinn's eyes shifted to Ashley. "Right?"

"You got it! Just ask Ashley!" She turned to Nicki. "That's my blog, *Ask Ashley*." Then to Quinn. "I take exception to your description of my popular blog. *Gossip* implies that what I write isn't true."

"Most of it isn't."

"Clearly a matter of opinion." Ashley's smile at Nicki was genuine. "It was really great to meet you." And to Quinn, "Always a pleasure. Bye, ladies. Come on, Nat. Let's go."

Quinn watched her go, shaking her head. "She's so fake."

"Wouldn't know it to look at her. She seemed nice to me."

"Bright smile. Dark heart."

"Wow, what'd she do to you?"

"Not to me. To Niko. Ask Julian about it. I don't want her messiness to junk up our day."

# Chapter 7

Julian pulled into his driveway and parked the car. Kept it out of the garage in case Nicki wanted to go out to dinner. He walked up the town house steps, pulling out his phone to check the text message that had just come in.

Who's Ashley?

He read it and frowned, called out to Nicki as he came in the door.

"Nicki! Babe?"

"Up here."

He walked upstairs. Nicki sat against the headboard, checking her phone. "Ashley who?" was his greeting as he walked over to the bed, kissed her forehead and sat down.

"The one Quinn doesn't like."

"Ah. That Ashley. So you did get out."

"Yes, Quinn came by. Took me around town, driving like a maniac."

"That sounds like her."

"We went by London's store. It's nice."

"That's where you ran into Ashley?"

Nicki nodded. "She and another woman came in right after we did. Who is she?"

"Somebody we grew up with—my older brothers, really. A lot of guys dated her. She had a crush on Niko that bordered on obsession."

"He dated her, too?"

"They messed around. When he met Monique, things got a little crazy. Ashley tried to sabotage the situation. But everything worked out."

"She asked for a selfie. Quinn said I'd probably be on her blog. Have you read it?"

"I checked out a couple things she wrote about—mostly fluff pieces. Gossip. She probably will write about you. A Broadway performer in our little hamlet—why wouldn't she? But I don't think you have anything to worry about." He glanced at his phone, tapped the screen and shook his head. "It must be the day for silliness."

"Somebody sent you a nonsense text?"

"When I let you go earlier, thinking my client had arrived? Wasn't my client. It was an old classmate named Natalie Moore."

"Classmate or girlfriend?"

"What did I say?"

"I heard what you said. I'm getting clarity on what you meant."

He reached for her hand, kissed it. "A classmate who I hadn't seen for years, since I was fifteen, sixteen years old. Anyway, to find an assistant, I signed up with a local staffing agency. Turns out she owns it."

"Didn't you hire an assistant?"

"Yes."

"Then why is she coming to your office?"

"It's a long story." Julian removed his shoes, sat against the headboard beside her and told her about the earlier encounter.

Julian had just pulled up a patient's file when his intercom buzzed. "Yes, Katie."

"Doctor, Natalie Moore is here to see you."

Natalie? What did she want? "Is my eleven o'clock here?"

"Not yet."

"Okay. I'll…" He looked up as his door opened. Natalie

sauntered in on four-inch heels, balancing her petite frame like a pro on stilts. When they'd met for lunch, she'd worn a suit and her hair in a loose bun, and aside from a flirtation or two, their interaction had been totally professional. Today the thick mane of brunette curls cascaded over her shoulders and down her back.

Julian's calm belied his ire. "Natalie, what are you doing?"

"Don't worry. I won't be long."

Hopefully as short as her skirt. If someone came to an interview in the tight mini she wore today it would be totally inappropriate, along with her behavior of entering his office without being invited and sitting down before being asked.

"Had you waited, I would have asked Katie to schedule you an appointment, the same as others who need to speak with me."

"Oh, Julian, don't be so formal. I heard you have a patient coming. Is it another one of my dad's?"

"Is that why you're here?"

"That's part of it. Dad has lost several since you've opened your office. What are you doing, offering a grand opening sale? Or is it the disparaging comments you've made about doctors as drug pushers that have patients leaving him to darken your door?"

"Natalie, my practice doesn't concern you. Why are you so interested in it?"

"Why are you evading my questions?"

"I'm not doing this with you. Your father's a grown man. If he has questions, he can ask them. As for the formalities of this office, they are there for a reason. We grew up together, but those interactions were a long time ago. We were children, and this is not school. If you need professional help in the future, make an appointment. Am I clear?"

"No need to be rude, Julian." Natalie rose from the chair and started for the door. "My dad has too much class to confront you, but let me be clear. People are watching. They see my dad's clients coming to this building, some who have been with him for years. What you're doing is unethical. And I'm going to find a way to expose it."

Julian stood. He'd had enough.

"I'm leaving. But you've been warned."

"Warned? What did she mean by that?"

Julian realized sharing with Nicki what had happened earlier might not have been the best idea. Her fiery nature was one of the things he loved about her. That she didn't sugarcoat or hide her feelings was a plus, too—most of the time. Might not be particularly advantageous while living in a small town. If Nicki met Natalie after what he'd just told her, it might not go so well.

"I don't know what she meant. But whatever it is means nothing to me." He spoke lightheartedly, adding a smile to further convey his nonchalance. "Let's talk about what's really important. You, and how you're feeling. Better, I'd imagine, since you went out."

"The ankle is still pretty painful, unless I'm taking the meds. Which I don't like taking because they knock me out. That's why your cabinets and pantry are still bare and dinner isn't ready."

"You'd planned to do all of that today?"

"It was a good plan in my head."

"What about now? Feel like going out to eat?"

"Would you be all right having something delivered?"

Julian ran his hand across her thigh, slid it between her legs and let it rest near her mound. "If I do, what's in it for me?"

"You mean…" Nicki's eyelids dropped, her voice, too, becoming low and sexy. "Besides a sandwich?"

Julian tried to hide it, but a smile escaped and grew as he chuckled. "It's good to see you happy."

"I'm hopeful about my appointment with the specialist on Friday, and the chance that he'll have good news. You can still take me, right?"

"Of course. What if he agrees with your New York doctor and you have to be out for four to six weeks?"

"Then I'll probably get replaced, and that will not make me happy." Nicki's shoulders slumped.

"Let's hope for the best and see what happens." Julian stole a quick kiss and slid off the bed. "What are you in the mood for? Italian, American, Mexican, Chinese?"

"Whatever you're having is fine with me."

"What I want most on the menu is you."

"Whatever."

"I'm going to take a shower. Order something for both of us." He turned on the water and quickly undressed. Under the pulsating jets and the hot water, the knots in his neck and shoulders began to dissipate. She'd answered dismissively, but Julian knew his comment made her wet. Or at the very least caused a little squiggle. In the six off-and-on years of their relationship, he'd studied Nicki as diligently as he had his textbooks. How to please her. What made her smile. Being on stage, performing, was one of those things. If Friday's prognosis knocked her out of the show, Julian didn't have a cure to fix it. The situation with Natalie was another matter. He hoped today was the end of her bothersome antics and threats to his practice. Because this wasn't school, and he wouldn't be bullied. If she pushed, Natalie would see that Julian had grown into a man well able to take care of his woman, and himself.

# Chapter 8

Friday morning, Nicki was nervous. She hadn't slept well last night, and when Julian offered to leave early and have breakfast she declined. Her stomach was in knots. She couldn't eat a thing. They headed to San Jose and the specialist who'd see Nicki, forty-five minutes away. On the drive, Julian tried to lift her spirits by reminding her of what was planned for after the appointment. The event for which London and Ace had been planning, New York Fashion Week, was in full swing. Later, she and Julian, along with most of the Drake family, were flying over to attend Ace's show. London was walking the runway for her husband's line. But even returning to the city she loved was filled with mixed emotions. How would it feel to be in New York if she'd been replaced in the show?

They reached Dr. Allen's office just before the 10:00 a.m. appointment. Nicki refused Julian's offer to help her out of the car, as if maneuvering on her own would bring her one step closer to healing. She'd filled out the patient paperwork online, so once they were inside, the cheery receptionist quickly directed Nicki and Julian to the inner offices. A medical assistant took Nicki's vitals and several digital photos of her ankle before escorting her into another room to take X-rays. Minutes later Nicki rejoined Julian back in the examination room. Not long after that, the doctor came in. He was younger than Nicki imagined he'd be, but his deep blue eyes were piercing and kind.

"Good morning, Nicki, sorry to keep you waiting. I'm Dr. Allen." He shook Julian's hand as well. "I hear you're a dancer."

"Yes, that's why I'm really anxious to hear what you've

got to say about the X-rays. I'm in a show right now—or I was until the accident—a show that has a good chance for a long run on Broadway. So I'm hoping you have good news."

"No news yet. Let's take a look. If I can have you sit up there for me." He motioned to the elevated hospital bed. "Here, let me help you."

Both he and Julian assisted Nicki to her feet. She took a couple hops over to the bed and perched on it. "Do I need to lie down?"

"No, you're fine. Let me get a look at that ankle."

Dr. Allen sat on a stool with wheels and rolled up to where he was eye level with Nicki's extended leg. He placed one hand under her leg to support it and used the other to gingerly touch her ankle in various places. "It's still quite swollen," he observed. "Have you kept it elevated as much as possible?"

"I don't remember the other doctor telling me to elevate it. But I have spent a considerable amount of time in bed, so…"

"That's not the same. The foot needs to be elevated when sitting and also when lying down by using pillows to place it higher than your head. The deep bruising here—" he pointed to an area on the right side of her ankle "—and here—" his finger continued to midshin "—causes me the greatest concern. They allude to the possibility of damage beyond a major sprain." He swiveled his chair around, reached for a remote and pressed a button. What looked like a simple whiteboard was actually a projector with the X-rays of Nicki's foot and ankle now on display.

Reaching into the pocket of his white jacket, he pulled out a pointer and rolled closer to the screen, identifying certain areas as he spoke. "To isolate the injuries and causes of pain, I checked both the medial and lateral ankle, the base of the fifth metatarsal, the Lisfranc region—that's right here—and the medial, lateral and posterior tendons. I also checked the syndesmosis—that's the area back here by the heel, for stability—and the fibula. There are signs of stress but no significant tearing. Which is good. The bruising on the side of your ankle that concerned me is due to an avulsion fracture, which means a small piece of bone has separated from the main mass of bone that is connected to this tendon." He ran the pointer down a long, thick line within several others.

Julian leaned forward, studying the screen. "That sounds more serious than a grade-two sprain, Doctor."

"It is."

"What does that mean?" Nicki didn't try to hide her rising anxiety. "Will I have to have surgery?"

"I don't want to recommend treatment based on these radiographs alone, so I have ordered an MRI to provide a more definitive image."

Nicki's eyes widened. "You mean go inside that tube thingy?"

Dr. Allen smiled. "No, Nicki. We have a scanner that functions without you having to be fully enclosed."

Her relief was evident. "How soon can we do that?"

"As soon as we can get you down there."

"And how long for the results?" Julian asked.

"Hopefully by Monday."

"Is there any way they can come sooner? I told the director of my stage production that I'd have an answer today about how long it will take for my ankle to heal."

Again the slight smile that Nicki realized was more from habit than anything else. "Unfortunately we cannot get MRI results back in less than twenty-four hours. But I think it's safe to say you won't be out for more than four weeks."

"Four weeks! Doctor, I can't."

"Perhaps less if the MRI reveals that the bone isn't actually fractured. Even then, it will be at least a week before you can begin physical therapy and at least two weeks to fully heal. You being in shape as a dancer is helpful. It will speed your recovery. I wish I had better news, but we don't want you to go back to work prematurely and risk permanent injury. In the meantime, keep the foot elevated when possible. Pay attention to the swelling, which should go down considerably in the next couple days. Also begin testing the ankle, gently, for its flexibility and level of pain."

Julian stood as the doctor did, holding out his hand. "Thanks, Doctor."

"You're welcome." He walked over to Nicki. "Chin up, Nicki. As bad as this is, when it comes to bicycle accidents I've seen much worse."

"Thank you, Dr. Allen."

"I'm happy to help. Someone will be in shortly to take you down for the MRI. After that, you're free to go. I'll call you on Monday as soon as there's news."

Back in the car, Nicki wasn't happy, and not even Julian's positive perspective could cheer her up.

"Look at the good side, babe. Not getting this second opinion could have led to permanent damage. This way you heal correctly, and come back at one hundred percent."

"Come back to what? Auditions for another marginal play or the rigors of regional theater and months on the road in a tour bus? Like I've done off and on for the last seven years? With that role in *A Hair's Tale*, I thought those days were over." She dug through her purse, mumbling, "Looks like the only thing that's over is my part in it."

She pulled out her phone, scrolled through the contact list and tapped the screen.

"Who are you calling?"

"Milo, the director."

"Sure that can't wait until Monday, when you have news?"

"Probably." When Milo's voice mail answered, she hung up without leaving a message. "It'll be better to talk to him then, anyway, and tell him I'll be back dancing in three weeks or less."

"I know that's what you want, babe. But best not to get your hopes up until you have more information."

"I'm just being positive, like you said. You did say that, right?"

"You're right. I did. Just don't want you to be disappointed."

"I'm going to make sure of that myself. Where there's a will, there's a way, and one way or another, a couple weeks from Monday, I'll be back on that stage."

Her mind might have doubted, but Nicki's voice was strong and filled with conviction. Misdiagnoses happened. Doctors had been wrong before. Nicki hadn't come this far to let a tiny bone fragment stop her. Tickets continued to be sold out. The show got rave reviews. There was a sense of certainty in her gut. *A Hair's Tale* was going to have a long run on Broadway. And so was she.

# Chapter 9

When they'd first met, Nicki found Julian's wealth intimidating. So he'd downplayed it. As she watched the private jet's stairs transform into a ramp that could accommodate the wheelchair upon which he'd insisted, even she admitted money had its privileges.

Once on board the sleek Challenger 850, her appreciation continued. The stark brightness of the cabin with its white walls and ceiling was complemented perfectly by the black flooring, dark gray leather seats and various shades of gray that continued throughout. Splashes of red interrupted the black, white and gray theme, just enough to bring interest to the palette without lessening the sophistication of the cabin's smart design.

Nicki immediately thought of the town house and its similar color scheme and wondered if they'd been remodeled by the same designer. The wheelchair was folded and stored up front. Nicki had no problem using her crutches to navigate the aisle. It was one reason Julian had wanted to arrive early, before the plane's fourteen seats were totally filled. And according to him, they would be. They bypassed two rows of forward-facing chairs and a meeting area with chairs facing each other and a love seat between them. Across from the meeting area was a full bathroom, complete with a marble shower. Beyond that were tables on either side of the aisle framed by two sets of chairs. Perfect for dining or playing games. Nicki directed Julian to the chairs facing the front. He then reached into one of the overhead bins and pulled out a couple pillows to place under her ankle and elevate it, as Dr. Allen had instructed.

Nicki turned the chair so that Julian could place her leg on the pillows on the chair beside her.

"How is that? Are you comfortable?"

"Yes, that's fine."

"Are you sure? Is it hurting? Do you need to take some medication?"

"It's throbbing a little, but I don't want to take anything."

The flight attendant came over. "Dr. Drake, could I get you or your guest something to drink or a snack?"

Julian looked at Nicki, who shook her head. He sat across from her. "No, thank you. We're fine for now."

"This is my first time on a private plane, and I can't believe how different it looks from regular ones. With love seats and tables, a full bath! It's more beautiful and well appointed than most homes I've been to. And here I've thought myself big-time when paying fifty extra bucks to upgrade for more leg room! After this trip, flying regular will never be the same." She looked at him, her face a question. "Is this how you fly when we're not together?"

"No, and it's not the way any other of the family flies all the time, either. This is the company plane, used almost exclusively for company business. On some occasions the paths of business and pleasure cross and the plane can be used to accommodate both."

"But you usually fly first-class."

"So do you when you're with me."

"I know."

"So what's your point?"

"I guess I forget sometimes how rich you are."

Julian turned to face her fully. "I'll tell you what my dad told me when I was younger. He's rich. We kids borrowed money that came from the rich dad."

"Thanks for trying to be humble, but you're rich, too."

"My financial portfolio is healthy. But it wasn't all

handed to me. My parents gave me a good foundation that I've worked hard to build on."

A sudden din of voices announced the next group's arrival. Nicki looked up as Julian's sister Teresa and her husband, Atka, entered, joking with Niko, Monique and their pregnant sister-in-law Charli, followed by Terrell.

Julian stood as the couples waved and sat, all except Niko and Terrell, who continued toward them. "Wow, Niko. Back-to-back New York trips in less than a month? London's got clout."

"She must not be the only one," Terrell interrupted, "because one glance and everyone knows you're not into fashion."

Julian responded to the good-natured ribbing with a fake punch to his brother's gut.

"How are you, Nicki?" Terrell leaned over for a hug. "Sure you're able to be in New York and not get on stage?"

"Not at all."

"We can't have you trying to dance before that ankle is ready. Julian, you'd better watch her."

"I'm on it, bro. Don't worry. Where's Aliyah?"

"She had to work."

"And she let you roll solo?"

Terrell put a finger to his lips. "I snuck out the house. Don't tell anyone."

They laughed as Ike Sr. and Jennifer entered the plane along with Ike Jr., Quinn and another couple.

"Who's that?" Julian asked.

"That's Quinn's dad and stepmother. You don't remember them from the wedding?"

"Obviously not."

"Don't even know your own kin," Terrell joked, shaking his head.

"There were almost three hundred people there when

Ike and Quinn got married." Julian looked not one bit embarrassed.

"True, but only one set of parents for Quinn."

"And your point is?"

"That you're stupid," Terrell deadpanned.

Julian looked at Nicki. "See what I had to endure growing up?"

"All that IQ going to waste, being squeezed into forgetfulness inside that small head."

"Brother, I'm concerned. Have you been treated?"

"For what?"

"For the oral acid malabsorption causing diarrhea of the mouth."

"Very funny, Doctor," Terrell said, not laughing.

"Cut it out, you two," Nicki warned. "You're lucky to have each other."

Terrell looked confused. Julian explained, "The misplaced longings of an only child."

"Ah, got it." And then to Nicki. "Come spend a week with all of us together. We'll change your mind."

Quinn brought back her parents, introduced them to Nicki and reacquainted them with Julian. They then joined Ike in the area with the love seat.

"They going to the show?" Julian asked Terrell, now joined by his sister-in-law Charli, Atka and Teresa, all sitting at the table across the aisle.

He shook his head. "Handling some East Coast business. Just bumming a ride."

"Nice to have friends in high places," Nicki said.

"Not friends, family," Terrell corrected. "They've only got it like that because Quinn is a Drake."

The flight took off, the group settled in and for the next five hours, Nicki observed and enjoyed some of the undeniable advantages of being a Drake. Besides the private plane and the attendant's stellar service. Dinner was like that from a Michelin-starred chef. Salmon flown in fresh from Atka's Alaskan fishery, lobster tails from Maine. Alkaline water, top-shelf drinks and a cheesecake ice cream with a hot fudge and pecan drizzle that was so decadent and delicious Nicki wanted to lick the bowl.

Even better than the luxury, service and food was the obvious love shared between all of the family. Everyone made sure Nicki felt at home. One by one they came back, said hello and asked how she was doing. Jennifer made a date for them to do lunch the following week. Although Nicki hadn't talked much with Ike Sr.—his presence was very commanding—his greeting was warm, his smile sincere. There was nonstop teasing. Nicki laughed till she cried. And between the couples lots of subtle affection— touches, hand holding, a quick kiss or two. Growing up it had just been her and her mother. Other than in movies, Nicki was sure that she'd never seen true love such as this. She thought about how she'd turned down Julian's proposal and Paige's reaction when she told her. How she'd said no to marrying a smart, wealthy, well-mannered man with values, who came from a loving, close-knit family filled with successful businessmen and celebrities. It seemed like a good idea at the time, but now turning him down felt like the worst mistake she'd ever made. In life, some things only came around once. As they neared her favorite city and the plane began its descent, Nicki felt sure that Julian proposing to her was one of those things.

# Chapter 10

There were some things that money—even a lot of it—couldn't buy. Like one's way out of a traffic jam on the Triborough Bridge caused by an accident blocking all lanes. While the women attended the fashion show, the men were headed to a business meeting/national strategy session/fund-raiser for Niko's senatorial campaign. Julian was calm, as usual. His brothers? Not as much. Ike Jr. and Atka talked business, but after every few sentences they'd bring up the delay. Terrell fidgeted. Niko constantly checked his watch. Ike Sr. exchanged trivialities with Quinn's father, Glen.

During a break in their conversation, Julian tapped his dad. "I have a question."

"Yes, son?"

"How familiar are you with Claude Johnson?"

"The psychiatrist?" Julian nodded. Ike Sr. shrugged. "About as familiar as I am with most people in Paradise Cove who've lived there most of their lives. Chatted at a few chamber meetings, maybe a couple times at the club. Fortunately haven't had the need to schedule an appointment yet." Ike Sr. chuckled. Julian smiled. "Why do you ask?"

Julian told his dad about Natalie's visit and accusations. "It's almost as if she's trying to create the illusion of something that isn't there, like I'm purposely trying to sabotage her father's practice."

"Is it true? Have some of his patients left his practice and come to you?"

"Yes, but not enough to warrant her egregious attacks."

Ike Sr. rubbed his jaw, his eyes narrowing as he pondered the situation. "I do recall some type of scandal a while back involving one of his patients. Jennifer most likely could fill in the details. That woman has a way of knowing just about everything that goes on in our town. Junior." Ike Jr. looked over with brow raised. "Do you remember what happened with Claude Johnson around four or five years ago?"

"The doctor?" Ike Jr. asked.

"He was charged with writing fake prescriptions. Supplying medication beyond the scope of his practice to patients he barely treated and some not at all," Niko said.

"Unfortunately, that's a lucrative market," Terrell said. "On the streets, some can pay as much as thirty dollars a pill."

"How do you know anything about him?" Ike Jr. asked Niko. Ike Sr. looked as if he wanted to know that, too. In fact, every eye in the limo was now trained on the mayor. "That I know about it is only a fluke. The attorney who helped squash the story and clean up the mess is married to Greg's sister."

"The city's finance director?" Ike Sr. asked.

Niko nodded. "Small world."

Julian asked the question on everyone's mind. "What happened?"

"Ultimately, the case got thrown out. The main pieces of evidence were obtained illegally, without the proper search warrant. He got written up on some lesser action but was allowed to keep his license. Obviously."

"So that's why," Julian mused.

"Why what?" Niko and the rest hadn't heard what Julian had shared with his father.

Julian shook his head. "Nothing."

"Why his daughter is upset that Julian has opened a practice in town," Ike Sr. shared.

"No, she's probably upset at not getting more alimony." Said without even looking up as Terrell texted on his phone.

"I asked about that, at least indirectly. Commented on the fact that she was married, given the new last name, and that she'd moved back to PC. All she said about her divorce was that it was a long story."

"From what I heard, when it comes to the telling, looks like her husband won. But she came back and opened a business. Can't be doing too bad. Where'd you run into her, Julian? And with all the work you're putting into your own practice, when did you have the time?"

"Irony. Went online and did a search for staffing companies. Contacted the one that was in PC. Wasn't until they called back and I recognized her voice that I learned it was Natalie's company."

"That's right, you would know her. She was a year behind me and one ahead of you."

"Yep."

"I'd be careful around her if I were you," Terrell cautioned. "She might be trying to set up a lawsuit and get some Drake dollars to supplement her income."

Julian nodded and remained quiet as the conversation shifted and traffic on the bridge began to move faster. He was already one step ahead of Terrell. Because when it came to caution regarding Natalie Moore, his brother hadn't said nothing but a word.

She'd never seen anything like it. The glitz. The glam. Bright lights and beautiful people. She'd spent her whole life in New York, liked clothes as much as the next girl. Had passed by the Fashion Institute of Technology dozens of times and shopped Fifth Avenue stores. But she'd never before considered the actual world of fashion. From where she sat, it was as dazzling, entertaining and fun as a Broadway show.

From the third row of an old synagogue, among a crowd that was standing room only, Nicki took in the high-tech fashion show. Neon lasers, pulsating music and plastic shaped into clothing and made to look like stained glass set the tone for Ace Montgomery's second offering of women's wear called OTB Her. OTB stood for Out of the Box. She remembered that from last year's billboards of London plastered all over town. That was when he'd introduced a collection for women, with London being the face for his line. Now, as then, she commanded the show. Any doubters need look no further than the show's finale. London wore a beautifully painted stained-glass maxi that lit up on the runway when she reached midway. The crowd's cheers turned to roars when she spun to reveal glass shoes that lit up as well.

Backstage was a crush. Quinn and Teresa walked on each side of Nicki as she moved toward the crowd surrounding London as quickly as her crutches would allow. When London saw her family, she pushed through reporters and fans and other celebrities to greet them.

"You were wonderful," Nicki said as London gave her a big hug. "I can't believe I've missed out on this my whole life!"

"You've never been to fashion week?" London asked.

"Never."

"Well, you haven't missed out on anything like what you saw tonight. What Ace is bringing to the fashion world hasn't been done before."

"Ace, how much do you pay her to say things like that?" Julian asked.

Nicki turned and saw that Ace had walked up behind them. She remembered the underwear ads from his modeling days and being in awe of him like the rest of her friends.

Back then she'd never imagined seeing him in person, much less meeting the handsome star. Even if she'd stayed in touch and could tell her high school friends the truth, they probably wouldn't believe it. As good as he looked in magazines, he looked even better in person.

"Ace Montgomery," he said, holding out his hand.

"Wait, y'all haven't met?" London looked between the two.

"No."

"Never."

"What about the family reunion?"

"I was only there a day, remember?" Nicki responded.

"What about...oh, never mind. Babe, this is Julian's girlfriend, Nicki Long. Nicki, Ace Montgomery."

"As though he needs introducing at his very own show," Teresa joked.

"Your clothes are amazing," Nicki said. "Have you thought of designing for Broadway?"

Jennifer had been talking with another of the models but overheard this comment and exclaimed, "An excellent idea!"

"I hadn't thought of it," Ace said. "But now I will."

A photographer walked up to them. "Excuse me, guys. Could I get a picture?"

In trying to orchestrate a pose, her crutches made Nicki feel hampered. "Just a second," she said to the photog. "Here, can you hold these for just a sec?" she asked someone standing behind her.

With her booted foot bent and hidden behind her, Nicki looked as chic and fit as the rest of the group and felt happier than she had since the bike incident. Felt great when they met back up with the guys and the next day that she and Julian spent with her mother, Marie.

By Sunday the swelling in her ankle had gone down noticeably. She only took two pain pills all weekend, the second one not until just after the plane headed back west. By that night, however, she would feel another kind of pain, and her foot would have nothing to do with it.

# Chapter 11

The tone of the message should have been her first clue. That her director asked her to call back no matter the time should have been the second. But when the Drake company plane touched down in Paradise Cove Sunday night, Nicki had to be awakened from a deep sleep due to the pain medication she'd taken. All she had on her mind when she pulled out her phone to take it off airplane mode was a bed and a good night's sleep.

"What's wrong?"

They'd reached Julian's car and were headed toward the townhome when she listened to the message a second time.

"Probably nothing," Nicki mumbled.

"That's not what your face says."

"Milo wants me to call him, no matter the time. Said it's urgent."

"That could be good news."

"I guess. He didn't sound too happy."

Nicki opened the browser on her phone and typed in the show's name. Familiar links she'd seen before showed up on the screen. Show's official website. Theater where the show played. Places where would-be patrons could get tickets. Nothing unusual or out of the ordinary. Then why, thought Nicki, had her heartbeat increased?

"Wonder what he wanted."

"Why don't you call and find out?"

She tapped the screen. Seven minutes past eight in California. Just after eleven on the East Coast. The show was over, Milo probably backstage. She could call and hope to get voice mail. Then again, if she didn't find out what he wanted, there'd be no sleeping tonight. That was for sure.

Her thumb hovered over the screen to hit Callback. Just before tapping the icon, she got a better idea. Swiped through to her favorites and tapped the smiling face on her screen. After the third ring, her heart fell. Paige was probably backstage, too. Or still had the phone silenced, as they all did until after leaving the theater.

"Nick! Oh my God. I was just getting ready to call you. What the hell?"

"What do you mean? What's going on?" Nicki's voice sounded as panicked as she felt. Julian looked over, immediately concerned. She put the call on speaker, getting the feeling that whatever Paige was about to say was something she'd only want to hear once.

"You don't know? Your picture is all over the internet!"

"Me? What? Where?"

"At the OTB show with the supermodel London! And her husband, Ace Montgomery!"

"And?"

"And now it looks like you're out having fun and hob-nobbing with celebrities when you're under contract to work. Somebody told Milo, and he is not happy, to say the least."

Crap! How could she have been so careless? London was a celebrity. Of course the photographer would sell the pic. Caught up in the show's success and the night's excitement, she hadn't thought twice about being in the picture, had actually enjoyed being snapped as part of the group. Why shouldn't she? London was Julian's sister. And why would Milo get angry about her seeing a fashion show? Was she supposed to stay locked inside and not have any fun because she was injured? Anger replaced fear, which Nicki preferred greatly, especially since she now knew what was so urgent and why Milo had called.

"Does he know that London is my boyfriend's sister?

It's not like I was just out indiscriminately painting the town. But even if I were, wouldn't that be my business, not to mention my right? Milo knows why I'm not dancing. My foot is sprained severely, but I'm on crutches, not in a coma! Watching models walk the runway doesn't require physical labor. And there's nothing in my contract that stipulates if injured I should become a hermit until I can dance in the show again."

"No, but it's not cool to use the injury as a way to get out of doing a show to hang with your boyfriend. And that's what one of the stories implies."

Nicki couldn't talk for scrolling the screen. She'd put her name in the search bar, and all hell came up.

"Hello? Nick, you there?"

"I've got to go, Paige. Whoever said that is lying, and I've got to find out who it is."

"I knew it didn't sound like you."

"As long as I've been wanting to dance in a hit like this? And he thinks I'd skip out for any reason, especially to see a guy I've dated for years?"

"I know. It sucks."

"I've got to go."

"Okay, but call me back after talking to Milo."

Nicki ended the call while reading one of several links that mentioned her name.

They'd reached the house. Julian pulled into the garage and cut the engine. "So... Milo saw the picture we took?"

"Yes, and several more by the looks of it." She held out her phone so that Julian could see the photos. A side view as she chatted before the show. Another as she clapped and smiled. A shot of her and London hugging backstage. And the group shot, with everyone looking happy. No one looking injured. Nicki noticed not one shot included the boot on her foot or was taken as she walked on crutches. Coincidence? Sabotage? If so, by who? And why?

"There were cameras everywhere. And flashes, both from them and the lights in the show. Never thought for a second that I was the subject. There were at least a dozen photographers backstage alone. Not to mention cell phones. It could have been anyone."

"Whoever it was, the end result is the same. It's put you in a negative light. I don't like that at all."

Nicki sighed but said nothing as she continued scrolling the internet.

"Come on, babe. Let's go inside."

"Hang on. I'm looking for..."

She found the post Paige had mentioned, and the words she read cut short those she'd planned to say.

How can someone too injured to dance go to New York Fashion Week and prance? For the answer... Ask Ashley.

No question on the identity of Ashley. Next to the group shot taken on Friday night was the one from London's store, the selfie she'd taken with the woman Quinn said had a "dark heart."

Julian leaned closer. "Dang, honey. I forgot that you took a pic with that girl."

"I take selfies all the time. Quinn warned me about her, but I didn't think anything about it. I see now how that was a bad idea."

Her eyes slid from the picture back down to the text. "'Officially she has a sprained ankle. But while her cast mates were dancing it up at the Royal Theater, Nicki Long was strutting it up with celebrities...allegedly.' Not *allegedly*, you witch—"

"Babe..."

"What? She's inferring something that's totally not true."

"Exactly why you can't let her get to you, Nicki. People like her write what they hope people will read." Julian covered her hand with his and the phone along with it. "No, baby. Don't upset yourself further by reading more of that crap. You're the brightest thing shining around here, and she's just trying to catch a little light. That's all."

How could a woman stay angry with comments like that? Nicki was still beyond furious, but she appreciated what Julian was trying to do.

"You're right. They're lies. Unfortunately, some people don't know that. Like Milo. He obviously believed what he read." A sigh escaped her, as heated as the hot air Ashley blew in that article.

"I didn't know how I'd feel about being in New York and not dancing. But with you and your family, I had the best time! Was the happiest I'd been since the accident. And now this. Hurts worse than my ankle."

"We'll get it straightened out, babe. But not here. And not tonight. Let's go inside." Nicki opened her door. "Hang on. Let me help you."

Julian hopped out and came around to her side of the car.

Still holding her phone, she slipped the purse strap over her shoulder. "Where are my crutches?"

"Don't worry about that. I've got you. Put your arms around my neck."

His slender frame was misleading. But those close to him knew Julian's toned body was mostly muscle. Very little fat. Regular workouts and a decade in martial arts kept him in top form. He scooped her up effortlessly, opened the door and walked them inside.

"Thanks, babe. You can put me down now. I can make it from here."

"Without your crutches? I don't think so." Once up the stairs and inside the master suite, he walked to the bed and set her down gently. "Now…isn't that better?"

"Personal service all the way to my bed. What more can I ask for?"

"For that service to continue once you're in the bed. Glad you asked, pretty lady. Because that's exactly…" He kissed each cheek. "What…" Nuzzled her neck. "I plan to do." Slid his tongue inside her mouth. Nicki welcomed the onslaught. Julian was an excellent kisser. She'd like nothing more than to get carried away on the wings of ecstasy. But there was something she had to do.

She ended the kiss. "Let's put that on pause for when you come back up."

"What? The luggage? I can get that later." He leaned in again.

She pulled back. "I've got to call Milo. I really don't want to. Paige says he's angry. I'm not in the mood."

"Then don't call him."

"I have to. He said to call him ASAP, no matter the time."

"And you'll do that. But not tonight when you're exhausted, and reeling from someone lying about you on the internet. I think tomorrow morning is soon enough. Nine o'clock here will be noon his time."

"Thank you, Doctor. You have such a bedside manner."

"You have no idea. Just wait till I get back."

She watched him stroll out of the room. Strong, confident, saving the day. She lay back, rested against the pillow. Still very troubled about what happened, but she felt better somehow. One of the women had commented on the flight home that there was something about those Drake men. Julian's calm, steady demeanor and logical perspective was the perfect complement to her rash, more spontaneous attitude. He was right. Tomorrow would be soon enough for a conversation with the director. She'd call him on the way to get the MRI results. What more could happen between now and then to change anything?

Her cell phone pinged, indicating a text. Nicki yawned as she lifted the phone and read the screen. Vince. She sat straight up. Why was he texting? What did he want? No doubt he'd seen the stories like everyone else. She didn't want to do it but read the text anyway.

Nicki, you're balling! London's your sister? Now I know you can do a favor for a friend. Wouldn't even ask but the timing is crucial. Give me a call when you get this, ASAP.

Nicki deleted the text. Fell back on the bed. Just moments ago she'd wondered what else bad could happen. She'd just found out.

# Chapter 12

Bad moods were rare for Julian. Most people dreaded Monday mornings, but they'd never been a problem for him. Whether he had a class, his internship or a patient appointment, he usually looked forward to whatever the day would bring. But there were a few things that could affect his attitude and quality of life. One of them was Nicki being unhappy. Two was not knowing exactly why. The injury was part of it, sure. But he was more focused on what had happened the previous evening. The change in Nicki's mood when he returned from the car. The mood that had shifted again this morning, as with stilted conversation she tried to cover up what bothered her.

"I appreciate you taking me back for the MRI."

"Of course. It's no problem."

With no patients scheduled on Mondays, driving her to the specialist didn't mar his day at all. There was nothing he would have handled at the office this morning that couldn't be done later at home. Being behind the wheel instead of behind a desk right now worked to his advantage. Preoccupied with the mystery going on in his home, he might not have accomplished a thing anyway.

After returning with their luggage, she hadn't wanted to make love. What could have happened to change her feelings so abruptly? Not the sudden return of pain in her ankle, as she'd claimed. Or fatigue from a pain pill when she tossed and turned half the night. There was more to it, but he hadn't pushed. Silence, Julian had learned, was a valuable tool when desiring to learn someone's true feelings. People usually shared much more information when given voluntarily without being pushed.

"I'm sorry for fading out on you last night."

"You're feeling better this morning. That's all that matters. Still no pain?"

"No, and I haven't had to take a pain pill. Makes me cautiously optimistic that I'll have good news for Milo."

"You think so?"

"Yes. Paige texted this morning and said my understudy is still being listed as a substitute and not my replacement. The grade-two sprain that was diagnosed in New York can take four to six weeks to heal. I'm hoping that my being in shape can cut off a week or two and I can be back in the show sooner rather than later."

"You don't want to risk a greater injury by going back to work prematurely."

"Wearing a protective bandage can help. And I won't start out full on—maybe eighty percent."

"I know how much you want to be back on stage, babe. Here's hoping that your dream comes true."

They reached the diagnostic center. Much like on Friday, Nicki and Julian didn't have a long wait. This time they were directed to an office instead of an examination room. Dr. Allen entered with a smile on his face. Julian hoped Nicki would leave with one on hers.

"Good morning, Nicki. Julian."

"Good morning," Julian said.

"Morning," Nicki said. "You'll tell me whether it's good or not."

"I've heard that any morning you wake up on this side of the dirt is a pretty good one." He sat behind the desk. "How was your weekend?"

The worst possible question, Julian thought, as he watched mixed emotions flit across Nicki's face.

"Long," she finally said. "My director is waiting to hear from me. I'm hoping not to be replaced."

"Then I won't keep you waiting. The bruising that garnered my concern was indicative of a more serious problem than the grade-two sprain that was initially diagnosed. You have an avulsion fracture."

Nicki's whole body slumped as she sat back against the chair. "A chipped bone?"

"A bone fragment has separated from the larger bone and the adjoining tendons. I'm sorry, Nicki. I know this isn't what you wanted to hear."

"What's the shortest amount of healing time?"

"I'd recommend no less than six weeks, especially since you were misdiagnosed and the ankle wasn't casted immediately. There's been no time for the bone fragment to reattach and set. I do believe it's close enough to that larger bone that a soft cast will stabilize it and surgery will not be required."

"A cast or surgery. Those are my options?"

"Absolutely not. You can continue to wear the boot and take your chances on whether or not the bone will heal correctly. You might even be able to do moderate dance. But maybe not. Either way you'll more than likely end up with chronic pain that can only be alleviated through surgery."

Nicki put her head in her hands. Julian reached over to comfort her. Nicki shook him off. "I'm okay." She took a deep breath and lifted her head. Her eyes looked misty, but no tears fell. "I'll do the cast."

Dr. Allen nodded. "That's a good and wise answer. The sooner you are on the road to healing, the sooner you'll be back to doing what you love."

Less than hour later, Julian helped Nicki to the car. He'd have broken his own ankle to help hers heal, but all he could do was support her as much as possible in any way that he could. They got buckled in and were soon on their way back to Paradise Cove.

"Are you hungry?" Nicki shook her head as she looked out the window. He watched her hand squeeze into a fist, knew she was resisting the urge to cry. His heart broke a little. The therapist kicked in. He remained quiet, giving her space until they merged onto the highway. It was midmorning. Traffic was light. The sun was bright. A total contrast to the gloomy, heavy atmosphere in the car.

"Baby, I'm sorry this happened to you. I can't imagine how devastating it must feel to work as hard as you have and reach your goal, only to have one of life's crazy flukes derail your plans." Julian didn't expect a response and didn't get one. "While dealing with day-to-day struggles, we often get used to hiding our feelings. We're told to be strong. Suck it up. Keep it moving, and all that. But you know I'm a safe zone, right? Where you can acknowledge the sadness, let the tears flow. It's best to get it out, babe, because otherwise those feelings will expand, deepen and cloud every thought and situation that you encounter."

She remained quiet. Julian let her be. As outgoing as she was in social situations and especially when she was on the stage, he was familiar with the side that she now revealed. Quiet. Private. Figuring it out on her own, in her head. Ironic, he thought, as Nicki reached for the cell phone in her purse. Patients paid a high fee to receive his counsel. Nicki could receive it for free, yet often kept her own.

"Might as well get this over with," Nicki mumbled.

Julian glanced over as she tapped her cell phone screen. "The call to Milo?"

"I've anticipated being fired before, but never considered having an injury cause me to leave a show. I've danced for almost fifteen years straight and never had to quit one. Why now?"

Julian remained quiet and instead heard Nicki leaving a message asking Milo to call her. After finishing the call, she adjusted her body, reclined the seat slightly and closed her eyes. Whether from exhaustion or avoidance, he didn't know. Remembering her restless night, he figured it was probably some of both.

He sympathized with Nicki, but it didn't extend to sadness. Everything happened for a reason. Julian felt this was no different. Her career was always the excuse she'd given for not moving west. For now, that barrier was gone. He hoped she'd stay in Paradise Cove during the recovery process, for the six to eight weeks Dr. Allen recommended. Perhaps in that time she'd come to love the town as he did, enough to leave New York for good. It was a selfish thought. Julian knew he should feel bad for having it. But he didn't. The only niggle that remained was from last night's situation and Nicki's mood swing. Why was he still so focused on that? Why had it bothered him so much?

More than likely it was due to the show, he decided, and the thought of having to leave it. He spent the next several miles shifting his thinking and imagining a life with Nicki in Paradise Cove. For that to happen, he'd have to get up the nerve to propose again. Nicki had no idea how she'd hurt him when she turned him down two years ago. He wanted to ask her. He wanted her to be his wife. But he didn't think his ego could survive a second no. Another rejection and their relationship would be over. And if she returned to New York? What would he do then? How long was he willing to endure a long-distance relationship and a life lived alone?

Not much longer, he realized. As they neared PC, Julian had a sobering thought. Their relationship might be ending right now.

# Chapter 13

Nicki looked at her phone for the tenth time in five minutes, then placed it on the kitchen island, determined to walk away and leave it there. It was the only way she'd stop checking the ringer volume or text messages to ensure she hadn't missed a message or call from Milo, returning her call from yesterday.

She reached for the crutches leaning against the granite countertop and headed out of the room as fast she could hop. It was hard to run away from one's thoughts on crutches. As she passed the dining space into the living room they followed her. So what if it had been almost twenty-four hours since she'd left Milo a message. There were any number of reasons why he hadn't returned her call. It could have nothing to do with the fashion show pictures and the past weekend's gossip. Milo would never doubt her passion for dancing, uncompromising work ethic or belief in the show. Until the accident she'd never missed rehearsal. Never been late. More often than not, she'd been one of the first ones there and one of the last to go home. She'd worked herself ragged to get a difficult sequence perfected, the timing just right. Milo knew about her dreams of Broadway, had said she was one of the hungriest performers he'd ever seen.

As for not calling on Friday? That was no big deal, either. The reason was simple. She hadn't any news until yesterday—which was the worst news possible, with dire consequences. But a short time after receiving the cast and leaving the hospital, she'd put on her big-girl panties and called the director. He needed to call her back. ASAP. The waiting hurt worse than her ankle ever did.

Reaching the expansive glass doors, she slid one of them open and walked out into the crisp morning air. The coming of autumn had not only brought cooler temps, but colorful foliage on the red maple and sweetgum trees planted in the backyard. Nicki noticed how the leaves' colors complemented the patio's natural stone tile, highlighted the red and orange shards amid the tan and gray. They reminded her of the trees in Prospect Park near her childhood home. She used to collect them as she played on Saturday mornings and take them to school for Monday's show and tell.

Time to go back, she thought as she watched a bird sail over the fence and perch on one of the higher branches. She didn't want to be a burden to Julian, or draw his family's pity. Even with crutches she could navigate Brooklyn. She had more resources there—she knew her neighbors. Could grab a bus, train or taxi down the street from her house. Maybe Julian could come for a visit in November, celebrate Thanksgiving in New York. Almost eight weeks away. A long time to be without her man. The only thing good about the thought was that by then she'd be back dancing.

She reached a patio chair and leaned her crutch against the table. Just as she was about to sit down, her phone rang. "Just like a watched pot," she mumbled, grabbing the crutch and hightailing it back to the kitchen as fast as she could.

"Hello?"

"Hey, superstar."

Crap! Vince. Too late, she glanced at the screen. Wouldn't have helped. The call hadn't come in as private but with a number she didn't recognize but probably would have answered since it began with a Brooklyn area code: 929.

"What, you don't have any conversation for an old friend?"

"No, Vince. We've already had what should have been our last conversation two conversations ago."

"You didn't get my text?"

"I got it but I didn't understand it. Taking a picture with a group of celebrities doesn't put money in my bank account."

"Not just celebrities. Your sister."

"London isn't my sister."

"Your boyfriend's sister. Same thing."

"Who have you been talking to?"

"The internet. Info at your fingertips, girl. No secrets anymore."

Nicki wished she'd remembered that after giving Vince her number. Had she done so she would have realized two very important words he'd left out of the description "pro basketball player"—*former* and *broke*.

"Who I'm dating and his family tree have nothing to do with what you asked me months ago. I didn't have money to loan you then and I still don't."

"Ask your man for the money. He should be able to take care of you at least as good as I did."

The comment was audacious and wrong and rolled off his tongue much too glibly. As though it wasn't being said for the first time. So quickly did she want to rebut the lie, Nicki almost bit her tongue. "Oh, so that's how you've re-written our very brief history together. I wondered how you could possibly come to someone you barely knew a month and ask for that much money. It's because you've fabricated an experience that didn't happen. I've taken care of myself since I was seventeen years old and worked hard for every dime I've earned. Just like I worked for and won the audition in Atlanta. The director exposed your lie two years ago. I didn't owe you then, and get this straight—I don't owe you now."

Vince laughed as though she'd just told a joke. Nicki wasn't laughing at all.

"Your attitude doesn't surprise me. Nor does your gall.

Next time it won't be me saying this. It will be my attorney or a judge. Lose my number."

"I'm not playing with you, Nicki. I borrowed money from the wrong people. Now I owe them. And you owe me. I intend to collect. Don't make me—"

She ended the call and seconds later heard the garage door opening. Unexpected since Julian usually called before coming home to see what she needed or suggest eating out. Earlier than he usually broke for lunch, too. Had something happened? Was he okay? And what if Vince decided to call again? That's exactly what he did. She refused the call and muted her phone just as Julian walked into the kitchen.

"Hi."

The barest of pauses between strides. "Hey, babe." He walked over. Hugged her. "Your heart's racing. I excite you like that?" His eyes were intent, but he smiled.

"Of course." She playfully pushed past him and put the wide granite island between them. "But I'm on edge, too."

"The director called?"

"No."

"That's got you nervous." Nicki didn't answer, just kind of half shrugged. "Totally understandable that it would. Think you should call again?"

"I don't want to appear as anxious as I feel. Wasn't expecting you, either, so hearing the garage door startled me."

"It was a spontaneous decision. A nice day, and I felt like getting out of the office. But perhaps I should have called."

"I'm glad you're here. Crutches are helpful, but I like you carrying me much better." One second she was standing, the next her feet had left the floor. Nicki let out a sound of surprise.

Julian had picked her up as though she weighed nothing, carried her across the room and set her down on the couch.

He flopped down beside her. "Better?"

"Actually, yes. Thank you."

"With nervousness probably putting your stomach in knots, is it safe for me to assume that you haven't eaten?"

"I had a protein shake earlier. Does that count?"

"Like I figured." Julian eased off the couch. "I'm going to run down to the deli. They've got great soups, sandwiches and salads. Going to bring you back something and you're going to eat it. Okay?"

"Sure." Julian walked away, but when Nicki's phone buzzed he came back into the living room. His eyes asked a question. In answer, Nicki held up her cell phone, which showed the face of a smiling man with curly black hair and a bright feather earring in his right ear. Milo.

Nicki answered the call and put it on speaker. "Milo?" She watched Julian sit on the short side of the L-shaped sectional with her directly in his line of sight.

"Hello, Nicki. How are you?"

"I've been better."

"From what I hear, things are fine."

Nicki looked at Julian. She was almost sure what Milo was talking about but refused to be the one to mention the pictures from fashion week.

"What did you hear?"

"That you were in New York last week. Partying it up at the OTB show. Can't dance on that ankle, but it appears you can walk just fine. You should have stopped by."

"Watch the show I'm supposed to be in, with someone else dancing my part? I can't believe you'd suggest that, Milo. Sitting this show out is the hardest thing I've ever done. Yes, I was in New York. London is my boyfriend's sister. They thought going to the show would cheer me up. But I was and still am very much on crutches, with an injury that's even worse than I thought. So please don't believe everything you read, Milo. This is hard enough."

"Perception is reality, Nicki. Especially in this town. You were supposed to call on Friday. You didn't. Then you're snapped at fashion week, leaving me to have to explain to investors why you were too injured to work but not too hurt to party. That was pretty difficult, too."

"I'm sorry, Milo. You're right. I should have called. I didn't because there was no new information. The doctor wanted to do an MRI before making an official diagnosis. We just got the results yesterday. I called right after."

"What's the verdict?"

"Chipped bone. Soft cast. Out for at least four more weeks."

"Ouch."

"Exactly."

"I'm sorry, Nicki."

"Me, too. I know that's a long time, but I'm hoping there's a way you can save my spot and let me come back. I've worked so hard—"

"You know I can't do that. This is a short run, only sixteen weeks. In three weeks Arielle will have been in the role longer than you. The audience loves her. So do the investors. It's rotten timing. Lousy luck. But there's no way I can guarantee you that spot."

"But the investors love you too, Milo. And you know how dedicated I am to this show! If you tell them you want me in that role, they'll listen. Maybe it won't take six weeks. If it guarantees that I won't lose the role, I can work my ass off and be back in four."

"It's too late, Nicki. Asking you to call on Friday wasn't just to inquire about your health. It was to inform you that while you were great, and you know how much I love how you dance, the investors prefer Arielle. Especially the one based in LA who wants to transition the show from Broadway to the big screen. She's pulled for her from the very beginning. Thinks the camera will love her. Arielle will take over the part permanently, beginning this week."

Milo kept talking, but Nicki didn't hear much more after that. The call ended. She was vaguely aware of Julian coming to sit next to her, his arms going around her. A river of tears came up from her belly. She batted her eyelids and swallowed the pain. The tears lodged in her throat. She wouldn't cry. What good would it do? It was time to go home. The faster she went back, the faster she and her agent could start working on the next gig. Finding upcoming shows. Taking meetings and networking. She would not let a chipped bone chip away her dream of Broadway and stardom. She was too close to stop now.

Julian kissed her temple. Nicki grabbed her throat lest the cry escape.

"What are you thinking, baby?"

"Calling my agent," she replied, her voice raspy with pent-up emotion. She cleared her throat. "Setting up meetings. And making a reservation to fly back home."

Nicki knew it wasn't the answer he wanted to hear. She didn't want to leave, either. Mostly because of how much she loved Julian, but there was another reason. Vince was in New York, along with the thugs, the threats and the fear that one of their angry taunts would be carried out.

# *Chapter 14*

The next morning Julian arrived at the office with what he thought were big problems. By the afternoon his perspective had changed. His first appointment was slowly rebuilding her life after relocating to PC following the unspeakable trauma of discovering a teenage son who'd committed suicide. The second appointment battled guilt over surviving an accident where his best friend was killed. It had happened years ago, but the pain was as fresh as if it had happened yesterday.

Julian released his last patient with a referral to a psychiatrist. There were times when medication was mandatory and the war vet's severe PTSD and dysthymia presented one of those times. He'd gone out for lunch, walked around the square to clear his head. He sat and thought about the dilemmas that hours ago had felt enormous. Nicki leaving was no small matter, and the increasing number of patients wanting to switch from Dr. Johnson's care to his was disconcerting at best. But in comparison to what some people in the world had to deal with, Julian counted himself a lucky man.

The sound of a cell phone broke into his thoughts. A programmed series of chimes informed Julian that it was the call he'd expected. He retrieved the phone from where it sat on the desk and walked back to the window.

"Hello, Mom."

"Good afternoon, son. How are you?"

"I'm good."

"Julian, I've known you since the day you were born. You're handling business effectively as always, but what's been said about Nicki has got to upset you. How could it not?"

With what had happened since then and his shift in perspective, he'd almost forgotten about Ashley's blog. "I'm not happy about what was written. But there are way worse problems than gossip, Mom."

"What do you mean?"

Suicide. War. Chronic depression. "Nicki's out of the show."

"Oh no! What happened?"

He told her. "Ashley's post was untimely and in poor taste," he finished. "But it was the chipped bone that got her released."

"Nicki must be devastated."

"It was her worst-case scenario."

"That still doesn't excuse what Ashley's done and continues to do. Did you know she talked to *XYZ*?"

"I did not." Nor did he care, at the moment.

"We should have handled that Ashley matter years ago after what happened with Niko. But your father talked me out of it. Felt as you did, that she and her mother were minor, insignificant and should be ignored. Now your lady has become fodder for tabloid media, and that conniver who's been trying to come up for years sees another bootstrap to try and ride up on since she can't seem to use her own. Well, I know you are not going to stand for that, and the members of your family, darling, stand with you."

"Mom, you know I'm not good at this kind of stuff. I don't fight with people like her. I treat them."

"I treat them, too, dear. We only differ on the prescription."

"Besides, Ashley isn't the one behind that smear campaign. Someone angry at me used her as a pawn."

"Go on."

"No need. I'll handle it."

"Of course you will. You always do. You're the only child of mine who can do so without my having one inkling about what's going on. It's something that I find equally admirable and annoying." Julian truly laughed for the first time all day. "What will Nicki do now?"

"Go back to New York. Start looking for work."

"But you just said she's out for at least six weeks. Why does she feel the need to go back so quickly?"

"It's home. She feels more comfortable there. Able to do things, move around, with a support system of her neighbors and friends, and her mother in New Jersey."

"Does she know about her support system in Paradise Cove? What happens to one of us happens to all of us. Tell her that. Never mind, I will. Please remind her of the lunch date we discussed over the weekend. Let her know I'll be calling tomorrow to firm up those plans."

Julian knew Jennifer. There was a motive for this meal. "I'll let her know."

"Good. I'm excited to share an idea with her."

"As long as whatever you have in mind can happen from New York. She's planning to leave at the end of the week. I doubt those plans will change."

"Is that what you want?"

Julian thought about what he'd wanted, and what had happened that night in Times Square when he'd worked up the nerve to act on his desire. Hadn't turned out so good.

"Julian, did you hear me?"

"I heard you. I want Nicki to be where she's happy. At the end of the…hold on, Mom." He muted his cell phone and pushed the intercom button. "Yes, Katie?"

"You have a visitor, Dr. Drake."

Julian slowly stood, his voice calm. "Who is it?" Nata-

lie? At the mere thought his back stiffened, despite his resolve not to react. He was so not in the mood.

"It's your brother."

His body relaxed. "Which one?"

The door opened. Ike walked in. "Your eldest brother,
Doctor. The one who matters most."

Julian unmuted his cell phone. The unexpected inter-
ruption brought out a smile. "Mom, I have a visitor. Let's
talk later."

"Sure, son. Love you. Goodbye."

Julian motioned for Ike to have a seat, then sat behind
the desk. Ike bypassed the two modern chairs facing Julian's desk and walked into the seating area where he saw
patients. There was a fabric-covered love seat done in a
geometric charcoal and gray print with blue microdots
breaking the monotony. A similar chair to those facing
Julian's desk was by the love seat, in the same color blue
as the dots on the couch. On the opposite wall was a leather
chaise. Across the back was a colorful fleece throw for
those patients who felt more comfortable lying down when
baring their souls and their problems.

Ike nodded his approval as he returned to the desk.
"Very nice, little brother." He sat, continued to look around
with an expression of wonder mixed with pride. "These offices have the look and feel of a bona fide psychologist."

"Imagine that."

"Not cold and impersonal, though, like those stereotypi-
cal ones you see in the movies. It feels comfortable, warm.
Mom handled the interior decorating, I assume?"

"It's signature Jennifer."

"I've often said the only difference between Mom and
the people she hires is their degree." Ike looked at Julian.
"I'm proud of you, man. Still remember you at family gath-
erings off in some corner with a computer or book. So

quiet. Missing nothing. I should have known you'd grow into someone focused on the mind."

"You clearly had heading up the family business on lock, so I had to find my lane."

"Ah, so that's how it happened?" Ike stretched out his legs, clasped his hands behind his head. "You were never all that into the business, though you would have made an excellent CFO. Sales? Not so much. On account of to sell a property you have to talk and all."

"Which is why Terrell as sales VP is a perfect fit." Said with that almost smile. He looked at his watch. "So, Ike, to what do I owe this pleasure? Since it hasn't happened before, I appreciate you coming by the office, but I doubt it was just to check out the decor."

"That was part of it. A visit to see the end result of a decade in college was long overdue."

"And the other part?"

"I wanted to see how you were holding up, not how you said you were doing, because that answer is always 'good' or 'fine.' But you're the quiet one. You don't do drama. So I came to see for myself how this weekend's scandal has affected you."

"I learned how not to do drama by watching you. Terrell is who I expected to come by."

"Come by to add to it?"

Julian nodded with gleeful eyes. "But then again, guess life has never been the same for you since Quinn shook you up."

"Are you equating my wife with drama?" Ike asked in a way that suggested Julian should be careful of his answer.

"Absolutely," Julian replied, totally carefree.

"You'd be right. I know you know, but I wanted to tell you personally that anything we can do to help, anything you or Nicki need, just let us know. Maybe you guys can come over Friday night. Quinn would love that. She once dreamed of being a ballerina. I think she's a little star-struck."

"She's flying home on Friday."

"How'd you run her away, bro?"

"She misses New York."

The intercom beeped. "Excuse me, Dr. Drake?"

"Yes."

"Could you pick up, please?"

Julian knew the call was about a patient, and Katie was following protocol to maintain privacy. "Okay."

"It's Frank Snyder calling. Again."

"Take a message. And can you pull his file and draft a formal letter with my explicit instructions for him to continue seeing his present psychiatrist?"

"Sure, Doctor."

"And please do the same for the folders placed in your inbox. There should be three or four. Thanks."

He replaced the receiver, brow furrowed.

"Problem?"

"A situation." Julian leaned against the chair back, idly rubbing his chin as he pondered the call. "Several of Dr. Johnson's patients wanting my help."

"Current patients?"

Julian nodded.

"Why?"

"Speaking generally, there are many reasons why it happens. Feeling uncomfortable, not with the treatment but with the person. Not connecting. No rapport. Or too comfortable, not feeling challenged, not progressing at the rate or level one thinks they should. Trust is paramount to healing, and what establishes that trust is subjective. Not long ago an associate of mine lost a client because he's a Mets fan and the patient was a Yankees season ticket holder."

Ike shrugged. "It's a free country. If people want to change therapists and come to you, it's their choice, right?"

"Yes."

"Why is that a problem?"

"Because in a town this size, Johnson knows what's happening."

"Did he confront you?"

"He didn't have to. Natalie did."

"I don't know her."

"We went to grade and middle school together."

"Look, don't give the competition another thought."

"I'm not competing with anyone."

"When there's a shared goal, a choice to be made and money involved, it's competition. This isn't personal, it's business. Sounds like Dr. Johnson might have a problem. Because when it comes to competition, Drakes always win."

"Thanks, Ike." Julian stood. "I'm glad you stopped by."

Ike stood as well. "I've overstayed my welcome so you're kicking me out?"

"No, I'm escorting you out. Duty calls."

Julian returned to his desk, glad his brother had decided to stop by. Ike had lifted his spirits and given him resolve. His brother was right. Drakes didn't lose. When it came to wanting something, they went all out to get it. And Julian wanted Nicki to stay in PC.

He looked at his watch. Five minutes until his client arrived. He turned to his laptop, checked his schedule, made some changes and then clicked on a search engine. Nicki might go home on Friday. But it wouldn't be for his lack of trying to convince her otherwise.

# Chapter 15

Vince hadn't followed Nicki's suggestion to lose her number. Instead he'd texted or called almost a dozen times since yesterday. That she knew of—could have been more. He'd only left one voice mail, ratcheting up the danger he faced. Demanding she call him. But there'd been a few calls from unknown numbers, too. She hadn't answered, and no messages had been left from those numbers. Even if she'd had an inkling to, which she hadn't, what was revealed in the texts wouldn't have changed her mind.

Nicki reached for her tablet and clicked on the app she'd downloaded that morning—a way to save the text messages in a printable document, a backup in case they disappeared from her phone. She typed in her password. The app opened up to Vince's messages. Exchanges that had changed in topic and tone. Growing more erratic. More threatening. More desperate. Making Nicki more uneasy with each note she read.

The phone on the counter vibrated. Nicki jumped, startled. She chanced a glance, hoping that instead of the 929 prefix of Vince's number, she'd see the friendly face of a number she'd saved. A wide, impish smile and bright green eyes looked back at her.

"Paige! I'm so glad it's you."

"I'm glad you answered. You didn't last night."

"I'd silenced the phone. Checked messages this morning, though, and didn't get yours."

"Didn't leave one. Figured you'd call back when you saw the missed call."

"I've been trying not to look at my phone."

"Oh no! Is it the reporters? Are you being hounded about

the fashion show pics or this morning's press release? I'm so sorry for you, Nicki. It just isn't fair."

"That I've been released from the show? They announced it?"

"Sounds like you knew already."

"Milo called me yesterday."

"What did he say? Because I thought he'd agreed to hold your spot for the four weeks it would take to heal."

"Looks like it's going to take longer than that. Besides, the investors like what Arielle brings to the role. They're considering a film version of the show and want her in it."

"How do they figure when you are clearly the better dancer? What she brings to the role? What does that mean?"

"Doesn't matter. Like I said, the injury is worse than first diagnosed. It'll take six to eight weeks to heal. She would have replaced me anyway."

"Your ankle is broken?"

"Fractured. The doctor in New York didn't see the full extent of the injury. The specialist Julian's family recommended, a doctor who specializes in sports injuries, was concerned about the bruising still visible after two weeks. He did an MRI and discovered that a piece of bone had been chipped off."

"Yikes!"

"Yep. And that I've tried to put pressure on it didn't help. Now I'm in a cast for the next two weeks to keep the ankle immobile so the bone can reattach. Where'd you read the announcement about the change?"

"The cast got an email last night."

"It's probably everywhere by now."

"This is such a bummer, Nicki. What are you going to do?"

"Paige, to be honest, I don't know. With everything going on, it may be a blessing in disguise."

"How so?"

"Vince is still contacting me, to the point where I'm getting a little freaked out."

"What is he saying?"

"He only left one voice mail, demanding I call him. But he's left these texts." Nicki tapped on the messages icon. "The first one said, 'You hanging up on me now? This is not a game!' I didn't respond. The second one. 'Come on, Nicki, I need this. These guys want their money now!' The third one. 'They'll back off if I send at least half. Can you loan me ten K? Today? Use PayPerson with this number.' The fourth one. 'I'm going to get my money one way or the other.'"

"Oh my gosh, Nick! That's an all-out threat!"

"Yep, and it's this last one that really got me. It says, 'Those guys think you're the problem. Do they need to pay you another visit?'"

"Okay, that's it. He's taken this to a whole other level. When are you coming back? As soon as you do, you need to go to the police, tell them everything and get a restraining order."

"Agreed. But will that be enough?"

"What else can you do?"

Nicki saw that a new message had come in. She tapped her screen to open it and read the text from Julian. "Right now I'm going to get off the phone and get dressed to go out. Julian just texted me saying he'd be by in an hour and be ready to go."

"Have you told him yet?"

"No, and I have my reasons so don't go there. I already know how you feel."

"You need to tell him, Nicki. Not necessarily about the affair, but definitely about the threats. Promise me you will."

"I never thought about revealing the threats but not the affair. But you're right. There's no need for him to know that part of the story. You have my word, Paige. I'll tell him today."

A short time later, Julian breezed into the house with the signature subconscious swagger of a confident Drake. He'd gone from feeling sad about Nicki's inevitable leaving to being excited about the challenge of trying to convince her to stay.

"Nicki!"

"Yeah, babe. Up here!"

"You ready?" He took the steps quickly to see for himself.

"Just about."

He entered the master suite. "Where are you?"

"In here." Nicki turned while putting on an earring as he reached the en suite doorway and leaned against the jamb.

"I thought I told you to be ready, woman!"

"I am."

"Ready would have been downstairs on the couch waiting with purse in hand."

"Where are we going? Is this okay?"

Julian took in her outfit, brown velvet palazzo pants, matching cropped turtleneck, a tan leather ankle boot on one foot and a knitted bootie over her cast. Several strands of vibrantly colored wooden beads completed the fall look.

"It's perfect." He stepped in and gave her a kiss. "Let's go," he said, glancing at his watch as he reached for her hand. "Our plane is scheduled for takeoff in thirty minutes."

Nicki snatched back her hand and reached for the second wooden hoop lying on the counter. "Plane? Where are we going? And why didn't you tell me to pack?"

"Someplace special. Come on. We need to leave."

"Julian!" She reached for the crutch leaning against the wall. "Move! I need to throw a few—"

He grabbed her hand once again and halted her progress. "You don't need to do anything but grab your purse and maybe your makeup. I'll take care of whatever else you need."

"Take care of me having something to wear? How, by buying me a whole new wardrobe?"

"If that's what it takes to get you out of this bathroom and into the car. Now, are you going to use that crutch or should I carry you down? Never mind." He scooped her up and headed toward the door.

"Wait, Julian. My purse!"

"I'll come back for it."

"Don't make picking me up a habit. I can walk on my own."

"Why? I thought women liked being swept off their feet."

Minutes later the couple were off and headed for the landing strip that serviced private planes.

"Where are we going?"

Julian glanced over, turned on the car's music system, kept on driving. Nicki huffed and crossed her arms.

"Baby, listen." He gave her a sexy look. "Remember this?" He turned up the volume. "I'm addicted, and I just can't get enough."

Nicki pouted, gave him a side eye.

"Come on, babe. That crazy party you invited me to. What was that, our second date or third one?"

Nicki's pout deepened. "I don't remember."

Julian laughed out loud. A rare sound. "Yes, you do!" He bobbed his head to the beat. "Come on, you know you want to dance. This is one of your favorite groups. Then there's this one."

Bruno Mars's lilting voice oozed out of the speakers and made Nicki smile.

"You remember what happened after we heard this?"

"No."

"Liar!" Julian laughed again as he turned up the volume.

"Of course I remember," Nicki said after a time. "That was the night we first made love."

The night she found out twenty-one-year-old Julian was a virgin, and learned the conservative view he held when it came to sex. Not the act. Julian was a freak between the sheets. But that lovemaking was special, not something to be done with just anyone. "What's with this trip down memory lane? You trying to tell me something?"

"Absolutely."

"What?"

Julian pulled into the parking lot next to the hangar where private planes were stored when not in use. Looked into Nicki's anxious eyes.

"That we're getting ready to make more memories, even more beautiful than the ones we made that night."

# Chapter 16

Though Julian offered both a wheelchair and his arms as transporting devices, Nicki insisted on getting through the hangar to the landing strip on her own strength. It should have been a given since they hadn't driven to a commercial airport, but Nicki didn't realize they were taking a private plane until she saw the same sleek aircraft they'd boarded to New York a week ago. Even so, she asked the obvious.

"We're taking the company plane?"

"We are indeed."

"I thought you said it was only used for business."

"This is somewhat of a business trip."

"How so?"

"It will become clearer as the evening unfolds. Can you make it up the stairs or should I inform the attendant to convert it to a ramp so that you can use the wheelchair?"

"I can make it." Julian reached up and placed a hand at her elbow, a move that got him reprimanded. "I've got it, Julian. Just give me a second."

"I'm just offering support, Nicki. The last thing we want is for you to have a mishap that results in another injury."

Nicki reached the top of the stairs, quietly greeted the cautious attendant and sat down in the first available seat. She watched Julian enter behind her. He chatted casually with the attendant before the pilot joined them. The three laughed at something before the pilot shook Julian's hand and walked into the cockpit.

Nicki watched how comfortable Julian was in these luxurious surroundings, as if flying in this manner was normal. She wondered what it was like to have grown up in wealth and privilege. Nicki's mom had done an excellent job in providing for her only child. Nicki's father had died when she was young, tragically killed in a freak motorcycle accident. Nicki hadn't lived in excess by any means. Her mother hadn't spoiled her. She'd been given everything she needed and quite a few things that she wanted as well. Yet in the last few minutes, she realized, it was him who'd acted like one with stellar home training and her who'd played the spoiled brat. Julian was only trying to be helpful, obviously taking her on this trip to feel better about losing her Broadway job. She should be thanking him for being so generous. Instead she was acting like a witch.

He slowly approached her. "Is it safe for me to sit beside you or should I find my own row?"

"I'm sorry for snapping at you." Nicki patted the seat beside her. "Sit down. Please."

He reached for her hand, held it as he spoke but did not look at her. "I can understand you being upset. I know how much your career means to you. But I get the feeling that something else is going on, Nicki." He looked at her then. "What is it?"

"You're right. There is something else."

The attendant walked up. "We'll be taking off shortly. Can I get you something to drink?"

"We're fine, thanks." Julian spoke for both them.

"Actually," Nicki said, "do you have Patrón?"

"Yes, we do."

"Could I get a margarita?"

"Salt on the rim?"

"Um, no, thank you."

"Coming right up."

She felt Julian's eyes on her. "You all right?" She nodded. "You rarely ever drink."

"I know."

"You shouldn't mix alcohol with those meds."

"I didn't take one today."

"But you're not hurting?"

*Not in my ankle.* "No, I'm good."

They felt the plane begin to taxi. Julian buckled his seat belt. Nicki did, too.

The attendant brought back the margarita and handed it to Nicki. "I brought you a sparkling water, Dr. Drake. I hope you don't mind."

Julian lifted the glass slightly. "Good choice. Thanks."

Nicki looked out the window. Her stomach roiled with nerves. There was simply no good time to share bad news, no pretty way to dress up ugly. With steely resolve and another sip of the tasty margarita, she began speaking.

"There is someone trying to force me to repay money I don't owe." In the ensuing silence, Nicki imagined Julian's sharp mind rapidly turning. Processing what she'd said, adding in what she hadn't. "He needs money quick and—"

"He?"

"Yes."

"He who?"

"A guy I met a couple years ago. One of his cousins directed a show I did in Atlanta. He tried to say his connection is how I got the role. It isn't. I auditioned like everyone else. But he's using the claim to try to get money. I think he borrowed from a loan shark or someone shady who's pressing pretty hard to get their money back."

Julian's eyes narrowed as he pondered what Nicki said. He took a sip of water, then another, before turning to eye her closely. "That sounds weird, like there's more to the story."

"There's a little more to it. I went out with him a couple years ago. Right after we broke up. Met him at a party, felt lonely, gave him my number. We only went out a few times. When you and I got back together, I had already blocked his number."

"That was it?"

"Pretty much. He was a jerk, obviously. I wouldn't have continued with him no matter what."

"So with his number blocked, how'd he contact you? Did he come to the show?" He turned more fully. "Is that what happened the night I was there? On opening night, when you ran to the car as though someone was chasing you?"

Nicki looked out the window. The attendant started toward them but was halted by Julian's hand.

"He was there. Waiting on the sidewalk. Didn't approach me when he saw you. But he'd called me a couple weeks before, when I answered an unknown number thinking it was someone calling about the show. It was him. He'd seen the news that I'd gotten a role on Broadway. Guess he figured, like many others, that anyone on Broadway is making tons of money. I honestly thought it was a joke, until he started talking about the show in Atlanta and how he'd talked to the director and that's how I got hired. I told him I didn't have it and even if I did, I wouldn't loan him that kind of money."

"How much does he want?"

"Twenty thousand."

"He thinks you owe him twenty thousand dollars?"

"I don't owe him anything. Twenty thousand is how much he needs. He has a gambling habit. That's one of the things I found out just before you and I got back together. He's got to be desperate to come to me, someone he dated for a month two years ago. Anyway, the harassing phone calls have continued, and gotten worse in the last few days."

"So this has been going on since the show opened." Nicki nodded. "I hate that you've dealt with this alone all this time. It's disappointing that you wouldn't reach out."

"I should have, Julian. I realize that now. But I was embarrassed to even have gone out with someone like him. Honestly, I never thought it would go this far."

"Just how far has it gone?"

Nicki hesitated. Should she tell him about the guys at her place? No, he'd definitely not want her to return home. "Threatening phone calls that I've recorded to turn over to the police. Coming to the show, but only that one time. Once I'm back in New York, I'll get a restraining order. I think that will put an end to it. I don't think he wants to go to jail."

"I think you should consider staying here with me."

"I knew you'd say that."

"Why not? At least for now. You can't dance or even try out for six to eight weeks."

"But I can meet with my agent, check out what's available and be there if a director wants to meet."

"You can do all of that from here and handle the initial meeting over the phone."

"I just want to get back, that's all. But I'll think about it. Okay?"

"Okay."

"Still won't tell me where we're going?"

"You'll know when we get there. When is the last time you heard from this guy?"

"A couple days ago. I told him the conversation was being recorded and that I was going to the police. I don't think he'll call again."

"Let me know if he does."

"Okay."

"I mean it, Nicki. I'm all too familiar with your independent streak. But don't keep me out of the loop on this. I can't take care of you if I don't know what's going on."

"Okay, I will." Nicki leaned over, kissed his cheek and

then nestled against him. "I feel better having told you."

He nodded, kissed her temple. "Know something else?"

"Hmm."

"It's probably good I'm not a drinker. That tequila makes me horny."

"In that case… Kim! Can we get another margarita, please?"

"Don't, Kim!" Nicki gave Julian's arm a playful swat. "But I'd love some sparkling water."

"Sure, coming right up."

A comfortable silence fell between them as Kim brought out Nicki's drink and a tray of hot appetizers. Nicki looked out the window. Before dating Julian, she'd never been west. Was still struck at the stark difference between the East and West Coast topographies. Back east there'd be shades of green from various trees, even oranges, reds and tans from leaves changing color. The view of the west from the sky was filled with reds and browns, vast, seemingly uninhabited tracts of earth punctuated by cities that cropped up here and there. Like the one that seemed to be coming into view. Not Oakland, as she'd imagined, and another visit to the Drake condo in San Francisco. No, this city was bigger. And what was that layer of brown hovering several feet below the crowds? Was it…

"Los Angeles! You're taking me to LA?"

"Can't keep a secret from you forever, huh?"

"I've never been to Los Angeles and always wanted to go."

"We'll be there in about—" Julian checked his watch "—fifteen minutes."

"This was a perfect answer for my doldrums. Thank you, Julian. Really. I love you so much."

"You're welcome, baby."

The plane began its descent. Nicki craned her neck to

take in the vast metropolis known as the City of Angels. Hard to believe, but in the moment she actually felt happy. Something she'd thought impossible just hours ago. Paige was right. Julian should know what was going on. Nicki felt better that she'd told him and hoped what she said was true—that Vince would heed her warning and stop the threatening phone calls and texts. If he scared her like this while she was out on the West Coast, who knew what could happen back east.

# Chapter 17

There was so much to see! Julian had the driver take the streets instead of the highway so that Nicki could appreciate all the diverse and plentiful neighborhoods that made up metropolitan LA. Thirty minutes into their ride, they'd already passed more than half a dozen: Ladera Heights, Inglewood, Baldwin Hills and View Park. A native Angeleno, the driver gave exciting history about the famous Crenshaw Boulevard that ran from Wilshire Boulevard all the way into Long Beach and was once the cruising route for lowriders and hydraulic wonders, a street that rappers immortalized in catchy tunes. Who knew about Leimert Park's rich history, where so many famous comedians honed their craft? Past West Adams and mid-Wilshire, they headed east through Koreatown and into downtown.

"What do you think?" Julian smiled broadly. Clearly, he enjoyed watching Nicki's virginal journey through the concrete jungles of the country's second-largest city.

"Everything's so spread out. Looks different than I expected. Don't know what that was, but…"

"Probably what you've seen on TV. Beverly Hills. Hollywood. We'll see that, too. Tomorrow."

The driver turned onto a street lined with shops. Nicki turned to Julian. "Is this the garment district?"

"How'd you know?"

"Worked with a girl from LA once who told me about it. Said you could get great bargains down here, designer clothing at wholesale prices. Looks like everything's closed, though."

"It is," the driver interrupted. "Merchants pretty much close up when the business workday is over. Very few customers after around four o'clock. These streets change late at night. Not the safest place if most of your business is in cash."

Nicki turned to Julian. "Will we be able to come back tomorrow?"

"If you'd like. Though I think we might be able to get what you need tonight."

"How do you figure?"

Julian winked. "I know people."

The driver pulled over near the end of a street.

"This is it?" Julian asked.

The driver pointed at a brick building on the corner. "Right over there."

"Come on, babe. Here, let me help you." Julian reached for one of the aluminum crutches, unfolded it and then went over to Nicki's side and helped her out.

"Where are we going?"

"So many questions!"

"Because I'm not getting answers!"

They reached the door on the corner. Julian rang a doorbell. The door opened quickly. A perky blonde twentysomething stepped back as they entered. "Dr. Drake! Hello. You must be Nicki. Welcome to OTB's LA warehouse."

Nicki gasped. "OTB Her?" The warehouse assistant nodded and laughed at Nicki's obvious surprise. Nicki looked at Julian. "I can get an outfit here?"

"You're going to get several, but the clock is ticking and we've got a full agenda."

"I've already chosen some outfits I think you'll like, so if you come on back to the showroom and have a seat, I'll bring them right out."

An hour later Nicki and Julian reentered the limo, the trunk packed with originals from Julian's sister London's husband, model-turned-fashion-designer Ace Montgomery.

Nicki's eyes shone like a kid at the circus. "That was so amazing, Julian! Thank you so much."

"You're welcome, baby. It's good to see you smile."

"Where are we going tonight? Hopefully someplace I can wear that jumpsuit."

"That was my second favorite after the mini. Your ankle might be injured, but your ass has never looked better."

"Obviously, since you couldn't keep your hands off it back there while I changed."

"Wait till later tonight and see what my hands do," he said while trying to ease said hand under her top.

She smacked it away. "Behave! Where are we going?"

"To the hotel to shower and change, and then to dinner and…your next surprise."

"Another surprise? Something more than getting OTB originals? I could die right now and be a happy woman."

"Don't do that, babe. If you miss out on what's happening next, you'll really be mad."

She really would have, too. After a short ride from the OTB LA warehouse, Nicki and Julian checked into a Ritz-Carlton suite, enjoyed sushi and seafood at a five-star restaurant, and then headed to the Ahmanson Theater.

"LuLu?" Nicki read the program Julian received from one usher while another escorted them to their orchestra seats. Once settled into their seats, she read about the innovative dance troupe out of Britain, creating a buzz in LA sure to sweep the nation with a fun, fast, fiery musical that absolutely embodied the title, *lu*, the Yoruba word for "beat."

Nicki watched, transfixed, as the lead character mixed an intricate dance style with beats created by everything from percussion instruments to hands and feet, taking the audience on a journey of the heart. By intermission she'd fallen in love with the show and especially the intricate type of dance. By the time the performance ended, she wanted to be on stage dancing with them.

Julian pulled strings and got them backstage. Nicki met the director, a humble British talent who was also the show's choreographer and playwright.

"The show is fantastic!"

The director acknowledged the compliment with a slight bow. "Thank you so much."

"What type of dancing was that?"

"It's lulu dancing, moving to and with the beat. The steps are inspired by African dance moves, a combination of steps from various countries."

"You absolutely captured the soul of the dance. How long does it take to teach that?"

The director chuckled, with a nod to her ankle. "Well, it is not something you can learn tonight."

"I sure want to. It's some of the most exciting, unique, energetic dancing I've seen in a long time."

"The movements are rather contagious, or so I've been told."

"Absolutely. Had my foot not been in this cast, I would have been up dancing! Seriously. I don't know how the rest of the audience stayed in their seats!"

"She's not kidding about the dancing," Julian said. "My girl's a professional dancer. Nicki Long. She was on Broadway before the injury sidelined her."

"For real?"

*"A Hair's Tale,"* Nicki said.

"The lead's best friend." The director pointed at her and held out his hand. "That's where I've seen you before. Ngo Xhe," he introduced himself, pronouncing it "In. Go. Che."

"It's very nice to meet you, Ngo." She returned the enthusiastic handshake. "You've been to the show?"

Ngo shook his head. "I want to. Saw a clip of the show online. I think you guys were on a morning show?"

"Yes, we danced a piece on there."

"You should give me your information. We're fielding a lot of offers across the country from people interested in sponsoring the show. Who knows? We might end up on Broadway."

"Most definitely! I could totally see this show as a hit."

Nicki exchanged information with the young director. There was something about what he'd done that spoke to Nicki and touched her heart in a way she hadn't felt in a very long time. Maybe even since she was a child and first fell in love with dancing. Cast or no, she felt that she could float out of the auditorium and dance to the car.

A half hour later, Nicki and Julian returned to their suite. Tired yet exhilarated after the whirlwind day, she hopped over to the bed and fell back on it.

"Julian!"

"Yes, baby."

"Get over here."

He walked over and sat on the bed, reached down and untied his shoes before crawling on the bed beside her. "Yes, my love."

"Have I told you lately that I love you?"

"I don't remember hearing that lately, no."

"Well, I do. You are amazing. I don't know how you pulled this trip together so quickly, but I can't thank you enough. I've never had an experience like this in my entire life. You made me feel like a princess in a fairy tale."

She wrapped her arms around his neck, pulled his lips toward hers. "Thank you." The first kiss was light, wispy, cushy lips brushing against each other like a whispered promise. Nicki felt Julian press harder, as if he wanted to devour her sweetness. She totally understood and wanted to eat him up, too. They hadn't made love since returning from New York. But she refused to rush the moment. She pulled away from his mouth to lick his ears and nuzzle his neck. She felt him relax, imagined his practiced restraint. He'd gotten the message to follow her lead. Good. Just what she wanted.

Nicki slid her tongue between his parted lips and reached for his belt. He lowered the zipper on the front of her jumpsuit, obviously fine with the direction she headed. She felt a hardening against her thigh. Every part of him was on board. She reached inside his boxers and wrapped cool fingers around a hot, hardening shaft. His hand slid over and beneath the fabric of an OTB original. Tweaked one nipple with his thumb and forefinger while lapping the other with his tongue. Nicki moaned as his hand slid farther down. Felt the love in his touch. The want in his tongue. She wanted it, too. Wanted it now. Wanted to feel his naked goodness against her skin. Thigh to thigh. Chest to breast. Totally connected.

She sat up to undress.

"Here, let me get that for you." Julian kissed her shoulders and the nape of her neck as he eased the jumpsuit away. Continued the oral onslaught as he sought and found the clasp of her bra and loosened that, too. Always a multitasker, the doctor. One of many things that Nicki loved about him.

Once the material was off her shoulders, she lifted her hips. Julian eased the pants down her long, toned legs, ever careful of her ankle as he slid the silky material from even softer skin. His eyes smoldered as he took in dark chocolate nipples that complemented golden tones of caramel skin. He pulled off his shirt and undershirt. Slid off the bed to remove his trousers. His eyes were locked with Nicki's as though mesmerized. She felt powerful. Sexy. Decadent.

Rubbed her hand over the single piece of material that remained on her body. Spread her legs to boldly display what the thong barely hid. His eyes narrowed. Trousers dropped. Boxers followed. His weighty dick swayed gently as he placed a knee on the bed.

"Stop right there, Doctor."

Nicki's moves were graceful, seductive, as she shifted to her knees, bandaged ankle in the air as she crawled toward him. Her eyes dropped from his to the tip of the erection that bobbed its greeting. She licked her lips. Kissed it. Flicked her tongue over the tip. Wrapped her fingers around his long, thick tool. Caressed it lovingly with her fingers. With her tongue. Swirling. Licking. Long wet brushes from base to tip. Grazes of teeth against sensitive skin before lovingly taking him all the way in. He inhaled sharply, began to roll his hips. She felt hands on her butt. Fondling her starfish, making her wet.

"Baby." The word came out on a gush of wind, a gasp when she licked his jewels.

Nicki smiled and turned around. Swayed her butt to tempt a man who didn't need tempting. With the intensity of a soldier directing a heat-seeking missile, she felt Julian ease himself inside her. Slowly, creating delicious friction, pulling out to the tip and plunging in again. He set up a rhythm. She joined in the dance. Julian thrust and stroked again and again. Deeper. Harder. Faster. More. Nicki's body quivered. She went over the edge. Weak legs could no longer hold her. She plopped on her stomach. He followed her down and turned her over. Nicki might have been finished, but Julian was just getting started. He eased his tongue deep into her mouth. Slid his dick in deeply, too. Made love thoughtfully and thoroughly, skillfully, like he did everything else. She remembered his words from earlier, of making new memories. That happened seconds later, as he gave Nicki an orgasm she'd not soon forget.

"Baby, that was amazing."

With one last quick kiss, Nicki turned on her side, scooted back until her body was flush against Julian's and pulled his arm around her waist so they could spoon. She sighed, content in every possible way. Aware of the blessing in this moment. Wonderful afternoon. Fantastic evening. Amazing night. A man who wasn't perfect but who was perfect for her. And as if all that had happened wasn't reason enough to celebrate, there'd been no call or text from Vince. Life was one big hallelujah!

When she'd woke up that morning she'd been sure about returning to New York next week. It had always been home. Was all that she knew. Even being in Los Angeles for her best day ever, she really couldn't see herself living there. But as she heard the steady sound of Julian's deep breathing, signaling sleep, she realized her hard stance toward relocating had softened a bit. She wasn't ready to give notice to her landlord or tear up her MTA card. She knew it would be hard for her to live anywhere but New York. But she knew something else—a woman was allowed to change her mind.

# *Chapter 18*

Julian had a part two planned for his getaway with Nicki, and he'd hoped to have more time off. But an emergency appointment wouldn't allow it. Interrupted his plans. The next morning, after enjoying extra helpings of breakfast and booty in bed, he and Nicki were driven back to the airport. The company plane had been flown back the previous night, so Julian and Nicki boarded the first-class section of a commercial plane just after ten o'clock.

"It's okay, Katie. One o'clock is fine. Right, we're boarding now. I should be in the office around noon. What's after the one o'clock?" He stepped back so that Nicki could take the window seat in the second row, then sat down beside her. "No, thanks," he said to the flight attendant eager to serve him. "Not you, Katie. I was talking to the attendant. Okay, so have her come in at three thirty. Right, I know. That's okay. I'd rather he be allowed to keep his appointment. One o'clock, three thirty and five. Got it. See you soon."

Julian buckled his seat belt, leaned against the seat and closed his eyes.

"Tired much?" Nicki teased.

"Meditating."

"Yeah, right. I should let you catch some sleep. Sounds like your day will be busy."

"A little bit," Julian said through a yawn. "But seeing you happy was worth the loss of sleep."

"I owe you one for sure."

"I plan to collect." Julian repositioned himself so that he could rest his head on Nicki's shoulder. "Don't forget about my mom."

"What about her?"

"You're meeting her for lunch."

"I am?"

He nodded, squeezed her thigh. "She called earlier to reschedule your meeting. I forgot to tell you."

"Are you sure? She said she'd call me."

"She knew you'd be in Los Angeles."

"How long had you planned this?"

"It all happened yesterday. I booked the plane and Dad or someone at the company must have told her. Anyway, you're to meet her at the club at twelve thirty. I'll have the car service pick you up at twelve fifteen. Cool?"

"Sure."

The plane began taxiing down the runway. "Okay, pull that shade, babe. Time to catch forty winks while I can."

Forty winks was all he needed. Shortly before landing, Julian made good use of the hot towels the attendant gave them, along with a cup of strong black joe. He'd planned the trip to Los Angeles all for Nicki, but it had been good for him, too. The laughter. The loving. Nicki's love did that. Was just that powerful. Most women had no idea of their power, of just how completely they could rule a man. He was sure Nicki didn't. Which was probably a good thing. Because the girl had the ability to rock his world. And had.

Upon landing they both took their phones off airplane mode. Indicators dinged and beeped. Julian scrolled through to see what messages he'd missed. Nicki did, too, but only briefly before pulling out her compact and checking her face.

"You're still beautiful," Julian said, not looking up. "Nothing's changed since we left the Ritz."

Nicki kissed his cheek. "You're good for my ego. Think I'll keep you around."

"Is your ego all I'm good for?"

"Not at all. You're a man with many talented weapons. Your mouth is only one of them."

They landed in Oakland. A uniformed driver from the car service stood near the escalator, holding an iPad with "Drake" across the screen. They'd not checked baggage, and airport traffic was light. Within minutes they were settled into a town car's roomy back seat, headed for PC.

Julian pulled out his iPhone and began responding to emails. Nicki rested her head against the seat back and gazed out the window. As they neared Paradise Cove, Julian looked over and was surprised to see a slight frown marring Nicki's brow.

"Babe?" She looked over. "You okay?"

"Yeah, I'm fine."

"Why were you frowning?"

"When?"

"Just now."

"Oh, I didn't realize. Just tired, I guess."

The comment made him smile. "Good loving will do that to you." He reached for her hand. "Hey."

"Yes, love."

"The driver is going to drop me off at the airport to pick up my car. This car can stay with you to drive around PC. All right?"

Nicki looked at her watch. "Sure, that'll be fine. You said lunch is at twelve thirty?" Julian nodded. "Should I wear the OTB mini? Or is that too risqué for the country club's noonday crowd?"

"Depending on who's looking, anything you wear could be considered risqué. You could wear a paper bag and still be sexy."

"Thank you for loving me."

"Easy to do."

They reached the private landing strip, and after a quick

kiss, Julian hopped out and headed directly to his car. He'd kept a calm facade for Nicki's benefit but now couldn't wait to get to his office. Katie had texted that there was a situation involving Claude Johnson—or Dr. Demented, as she liked to call him. He'd chastised her appropriately. Said they were above name-calling. But intuition suggested that whatever awaited him from the doctor would not be good.

Nicki entered the country club just after twelve thirty and hobbled over to the host stand as quickly as the crutches allowed. She'd been told about Jennifer's punctuality and had rushed to get there. Considering the challenges of being injured, and the reason for the frown Julian caught on her face, she was glad to have pulled it together and arrived when she did.

"I'm here for lunch with Mrs. Drake."

"Of course, Ms. Long. One moment and the maître d' will escort you back."

On cue, a handsome older gentleman with salt-and-pepper hair and lively blue eyes appeared at her side, assisted her down the hallway and formally announced her once he'd opened the door to one of the smaller private dining rooms.

"Mrs. Drake, I present your guest, Ms. Long. First courses will arrive shortly."

Jennifer rose gracefully from the chair and walked toward her, arms outstretched. Or floated, Nicki decided, would be a better word. She looked like elegance personified in an ivory pantsuit paired with a navy knit shell and pearl accessories. Nicki was glad she'd changed her mind about wearing the mini and had instead donned a gold, poncho-styled sweaterdress.

"Nicki, darling. Love that dress. You look amazing."

"Thanks, Jennifer."

They shared a brief embrace and walked back to the table set for two.

"Isn't that from Ace's collection?"

"Yes, an original from their fall line. Julian arranged for us to go by their warehouse in LA."

"What a smart and thoughtful move. Especially if he brought me something back. Did he?"

Nicki play cringed. "I don't think so."

"Then I'm afraid there's still some home training to do." Said derisively but with eyes that sparkled with laughter.

"You've raised an amazing son."

"He is so very special. Thank you, but honestly, Ike and I can't take all the credit. A lot of what the world sees is Julian being Julian, guided by an inner, almost old-soul knowledge and sensitivity. I'm honored to be his mom."

"I know I was late, by the way. Sorry for that."

"Ah, so you've been warned." Jennifer waved off the comment. "No worries. I completely understand. It must be difficult to navigate the world on crutches."

"I have a whole new appreciation for the disabled. My ankle will be healed in weeks. Can't imagine it being a way of life."

"It is always good to be thankful."

The waiter arrived with warm bread, butter and jams. The ladies shared small talk, mostly on Nicki's ankle and how soon it would heal.

"I never welcome misfortune," Jennifer continued, breaking her bread into bite-size pieces before buttering each individually and placing it daintily in her mouth. "But I must say it's delightful to have you here, and a part of me is hoping you'll stay."

Nicki felt that was a perfect time to eat bread herself. With a mouthful, she couldn't respond.

"I know the chances are quite slim. Yours is a talent that

belongs on Broadway. What I'm hoping, however, is that while you're here, you could help me plan a new component for the community center involving the arts. Specifically music, theater and dance. Unfortunately, the arts have been cut from the budgets of most public schools. I believe they're as important as math or science, maybe more so depending on the child."

"I agree. It's how I honed my craft in those early years and cemented my desire to become a professional dancer. Mom certainly wasn't able to afford private lessons. Those offered through the public school I attended probably helped save my life."

"How so?"

"Kept me off the street, busy, focused. Couldn't dance and be pregnant, so kept me sensible there as well. I think your idea is an excellent one, and I'd be happy to help. Can you share more?"

"The position I have in mind for you is that of artistic director."

Jennifer continued, and for the next hour she and Nicki shared their love of the arts, teaching children and creating dreams. By the time dessert arrived, Nicki had agreed to create a dance curriculum, and while making it clear her goal was to return to Broadway, she did agree to give the AD position some thought. She also promised to stay in Paradise Cove for the duration of her rehabilitation. With Vince and the threatening texts resurfacing, proving to be as hard to shake as the common cold in a New York winter, being on the other side of the country once again seemed like a good idea.

# Chapter 19

Julian walked his last patient to the door. "All right, Frank. Good work today."

"Doctor, I can't thank you enough for finally agreeing to see me. I know you wanted me to stay with Johnson. But I tell you something—" The middle-aged man turned around, his eyes shiny with tears. "I feel better with you after one hour than I did with him in ten years."

"I wouldn't discount the work that's been put in to make you better. Often results aren't seen overnight. That being said, your focus should be on the present. Feeling better today. Maintaining a positive outlook today. Where's your journal?"

"Oh, I forgot it in your office."

"Wait right there." Julian went back and retrieved the journal the persistent Frank Snyder had selected, a black faux-leather design with bold white letters stenciled across it: Strive for Progress, not Perfection. "Here you go, Frank. See you next week."

Julian shut the door behind Frank and enjoyed a deep stretch. The day had been long but productive. He was especially pleased with the last appointment. For months he'd declined to treat Frank Snyder, one of the many patients formerly treated by Dr. Claude Johnson who'd practically run to his office and demanded he take them. Actions that undoubtedly led to what had awaited Julian back at the office—a cease and desist letter from Johnson's attorney.

While a bit disappointed, Julian wasn't surprised. He'd hoped Natalie's false allegations had been from her own overactive imagination. But apparently the apple hadn't fallen far from the tree, passing on lies her father obviously believed. Because he wasn't a lawyer, Julian scanned the letter and emailed a copy straight over to Niko's wife, Monique, a tiger in the courtroom before marrying his brother and reducing her workload. The hotshot attorneys were out of town, campaigning in Sacramento, but she promised to look at it once back in their suite. Julian wasn't worried. He'd done nothing wrong. But with people like Johnson, and by extension his daughter, all future interaction would require a paper trail.

He walked back into his office and had just placed his laptop in its carrier bag when he heard the door open. What else had Frank forgotten? He did a quick check around, turned to walk into the reception area and came face-to-face with...Dr. Claude Johnson.

Julian recognized him immediately. He looked older, of course, and shorter than Julian remembered. The piercing gray eyes had dimmed, and the few wisps of blond hair left on top of his head were combed over in an attempt to hide the obvious passage of time.

"Dr. Johnson, hello."

"Who were you expecting, another one of my patients?"

"My client roster is confidential, as you know, but in a town this size I'm sure you're aware of or can deduce that some who've stopped coming to you have made their way to my office. That being said, considering what was delivered by courier today, I wasn't expecting you. Why are you here, and not your attorney?"

"Last I heard it was a free country. Or have the Drakes bought up the entire town and are now handing out passes to walk around?"

Julian had enjoyed an amazing but exhausting twenty-four hours in LA, followed by several hours of intense counseling. Lunch had been a salad at his desk in between patients. He didn't need this right now.

"Dr. Johnson, I've been taught to respect my elders. But this is my private business and you are trespassing. Please see your way to the door."

"Can talk behind my back but not to my face. I figured as much."

"Our inability to converse is entirely your doing, a tone set by what you had delivered today. Any communication between us will now be through our lawyers." Julian walked past Johnson and opened the door. He was done talking. His opening the door was a very clear message.

A shade of red crept up from Johnson's collar, evidence of bottled rage. He reached the door and turned to Julian. "Stop trying to steal my patients. Go out and find your own."

He kept his usual cool, but by the time he arrived home to pick up Nicki for dinner, Julian was in a mood. He tried to hide it from Nicki—wasn't successful. Her first comment as he drove them to the restaurant made it clear.

"We could have ordered in, you know. Or I could have cooked something."

Julian glanced over. "When'd you start cooking?"

"I can cook." Another glance, this one accompanied by a wry smile. "What? I can. I mean, there hasn't been a stint in culinary school so it wouldn't be a five-course meal. But I've perfected a few dishes."

"Name one."

"I'd rather you name what's bothering you."

Julian didn't hesitate. "Claude Johnson."

"Who's that?"

"One of two other therapists in town, the older one who had the market cornered for about thirty years."

"The one whose daughter accused you of stealing clients?"

"You remember that, huh?"

"An old classmate—" she used air quotes "—coming by your office on behalf of her father? Yeah, girlfriends tend to remember ploys like that." Julian recalled Natalie's appearance and actions from that day. The heels and mini, flirty hair and mannerisms. He gave a thoughtful nod. "The doctor, what did he want?"

"I really don't know, especially since a cease and desist from him was what greeted me today when I reached the office." He shared details about the letter, that he'd sent a copy to Monique and the brief conversation with the doctor.

"What did Monique say?"

"She and Niko are in Sacramento on business, so she couldn't check it out right away. She did suggest I create a log of interactions with both him and Natalie, which I did before leaving the office. A man is no better than his reputation. Which is why I refuse to have mine sullied by Johnson's lies."

"It's rare I see you get this worked up, babe. Don't let those haters steal your joy." Nicki reached over to rub Julian's shoulders. "You're a good man, a great therapist, and people around here know it. It'll take more than a couple rumors from a washed-up psychiatrist to change their minds."

They reached Acquired Taste and entered a fuller parking lot than expected, given it was a weeknight. Julian pulled into one of two reserved parking spaces, helped Nicki into the restaurant, then moved the car to a regular spot. When he returned, a menu, a shot of premium tequila and a saucer of accompaniments were on his place mat. The same sat in front of Nicki. He looked at her with a raised brow.

"To take the edge off," she replied with a smile. "Because neither of us are drinkers, I figured one shot is all we'll need."

He sniffed it, bunched up his nose. "What is this, gasoline?"

"Close. Enough to smooth out our ride but not rev up our engines."

"What if I want to get your engine revved up?"

"Baby, you can do that with a single look or a simple kiss. Those scrumptious lips, long curly lashes around those bedroom eyes…" She licked her lips seductively and lowered her voice. "It's happening right now. I'm getting hot. And wet."

Julian's arm shot up as he looked around. "Check, please!"

"Ha! You're a sex fiend."

"Yes."

She held up her shot glass. "Let's toast to sex fiends, and how much I love the one currently sitting across from me."

"Wait." Julian nodded toward the saucer. "What's all this for?"

"Oh, right. There's an art to this. So, we're supposed to place a little of the salt on our tongue, drink the shot straight down and follow up with a bite of the lemon slice. The salt and citric acid will cut the tequila's burn. So wet your finger—" she licked her forefinger "—like this." Julian licked his finger. "Now stick it in the salt."

Again, he complied.

"Now, you lick the salt off my finger and I'll lick…well, for now, I'll lick your finger."

Julian smiled broadly. "Stop that nasty talk. It's making me uncomfortable."

"A little too much for my conservative doctor?"

"A lot to try to keep calm between my legs."

"Ah, got it."

She held out her finger. He placed his near her lips. Each licked the other's finger. Julian's action was straightforward. Nicki took longer, swirled her tongue around Julian's pointer and suckled as she eased it from her mouth.

They picked up their glasses, downed the tequila and bit the lemon. With closed eyes Julian absorbed the tequila's heat and the lemon's tartness. A few seconds later he smiled. "That wasn't too bad."

Nicki's face told a different story. Her eyes were scrunched, her lips pulled into a grimace. She finally spoke, her voice low and raspy. "That burned everything from my mouth to my anus."

At that very moment the waiter arrived. "May I take your order?"

"Ooh!" Nicki started after the question. "I thought he was going to offer to take something else."

Nicki and Julian cracked up.

So into themselves they took little note of who dined around them. For two women in particular, the oblivion fit perfectly into their plan. A few choice snaps and they left unnoticed, their targets not knowing they'd been there at all.

The next morning Julian woke up to texts from his siblings and a missed call from Jennifer, all regarding a picture making its way across the web and a story on the gossip blog *Ask Ashley* titled Dancer Dates Drunk Doctor?

# Chapter 20

The Drake clan circled the wagons. Sunday brunch got moved to Friday night. Attendance wasn't mandatory. Didn't need to be. When Jennifer called, the clan came. Being out of town was the lone reason one would be absent. London and Ace were doing a show in Dubai. Niko's narrow lead in the polls and crisscross campaigning across the state meant he and Monique wouldn't be there, but that didn't stop their making an important contribution. In addition to the response she'd written for the cease and desist letter from Dr. Johnson, she'd given Julian legal options for dealing with Ashley's gossip.

Julian and Nicki were there with his parents, Ike Jr. and Quinn, Warren and Charli, Terrell and Aliyah, and Teresa and Atka. The table had been set informally, the household staff sent home to enjoy their weekend off. Jennifer entered the dining room bearing two trays, a very pregnant Charli waddling behind her. Julian hopped up to take the bowl from his expecting sister-in-law.

"I've got this, Doctor," Charli replied, batting his hand away.

"Are you sure?" Terrell asked.

"Bro, you took the words right out of my mouth."

"Mine, too," Quinn and Aliyah chimed together.

Everyone laughed. The women set down the evening's first course—jalapeño–and–goat cheese hush puppies, stuffed artichokes, and spicy chile crostini with a variety of sauces.

Terrell accepted a tray from his mom, removed a stuffed artichoke and then passed it on. "Is the third time the charm, making this the last little dogie for the ranch, sis?"

"I beg your pardon." Charli acted appropriately incensed.

"What? Y'all are ranchers. I thought a pet name quite appropriate."

"Then call him a kid, but not a dogie. God's will, he'll be neither motherless nor neglected."

"Oh, is that what the word means? My bad."

"Simple city-dweller ignorance," Charli said, nonplussed, as she filled her plate with a serving of each appetizer. She picked up a stuffed artichoke and smiled. "You're forgiven."

"You need to serve Quinn some of whatever you're drinking. It's time for me to pass on the name and usher in Ike III."

"Yes, and give some to Aliyah," Terrell added. "We're going to have a baseball team, so best get started."

"Easy for the man to say," Aliyah said. "Let's get you through that first one's midnight feedings and diaper changes and then see how you're talking."

The first courses were removed. Teresa helped Jennifer bring out piping-hot bowls of seafood chowder, flown in from a favored New Hampshire restaurant just that morning. Jennifer set down the last bowl and took her seat. She immediately reached for the soupspoon for a taste.

"Delicious."

The others followed suit and agreed.

"I'd have you all over every night if I could," she continued between spoonfuls of soup. "But there is a specific reason I invited you over tonight."

*"Ask Ashley,"* Aliyah answered quickly.

Terrell lifted his linen napkin and sat back as he wiped his mouth. "I told y'all how to handle her when she started tripping years ago. Money. Give her some money to shut her up or threaten her livelihood to shut her down."

Jennifer emitted an uncharacteristic humph. "What livelihood?"

"Exactly," Teresa said. "What we need to do is give her a taste of her own medicine." Teresa ran a successful blog with a million opt-in readers.

Terrell looked up surprised. "Not on your blog."

"Why not?"

"Because the name of your blog is *Tip-Top Taste*. Ashley has none."

The men chuckled.

"Attention is what she wants," Aliyah said.

"Craves," Warren added.

Teresa stirred her soup. "She tries to push our buttons because we ignore her."

Jennifer agreed. "Precisely. Not quite the effect we were seeking."

"Perhaps," Nicki said. "But I agree that we shouldn't give her any of our energy. Unless it's in the form of a Brooklyn beat down like the bullies in grade school."

"That's what I'm talking about!" Aliyah laughed and raised her hand to high-five. As a native New Yorker, she totally understood.

Julian cleared his throat. "Sorry to break up the New York lovefest, ladies. But there will be no fisticuffs. That's not the way we Drakes like to make the news."

"What do you suggest, son?" asked Ike Sr.

"That we send a letter to both the blog and the company that hosts it demanding an apology and retraction, threatening to take legal action if our order is ignored. That was Monique's suggestion, the same as she gave when it came to the doctor, and in that case it seems to have worked very well."

It was true. The day after Dr. Johnson's unexpected visit, Monique took over. She'd taken affidavits of support from the patients who'd chosen Julian as their therapist. His notes were transcribed and filed along with his letters recommending to some that they stay with their current doctor. Finally, she'd expressed Julian's desire not to have unexpected visits to his office by either Dr. Johnson or Natalie. He'd not seen or heard from either since.

Teresa stood to help Jennifer gather the soup bowls. "I don't know, I'm kind of leaning toward that Brooklyn-style beat down."

Julian's sensible solution prevailed. He texted a note to Monique right from the dinner table. The conversation shifted from gossip to Gallup polls and what each family member could contribute to ensure Niko's win. As they left the estate, Jennifer reminded Nicki about their meeting on Monday. Problems solved or at least addressed, the dancer and doctor spent a quiet weekend making more memories.

That Monday, Nicki left the town house feeling optimistic. She'd had a phone consultation with Dr. Allen, which was very welcome good news. He told her if the bone had set and begun to heal, the cast could be removed. She'd still have to wear an Aircast or boot, but at least she'd be able to rent a car to get around instead of being chauffeured. Not that she didn't enjoy the perks of having a car at the ready, transportation a mere phone call away to take her wherever she desired. But she also liked being independent and looked forward to being able to check out the town and surrounding communities on her own.

She adjusted the shoulder strap on her oversize bag, secured her crutches and walked out of the house.

"You got it, Miss Nicki?"

"Yes, thank you, Devante." He opened the car door. "And what did I tell you about calling me 'miss'? I thought we handled that last week during the drive to the club."

"I'm sorry mi—I mean, Nicki." His nervous laugh revealed straight white teeth set in the handsome face of a man she guessed to be in his early twenties. He closed her door softly, then hurried around to the other side of the car. "To the community center, right?"

"That's right. How far is it?"

"Ten minutes or less." He backed out of the drive and headed toward the town's main drag.

"Not far at all."

"No, ma'am. Nothing is really far in this town."

She didn't correct him this time, though the formal title made her feel old. She knew he was only being respectful. "Where are you from, Devante? With those 'miss' and 'ma'am' manners, I'd guess down south. But you don't have an accent."

Another smile. "No. I'm not from down south."

He was cute. A good kid. She liked him. "Where, then? You seem to know your way around the city, but I get the feeling you're not from here."

He eyed her through the rearview mirror. "I'm from LA."

"Ah, that's where the city swagger comes from. I didn't think you'd grown up here."

"Is that a good thing?"

"Swagger? Oh, yeah. Definitely. Have you ever been to New York?"

"No. I've never been out of California."

"Wow, really? You'll have to get out and see a little bit of the world."

"One of these days."

"How'd you get here, if you don't mind me asking?"

"To PC?"

"Yes."

"Flew in on Southwest Airlines. Then it was straight down the 101 to the 77."

She met his twinkling eyes in the rearview mirror with a smirk and a shrug. "Hey, I'm not trying to get in your business. Just making conversation with one of the few people in this town who seems to be real, unlike some of the fake, shallow people I've run across." Her thoughts were on Ashley and the link Paige had sent to the misleading blog post highlighting Julian and Nicki's Thursday night dinner at Acquired Taste. The story had been picked up by a New York–based blogger and by Monday had even gotten a mention on a national network. Ashley had gotten some of the attention she wanted. That it was from a story based on a thinly veiled lie, Nicki thought, a bit sadly, probably didn't matter to her at all.

"So you've checked that out, too, huh?" Devante waited for a car to pass, then turned left onto one of only four major thoroughfares in all of Paradise Cove. "You know Monique, the mayor's wife?" Devante clucked and shook his head. "What am I saying? Of course you do."

"Yes, I know her, though not very well."

"You know she's an attorney, right?"

"Yes."

"She used to practice in LA. Around the same time I was being a hardhead, getting into trouble, trying to prove my manhood and other stupid stuff. She saved me. Kept me from a long lockdown, know what I'm saying?"

"Out of prison?"

He nodded. "Brought me up here. A whole different world from where I came from. Mr. Niko started mentoring me. Then Mr. Terrell and Mr. Ike Sr., they all helped show me what a real man looked like."

Devante turned into the parking lot of the community center. He pulled up to the entrance, but Nicki continued the conversation. Just when she thought she'd seen it all, the Drakes found another way to impress her. "You work for one of them now?"

"I'm going to college full-time and work for them part-time running errands, driving, cleaning the center, whatever they want me to do."

"What's your major?"

"Criminal justice. Want to be able to help some other young guys the way Monique and the Drakes helped me."

"You're clearly a good man, even if you did some bad things. I'm glad the system didn't claim you."

"That's for sure. It's claimed too many. Here, let me get that door for you."

Nicki tipped a reluctant Devante, thinking that the criminal system often punished good men like him when jerks like Vince got to walk around free. Some bad apples could do just about anything, could go anywhere they wanted. Which for Nicki would soon present a problem even more bothersome than the *Ask Ashley* blog.

# *Chapter 21*

Nothing could dim Nicki's outlook that Monday. She left the Drake Community Center feeling better than she'd felt since her date with a runaway bike. Her mood was so bright she had Devante stop at the new organic grocer. Julian had doubted she knew her way around a kitchen, but she planned to show him a thing or two. He'd arrived at the center shortly after she left, had called while she scanned fresh veggies. Told her what time he expected to arrive home. Asked what she wanted him to bring home. Her answer didn't require him to stop anywhere. She didn't even need tequila.

An hour later, freshly showered and changed, Nicki stepped back and admired her handiwork. Jennifer had scoffed at Nicki's choice of black china, but Nicki's taste often went against the grain. She liked how the dark backdrop made the colors of her simple salad pop. The dark green spinach, red cherry tomatoes and yellow sweet peppers drizzled with a creamy homemade vinaigrette. Walking past the dining room area into the kitchen, she lifted the lid of a cast-iron pot. Inhaling the mixture brought out a big smile. The Italian sausage and fresh herbs in the cheesy tortellini dish gave off a highly complex aroma. Who'd know that she'd used words like *fast* and *easy* when searching for something to show off her limited cooking skills? Certainly not Julian. If he wasn't properly impressed with her homemade dinner, then her outfit and the dessert she planned to serve bedside would certainly raise her score.

Nicki poured herself a glass of sparkling juice, picked up her cell phone from the kitchen island and walked into the living room to catch the news. Normally not much of a TV watcher and totally uninterested in politics, she'd been drawn into the California senatorial race and watched nightly results along with every other Drake in the States. She clicked the remote and switched to a local station. Minutes into watching an editorial piece comparing Niko and the rest of the candidates, her message indicator pinged.

She tapped her phone, still focused on the announcer, who seemed to offer a balanced, unbiased perspective on those running for office. She looked down. Unknown number. The same message that had showed when Vince's texts started up again the day she met Jennifer for lunch. Her heart sank. *Please don't let it be him. Not here. Not now.* Begrudgingly, she opened the text.

So you're in Paradise Cove with your doctor boyfriend and his rich clique. Looks like the nerd doctor has a wild side! Went online and checked out the town. Quaint, upscale, a bit on the small side. But perhaps a perfect place to get away from these fools still jocking me about the money I owe. Saying they're now going to start charging interest. Lucky for me the timing might be perfect. If I come there will you show me around?

Nicki tossed down the phone in disgust. She'd show him around, all right. Show him the main road that led out of town. She tried to refocus on the news show. Hard to do with Vince's words running around in her head.

"He wouldn't come here. That party boy? No way." Nicki's shoulders relaxed. Easy breathing returned. Ten minutes in a place like Paradise Cove, and Vince would be bored to death.

Jennifer was known as a magician and miracle worker, able to pull off the impossible time and again. But what

Julian witnessed at the community center when he crossed paths with his girl increased his regard for his mother. Exponentially. He was just about ready to put her on par with a saint. The Nicki he'd fallen in love with had come out of the dark.

He'd first noticed a change after Nicki and Jennifer's country-club lunch date. She'd greeted him that night with a light in her eyes, an excitement that he'd only seen before when discussing her passion or just after she got hired for a Broadway show. An excitement that emanated like fire from her body that scorched and sizzled when they made love. For the first time in six years, the very first time, Julian had allowed himself to truly believe. To actually entertain the idea that his girl—the woman who stole his heart the first time he saw her dancing across campus to a song in her head that only she heard—might leave New York and move to Paradise Cove. He hadn't felt this optimistic since…since that magical night in Times Square. That was the best time ever. Until it wasn't. Until she clarified what her hug under the flashing neon lights meant. That she didn't want to embarrass him, but she didn't want to marry him, either.

As Julian entered the parking lot of the Drake Community Center and pulled into one of the reserved spaces, his joy had dropped a bit. There was room for optimism, but maybe not a dance in the end zone. Then he'd arrived at the center and saw that light in her eyes. Against his will and self-delivered admonitions not to, that optimistic belief bubbled up again.

Walking into the center, he passed the administrative offices, waved at Miss Marva and continued to Terrell's office farther down the hall. He tapped the open door.

"Come on in, JuJu." Terrell greeted him as he typed on his laptop.

Julian's expression was a cross between a smile and a wince. "Cut out that bull crap. I hated when you called me that as a kid."

"And as an adult?"

"I hate it even more." They both laughed at that. Julian plopped into one of the leather chairs facing Terrell's desk.

"I thought you were here for a therapy session."

"I am."

"With Lopez?"

Julian shook his head. "Marion, the kid from Sacramento."

Terrell stopped typing. Swiveled his chair around to face Julian. "Marion Tucker. Moved here to live with his aunt. Real chip on his shoulder, that kid."

"That chip is a shield. You know why he moved here, right?"

Terrell nodded. "I'm glad you're here to help him, bro."

"Me, too. I'm told he hasn't been the same since his best friend got killed. And right in front of him? Stray bullet fired from an officer's gun?"

"That's why his aunt petitioned the court for temporary custody, to try to save his life. She's got a difficult journey ahead of her."

"There's still time. Fourteen is an extremely critical age for any youth, but especially for today's young black male. He's a tough case. Lots of anger, sadness, pain. But it's not too late to save him. The aunt bringing him to a smaller town from a big city was a good move. Less distractions and opportunities for trouble. Even better that she brought him here, where he can see positive male role models."

"Speaking of role models, remember me telling you that I was going to place an ad on CarlsList for an athletic director?"

"No, I don't remember. Doesn't mean you didn't tell me, though."

"Yeah, that's right. With Nicki around you tend to not think straight."

"Yeah, whatever, man."

Terrell chuckled. "Well, I did. Posted it there in the hopes of attracting someone from the bigger cities—San Jose, Sacramento, even Oakland."

"And?"

"I got interest from a big city, all right. All the way out East."

"Really? Who?"

"Vince Edwards."

Julian thought for a moment. "The basketball player?" Terrell nodded. "He's living here?"

"Not yet. But he's checking the town out as a definite possibility."

"But he's East Coast, Philly—hated the West Coast during his playing years."

"I think what he hated was the Lakers and that whooping the guards put on him every time he came to town."

"Ha! That's probably true. I'm surprised he was looking at CarlsList."

"Tell me about it. And even so, I'm surprised he was looking for jobs on the West Coast. Guess you have to follow the money, and goodness knows he burned enough bridges back in his playing days to need a scenery change."

"How long has he been out of the game? Four, five years?"

"Something like that. Did a little search after the call. Read that he played a couple seasons over in Europe. Got into tax trouble with the IRS. Had to file bankruptcy. Lost that big old house featured on *Ballers Got Bank*. Remember that?"

"No, and from the sound of it, that's a good thing. Damn. It's a shame to make the kind of money he did and end up broke."

"Without proper financial guidance, it's the only thing that can happen. You can't learn how to manage money if you've never had any."

"Is he coming in for an interview?"

Terrell nodded. "Next week. Could be a good addition to the center. He's been out of the league for a while, but he's still a star to the kids."

"A star, maybe, but not necessarily a good role model. If he was, he'd still be playing instead of being a talented but poisoned point guard no one wants to sign."

"I thought about that, but he's older. Wiser. Figured there'd be no better way to show what not to do than somebody like him whose questionable choices cost him millions of dollars and a career. He grew up poor, troubled, like Marion and many of the other kids this center serves. They'll listen to someone like him."

"You know Mom talked to Nicki, wants her to be the center's artistic director."

"Is that a possibility?"

"Looks like it might be."

"I didn't think Miss Broadway could breathe for too long outside New York's air."

Julian summoned up his best Terrell impression. "I'm giving her a special kind of oxygen."

"Wow. Just say no, okay?"

Julian grinned broadly. "I did you pretty good, huh?"

"Keep your day job, JuJu."

Julian stood and headed to the door. "Uh-huh. Call me that again, and I'll tell Aliyah about the time down at Grandpa's when you thought Teresa's jump rope was a snake and peed the bed."

"On that note, Dr. Drake, I believe your counseling session begins shortly."

"I thought so."

Nicki heard a car in the driveway and the garage door raising a few seconds later. She turned off the TV and, ignoring the crutches, hopped into the dining room and lit two tapered candles placed on either side of a vase of fresh sunflowers. The door from the garage opened as she reached the dimmer. As Julian turned the corner, the lights faded.

His stop was abrupt, almost midstride. "Wow."

"Like my outfit?"

She watched the slow sweep of Julian's eyes over her body. "I love it."

A squiggle of excitement flip-flopped in her gut. Julian walked over to where she stood by the dimmer. Reached out and fingered the nearly sheer minidress made of silky organza. Slid his arms around her waist and pulled her close.

"I love you."

He kissed her. Pulled back and kissed her again. Soon tongues dueled. Nipples pebbled. Sexes dewed and stiffened.

"The food," Nicki murmured, pulling away. "I made tortellini."

"You made it. Like, cooked it?"

"All by myself. And set a beautiful table, which you haven't mentioned, by the way." She swept her hand across the room. "The mood I've set. The romantic atmosphere."

Julian turned and took in the plated salad. The flowers and dim light. "It's real nice, baby, but can I be honest? From the moment I turned the corner, all I saw was you."

He wrapped her in his arms again.

"Good answer, Doctor." Nicki deftly escaped him and

walked toward the stove. "Good tactic, too. But you'll have to eat dinner before getting dessert."

Dinner was scrumptious. Dessert was even better. Nicki forgot that Vince had texted. The ex-ballplayer being interviewed to work at the center never entered Julian's mind. All on the lovers' minds that night was each other.

But that same night, on the other side of the country, the doctor and dancer were very much on someone else's mind.

# Chapter 22

The next morning, Nicki was up before Julian. A rarity. But after waking sometime shortly after the birds, ideas for the community center's arts program began to fuel her passion and chased sleep away. Plus, her ankle was healing. A clear cure for the doldrums. She'd put a little weight on it late last night. Not for long, and there'd been discomfort, but that she could at all was a clear sign of progress. That and the lessening need for pain medication. She'd gone the whole weekend without a pill. The haze receded, and when she went into the bathroom for a quick shower and looked in the mirror, she felt and saw her true self for the first time in weeks.

Downstairs she put on water for tea, then sat on a tall chair at the island and turned on her tablet. She started a search for nearby dance colleges with artistic programs. She and Jennifer hadn't discussed an overall budget for the program or even specifics about what she would be paid. Even if there were no funds currently available, Nicki still believed she could find talented students in college programs willing to teach for credit and experience. She quickly found several that offered degrees in theater, dance and performance. Perfect for the artistic mediums she suggested first be offered at the center—theater, music and dance. She focused on those closest to Paradise Cove, found the email addresses to who she thought were the appropriate faculty and began formulating an introductory letter.

The kettle whistled. Julian ambled down the stairs and entered the kitchen just as she poured a cup.

"Tea?" she asked, still holding the kettle.

He walked over and kissed her forehead. "Got any with caffeine?"

"Green tea. Even better."

"I believe it, if that's what has you looking so perky." He slumped into the chair next to Nicki's tablet and suppressed a yawn. "Why are you up so early?"

"Couldn't sleep. Working on the dance curriculum for the center has me all excited. Working with others in the art is the next best thing to dancing myself."

He nodded toward the tablet. "Can I look?"

"Sure." She bought the covered mugs over and set them on the table. "I'm looking for college students as teachers who might work for credit instead of pay."

"Thinking like a true nonprofiteer, babe."

"I've gone through life on a shoestring budget. Can pinch Lincoln off a penny and Roosevelt off a dime."

Julian took a moment and read what Nicki had written so far. "Who's this letter that you're drafting for?"

"Faculty members at the schools I've chosen—Santa Rosa Junior, University of the Pacific and both San Jose and Sacramento State." Nicki poured agave and lemon juice into the cups. "I'm also thinking about tapping into the community of retired artists for people who can mentor as well as teach."

"Speaking of mentoring and teaching, guess who might be heading up our athletic department?"

"Who?"

"You might not even know the name, since you're not into sports. A former pro basketball player named Vince Edwards."

Nicki almost spewed out her Citrus Sunshine and wished she could be so lucky. She also wished she could respond, say something witty. Or even better, something real. Clearly this was the moment of truth. But if she told him,

then what? They'd call off the interview? Which would in-
cite what kind of reaction from Vince? One where he told
Julian what Nicki had failed to disclose? She should have
told him everything as soon as it happened. She realized
that, but now the timing sucked.

"Nicki, did you hear me?"

"Hmm, sorry babe, got distracted. Something about a
basketball player coming to the center?"

Julian swiped a finger over Nicki's cheek as he slid off
the school. "Never mind, babe. I have to get going, but we
can talk later. That tea was good, but tomorrow I'll expect
the chef to serve breakfast."

Nicki laughed as she got up and walked him to the door.
"One good meal and I'm a chef now?"

"You are in my book." He pressed his lips against hers
in a quick kiss. "It's good to see my Nicki back. Love you,
baby."

"Love you, too."

Nicki held her poise until Julian had backed out of the
driveway and started down the street. Then she let out an
anguished sound of frustration, a cross between a growl
and a screech. The interview must have been scheduled
before he'd texted her yesterday. The community center
looking for an athletic director was the perfect timing of
which Vince spoke.

She'd never thought much about reincarnation but Nicki
felt she had to have done something heinous in another
lifetime. Like murder. It could only be karma from some
egregious past wrong that would have put her and Vince
Edwards in the same place, at the same time, right after
she and Julian had broken up. Then have him ask for her
number, and worse, for her to give it to him? Seemed like a
good idea at the time. Hindsight revealed she couldn't have
been more wrong. Now he was coming to Paradise Cove,

turning what she'd thought might be a heavenly situation after all into the pits of hell.

She picked up her phone and scrolled to the last unknown number. Trying to dial it back didn't work. She hit star sixty-nine. That didn't work, either. Crazy that the one time she actually wanted to talk to him, the jerk could not be reached.

She let out another groan followed by a few choice expletives. Then she reached for her phone and checked the time. Just after nine thirty, the screen indicated. Half past noon in New York. She called Paige.

"Please answer," she mumbled, pushing the speaker button and nervously tapping her foot while the phone rang.

"Nicki, hi!"

"I can't get rid of him" was her greeting.

"Huh. Who? What?"

"Vince Edwards. The asshole. I can't figure out what I've done to deserve this type of punishment. I date the guy for a month. Do a show in Atlanta that just happens to be directed by some distant relative, and all of a sudden I owe him a favor."

"Twenty thousand favors."

"To be exact."

"According to him."

"Who does that? And why did he ask me? Why didn't he ask one of his rich baller friends? His mother or father? A bank? I thought extortion was just about the worst he could do, but guess what? He can go even lower. I'm seriously about to lose it, Paige. Why won't he leave me alone!"

"Whoa, Nick. You're scaring me. Slow down. Start over. Tell me what's going on."

"Vince is coming to Paradise Cove."

"Holy crap, Nick! That's crazy!"

"Yeah, because *he's* crazy."

"You didn't have the money here. What makes him think you'll have it there? Julian? He wants you to get it from him?"

"Clearly his main goal is to ruin my life." She told Paige about the community center expansion and the athletic director position. "I can't believe he even saw it. Though he is handy with a computer and the internet. He told me that himself. And thanks to *Ask that A-hole Ashley*, he knew where I was."

"From there he could have put any one of several word combinations in the search engine and pulled up that ad. What is Julian saying? He's cool under pressure but this has got to have him pissed." Nicki sighed and leaned against the island counter. "Nicki...you did tell Julian about Vince, right? Yeah, you told me you did."

"I told him about a guy I dated briefly trying to extort money. I didn't go into detail."

"He doesn't know it's Vince?"

"I didn't think it was important."

"Do you think it's important now? Like, before he gets to Paradise Cove. Before the interview? Before something crazy happens, like he gets the job. Something crazy like that. I don't get why you're being so tight-lipped about this. You already told him you dated."

"But I didn't say I slept with him."

"So what? You and Julian were broken up. You were an adult on a date. It's what we do. Tell him, Nick."

"I already hurt him so badly when I turned him down. To know I was with another guy when we were only broken up a month? It'll really upset him, Paige. Especially now, since it's information I withheld when sharing the rest. Julian isn't like the other guys. Sex isn't a casual thing with him."

"Then what are you going to do? Roll the dice and hope Vince doesn't get the job?"

Nicki stood straight as an idea came to her. "Maybe I can get him to not need it. Thanks for being a sounding board, girl. I gotta go."

"Nick—"

Too late. She'd already pushed the end button. Before she could think herself out of the tricky yet possible solution that had popped in her head, she called Jennifer.

"Hi, Jennifer. It's Nicki."

"Hello, Nicki. How are you?"

"I'm okay, thanks. I was calling about the artistic director position."

"Yes?"

"While my long-term plan is to return to Broadway, and I want to make that very clear, I am now giving serious consideration to the position you offered."

"Nicki, that's wonderful!"

"I can only make a one-year commitment. Are you okay with that?"

"Absolutely. You can get the program up and running and hire an assistant to take over the reins. Have you told Julian?"

"No, I just decided."

"I'm so happy, Nicki. He will be thrilled!"

"I know—can't wait to tell him. Until then, can we keep this between us?"

"Of course. I wouldn't want to ruin this very special surprise."

"Um, there's another question I need to ask, and this one is a bit awkward."

"What is it, dear?"

"I need the specifics regarding salary, if you don't mind."

"Of course, Nicki. How remiss of me not to have included that in the discussion. It's not along the lines of what someone with your experience and renown is worth, I'm afraid. The starting salary we're offering is only thirty-five thousand annually, but there are perks, including a five-thousand-dollar signing bonus over and above the annual compensation."

Jennifer continued detailing the benefits, which included comprehensive health insurance and paid vacation days. Those facts barely registered. Nicki didn't hear much past the words *five thousand*. She wrapped up the conversation and ended the call. Her next move was going to be trying to reach Vince to make him a five-thousand-dollar offer she hoped he wouldn't refuse.

# Chapter 23

She sent Vince a text with a payment plan. Five thousand now, and five more for the next three months. He didn't reply. A second text and again, nothing. She learned the one thing worse than hearing from Vince Edwards was not hearing from the extorter at all. Not knowing his movements. If he'd considered her offer. When or if he still planned a trip to PC.

When she finally received a text a few days later, his answer wasn't what she wanted—he said no, with a smiley face and a LOL. He countered, once again demanding the whole twenty grand. She countered back and offered ten. It would take going into her savings and her first couple checks. Didn't matter. Right now his absence was more important than a nest egg. He wanted her to wire the money. She wanted him to sign off on it first. Have it in writing that he'd no longer harass her, he wouldn't come west and she'd pay him in full.

That exchange had happened days ago. He'd never responded. Her stomach nerves had been coiled ever since, in knots tight enough to puke. Couldn't let the feelings show now, though. She'd signed the agreement to become the community center's artistic director. Today's Sunday brunch was being held in her honor at the country club instead of the Drake estate. Time to put on a positive game face. All eyes would be on her.

"How do I look?"

Julian took in the simple dress that on Nicki's toned, curvy body looked elegant and chic. The deep cranberry color brought out the golden tones of her skin. The curly black locks usually kept bound were loose, framing her face and tickling her shoulders. A low-slung belt accented her small waist, and its gold trim was complemented by the jewelry she wore.

"You look beautiful, babe. I feel like the shy, nerdy kid who snagged the cute, hot girl and wondered how he got so lucky."

"You sure? I'm nervous."

"Really?"

"A little bit."

"Why? It's going to be mostly family there."

"I know. But today it becomes official. I'm going to be here for at least a year."

While the Friday night dinner had closely resembled it, Nicki had avoided the famed Drake Sunday brunch. Having been in their town a month, this was a fete, and a calculated one at that. Individually, each Drake exuded a certain type of power and confidence. As a group they could be quite intimidating, especially for someone like Nicki, who'd grown up an only child and cherished her privacy. That she and Julian had dated for two years before she met the family had gotten her labeled "the invisible girlfriend" and made the first meeting awkward. It had taken that long for her to admit she was actually in a relationship, something she'd sworn wouldn't happen. Her first and only love was dancing. Until Julian Drake walked into her life.

"Baby, why are you tripping? You know everybody. You'll be fine."

"Yes, but I'm not used to seeing everybody at once."

"What about the other Friday?"

"That wasn't the whole dynasty!"

"Ah, come on now. We're not so bad."

"Easy for you to say. You're a Drake."

"I could easily make it happen for you to be one, too." He glanced over, waited. She remained silent. "I tried that once before. You weren't ready." He waited for an answer. "Nothing to say?"

"You already said it. I wasn't ready. I grew up dreaming about being a dancer. Guess I never thought about being a wife."

"And now?"

"I still haven't thought much about it."

"Maybe you should."

With a last look in the mirror, Nicki reached for her purse. "Come on, babe. We should go. I don't want to be late."

She reached out to smooth his lapel.

"I love that you picked a shirt that matches my dress. Love that color on you, too." She leaned over, kissed his cheek. "Who knew a man with glasses could be so sexy?"

"You know what they say. The sexiest muscle on a man is his brain."

"That isn't what poked me in the back this morning."

"Touché."

A short time later they reached the Paradise Cove Country Club. Julian pulled up to the valet, and they were soon ushered into the large private dining room, beautifully decorated in autumn shades. Deep purple cloths and pumpkin-colored linen adorned three round tables. On them were settings of white china and Waterford crystal goblets trimmed in gold, eight settings per table. Elaborate bouquets with fresh autumn flowers were in six-foot-tall vases. The room was stunning. Perfect. Surpassed only by the beautiful people casually chatting inside—the Northern California Drakes and a handful of choice supporters. Nicki was glad to learn she'd been seated with Terrell and his wife. Their shared New York background had created an instant affinity. Nicki appreciated Aliyah's East Coast authenticity, and with Terrell at the table there would never be silence or boredom.

As waiters unobtrusively served the first course, Jennifer stood to address the room. "Good Sunday, family."

"Good Sunday."

"As many if not most of you already know, the past week has been one of awesome progress for the Drakes, our community center and Paradise Cove. Ike and I would like to publicly thank Wayne and Lillian Channing—" she nodded toward them "—our dear friends, longtime neighbors and staunch supporters of Niko's political career. Last week's polls calmed my nerves and alleviated Ike's ulcer a bit, as Niko's lead reached double digits." The room applauded. "The news is encouraging but we can't ease up. Son, no matter what happens, know that you have been an exemplary mayor of Paradise Cove and a stellar example of true leadership. We're so very proud of you.

"I am also delighted to make official an addition to our family. Oops," Jennifer hurriedly continued with mock dismay. "I meant faculty—to the Drake Community Center faculty." The room joined her in laughter. Julian placed a firm arm around Nicki as Jennifer pointed out, "Nicki Long."

Applause and whistles followed.

"Until recently Nicki was a lead dancer on Broadway, starring in the hit show *A Hair's Tale*."

Jennifer was interrupted by a ringing cell phone.

"Hold up, Mom," Terrell blurted. "That might be Broadway calling her back!"

"Don't answer," Jennifer pleaded dramatically. "Please, don't answer!"

Humored responses and chuckles followed as an embarrassed Nicki hurriedly reached for her clutch, pulled out the phone and silenced it.

"Is everything okay?" Jennifer asked. Nicki nodded. "Good, because unfortunately a few weeks ago, that was not the case. Nicki was injured in a bicycle accident and was forced to leave the show. Paradise Cove and our center are the grateful beneficiaries of her misfortune, as she has just signed on to a yearlong term as Drake Community Center's artistic director."

Nicki forced a smile as the diners applauded. She felt Julian's arm slide around her shoulders and tried to find comfort within the embrace. Tried to present a cheery, peaceful demeanor despite the text she'd glimpsed just seconds before. From Vince. Four short words that stabbed her heart like a knife.

See you in PC.

# Chapter 24

In his next text, he agreed to take the money. Added he was still coming to town. The center had paid for the flight. Her nerves became so frayed that simple breathing was difficult. How did criminals operate without having a breakdown? Between the covert back-and-forth text exchanges with Vince and assuring an astute Julian she was okay, Nicki was almost ready for a shot of tequila. Instead, she turned her mind to more positive news. Like how within a few hours her cast would be gone. And perhaps convincing Paige to come out for a visit. *A Hair's Tale* was nearing the end of its first run and Paige had never been to PC.

Julian flopped on his back, barely awake. "You sure you don't want me to stay and go with you?"

"No, thank you, babe. You've been amazing these past four weeks. I've been coddled and spoiled and a part of me could get used to that. But that independent part that you love so much is screaming for control!"

"That sounds like you're still going to rent a car."

"I am. For a whole week, at least!"

Nicki watched Julian get out of bed and walk into the bathroom shaking his head. She couldn't see the problem. He wanted to run out and buy her a car. She wanted time to try out different models and find which model fit her, what style she wanted. She also wanted to secure a loan and make the payments instead of allowing Julian to plunk down a big stack of cash. Julian didn't know that part. He already did so much, basically took care of everything. Nicki appreciated everything he did but wanted to be a bit self-reliant. With her five-thousand-dollar advance going to el jerko, money was going to be tight. Of course, Julian didn't know that, either. Thankfully he never would. Vince would refuse the job if offered, leave town and the nightmare would be over.

Devante drove her to the medical institute. Just thirty short minutes later, Dr. Allen had removed the cast, X-rayed her ankle and given a positive update. The bone was healing quickly and correctly. He didn't want her to put too much pressure on it yet and had given her an Aircast to keep it protected. But he'd given her the green light on driving. Next stop, rental car company.

She chose a black Hyundai Sonata. Sleek. Sporty. And undoubtedly less expensive than any car Julian would have chosen for her. After assuring Devante that she'd be fine, she plugged an address into the GPS, stopped at a drive-through for a shake—and to put distance between her and Devante—and then headed back to Paradise Cove. It seemed she got there in no time. She pulled into the strip mall parking lot where she'd suggested they meet. It was nearing lunchtime, the parking lot fairly full. She parked on the back side of the mall, near an insurance company without much traffic. Less chances of being seen by any of the town's busybodies. Which Nicki had learned in a small town meant just about everybody.

Ten minutes passed. She was early. No big deal. Ten more minutes. A little late, but no need to panic. Or was there? Nicki had assumed Vince would be driving a rental. But what if someone from the community center picked him up? She sent a quick text, asking what kind of car he was driving and whether or not he was on his way. She also described her Sonata and where she was parked. Thirty harrowing minutes later, a late-model car whipped into the lot. She honked her horn. He spotted her and parked in the empty space next to her car.

Vince got out of the car, or more like uncoiled six

feet and five inches of strong bones and chiseled muscle from inside the low-key sedan she'd insisted upon when a sporty convertible or luxury model was what he would have rented. The whole point of being in PC was to hide, she'd reminded him. To be on the down low. To blend in.

She watched his slow, easy gait as he walked to her car. He could have driven a Ford truck like Julian's brother Warren and the rest of the ranchers. But he still would have stuck out like a rooster in a coop of guinea fowl as soon as he smiled. The same pearly whites that were on display as he opened her car door and sank into the seat beside her. The same boyish grin that separated women from their panties. That had caused Nicki to ignore her head's knowledge and her gut's warning against such and give the guy her number.

"Hey, beautiful."

His attempt at a kiss was stopped by a strong hand on a hard chest.

"Don't."

"What?" Vince asked, hands raised in mock innocence. "I was just going for your cheek, a friendly kiss."

"I'm not here to be friendly. I'm here to try to settle this craziness so you can get out of my life."

"Wow…"

"It's not personal, Vince. And that probably didn't come out the way that it should. This is a small town. That's the reason. And the Drakes are very much a part of it."

"Hell, looks like they own it."

"I came here to start a life with the man I love very much, who I've been with for years. And for you to follow me—"

"It's a free country. I need a job. Saw one that fit me. Applied. Simple as that."

"Not that simple, and you know it." Nicki reached for

her bag in the back seat and pulled out a sheet of paper. "I have the money—ten thousand, as promised. There will be two more payments of five thousand each. To have proof of this agreement, I've had what we agreed on put in writing. Not a lot of legal jargon. Quite concise. You agree to cease all contact with me following the receipt of this first payment. You also agree not to take the job at the community center and not to remain in Paradise Cove. We can wish each other the best and go our separate ways. I admit I really dislike being in this situation, but I don't hate you. There were some fun moments in that brief time we spent together. I'll choose to remember them." She held out the piece of paper and dug for a pen. It wasn't until she found one that she looked back up and realized Vince hadn't reached out for the paper she held.

"You've got to sign the agreement, Vince. I can't give you the money without it."

Vince huffed, looked over at her with narrowed eyes. "What if I said I don't want the money? What if I said it's too late for that?" He craned his neck from left to right and looked behind him. "I've never lived in a small town before. Looks like this one might grow on me."

"Vince, don't…"

He snatched the paper, folded in half. "Give me a day to think about it. Meet with Terrell. Then I'll decide what I'll do."

He opened the door.

"Vince, wait!"

"I've been waiting. It's your turn now."

Nicki sat stunned. What just happened? Away from the city, closeted in a small town, her bullshit radar had clearly quit working. Vince's flip of the switch caught her totally off guard. But she was no fool. Clarity came quickly. That asshole had never intended to settle this drama. He wanted to throw his *hell no* in her face. That in itself was bad enough, but life could get worse. He could be on his way to the center right now, ready to spill the beans about dating her to the first Drake who'd listen. Nicki started the car and tapped Julian's number seconds later. The music playing right now might be a treacherous dirge, but it was time to face it.

"Hey, baby."

Julian sounded so happy to hear from her. It hurt to know the joy wouldn't last long. "Hi. Are you busy?"

"Not right now. Just waiting to hear about your trip to the doctor, and how it feels to once again walk on two feet."

"It feels amazing."

"Really? You don't sound too happy."

"Actually, I'm not. We need to talk."

"What's going on?"

"I don't want to discuss it over the phone. Can I come by the office?"

"My next client arrives in about twenty minutes. How far are you from the office?"

"I'm back in town, so not that far. But I don't want to have this conversation in a rushed atmosphere."

"You're worrying me, Nicki. What's this about? Second thoughts on the AD position?"

"No, I'm really excited about developing that program."

"What then? Did you wreck the car?"

"No."

"Rob a bank?"

She smiled. "No."

"Then what? Listen, never mind. This is my last patient until after lunch. Why don't I head home afterward and we can talk there?"

"Okay. But just don't…" How would it sound for her to ask that he not talk to his brother? Not good. Really bad, in fact. "Never mind. I'll pick us up something for lunch. See you then."

The weather turned gloomy as quickly as Nicki's day. She hadn't known there was rain in the forecast. Didn't know bullshit was scheduled, either. A day full of surprises.

Since the weather had turned chilly, she decided on soup. Stopped by Julian's favorite deli and found that a lot of other residents had the same idea. She pulled up in front of the town house thirty minutes later. Felt she'd been inside only moments before hearing Julian's car. Busying herself with gathering dishes and reheating the soup, her back was to Julian when he entered the room. As if not looking at him would delay the inevitable. It did not.

"All right, Nicki. Tell me what's going on."

She turned. "Oh, hi, babe. Don't you want to sit down first? I just need to nuke the—"

"No, that can wait. The only thing I want right now is an explanation."

"Okay, but I might as well warn you. This won't be easy for me to say or for you to hear. It's about that guy who's been bugging me, trying to extort money." She paused for a response or a reaction. There was none. "It was Vince Edwards."

The merest crease appeared on his brow, but his voice was calm. "The ballplayer?" Nicki nodded. "The one coming in town to interview at the center? You two dated?"

"Briefly. Barely a month, as I told you before. Before you and I got back together, I had already found out what a jerk he was and had broken things off. Hadn't heard from him since ending it with him two years ago, until just before the show started on Broadway. Obviously he found out I was in it, made up a lie about me owing him and started the harassment."

"Why you, though? A guy like him has probably dated hundreds of women."

"I've asked myself that question a thousand times, almost every time I've had the misfortune to answer his call. I wouldn't knowingly. But a few times, especially around when the show was just getting started, I answered unknown and private numbers. That's how this started."

"When you say the two of you dated, did you sleep with him?"

Nicki nodded, answered softly. "Yes."

"Why didn't you tell me this before?"

"Because I know how you feel about that. Besides, I told you he and I dated."

"You told me you dated, but you didn't tell me you *dated*." He put a sarcastic emphasis on the last word. "You tried to make it sound casual, as in went to the movies or out to eat. Not like something that was intimate, the two of you connecting by having sex."

"Trust me, there was no connection—"

"There's always a connection." His tone was emphatic, but his voice did not rise. "Despite what society says, there is no such thing as casual sex. We were barely broken up a month, Nicki. How'd it happen?"

"I don't even know. Angry. Stupid. A rebound reaction, and one of the worst mistakes I've ever made." She looked directly at him for the first time, her eyes shiny with unshed tears. "It was only after finding out the truth about him and what a jerk he was that I felt truly ashamed for being an easy target, one of hundreds of women, as you said, who'd ignored the signs and drank the Kool-Aid."

"Yet he's not in any of their towns trying to get hired on where they've just taken a job. He's here. With a scheduled interview at the center that bears my name. And I'm just now finding out. That's messed up."

"I never thought the harassment would go this far. Thought him saying he'd come here was just a threat."

"Wait, he told you about coming here? When?"

"The day of the brunch. He sent a text."

"So you knew before I did. Before Terrell. You knew he was coming here and kept me in the dark!"

"I thought it was just a threat to get me to pay him. So I agreed to give him money. I didn't want you to know. He promised that afterward he'd leave me alone. But he lied."

"When did you last talk to him?"

"Today. I met with him to—"

Julian held up a hand. "You met with him? Here, in Paradise Cove?"

"In the strip mall parking lot to give him the money. But to get it he had to sign an agreement that put his promise to leave me alone in writing."

Julian leaned against the island. Was silent for a very long time. The silence made Nicki feel horrible. Then he started talking, and she felt even worse.

"Before I was confused, but now everything makes sense. The distractedness. The distance. You being nervous and jumpy and preoccupied. Sleeping with me every night while keeping secret communications with another man."

"Julian, it wasn't like that—"

"I asked you what was going on. Not once. Several times. On any one of those occasions, you could have trusted me, confided in me, but you didn't. You let my family entertain the notion of hiring your extortionist as a mentor to young children."

"Baby…"

He shook his head. "Don't. Not now. When I needed you to talk, when there should have been conversation, you were silent. But knowing I might find out the truth, you decide you want to bare all and tell me everything. Well, guess what. It's too late. I don't want to listen. Not to another word that you have to say."

Except for a word here or there, Julian never raised his voice. He turned and walked out of the house. Seconds later she heard the car leave the driveway.

When she went to bed, he still hadn't come home. Wasn't there when she awoke the next morning. There wasn't a word for how bad Nicki felt. Everything Julian had said was correct. There was no good excuse for why she hadn't told him everything from the beginning. That she hadn't had caused a horrible ending. The worst part about it was that she couldn't even put the fault for what had happened all on Vince. The person mostly to blame was herself.

# Chapter 25

Before he'd only had a clinical perspective. But at this moment Julian knew from personal experience how a person could snap. He hadn't even known he could get this angry, let alone having ever experienced it before. As angry, hurt and disappointed as he was in Nicki, it was the dog Vince Edwards at the pit of his rage. He'd disrespected Julian's woman. Misled his family. No one mistreated his family like that and got away with it. Not on Julian Drake's watch.

He tapped the steering wheel and called his office. Cited an emergency and canceled his next appointment. Then he called Terrell.

"What's going on?"

"I need your face not to show what your ears are hearing."

A short pause. "Okay." The teasing quality had totally left Terrell's voice.

"Is Vince Edwards scheduled for an interview today?"

"Yeah, he'll be here in about an hour. Hold on a minute." Julian heard a series of noises, imagined his brother closing the door. "Okay, man, talk to me. No one can hear us. What's going on?"

"Something you're not going to believe." Julian took a deep breath, forced himself to stay calm as he relayed an abbreviated version of what he'd found out from Nicki. "She tried to explain, but I'd heard enough," he finished. "I thought nothing could hurt like her rejecting my proposal. But this type of betrayal? It's on another level. If you don't have trust, you don't have a relationship."

"It's a rare moment when I'm speechless," Terrell said

solemnly. "But I've got to tell you, bro. This is one of those times."

"Hard to find words for this situation. I finally get what I've always wanted—Nicki living here in Paradise Cove—then find out that a dude she slept with has followed her here, and some twisted game has been playing out the whole time that she's been with me. And the only reason she tells me is because he might mention it to you? That's a wrap, man. Done deal. It's over."

"Where are you headed now?"

"Your office, for the interview. I'm almost there. I've got a few questions to ask Vince Edwards. See what kind of threats he has to offer up when facing a real man."

Julian pulled into the parking lot a short time later and saw Jennifer's car. He wasn't surprised. The intensity with which he'd relayed the story about Nicki had probably frightened his brother into calling backup. The mere thought calmed Julian. A little.

A quick knock and he opened the door to Terrell's office. He and Jennifer were sitting at a small conference table. Warren was there, too. After hugging his mom and fist-bumping Terrell, he placed a hand on Warren's shoulder. "How'd they get you away from Charli? Tell you there was an angry bull loose that you might need to rope?"

"More like a coyote threatening the livestock that might need to be shot."

"Warren," Jennifer admonished, "do not say something like that, even in jest."

"Sorry, Mom."

Julian plopped into a nearby chair. "Guess y'all have already gotten the 411."

"Terrell told us what he knew," Jennifer answered. "But there's got to be more to the story."

"How do you figure?"

"Because I believe I know Nicki," Jennifer answered calmly. "She doesn't strike me as a cheater. Or a schemer who'd act with duplicitous motives."

"An hour ago I would have said the same thing. But the Nicki you know did all of that, right under my nose."

"I heard, son, and that's horrible. There is no denying or excusing the fact that she should have told you everything immediately. Up front. But I don't think she acted maliciously. You're angry and can't see it now. But from an objective stance, there is room for other perspectives. Don't get defensive," she hurriedly added. "I'm on your side. I just caution you to not be too hasty. To get the whole story, hear all angles, before making up your mind."

Jennifer left for a meeting. The brothers were mostly quietly waiting, until Terrell received the call that his appointment had arrived.

"You cool?" Terrell asked Julian.

"I'll make it a clean kick," Julian answered, referring to skills he'd honed for years as a black belt in martial arts.

"You heard what Mom said," Warren chided. "Don't joke like that."

"He's not joking," Terrell said, real concern on his face.

"I have no plans to get physical," Julian said finally. "If he has any sense at all, he won't say the wrong thing and have to get punched in the throat."

"Keep an eye on him," Terrell told Warren as he reached for the phone.

"Hello, Beatrice. Will you escort our visitor back to my office? Thank you."

A murmur of voices followed by laughter preceded a short knock on the door. A new, obviously besotted assistant announced Vince, who strolled into the office as though he owned the world. The door closed behind him.

He walked toward Terrell, now seated behind his desk, with hand outstretched. "Mr. Drake!"

Terrell didn't stand and barely smiled. "Have a seat, Vince."

The rude behavior was obviously unsettling. Even more so when Warren stood and walked toward the door and Vince realized he and Terrell were not alone. He looked at Julian, then back at Warren, now standing in front of the door as if to guard it.

Vince's smile dimmed as he sat. "I didn't realize this was going to be a group interview."

"There's a few things we didn't realize, either, my man." Terrell's tone was not unfriendly. "A situation involving my brother Julian—" he nodded toward the conference table where Julian now rested a hip "—and a person very important to him named Nicki Long. We need you to clear up a few things."

"And then we'll need you to get the hell out of this town," Julian said as he slowly walked over. "And not contact Nicki again."

Vince sat up straight in the chair. "Careful, brother. That sounds like a threat."

Julian offered a smile that didn't reach his eyes. "Oh no, Vince, only cowards do that. Real men like the Drakes don't make threats. We make promises. And we keep them. Harass Nicki again and you'll find out."

Thirty minutes later, Vince returned to his rental not quite sure how three men, talking calmly and smiling, put more fear in him than the punks he owed money had done while armed with guns. He'd never admit it. Was already creating an alternative truth in his head of why he decided not to work at the center. As for that witch Nicki, she wasn't worth him getting in any trouble. Especially here, in a town where he didn't know anybody and the Drakes were influential. Get arrested and there was no telling what would happen to him in jail. Vince would leave, but he'd remember the way he'd been treated. He'd come back here one day and bring his boys, the ones with records who were violent for real. Then he'd see how cool those Drake fools acted. Private school sissies raised on trust fund milk. He'd come back with backup, and even the score.

He checked the internet then plugged an address into his GPS. Minutes later he pulled into the parking lot of what seemed to be the town's lone restaurant. "Rinky-dink Hicksville," he muttered, anger increasingly replacing fear the farther he got from the center. "About all punks like those Drakes can handle."

He stepped inside and was surprised at the classy decor. There were only a few patrons. Not surprising, since it was almost two o'clock and most lunch hours had ended. There was no one at the host station, so Vince walked over to the bar and grabbed a seat. Pulled out his phone to check messages. The bartender was on the other side of the L-shaped counter, his back to Vince as he chatted with an attractive woman typing on a laptop. The woman looked up, made eye contact and smiled. A few seconds later, the bartender turned and walked over.

"Sorry about the wait, sir. What can I get you?"

Vince answered without looking up from his phone. "Rémy Martin, neat, and a glass of seltzer."

"Vince Edwards?"

Vince looked at the bartender, a handsome blond kid who didn't look old enough to serve liquor.

"Yeah, that's me."

"Man, I thought so! Dude! What are you doing here? I mean, it's cool and all. Of course, you can be anywhere you want. I'm just shocked. Sorry, my bad for rambling. Just a huge fan."

Vince's smile was slow and easy. The kid's excitement helped cover the negative feelings brought on by the Drakes questioning his manhood. Now he was being treated the way he was used to—as the superstar he was.

"What's your name, kid?"

"Jake." He held out his hand.

Vince shook it. "Nice meeting you, Jake. You sure you're old enough to work the bar?"

"Ah, man. I get that all the time. When I'm out socializing, I walk up to the bar with driver's license in hand."

"Ha!"

"Because I already know the drill. Vince Edwards! My buddies aren't going to believe this. Hey, mind if I get a selfie?"

"I'll think about it while I sip my drink."

"Oh, right. Drink. Sorry. Coming right up."

The bartender left to fix his drink. Vince watched him for a sec, then glanced over at the pretty lady. She was looking at him and, when caught, didn't immediately avert her eyes. Didn't walk over, either. Didn't matter. Vince knew the way he had with women. Knew she was trying to play hard to get. Another time and he might have joined her in the game. But he had business to handle. First, coming up with a way to get those fools their money. Then dealing with Nicki's boyfriend and his brothers.

"Here you go, sir, on the house."

Vince toasted with the snifter. "Appreciate it." He knocked it back in two gulps, gritted his teeth against the slow burn as the cognac trickled down his throat and chased it with the seltzer water. Checked out Jake talking with the woman again. Telling her a star was in the building. He was sure of that.

"Let me get another one, Jake. And a menu."

"Sure, right away." Jake brought over a menu.

"Make it a double this time."

"You got it."

Vince picked up the menu and leaned back against the bar seat. Soon there was movement in his peripheral vision. He knew that chick wouldn't be able to ignore his presence. Women never could.

Her floral-smelling cologne arrived before she did. "Bad day?"

He took his time looking up from the menu. "How do you figure?"

"Double shot at two in the afternoon. Mind if I sit here?"

He shrugged. "Chair's empty."

She perched on the seat, revealing a backside worthy of his attention. Pretty girl. A barracuda. He'd seen her kind time and again. He wasn't interested, but he wouldn't ignore her. He was a gentleman, after all.

"Anything worth ordering on this menu?"

"Best choice is the rib eye, medium rare." She opened her laptop and began typing.

Vince watched her fingers fly across the keys. "You must be a writer."

The woman smiled and revealed perfect white teeth and a dimple. Vince loved dimples. "A blogger. Why?"

"You type fast."

She nodded. "Jake says you're a basketball player from the East Coast."

"That why you came over? To blog about me?"

She stopped typing. "Not necessarily. I blog about celebrities. Jake knows you but I don't, so…" Her turn to shrug.

"That can easily be rectified." Vince held out his hand and flashed his panty-dropping smile. "Vince Edwards."

She countered with a look that Vince was sure had separated men from their money. "Ashley DeWitt."

"Nice to meet you, Ashley."

"Likewise."

"Now, since you know me, will I be in your blog?"

"Depends on what kind of juicy tidbits I can pry out of those tasty-looking lips. Do you have any?"

He thought briefly. Looked over and smiled. "I might. Are you familiar with the Drakes, the family that owns the community center?"

"Very familiar. I dated the mayor." Vince was obviously confused. "Ah, right. You're from out of town and might not know. Niko Drake is presently our town's mayor. But he looks poised to become the state's next senator."

"Is that so? What else can you tell me about them?"

"What would you like to know?"

Vince looked out at the near-empty dining room. "Why don't we discuss it over lunch? My treat. You might have information that could be beneficial to me, and I might give you a tip on a hot story."

Ashley slid off the stool with a hand on his thigh. "Follow me, Vince Edwards."

Vince picked up his drink and followed Ashley into the dining room. The Drakes wanted him gone by nightfall. But Vince might not be ready to leave so soon.

# Chapter 26

Nicki sat in the middle of the master suite's walk-in closet, trying to squeeze way more clothes into a piece of luggage than it was designed to hold. It didn't seem as though she'd shopped that much since arriving, but the pile of clothes still needing to get packed told a different story. Was there time to run out and buy another suitcase? Maybe, but Nicki didn't want to stop to do that and have to come back. Somewhere between when she arrived and today, the town house had begun to feel like home, one she'd decorated. It was going to be hard enough to leave as it was. She only wanted to do it once.

She pulled out a stack of folded clothes and started to roll them, belatedly remembering that more clothes could get packed that way. Didn't surprise her that the thought hadn't come earlier. Considering how her whole world had been upended in the past forty-eight hours, she was amazed she could remember anything.

After thirty more minutes of trying the impossible, Nicki gave up on her single-piece-of-luggage concept. She'd place the extra items in a recyclable bag and buy another piece of luggage at the airport. There was plenty of time for her to catch the red-eye. But she needed time to go to the rental agency and have Devante added as a driver so that he could return the car after dropping her off at Oakland International. Thank God he'd given her his card that included a cell phone number. Aside from the Drakes, he was the only person in town that she knew. With any luck, she'd be able to depart without having to see the family.

A bit cowardly, she readily admitted. But easier. Necessary. It broke her heart to have hurt Julian the way she did.

The man was in pain. Evidenced by how he hadn't come back to the town house or returned her calls. After waking up to his empty side of the bed for the second day in a row, she got his silent message. There was nothing left between them to talk about. Her lies, no matter how well intended, had backfired and cost her the love of her life. It was over. Julian was done.

Feeling the onslaught of tears and refusing to shed any more, she jumped up and went into the bathroom for her toiletries. While gathering them she mentally went over the email she'd sent Jennifer. The one resigning from a position she hadn't started. Apologizing for any inconveniences caused by her departure. Admitting she hated to leave but knowing it was for the best. And the one she'd sent Julian, stating all of that and the depth of her love. After one last look around, she ran a finger across the smooth, cool marble countertop and headed downstairs for a recyclable bag. She reached the landing and was startled when the doorbell rang. Walked over, looked out the peephole and opened the door with a sigh.

"Mrs. Drake, hello."

"Nicki, we've come much too far to revert to formalities."

"You're right, I'm sorry. Just wasn't expecting anyone."

"It is how I intended. Wasn't sure that had I asked you would have agreed to the visit. May I come in?"

"Sure." She stepped back so that Jennifer could enter. "Can I get you something? Water or tea?"

"Tea sounds lovely, dear. Chamomile if you have it."

Nicki went into the kitchen, grateful for the chance to get over the shock of Jennifer showing up at the front door. Time to put on her grown-girl girdle and take the verbal lashing Julian's mother had undoubtedly come to deliver. After setting the kettle to boil, she joined Jennifer on the sofa.

"The water will be ready in a few minutes."

"Good." An awkward silence followed as Jennifer eyed Nicki thoughtfully. "I must admit, your email came as quite a surprise."

"This week has been full of them."

"More for some than others, I'm told."

"Whatever it was that Julian told you, know that every story has two sides."

"That is correct. The story told from his point of view is quite damning. I'd like to hear yours."

The kettle whistled. Nicki prepared the drinks and carried the mugs back into the living room.

She took a sip and a breath. "I love Julian very much and would never set out to purposely hurt him. Whatever you think of what I'm about to share with you, please know that, Jennifer. Your son is the love of my life.

"In the twenty-twenty vision of hindsight, it's clear that I should have told him everything up front. I didn't lie, not outright. I just didn't tell him everything at once. I told him I'd dated someone while he and I were broken up. He didn't ask for a name, and I didn't offer one. He didn't ask whether or not we'd slept together, and I thought it best not to share that, either. It was a fling borne out of the hurt from the breakup. And it was over. So why tell him about it? We were back together, and for me, that's all that mattered."

Nicki continued to pour out her heart. Jennifer sipped tea and listened.

"With everything that's happened," she finished, "I knew there was no longer a place for me at the center or in this town. Julian doesn't want to be around me. His actions have made that very clear. So I felt it best to leave quickly, quietly. Go back home and begin to pick up the pieces of my life."

"I appreciate your honesty, Nicki. Thank you for sharing

your side. Out of all of my sons, Julian is easily the smartest and the most sensitive. You're right. He is deeply hurt by your betrayal, especially since it happened while the two of you were in such close proximity, and because it went on for so long. It seems clear that had you the opportunity for a do-over, you'd handle the situation differently. But…"

Jennifer paused as her phone chimed. She reached inside her designer bag and pulled it out. "It's Julian. One moment." She tapped the screen. "Hello, son." A pause to listen. "Actually, I'm at your house, talking with Nicki." She glanced at Nicki, her brow slightly creased. "What? When? Hold on a moment. Nicki, can you turn on the television to local news?"

Nicki opened a compartment of the coffee table, pulled out the remote and tapped the power button. Then she changed the channel to the local station, where a banner along the bottom of the screen announced breaking news. "We've got it, son. Let me call you back."

Just as Jennifer ended the call, a picture of Vince came on the screen.

Nicki turned up the volume.

"Edwards claims the original dispute was between him and ex-girlfriend Nicki Long."

"What?"

"…a professional dancer most recently seen in the hit Broadway musical *A Hair's Tale*, now dating local resident Dr. Julian Drake. According to the former basketball star, the Drakes lured him to Paradise Cove under the false pretense of potential employment and then allegedly proceeded to threaten his life. Edwards says they backed down when he vowed to take the dispute public and was then offered money by Long to stay quiet and leave town."

"Oh my God!" Nicki jumped up from the couch. "He's such a liar!"

The TV cut to a location shot of Vince. "I was shocked," he said, looking at the reporter who was offscreen. "I was excited about the chance to mentor the type of boys who grew up like I did. And to be blindsided like that, when expecting an interview? And then this bribery attempt?" He held up the paper that Nicki had given him. She wanted to throw up. "From everything I'd read, the Drakes are an upstanding family. But behind the suits and professional facade, they're just a bunch of thugs."

"What do you plan to do, Mr. Edwards?" the reporter asked.

"I'm not going to do anything," Vince said with a smile. "I have an attorney to fight those kinds of battles. They'll be hearing from him very soon."

"Just when I thought he couldn't sink lower…" Her voice trailed off as Nicki seethed.

"For some there is no limit to the depths they'll go when money is involved."

"Right. Money he was trying to get from me, which is why he badgered me and why I finally agreed to paid him. Not that crap he just spouted on TV."

"Of course, but the truth wouldn't warrant a lawsuit." Jennifer appeared unmoved, her countenance almost one of boredom.

Nicki grabbed her phone. "What's the name of that station, Jennifer? Their call letters. Do you know?"

"Stay calm, Nicki. This isn't the first time we've danced with a frivolous lawsuit, which is certainly coming."

"I still need to contact them and set the record straight."

"What are you going to do?"

"I'm going to go down there and tell the truth about what happened. I will not let him tarnish Julian's name. Or the Drakes'."

Jennifer appraised Nicki with a spark in her eye. "Spoken with such conviction, one would mistake you for a Drake yourself."

"I'm afraid I've ruined those chances."

"Maybe. Maybe not. But one thing's for sure. You're not going to help the situation by running away."

"I'm not running away."

"That's exactly what you're doing."

"I'm leaving a place where I'm no longer wanted."

"You're leaving a man who is angry and hurt, and rightfully so. But as you said, there are two sides to every story, at least. As a woman, I understand yours. Brief fling. Over and done with. Forget about it. Move on. It makes sense that you wouldn't tell Julian. But once the threats continued, and you knew Vince was on his way here…"

"I used the advance to try to stop him. It was money, not me that he wanted. Vince promised me if I gave him the money, he wouldn't take the job at the center and he'd leave me alone for good. Knowing the kind of man he is, I couldn't give him the money without proof of that promise. That's why I wrote the agreement. I thought the problem had been handled. That's why I didn't tell Julian. It's too late for all that now. He doesn't want to talk to me—he hasn't come home for two nights straight."

"He's at our home, honey, and he hasn't wanted to talk to me, either. He's an introspective man who needs time alone with his thoughts. Space to ponder and work out his feelings. I can tell you this much—he doesn't want you to leave."

"Humph. I can't tell."

"If my son is truly the love of your life, as you claim, leaving now, with things as they are, would be the worst possible move. Drake men are some of the strongest, proudest, most stubborn, confident—some would say arrogant— men I've ever known. Yet if one is fortunate enough to win their heart, no man will love you stronger or better. This, I know for sure.

"He doesn't want you to leave, Nicki, and quite frankly I don't, either. Nor do I want to force you to stay—which, technically and legally, since you've already signed the contract to work at the center, I could do. I will say that the timing is especially unfortunate given an exceptional opportunity I'd planned to share with you before…everything happened. One that I feel could have provided quite a boost in your professional career. Some might even have called it a chance of a lifetime. Not to mention a rather hefty paycheck. But never mind."

"What is it?"

Jennifer hesitated. "I'm really not sure I should tell you, Nicki. Given your plans to return to New York."

"That's a wicked smile, Mrs. Drake. I think you absolutely should tell me."

"Oh, well. If you insist. It involves a director named Ngo Xhe. Have you heard of him?"

"I've met him. Julian and I saw his show in LA. It's fantastic!"

"So I've heard. One of my well-connected friends, a patron of the arts, is among several helping to sponsor a USA tour, performing in several major cities. I mentioned how wonderful it would be if he could put on some kind of show at the center, a fund-raiser during the holidays or the first part of next year. She wasn't sure he could actually do the show himself but thought he might be able to lend us some dancers. All of this would require coordination and expertise, of course, but considering the level of people who support our endeavors, the rewards through connections made and the networking possible could be quite significant. Dear, what time is your plane?"

Nicki canceled her flight. She called the network and

scheduled an interview while Jennifer fielded calls from family and friends. It hadn't taken long for everyone in town to know what happened. Those who hadn't seen the report on TV had found it online. By six o'clock the story had broken nationally. By the time Jennifer left an hour later, the Drakes' lawyers had been called to handle Vince, and the two women had hashed out plans for a Valentine's weekend fund-raising gala. That was less than four months away. The day had proved emotionally exhausting, yet Nicki was glad it had happened, and awed at how differently problems could be handled when one had power and money. If she'd shared everything with Julian the moment Vince's threats started, the problem would have ended a long time ago.

Nicki went upstairs to unpack the suitcase. Happy that she was staying in town and excited about her professional future. Her ankle was almost healed, she'd soon be back dancing, and without so much as a phone call let alone an audition, she was set to choreograph a holiday show with Ngo Xhe's dancers! Would she and Julian get back together? Only time would tell. Was the saga with Vince finally over? She certainly hoped so. But for now, and the next four months at least, she'd be too busy to worry.

# Chapter 27

Julian felt he'd lived four lives in less than a month. So much had happened. Everything had changed. The rift with Nicki. Vince showing up in PC. The all-hands-on-deck push for his brother during the final week of campaigning. An endless round of parties after Niko won. All this while still handling a full roster of patients. Counseling other people while feeling *he* needed therapy. Or a vacation, at the very least. Instead he sat in Niko's office having just agreed to take on more work.

"I know you've got a lot on your plate, Doctor, so I really appreciate you agreeing to serve as a consultant."

"I'm still trying to figure out how you got me to do it. I came here totally prepared to say no—had a list of valid reasons and everything."

Niko chuckled. "Power of persuasion. Can't be a successful attorney without the ability to present a compelling argument. Plus, I know how passionate you are about the problems facing the health-care system. As the most populous state in the nation, I feel an even greater need to make sure the proper plans remain in place for agencies such as Medicare and Medicaid, no matter what's happening in Washington. Because of our large immigrant population, we have a lot of little ones who need access to preventative services and the area on which you're most focused, mental health."

"I must admit that's the driving factor in my decision to be a part of the Committee on Health. To be able to help contribute to bills that will decrease America's dependence on prescription medication. To expand the definition of post-traumatic stress beyond military personnel to one that includes average citizens growing up in American neighborhoods with worse violence than those in the Middle East is an opportunity I couldn't turn down."

"Being part of the solution."

"Exactly."

"Speaking of solutions, what's going on with you and your lady?"

"Nothing much."

"You haven't talked to her?"

"Not really."

"Why not?"

"She's been out of town. Went to LA right after the election. Was there a couple weeks working on the dance. After that she went back east to sublet her place and spend Thanksgiving with her mom."

"Her phone doesn't work outside PC?"

"We talked a few times, but there's a lot going on. Especially with her back working, choreographing the show..."

Niko eyed him intently. Julian fought the urge to squirm under his older brother's intent gaze. Like Julian, Niko was keenly intuitive and paid as much attention to what someone didn't say as what they did.

"So y'all haven't talked because she's working?"

"We've both been busy. On top of my usual workload, I've been back and forth to San Diego, fulfilling a promise I made to Dexter's wife Faye about counseling teens who'd been treated at her clinic. And I've been helping the state's new senator."

"Ah, no. Don't put any of that on me, bro. I'm never too busy to talk to Monique. My wife and I talk every single day. No matter what. No matter where. What about the ballplayer? He still in PC?"

"No, he left."

Julian purposely left out details on that exit, the persuasion used to ensure that Edwards left town. Terrell had refused to provide specifics regarding what happened. All Julian knew was that the solution had involved one of Ace's contacts from his old neighborhood in Oakland—someone whose background matched that of Nicki's nemesis. Someone who spoke a street language Vince understood.

"I don't know the whole story. It's not my business at all. But what I do know is how happy you were when you were dating Nicki. How in love the two of you appeared not long ago in New York, and here. Is what happened between her and that guy so egregious you can't get past it?" Julian shrugged. "I don't think so. Because if what happened had been a deal breaker, the two of you would have officially broken up by now."

"It's about a betrayal of trust. Of lies and deception. I love Nicki, no doubt. Wanted to spend the rest of my life with her. All she needed to do was tell me what was going on. Tell me the truth. Why did she lie? That remains a question in my mind."

"Have you asked her?"

"Of course."

"And…"

"The guy was extorting her. She didn't want me to know. Knew I'd handle the situation but was concerned about how I'd handle it."

"I can kind of understand that, brother. You know what they say. Gotta watch those quiet ones. Plus, you are a third-degree black belt. Sounds like her actions were to protect you."

"I'm sure that's the way it plays in her mind. For me, though, what most stands out is the broken trust. I don't know if I can get past that. Or if it's something I can live with."

"Only you know that, bro. But ask yourself this. Is Nicki the kind of woman you can live without?"

Julian's ringing cell phone broke the silence. He pulled it from his pocket. "My assistant," he explained. "Yes, Katie."

He paused, listened, watched Niko begin to check his phone. "Excuse me, what? Dr. Johnson?"

Upon hearing that name, Niko looked up.

"Where'd you hear this?" Julian leaned against the chair back, his face a mask of concern. "No, I appreciate you calling. Both of them? All right, Katie. Anything else?" He listened, nodded. "Right. No, I'll be heading home shortly, just waiting for rush hour to die down a bit, and in the office first thing in the morning." Julian continued to listen. "Put it in my inbox. I'll take a look at it. Okay. See you then."

He ended the call, stared into space.

"What's going on, man?"

"Something crazy."

"I heard the name Johnson. He get busted again?"

"No, his daughter Natalie just got arrested. She got pulled over for speeding. The police searched her car. Found a large stash of prescription drugs. Threw on the cuffs." A pause and then, "She wasn't alone. Ashley was with her and got arrested, too."

"I didn't know even know they were friends! So instead of the doctor, his daughter was dealing pills?"

"Possession of a controlled substance with intent to distribute is how they were charged. Is there evidence to prove it?" Julian shrugged. "I knew they were very close and believe Natalie used that friendship and Ashley's blog to come against me. The doctor wasn't charged, but announced his immediate retirement."

"Brother, your business is going to boom."

"Doesn't feel good making money on someone else's misfortune."

"Someone has got to service those clients. It might as well be you."

"At least now Natalie's actions make more sense. The fewer patients her dad had on his books, the fewer medications it would appear he needed, and if she was stealing inventory…wow, that's really too bad. Ironic that I get this news while in your office. This kind of drug proliferation is the very reason why I agreed to be a consultant for the Committee on Health. We've got to do something about prescription-drug abuse."

"That's why I asked you to come on board, bro. You are the man for the job."

Julian looked at his watch and stood. Niko did, too. "Heading out?"

"I think traffic's lightened up enough to make it a quick drive. Are you getting a place here? Commuting? How does that work?"

"Monique and I have talked about getting either condos or townhomes both here and in DC. I'll actually spend more time in Washington than I will here in Sacramento, which of course is fine with Monique. She has friends and colleagues on the East Coast and will likely travel with me on those occasions. It's a new chapter in our lives, one that we're going to write together."

"I always saw you two as the family's power couple."

"That title would probably go to London and Ace."

"They'd definitely get the paparazzi couple award."

Niko chuckled. "Yes, and our baby sister loves every minute of it."

The two men hugged. Julian walked toward the door.

"Ju."

He turned around.

"Call Nicki. Talk to her. Work it out."

"I hear you."

"Don't go with your head on this, bro. Go with your heart."

It was just over seventy miles from Sacramento to Paradise Cove. Julian spent sixty-five of them thinking about Nicki, Niko's instruction to call her and, even more, his question about living a life without her. In many ways it was as though his life officially began only after she'd come into it. Could he live without her? Yes. It would be difficult, but there'd never been anything Julian couldn't accomplish when he put his mind to it. What really mattered was the question he now asked himself.

Did he want to?

# *Chapter 28*

Nicki stood front and center in the Drake Community Center auditorium. She faced the stage, head high, arms raised with the focus of a conductor. Fifteen pairs of eyes were on her. Excited young teens who attended the center, talented and lucky enough to have been chosen to be a part of the Valentine-themed show's finale. Paige had flown over to help with rehearsals and because *A Hair's Tale* was on break could be in the show!

"Cue the music! Get ready, guys. One, two, three, four! Pow! Big movements. Smile. Turn. Pop. Two. Three. Four. Step. Step. Good!" She directed the dance with her body and soul. Shouting out counts. Steps. Encouraging them on. Joining in on the parts they'd all dance together. It was only the first two eight counts with several missteps, but considering these girls were not professional dancers, had only seen Ngo Xhe's show on tape and had only practiced the intricate dance steps for just over a week, they did well. Nicki didn't coddle them because they were beginners. She set high expectations and demanded their best. She assured them that excellence lived inside them. Helped them believe. In return they worked to prove her right. Over and over they practiced. Individually. In groups. And then back on stage. Finally, an hour later, she announced that practice was over.

She walked to the center of the stage. Paige joined her. "Gather round, guys." The teens and Nicki were joined by the ten professional dancers from Ngo's troupe at the heart of the ninety-minute program. The group formed a circle and grabbed hands.

"Okay, ladies, good job today. One of the things I want

everyone to focus on during tonight's visualization are the transitions from one formation to another. One line into two. Right now that's real sloppy. Understandable—it's only been a week and this is a new way of dancing. But it's important to remember that the steps, transformations, music all work together, so we need to see that happening in our minds. Then it becomes easier for our bodies to follow. Everyone understand?" She raised her hand as a sign for their answer. All around her hands shot up in the air.

"You all are visualizing, right? For five minutes before you go to sleep? Seeing the dance and you doing it perfectly?" Some teens responded audibly. Others nodded. "Well, a couple of you might want to add another five minutes, because clearly no practice outside here has been done. I'm not calling out any names—Carissa, Michelle, Angelique—I'm just saying…"

The group laughed along with her. "Those ladies know why they got pointed out, but we all can and will improve. That's why it's called practice. The more we practice, the more perfect we become. So have a great weekend, everybody. Get in a little rest and a lot of practice. Next week we'll add on the next set of eight counts to what was learned this week. Any questions?" She looked around the circle. "No? Then that's it. Good job, dancers."

The group of excited teens began to disperse. Several of them came up to hug Nicki. Others chatted or checked their phones as they left the auditorium.

Paige strolled over. "I love this type of dancing, Nicki. It's such fun!"

"Isn't it? I'm so glad you're here. Just wish you could stay the whole time."

"I wanted to, but with Mike a long stay was a no go."

"Problems?"

"No. But I'd promised him that my break from performing was to spend more time with him. Instead I'm here. With you."

"Performing," they said together.

"I'll watch the tapes and work on my dance. That and a week of rehearsals right before and I'll be ready to shine." Paige turned to leave. "You heading out?"

"No, think I'll work on my dance a little bit. What time is your flight?"

"First thing mañana. That's why I wanted a hotel close to the airport tonight."

"Devante will take good care of you." They hugged. "Love you, girl. Text me when you get home so I know you've arrived safely."

Once alone, Nicki sat and went through a series of stretches, then walked over to the sound system. Soon a mellow, piano-driven jazz piece filled the air. It was the solo piece that would anchor the program's first half. The stage bare save for Nicki and a spotlight. She walked to a point on the stage just beyond the curtain, raised to her full height of five feet, eight inches, and assumed ballet's fourth position. She wore denim-inspired dance pants and a faded, cropped, long-sleeved tee emblazoned with the words *Live Your Life*. On the next downbeat, she took a step. Leg straight, toe pointed, then into a twirl. Her moves were fluid, flawless, her body an instrument of beauty as she executed a series of steps. Split leaps. Pirouettes. Elevating the basic steps of Xhe's original lulu when the song's tempo quickened into a midtempo beat. She felt herself get lost in the music and movements. In this moment, nothing existed but the dance. Worries took a back seat. Problems faded. She was one with the music.

The routine crescendoed and then eased back into the romantic melody from which it began. Her movements became graceful, sensuous, expressing the emotion of love with her body better than others could do with their voice. As the last notes faded, she floated to the ground and ended with legs stretched, back arched, arm touching the floor behind her. The song ended. She held the position, ignored her body's complaint at being contorted. Stayed until she heard a single clap.

Her eyes flew open as she sat up abruptly. Another clap happened. And another. And more. She looked out, unable to see past the first few rows.

"Tangie?"

It would make sense for the dancer from Ngo's company serving as her assistant to have stayed to watch her work on the dance. The claps increased as a person walked into view. It wasn't Tangie.

"Julian."

He continued clapping until he stood directly before her. "Girl, you were born to be a dancer. That was…magic."

"Thanks. It's a work in progress, but I like how it feels."

"I don't see how it can get any better."

"How long were you watching?"

"I saw it all."

Her voice was calm but her heartbeat skipped and jumped with excitement. Had she manifested this man on the strength of desire? Could he feel that he was the muse who'd inspired her movements? Did he know that it was her love for him at the heart of the dance?

"I like your top."

Nicki looked down, then back up with a smile. "It's one of my favorites."

"Our first official date."

"Prudential Center. Newark, 2011."

"Rihanna was all of that, man. And when that song started up and T.I. came on stage…madness."

"Pandemonium. Everybody went crazy! I still don't

know how you managed to keep the shirt hidden until the show was over and we were back in the car."

Julian nodded, said nothing. His eyes narrowed, thinking. Nicki wished she knew what about. For a time, mere seconds, they'd been back in the couple flow. Easy camaraderie. Julian had almost smiled. Then a return to uncomfortable silence.

"I've hardly seen you here lately."

"I've been back and forth to Sacramento doing work with my brother, and to Faye's clinic in San Diego."

A few seconds passed. Then a few more. Nicki tried to read his face. Julian looked beyond her to a space on the wall.

"Has he settled in yet?"

"Taking to it like a duck to water."

Nicki reached over for a towel and a bottle of water. She blotted the perspiration on her forehead, took a long, healthy swig.

"How was Thanksgiving with Miss Marie?"

"Unorthodox." Julian raised his brow. "Chinese food and a guided tour of the African American museum in DC."

"Nice. Just you two?"

Nicki shook her head. "There were about fifteen or twenty of us."

"Surprised they were open on a holiday."

"I was, too. While there I learned that Christmas is the only day that they're closed."

The small talk continued, punctuated by pauses. Unlike Nicki's dance it was stilted, unsure. She knew why. Hard to have a conversation around the elephant standing between them.

"Julian, can we sit and talk, really talk, for a minute?"

"Actually, I was on my way out. Just happened to hear the music and came to see what was happening."

"Just a few minutes. We've hardly seen each other in almost a month. Living here with us not talking is driving me crazy."

"You've barely been here."

"I'm here now. I know you needed space and time and all that. But I want to make sure you understand everything. And then after that…the next move will be on you."

"All right."

He turned and walked halfway up the auditorium. Beyond the stage lights and into the shadows. Nicki followed, and when he sat down she took the chair beside him, turned to face him as directly as possible and began to share her heart.

"I never imagined myself living here. You know that better than anybody. As much as I love you—and that's more than I've ever loved anyone—Broadway always stood between me and that possibility. Then life happened, and just like that I'm not only living here but working and dancing. But it still feels like a situation that's contrary to reason, because I'm living in your home and hometown without you. I've signed on as artistic director for a year. But honestly? If this is how it's going to be between us, I'll break the contract, because I simply can't deal.

"I understand why you got so upset. I get it now. I've apologized. I meant it. That's all I can do. I can't do it over. I can't take anything that happened back. If we could rewind time, I would definitely do things differently. It would have made my life easier. I see that now. Once you and your family found out about Vince, the issue was resolved. It was like, one and done. But at the time I made the decisions I did, it was for the right reasons. I thought he was someone I could handle—I had no idea he would take it as far as he did. Especially since what he said was a lie and I didn't owe him anything. But there's another reason. Something else I didn't tell you."

He'd been looking straight ahead, but at this revelation, Julian looked her in the eye.

"A week or so after he started calling, I got home and realized there was nothing to drink. So I hopped up and headed to the store. No problem, right? It wasn't that late, around eleven o'clock. On my way back, these two guys who'd parked in front of my house got out of their car. Didn't think much about it, but they had my attention. I am a New Yorker, after all."

Nicki's attempt to lighten the situation didn't work.

"We got to a place on the sidewalk at the same time. When I tried to go around them, they blocked my path. They knew who I was, said Vince had sent them to collect his money. Thank goodness for my nosy neighbor, Miss Frances. She hollered a greeting, and they let me by. That's when the situation became serious in my mind, and I felt threatened. A part of me wanted to tell you. Paige kept insisting that you needed to know. But I knew if that happened, you would have been on the very next flight and things would have definitely escalated. I couldn't have lived with being responsible if anything happened to you. It was a few days later that the accident happened and I came here. Situation over. Problem solved. End of story. Until it wasn't. The problem that I thought was over followed me here."

She placed her hand on top of his. "I'm sorry, baby. And I miss you. Can we work this out and get back together? I'm going crazy being alone in the town house. The nights are too quiet, and beyond the dancing I'm totally bored."

"Sounds like you don't want a man. You just want company."

"Pretty much."

For the first time since he'd walked in, Julian smiled.

"I appreciate you trusting me enough to share everything. It's probably better that I didn't know about it before. That you didn't share that until after he'd left town. But don't ever do it again, Nicki. You hear me?" She nodded. "Don't ever try to deal with something like that on your own. Protecting you is my responsibility. It's what a man does."

"I get that now."

"Good." He stood, stretched. "I'm headed out to get something to eat. Want to join me?"

She stood, too. "I would, except I have a conference call with my agent in thirty minutes. Just enough time to shower and have a quick bite. Maybe we can hang out tomorrow night?"

"Maybe."

Men and their pride, Nicki thought as they parted. He wanted to come back on his schedule, his timetable. Jennifer had encouraged her to exercise patience. She'd also said that a love worth having was worth fighting for.

Reaching for her phone, she sent Julian a quick text.

Want to come over later and massage my sore muscles?

She waited. No answer. Started up her car and headed home. A few minutes later, her phone pinged. Once stopped at a red light, she checked it.

A text back from Julian.

Yes. I have a muscle that needs rubbing, too.

Nicki laughed out loud. Turned on the stereo, turned the music up loud. Her baby was coming over. They were going to rub muscles and spend the night doing her favorite dance with the best partner ever.

# *Chapter 29*

December and January had flown by in the blink of an eye. Nicki could hardly believe it was Valentine's Day weekend and the charity gala had finally arrived.

She peeked from behind the curtain to check out the crowd. San Francisco's War Memorial and Performing Arts Center was filled to capacity. When Jennifer told her she'd have no problem selling out three thousand seats, Nicki had her doubts—not only about the relatively short window to promote and sell tickets, but that it was five hundred dollars for the least expensive seat. But she'd done it. Not only would the Drake Community Center benefit, but so would Nicki, as part of the funds would be used for the arts program Nicki would run.

Less than six months ago, Nicki had had life all planned out, and it had looked nothing like the one she lived right now. Then, she'd been focused on back-to-back Broadway shows, saving money to build her portfolio, continuing a long-distance relationship with Julian and eventually talking him into moving his practice back east so that he could counsel, she could dance and they both could live happily ever after. Now, here she was about to lead a troupe of seasoned professionals and a few exceptionally talented Drake Community Center dancers in the lulu, Ngo Xhe's original dance.

Looking beyond the glittering gowns and starched tuxes that filled the orchestra level, Nicki spotted the Drake clan in their private box. Julian's parents sat in the middle of the first row, flanked by Ike Jr. and Quinn on their right and Niko and Monique to their left. Behind them sat Terrell and Aliyah, Teresa and London. Nicki guessed Ace and Atka were together, getting drinks or doing something equally mundane, like plotting a world takeover. Warren was home with the new baby. She didn't see Julian, who'd said that he'd come. They'd done well the past couple months. Just before the new year, he'd come back home. Had there been a flashback to the hurt she'd caused him? Had the news that Vince Edwards now coached at a high school near San Francisco made him doubt some or all of what she'd sworn was true? Nicki closed her mind against the onslaught of thoughts. There was time only for positive energy. She had a show to do.

Paige joined Nicki at the curtain, peeked over her shoulder. "Wow, it's crowded."

"Yep, a sold-out house."

"Not quite Broadway."

"It's even better." Nicki turned to Paige. "Never thought you'd hear me say that, huh?"

"Not in a million years. Not surprised, though. Love tends to wipe out the logical and accurate-thinking side of one's brain."

"And on that note…" Nicki gave a playful nudge as she walked past her. "Let's get dancing." She reached for Paige's hand, clasped it into her own. "And let's hope that in the very near future you lose your mind, too."

"I love you more than most, Nicki Long. But move to the West Coast? My honey would never."

"But you are going to audition for Ngo Xhe's next show, right? It's in San Francisco, but only twelve weeks."

"Definitely going to try out for that one. Mike can handle cross-country visits for that length of time."

"I'm so glad you're here."

"Me, too. And I'm happy for you. Love's got you glowing. Congratulations."

Backstage, the dancers gathered in a circle, waiting for

Nicki. She and Paige joined them, still holding hands, and clasped the hands of the dancers next to them. Nicki smiled at the professionals and took in the nervous, excited looks of the teens from the center.

"I was you once," she began, looking at her first crop of community center dancers. "Standing backstage at my very first professional show. Nervous, excited, not sure if I'd remember the steps. Petrified I'd mess up the entire routine." She paused and looked each girl in the eye. "You will remember. And if you don't, your body will. And if your body doesn't, it's still okay. Because your heart is in the right place. And so are you. Out there, on stage, even your mistakes will look like magic. Just keep smiling and flowing to the rhythm of the beat. Remember how absolutely beautiful, talented and amazing you are. Now, repeat after me.

"I am exceptional. I am amazing. I can do anything I want to do and be anything I want to be. Tonight, I am a dancer. Wait, I didn't hear you. Tonight, I am what?"

"A dancer!" the girls shouted, and the pros, too.

"That's right. We are dancers. Let's go out there and make the lulu come alive!"

Moments later the music began, pulsating percussion against a pitch-black stage. With a hidden light to guide them, the ten girls trained at the Drake Community Center danced across the stage—syncopated claps and stomps with their feet. Driving the movement. Creating the beat. The professional dancers entered next. Twirling and leaping, gliding and marching. Fluorescent red stripes on their black leotards came alive, as did more percussion instruments, then horns, then strings.

Three minutes into the first song, Nicki entered, a bundle of energy, a body of grace, combining years of training in modern dance with jazz, a little tap and a touch of ballet, mimicking the other dancers as they marched and then flawlessly inviting the audience to clap along and tap their feet in time to the contagious rhythm. During the first segment, the dancers introduced the story. About a group of girls, friends, outcasts all, who found their voices in their feet. On the final notes of the song preceding the first half's finale, dancers twirled and danced themselves off-stage, leaving the stage bare save Nicki and the spotlight.

She performed her solo dance. In her mind it was for Julian. Becoming one with the music, she poured her love for him from her heart to her limbs. Expressed the joy he brought her in every leap, her excitement in every spin. The music slowed and with it her movements. A series of dance moves took her to the back of the stage. In a final flurry of arms and legs in fluid motion, she returned to the center of the stage. As the last notes of the song played out, she was slowly lifted up from the floor. Higher and higher, until she disappeared into the rafters.

The unexpected move stunned the crowd, evidenced by their collective gasp. Seconds of silence passed, and then thunderous applause began. Nicki smiled as she hurried out of the harness that had lifted her safely to the ceiling's rafters and a narrow walkway to a ladder behind the back curtain. Her plan to end the first half on a high, showstopping note had worked better than she imagined. It would be topped only by her solo before the group finale, again the way she'd planned it. A cocoon for her students' first performance, and their inevitable faux pas. However they performed and whatever happened in between these well-polished acts would be forgotten. Nicki felt certain that the show would be labeled a success, both as a sold-out fundraiser and artistically, as a show she'd designed. A dancer and choreographer? Who knew!

With two forty-minute sets and a fifteen-minute intermission, the evening flew by. Sweaty and exhausted but pumped with adrenaline, Nicki smiled and preened and dazzled the audience, even as she mentally prepared for her heart-stopping finale. This would be the truest test yet of how well her ankle had healed.

"This is it, Nicki," she mouthed to herself while dancing over to the far side of the stage. "You can do it." Then, with a running start, she cartwheeled into a handless backflip over ten pairs of shoes. She heard another collective audience gasp as she landed on the other side, executed perfect piqué turns to the center of the stage and ended with a dramatic flourish of fingers as she dropped into a Chinese split.

The audience went wild. She stood, waved and exited the stage as each group of dancers took their bows. After Paige and the principal dancers were acknowledged, Nicki returned to the stage, the rousing standing ovation now minutes long. She clasped the hands of the dancers next to her as they took one final collective bow. As they did so, Nicki noticed Jennifer being ushered up the stairs to the stage. Turning, she applauded the woman who'd organized the night's performance.

Jennifer acknowledged the crowd, then pulled Nicki into a warm embrace. "Fabulous! Absolutely amazing," she whispered. "I'm so proud of you."

Then, taking the mike from an assistant who waited, she addressed the crowd, eyes twinkling. "I told you tonight's show would be worth every dollar. Was I right?"

The audience cheered their affirmative response.

"I want to thank everyone involved in helping to make tonight's event a huge success through supporting, promoting and making the arts available to all children and teens everywhere. To the Ladies of Paradise—the very active women's society of Paradise Cove—the businesses and corporations of Paradise Cove, San Francisco and surrounding communities, for your largesse in donations of both money and resources, to the professional dancers that hail from across the country, from New York's stages to California's showstoppers, and especially to the pop sensation and Broadway star who generously donated her time to perform for us... Paige McCall!" Jennifer waited as the crowd enthusiastically showed their appreciation. "Finally, to Nicki Long, a Broadway performer and our very own star, who now shares her time and talent with hopeful young girls who dream of a life on stage, such as the ones who've danced their way into our hearts tonight!"

A movement offstage caught Nicki's eyes. They widened a bit as she saw Julian coming up the stairs carrying a gigantic bouquet of large, perfectly formed red, yellow, pink and purple roses. Her heart skipped a beat. He'd been there. He'd seen the dance!

"For the show's choreographer and star," Jennifer gushed as Julian handed her the flowers.

The show's star, of course. Nicki's smile didn't falter as she accepted the bouquet.

"Because of tonight's success, we are well on our way to breaking ground for the Performing Arts of Paradise Center in Paradise Cove, opening by the summer of next year." Jennifer turned to Nicki. "Please, a few words to our patrons. She's not big on public speaking," Jennifer explained as she handed over the microphone.

"No, I'm not," Nicki agreed, clearing her throat to speak more loudly. "However, doing so is much easier tonight after receiving such amazing and genuine appreciation for this show. I've danced on Broadway. But nothing tops the way you've all made me feel tonight." She included Jennifer and Julian in her gaze around the auditorium. "Thank you."

And then it hit her. Of course. Why not? The idea was

crazy. Unorthodox. Scary. But what did she have to lose? All these thoughts whirled in her head in a matter of seconds.

Her eyes became misty as she eyed first him and then the crowd. Crazy how a broken ankle had prematurely ended a dream and at the same time catapulted her into a fantasy beyond any she could have imagined. For that she thanked everyone, even Vince. She thanked them, and she meant it. Julian, too. Even if he never asked her to be his wife again, she'd be his woman forever. But he hadn't asked her. And he probably wouldn't. So what if...

"Ladies and gentlemen, there's one more thing. I'm sorry, I won't be long, but there is one thing that tops even tonight's performance and your enthusiastic support." She turned to face Julian. "It is the love I feel for this man, Dr. Julian Drake."

Murmurs rippled through the crowd, followed by applause. She turned back to the crowd.

"A few years ago, in a wonderful moment in Times Square, he asked me to marry him. And I did something really stupid. I said no."

Gasps. Murmurs.

"I wasn't ready. I'm a dancer. A showgirl. My life is the stage. That's what I thought. But tonight, this is what I know."

She turned back to Julian as a single tear escaped and slid down her cheek. "My life on the stage isn't the same without you in it. I wish I'd said yes that night. Having hurt you the way I did, you'd be crazy to ask me again. So I'll ask you."

The audience became completely still. One could hear a feather fall.

"This wasn't preplanned, so I don't have a ring. What I do have is my love. My heart. And this question. Julian—" Nicki cried openly now. "Will you marry me?"

The entire audience held its breath.

She held up the mike. Julian slowly pulled it from her grasp, their eyes locked seemingly for centuries, though only mere seconds passed. He shifted, lifted the mike up to his mouth.

"No, Nicki. I can't do that."

# Chapter 30

Julian heard the crowd noise gain in intensity, watched tiny beads of sweat mix with the tears running freely down Nicki's face and over the tendrils that clung to her skin, saw her lips quiver as she struggled for control. He'd never seen her look more radiant or beautiful. Her smile wide and eyes bright, even tinged with the slightest hint of regret he'd glimpsed when handing her the flowers. He felt that she loved him deeply, even after she'd said no to marrying him that time he proposed. Knew that in her mind Paradise Cove was temporary. A mere speed bump on her road back to a career on Broadway. The place she'd dreamed of dancing since seeing her first live show there, *The Lion King*, at ten years old.

He knew all of this, and he knew something else. For a Drake the word *no* was a mere speed bump, too, when it came to something they wanted. Yes, he'd just told Nicki no. But he wasn't finished talking. He held up his hand. The audience fell silent, as though he was their conductor.

"You know I love you, Nicki. Feels like I always have, like, since the beginning of time. When I said no just now, it was because of being the type of man I am—maybe it's that Drake thing. I know you're independent. That it's the twenty-first century and traditions have changed. But I couldn't let you play my position. Sweetheart…"

He reached into his pocket, pulled out an aqua-blue box.

"You're the very beat of my heart, the lulu of my life. And while you may have many others in your long and illustrious dance career, I want to be your one and only permanent dance partner."

Several women in the audience joined Nicki in wiping away tears.

"I asked you once. If necessary, I'd ask a thousand times. But I hope that tonight, I'll get the right answer."

He got down on one knee. The audience could barely contain themselves, a symphony of whistles, claps, murmurs and shushes providing the background music to Julian's declaration.

He raised his voice above the din. "Nicki Long—"

"Yes!"

"Will you do me the honor—"

"Yes!" Nicki screamed again, now laughing and crying at the same time.

Julian smiled broadly. "Let me finish, love. Will you make me the happiest man in the room by agreeing to marry me and to becoming my Mrs. Drake?"

"Yes!" Nicki shouted for a third time.

Jennifer whooped. The dancers jumped. Nicki grabbed the microphone, shouted louder.

"Yes, Dr. Julian Drake. I'll marry you!"

There was no mistaking her words this time. She'd shouted them through tears before throwing her arms around his neck and planting a whopper of a kiss smackdab on his lips. Jennifer cried, too, and dabbed her cheeks with the back of her hand. Julian pulled out a handkerchief and wiped Nicki's tears before handing it to Jennifer.

The crowd applauding, the dancers cheering, he took Nicki into his arms.

"I almost passed out when you said no," she whispered.

"I shouldn't have scared you." He wrapped her arms around his neck. "I just wanted to secure you."

She kissed him again. He parted his lips. Her tongue scorched his mouth. His tongue darted out in search of hers, created an oral tango worthy of any stage. He felt himself harden—Nicki's nipples, too. Nicki giggled, embarrassed. He knew that she felt him. Knew they needed to maintain the position until both calmed down. He handed his mother the mike.

"Now that's a finale," Jennifer exclaimed. "Thanks again, everyone. Good night!"

She walked off the stage. The dancers, too. The audience slowly filed out of the auditorium. Nicki and Julian remained where they were, two hearts beating as one for several minutes. They basked in the moment, in no hurry to leave. It had taken almost six years and two tries to get this commitment. For Julian, this lifetime dance of decadent desire had been more than worth the wait.

Backstage was a crush. Nicki smiled until her face felt frozen. Posed, shook hands and gave hugs across the room. Finally she made her way to the dressing room, where in the privacy of the room filled with flowers she spent ten glorious minutes with Julian.

"Baby, I need to shower and dress real quick. We've still got the private party, remember?"

Julian tightened his hold, pulled her even closer. "I'm enjoying the private party we're having right now."

Fifteen minutes later, they left the building through a side door. Nicki shivered against the chilly night air and wrapped her coat even tighter around her.

Julian noticed and placed his arm around her. "You want to wait inside while I go get the car?"

"How far away is it?"

"Just down the street. But your head isn't covered, and I don't want you to get sick."

"I grew up in cold weather, babe. Let's just hurry. I'll be fine."

She threaded her arm through his as they rounded the building and, once on the sidewalk, picked up the pace.

"Nicki!"

She stopped abruptly at the sound of her name. She shivered again, this time not from the cold. But from recognizing the voice of who'd called out to her. A quick glance around confirmed the fear. Vince.

"Let's keep walking." She urged Julian forward.

Vince called out again. "Nicki, wait."

He stopped. "Babe, who is that?" She looked at him, aware as the answer dawned in his eyes. "Wait here."

He turned and began walking swiftly toward Vince, his hands balled into fists.

"Julian!"

Vince held up his hands, began a fast retreat. "Hey, man. I don't want any trouble. Just need to apologize to Nicki, that's all."

Julian stopped with a couple of feet between them. Nicki reached his side and grabbed his coat sleeve. Tension emanated from Julian's body. Coiled, controlled, ready to pounce.

She glared at Vince as he began to speak.

"I'm sorry, Nicki. About everything. Hopefully one day you'll be able to forgive me. I had a problem back then that had me out of control. It's no excuse, but I was addicted. To gambling. A habit worse than drugs. One I couldn't control. Ironically, you played a part in my healing. Ran into this girl on my way out of town, out of Paradise Cove. I'd hit bottom. A weak moment. Poured out my heart. She suggested a program called Gamblers Anonymous. I looked it up and found one here. So instead of going back to New York, I stayed out West. Got well. Now I hear she's in trouble. Anyway, that's a whole other story."

"You ran into Natalie?" Julian asked.

"I ran into Ashley, who introduced me to Nat. Do you know her? Never mind. I forgot. Small town."

Nicki shivered again.

Julian reached for her hand. "Let's go, babe."

She looked at Vince. "I forgive you, okay? And I'm glad you got help."

"Thank you." And to Julian. "I'm sorry, man."

Julian nodded. They turned and hurried to the car, Nicki easily matching Julian's long strides. She never looked back. There was no need. The only man she wanted was walking beside her.

\* \* \* \* \*

*If you enjoyed this sexy story, pick up
these other titles in Zuri Day's*
THE DRAKES OF CALIFORNIA *series:*


*CRYSTAL CARESS*
*SILKEN EMBRACE*
*SAPPHIRE ATTRACTION*
*LAVISH LOVING*

*Available now from Harlequin Kimani Romance!*

## COMING NEXT MONTH
### Available November 21, 2017

### #549 SEDUCED BY THE TYCOON AT CHRISTMAS
*The Morretti Millionaires* • by Pamela Yaye
Italy's most powerful businessman, Romeo Morretti, spends his days brokering multimillion-dollar deals, but an encounter with Zoe Smith sends his life in a new direction. When secrets threaten their passionate bond, Romeo must fight to clear his name before they can share a future under the mistletoe.

### #550 A LOVE LIKE THIS
*Sapphire Shores* • by Kianna Alexander
All action star Devon Granger wants for Christmas is a peaceful escape to his hometown. How is he to rest with Hadley Monroe tending to his every need? And when the media descends on the beachfront community, their dreams of ringing in the New Year together could be out of their grasp…

### #551 AN UNEXPECTED HOLIDAY GIFT
*The Kingsleys of Texas* • by Martha Kennerson
When a scuffle leads to community service, basketball star Keylan "KJ" Kingsley opts to devote his hours to his family's foundation. Soon he plunges into a relationship with charity executive Mia Ramirez. When KJ returns to the court, will his celebrity status risk the family that could be theirs by Christmas?

### #552 DESIRE IN A KISS
*The Chandler Legacy* • by Nicki Night
On impulse, heir to a food empire Christian Chandler creates a fake dating profile and quickly connects with petite powerhouse Serenity Williams. She's smart, down-to-earth and ignites his fantasies from their first encounter. But how can he admit the truth to a woman for whom honesty is everything?

KPCNM1117

# Get 2 Free Books,

## Plus 2 Free Gifts —

### just for trying the Reader Service!

## DONE WITH

Longarm stood back from the grimy glass to regard
the lone figure at the bar with interest. The local deputies agreed to stay outside and cover him, so Longarm moved along the walk to the batwing doors and
strode on in, not looking directly at the man bellied
up to the bar, dead center. But the solitary drinker
had been looking into a mirror in the back of the
room. So as Longarm casually approached, there
came a sudden blur of motion as the mysterious
stranger spun away from the bar to drop into a gunfighter's crouch and, worse yet, go for his gun as he
yelled a mighty mean thing about Longarm's poor
mother!

Longarm still had no idea who the cuss might be,
but nobody moved his gun like that without considerable experience. And as any experienced gunfighter
knew, given a head start, there was no way in hell a
tied-down side draw wasn't going to beat a cross-
draw in a stand-up saloon fight.

It got mighty noisy in the Fremont Saloon for a
spell of two or three full seconds, and as the smoke
cleared, the other lawmen charged in with their own
guns drawn . . .

## DON'T MISS THESE
## ALL-ACTION WESTERN SERIES
## FROM THE BERKLEY PUBLISHING GROUP

**THE GUNSMITH by J. R. Roberts**
Clint Adams was a legend among lawmen, outlaws, and ladies.
They called him . . . the Gunsmith.

**LONGARM by Tabor Evans**
The popular long-running series about U.S. Deputy Marshal
Long—his life, his loves, his fight for justice.

**SLOCUM by Jake Logan**
Today's longest-running action Western. John Slocum rides
a deadly trail of hot blood and cold steel.

**BUSHWHACKERS by B. J. Lanagan**
An action-packed series by the creators of Longarm! The
rousing adventures of the most brutal gang of cutthroats ever
assembled—Quantrill's Raiders.

**DIAMONDBACK by Guy Brewer**
Dex Yancey is Diamondback, a southern gentleman turned
con man when his brother cheats him out of the family fortune. Ladies love him. Gamblers hate him. But nobody pulls
one over on Dex . . .

**WILDGUN by Jack Hanson**
Will Barlow's continuing search for his daughter, kidnapped
by the Blackfeet Indians who slaughtered the rest of his
family.

**TABOR EVANS**

## LONGARM

### AND THE NEVADA BELLY DANCER

JOVE BOOKS, NEW YORK

This is a work of fiction. Names, characters, places, and incidents are
either the product of the author's imagination or are used fictitiously,
and any resemblance to actual persons, living or dead, business
establishments, events, or locales is entirely coincidental.

LONGARM AND THE NEVADA BELLY DANCER

A Jove Book / published by arrangement with
the author

PRINTING HISTORY
Jove edition / April 2000

All rights reserved.
Copyright © 2000 by Penguin Putnam Inc.
This book may not be reproduced in whole or in part,
by mimeograph or any other means, without permission.
For information address: The Berkley Publishing Group,
a division of Penguin Putnam Inc.,
375 Hudson Street, New York, New York 10014.

The Penguin Putnam Inc. Wide Web site address is
http://www.penguinputnam.com

ISBN: 0-515-12790-6

A JOVE BOOK®
Jove Books are published by The Berkley Publishing Group,
a division of Penguin Putnam Inc.,
375 Hudson Street, New York, New York 10014.
JOVE and the "J" design
are trademarks belonging to Penguin Putnam Inc.

PRINTED IN THE UNITED STATES OF AMERICA

10  9  8  7  6  5  4  3  2  1

# Chapter 1

A little knowledge had confused some minds when they'd been trying to come up with a suitable name for a silver strike in the Basin and Range Country of Nevada. Somebody had read somewheres how Cairo, Egypt, was a desert town set on a river and, so, seeing old Mose Kramer had struck pay dirt on the banks of Skeliton Wash in the rain shadow of the Trinity Range, they'd decided to name the township Cairo in hopes of it amounting to a city some fine day.

It hadn't. But just as the silver chloride had commenced to bottom out, the Western Pacific Railroad had shown up to save the dinky desert settlement from becoming yet another ghost town of the boom-and-bust Great Basin.

Hauling transcontinental passengers and freight across the arid wastes of the Basin and Range Country was thirsty work for a steam-powered Baldwin, and Cairo's Skeliton Wash, once they'd dammed it, offered the only boiler water for many a mile that wasn't a steam-line-clogging stew of alkali salts. So whilst there was less action to a jerkwater town than a mining town, Cairo still served up some noisy Saturday nights, seeing there was no place better to set up a saloon or house of ill repute betwixt, say, Lovelock on the Humboldt and Fallon on

1

the Truckee and a man needed someplace to raise hell after a weary week, looking for strays on the sage flats or color in the rocks of the snake-infested Trinities.

But hardly anybody who didn't belong there came to Cairo on a Wednesday before payday. So the old boys who spit and whittled over by the loading platform got word to Gandy Burgess soon after a tall dark stranger packing a McClellan saddle and Winchester '73 got off a westbound combination late that afternoon, wearing a Colt double-action .44-40, crossdraw. You could tell because, in deference to the summer climate of their range, he'd lashed his tobacco-tweed frock coat to the bedroll across his saddlebags. The grips of his serious shooting iron looked to have been tailored for his gun hand, too.

Nodding curtly to the poker-faced railroad hands in passing, the mysterious stranger headed directly across the sun-baked alkali dust of Front Street toward the inviting shade of the Freemont Saloon. So Gandy Burgess figured that was where he'd find the rascal when, not if, he had to get it over with.

Gandy Burgess ran the one livery stable in Cairo when he wasn't serving as their town law. Since the stranger hadn't ridden in aboard a pony, their part-time chief constable wearily pinned on his gilded copper badge and strapped on his own Colt '74 with a wry grimace. Gandy Burgess had come over the Sierra Nevada with the tracks of the Western Pacific, won a share in the Dusty Devil silver mine and somehow stayed on, doing one thing or the other in the hopes of a mite more peace and quiet than they'd been having of late. A man who'd lived through the uncertain years since the Mexican War got to where he no longer enjoyed sudden surprises in his golden years.

A man hardly made it to his golden years in gun-toting country by just barging in on well-armed strangers. So the old-timer entered the Fremont by way of its back door to stand behind a bead curtain across from the front entrance

2

and size the stranger up a mite before he made his next move.

U.S. Deputy Marshal Custis Long of the Denver District Court was even more experienced than he looked, so he went on sipping from the beer schooner in his left hand with a double derringer palmed in his big right fist as he quietly remarked, as if talking to the saddle and possibles next to him atop the otherwise deserted bar, "We'd be able to talk better if you'd come out from behind them beads and have some of these fine cool suds with me, pard."

When there came no answer, the man who seemed to have the Fremont to himself, since even the barkeep had vanished, soberly continued, "I just hate it when ponies spook for no good reason, pard. You would be a fellow lawman, wouldn't you? I'd hate to think I was the only law in town and you were the resident bully."

Gandy Burgess cautiously replied, from cover, "I'd be Chief Constable Burgess and you'd be . . . ?"

"U.S. Deputy Marshal Custis Long, riding for Marshal Billy Vail of the Denver District Court, out your way on a special assignment because I've poked through sagebrush and rid around alkali water before, I reckon."

Burgess grudgingly replied, "I've heard tell of you, Longarm. You'd be out here about that killer from Boston, if you'd care to show me some tin, mister?"

Longarm reached with his left hand to fish out his wallet and flip it open as he soberly replied, "Bite your tongue. The Justice Department don't issue us federal deputies those mail-order pewter badges. This one's German silver. My boss sports genuine Sheffield silver plate. I got my deputy marshal's warrant here as well, if you'd care to come on out from ahint that curtain, you shy little thing.

So the older man laughed despite himself and moved out into the light as he remarked, "You'd be the one and

3

original Longarm, I reckon. We heard how free you can be with your sarcasm, too."

Then he yelled for the barkeep as he strode on over, putting his six-gun away as he added, "We got Boston Ferris over to the lock-up with one of my own deputies keeping an eye on him. You'd be here in answer to that all-points we put out on the telegraph wires, right?"

Longarm replied in a sincerely puzzled tone, "Wrong. Might we be talking about a self-professed private detective riding out of Fort Smith in fringed buckskin with a brace of ivory-handled Schofields?"

The pudgy barkeep came out of the back room with a bar rag and a sheepish grin as the town law replied to Longarm, "We took his fancy buscadero gunbelt and silver inlaid sixguns away from him before we locked him in our patent cell and wired high and low that we had the son of a bitch on ice for anybody looking for him. Why do they call him Boston, anyhow? He talks like a Southerner and looks like a breed if you ask me!"

As the barkeep got back where he belonged Longarm told the older lawman, "Don't have to ask you. If we're talking about the same bad news he *is* a breed. Cherokee, some say, albeit he'd rather have it known his mama was an Osage princess because the Osage have a more ferocious rep. He don't talk like they do back east in the *town* of Boston because he was born and riz in the Boston mountain of the Indian Territory. Cherokee never wore fringy buckskins like Osage and other plains Indians. But I reckon old Boston Ferris has as much a right to fringy buckskin as Kit Carson or Buffalo Bill as soon as you study on it. He wears those fancy Schofield .45s lest anybody take him for an honest young puncher, too. They say it pays to advertise and when a man strides the world's stage as a hired gun he wants his guns to stand out. What'll you have and what's Boston Ferris done, here in Nevada?"

Burgess said he'd best stick to suds until after sundown

and as the barkeep drew him a schooner of draft he told Longarm, "I was hoping *you'd* know. When we asked him, about this time yesterday, in this very saloon, he declared he was bounty hunting and showed us a reward flier offering the ridiculous sum of ten thousand dollars for Frank or Jesse James of, for Gawd's sake, Clay County, Missouri!"

As the town law sipped some suds Longarm shrugged and told him he'd seen said flier, adding, "Whether anybody ever collects that handsome a reward or not remains to be seen. It's easy for some men to promise a gal they'll marry up with her when they're feeling hot and bothered."

Neither Frank nor Jesse have been seen around their old stamping grounds since their Northfield raid blew up in their faces back in '76. But I'd be mighty surprised if either of them turned up this far west. You *hear tell* of owlhoot riders here, there, and everywhere. But nobody's been able to place any members of the James-Younger gang west of say, longitude one hundred degrees for certain."

The older lawman pulled his face out of his suds to declare, "I can read and that's what I told the smart-ass hired gun when he tried to sell me a tale of Missouri bank robbers hiding out in Nevada. But if you ain't here to take Boston Ferris off our hands, what in blue blazes *might* have brung you to Cairo during the sleepy season on such range as there might be?"

Longarm wet his own whistle before he easily replied, "Coming down from the Humboldt Sink aboard the train I noticed most of the grass had been grazed or gone to cheat-straw, with your thin-spread stock down to brousing sagebrush and rabbitbush. But I was hoping that even if your whores and gamblers have packed it in until after the fall roundup, you could put me on to a dance hall gal famed far and wide for her oriental belly dancing."

Burgess blinked in surprise and asked, "Belly dancers, here in Cairo, *Nevada*? I have heard tell of such dancing

5

over to *Egypt* land, if we're talking about them hoochy kootchie gals who disport their fool selves in Turkish harem outfits with their wiggly bare bellies rippling like jelly in a way to give many a man a bodacious hard-on!"

Longarm smiled wistfully and said, "That's about the way I picture this federal witness or whatever. I'll know better what she might be once I can ask her whether she wants to hang tough or turn state's evidence. But I can't ask her toad squat before I catch up with her, so now it's your turn, pard."

The older lawman sounded sincere as he replied, "I don't have the least notion of what we're talking about! I've been here in Cairo going on ten years and I've been the law for half that time. So I've seen me some sights and heard me some talk in my time out this way. But I will be switched with snakes if I have ever seen or heard tell of any *belly dancing* gals in *this* town called Cairo! Are you sure they weren't talking about that *other* Cairo, where you'd *expect* to see such scandalous entertainment?"

Longarm finished his schooner and signaled the barkeep for a refill as he said, "Lord, you keep it hot and dry enough around here! I'd best start at the beginning, up the line to the east where they jerk engine water at the seat of Elko County. This quartet of owlhoot riders hit the Elko Post Office at dusk, making it federal in the first when they gunned an innocent bystander on government property as they were on their way out."

As the barkeep slid two fresh beers across the zinc to them Burgess nodded and said, "We heard about that robbery a week or so back. Elko wired ahead for us to be on the lookout. So we was looking. But didn't the gang ride into that roadblock at Battle Mountain, just a hard two days west along the Humboldt from the scene of their crime?"

Longarm said, "Three of them did, for certain. It was dusk and they were brush-popping through the tangle-

6

wood and canebrakes along the river until they were challenged in the tricky light and reined in their jaded mounts to make a fight of it. One posse rider and three of *them* went down in the exchange. Since four held up that post office in Elko one of 'em must have gotten away through the gunsmoke-filled willow branches in the gathering dusk. Two of the outlaws were killed outright. That posseman and one of the gang were still breathing as the smoke cleared. The lawman is still with us. The gut-shot outlaw died before dawn. But not before the sheriff of Lander County got a dying statement out of him. Sort of. Men don't always make a heap of sense when they're hurting bad and he took a .52 Spencer ball through his colon and gall bladder, according to his post mortem."

"We heard about that, too." The local lawman cut in, adding, "They wired us to be on the lookout for the fourth member of the gang, on account they never recovered the eight or ten thousand from that post office robbery. Needless to say, he never come through Cairo. Get to the part about that belly dancer."

Longarm did. He said, "It was more like twelve thousand, kept on hand to cash postal money orders. The lawman up the Humboldt in Battle Mountain noticed the money was still missing as they gathered up the remains. As I just said, they had a long talk about his recent moves with the semi-survivor, a wayward youth called Coleman, Tim Coleman. Better known over in the Mormon Delta as a stock thief. He confessed to sincerely regretting his throwing in with an older stick-up man he named as one Happy Jack Henderson. We have Henderson in our files as a morose and unreconstructed rebel with a mean streak. So that much of the dying outlaw's statement rings true. As the leader, Happy Jack would have been packing the swag. Coleman confessed he and the others were recruited over in the Mormon Delta by Happy Jack for what he sold them as an easy job."

"Easy my Aunt Fanny Adams." The local lawman

snorted, adding as if Longarm didn't know the Basin and Range Country, "There's hardly no ways in or out of the scene of the crime this late in the summer but by longhaul rail, with the Elko law sure to wire up and down the only line, or by bronc, as they rode no more than thirty or so miles a day within easy reach of the water and shade along the Humboldt. This of course led them into more lawmen who'd been wired to be expecting 'em, long before they could get there. When do we get to that belly dancer?"

Longarm replied, "That's who they were riding to meet, here in Cairo, according to that dying outlaw who'd already given away the name of his leader. They took his words down as Coleman confessed that Happy Jack had told them he meant to leave the heavy bags of money with his belly dancer in Cairo. The plan, as best they could gather the confused words of a dying man in pain, was for the bunch to *split up* in the railroad town of Battle Mountain. Not to *die* there. Coleman seemed a mite chagrined about that twist of fate. Happy Jack had told him he'd carry the money bags to this belly dancer in Cairo and go on as an empty-handed railroad passenger, the same as them. Coleman allowed he'd meant to backtrack from Battle Mountain by rail and get off in Elko as an innocently smiling cowhand in the market for a job. He knew nobody would hire him at this time of the year. But they'd been wearing masks during the robbery across from the depot, so what the hell and as soon as the heat died down he could always board a *westbound* train to join Happy Jack and that belly dancer, *here*."

But Chief Constable Burgess shook his graying head as if he knew and insisted, "Ain't no belly dancers here in Cairo. Ain't never *been* no belly dancers here in Cairo. Are you sure they couldn't have been talking about Cairo, Illinois?"

Longarm sighed and said, "Nothing is sure but death and taxes. On the other hand, if Happy Jack and that post

8

office swag made it all the way east to Illinois I might as well waste my time searching high and low for Frank and Jesse."

The local law polished off his second beer and decided in that very sober tone of a man who'd just commenced to feeling two beers, "I *am* holding a man who claims he came all the way out here looking for the James boys. What say we traipse over to the lockup and ask the son of a bitch what he knows about belly dancers?"

# Chapter 2

The patent cells that peppered the jailhouses of the West were made in Penn State to a patented pattern of boiler-plate and barred grids that were shipped flat in handy-sized crates and then bolted together as expanded boxes with solid steel walls, floors, and ceilings. Bunk beds, corner sinks, and such could be bolted to the otherwise blank walls. Back walls could be ordered with or without barred windows. The front of the cube was almost always a floor-to-ceiling zoo cage with a sliding door. The patent sold better out West because holding restless prisoners under light guard betwixt walls of 'dobe, logs or even mortared brick could be a bother. So those townships as liked things up-to-date found a patent cell more than paid for itself by allowing the rest of the town lockup to be built cheap of local materials.

The town lockup of Cairo, handy to the livery stable and corral run by its chief constable, was simple balloon frame, delivered by rail along with most of the construction along Front Street. A few of the older buildings, erected before the wedding of the rails in '69, had been built of freestone with mud mortar or, as in the case of the livery corral, logs snaked down from the higher slopes of the nearby Trinity Range. But neither the pinyon pine nor the juniper logs that grew at higher altitude in those parts could hold a candle to way less bothersome white pine lumber shipped in cheap by rail. Longarm, who dropped his saddle and possibles near the doorway, could smell the pine sap in the lockup as the town law led the way inside. For the dry heat out this way played hell with fresh lumber.

As if to punctuate Longarm's observation, the man seated on the floor of the patent cell in his underwear called out in an outraged tone, "I aim to sue you desert rats for subjecting me to this cruel and unusual punishment without charging me formal or showing me any warrant!"

The kid deputy reading a copy of *Captain Billy's Whizbang* behind the flat-topped desk in the somewhat cooler front of the airless frame building chortled, "He's been fussing like that since noon. I told him back then it was going to get hotter afore it got cooler, but he just keeps hollering for his mama, a lawyer, or whatever."

As Longarm and Burgess approached the bars the man behind them remained seated with his back to the boiler plate wall, painted an unconvincingly cool shade of park bench green. He said, "Forgive me for not rising, you son of a bitch. It's even hotter in here at waist-level."

Gandy Burgess turned to call out, "Bobby, open the front door and find something to prop it like so, seeing the sun's on the other side of the building, now."

Then he turned back to the prisoner seated on the iron floor to quietly say, "Don't ever call me a son of a bitch again. I mean that. This here would be a U.S. deputy who says he knows you. Talk nice and, come suppertime, you'll get some coffee and beans to go with your bread. Talk sassy and you may not even get the bread."

Boston Ferris, if that was who they were holding, stared up through the bars at Longarm to sullenly remark, "Never seen him before and I ain't wanted federal, or,

11

come to study on it, wanted for shit in any clime or place except this one-horse town."

Burgess smiled down at him to reply, "Oh, we have more than one horse here in Cairo. But you were about to tell Longarm, here, what you know about belly dancing, weren't you?"

The prisoner stared up owlishly to answer, "No offense, I sure want them beans. But this conversation is getting curiouser and curiouser, like Miss Alice told them other peculiar folk. I told you yesterday who I was and what I was doing out this way. I never said shit about any belly dancing because I don't *know* shit about such an exotic notion! I seen a belly dancing gal at the Omaha State Fair one time, but I sure wasn't expecting to see one out here at this desert jerkwater!"

Then he rose hopefully to his bare feet and moved closer to the bars as he added in a plaintive tone, "Might you really be that lawman they call Longarm? I've heard it said the one and original Longarm is a straight shooter. I'm a lawman, too, and these desert rats are holding me unlawsome as all get out!"

To which Longarm could only reply, not unkindly, "I have heard tell of you as well, Boston Ferris. Leaving aside the bullshit about your state permit to hire on as an armed guard, not a judge, jury, and executioner, I find it as easy to buy an exotic dancer in these parts as I do member one of the James-Younger gang. So let's start with your true reasons for being this far west."

Boston Ferris shrugged his bare shoulders and said, "It's like I told these other lawmen. I was tipped off by mail. I got me a letter saying one of the James boys was out this way, laying low as an honest stockman whilst they waited for the heat from their stopping that old Chicago and Alton train back east."

Longarm said, "*Back East* is the term you were groping for. I've heard about Frank and Jesse being spotted as far west as California and as high as the moon. But in point

12

of fact, those boys have yet to stray as far west as Colorado."

The bounty hunter cocked his dark-featured head to demand, in a mocking tone, "Do tell? And didn't I read in the *Rocky Mountain News* about the famous Longarm shooting it out with one of the Younger boys on the very steps of the federal courthouse in Salt Lake City, a far reach *west* of Colorado unless I have my atlas upside down!"

Longarm grimaced and said, "You and the *Rocky Mountain News* would be talking about a spitesome cuss called Cotton Younger, who might or might not have been distant kin to Cole Younger but never rode with him and the James boys, as far as were ever able to learn."

Boston Ferris shrugged tawny bare shoulders to insist, "You still shot it out with an outlaw called Younger, west of the Great Divide. So who's to say no outlaw named James could be hiding out in this neck of the woods?"

"I can!" said Gandy Burgess firmly. He added, "I've been here most as long as Cairo and I've seen men come and I've seen men go. They generally *ride* through if they're in town long enough for me to give a damn. But passing through on horseback or by rail I have more eyes than my own peeled for strangers and didn't I notice the two of you within minutes of your wide-spaced arrivals?"

The bounty hunter behind the bars tried, "I never said anybody named James was loitering right here in town. I said I'd heard he might be in this neck of the woods. I was told he'd set up as a poor but honest stockman somewheres within a day's ride."

"You was told a lie," insisted the lawman who lived there, adding, "As anyone but a total greenhorn should be able to see, such range as can be found for a day's ride of here is marginal and over-grazed by old-timers I've known for years. Takes many an acre of cheat grass and sage to support one cow, and cows browsing sage need too much water to range far from the same. There'd be no profit in beef along this stretch of the railroad if Indian Affairs didn't have that Fallon agency to the south and the Pyramid Lake agency to the north to feed. Costs more than scrub beef on the hoof can *sell* for, to ship it by rail any further."

He thought and decided, "Ain't a round-dozen cattle spreads within easy reach of Cairo and I know all the hands working 'em well enough to howdy. The sheep outfits grazing up in the Trinity would make for even worse hiding-out for an owlhoot rider. Sheepherders don't come into town on the weekends. They stay up in the hills getting drunk with the sheep until they herd 'em back down to the railroad in late fall."

The kid deputy at the desk looked up to gravely ask if they'd heard the one about the sheepherder tallying a flock as, "One, two, three, good morning, darling, five, six, seven . . ."

Longarm allowed he'd heard it more than once and turned back to the prisoner to ask, "Who did you say wrote you that Frank or Jesse might be out this way?"

Boston Ferris didn't look away as he replied, "Can't tell you. It ain't that I don't *want* to. She never signed her name. She sent it to this office where I pick up my mail from Fort Smith. She told me to come on out and that she'd be waiting to contact me at the one hotel and point me at that handsome reward, for half the pot."

Longarm demanded, "How did you know the letter was from a gal if it wasn't signed, and I've been meaning to ask why you ride out of Fort Smith with a license issued by a Kansas J.P."

The bounty hunter shrugged and replied with no shame, "I feel a lot more comforted in Fort Smith amongst kith and kin. But that muley old Judge Parker had black-listed me with the whole Arkansas bar association since I had to gun that Black Seminole horse thief in self-defense. As to how I could tell it was a lady wanting me to join her out this way, her letter was in purple ink on perfumed stationary, writ womansome."

The town law nudged Longarm and motioned toward the open front door with his eyebrows. Longarm told Ferris, "Don't go 'way. I may have some more questions to ask you."

As he followed Burgess out to the now shady plank walk, Longarm said, "Great minds run in the same channels. Happy Jack Henderson and Boston Ferris were both supposed to meet mysterious shemales here in Cairo. But, like you said, you and your pals notice when a stranger in pants shows up in a settlement the size of this one, no offense."

The older lawman pointed out, "The mystery condenses by half if we picture the unknown letter writer and Happy Jack's belly dancer as one and the same!"

But Longarm shook his head and said, "No it don't. It makes the whole can of worms more mysterious. Ferris says the lady who wrote to him wanted a piece of the bounty on the James boys. Happy Jack told that pal who died he was headed here to leave their swag for safe-keeping with a belly dancer who liked him and—"

"Somebody has flat-out lied," the older lawman firmly cut in. He continued, "The tales as told don't make a lick of sense. There ain't no members of the James-Younger gang hiding out in these parts and we'd have surely noticed a sassy belly dancer if she'd ever come out this way."

"Unless she was dressed more sedate." Longarm pointed out, adding, "Happy Jack told the shot-up Tim Coleman he meant to leave the heavy moneybags in the keeping of a belly dancer he knew. Coleman never said the sporting gal he knew here in Cairo had to be known by you Cairo gents as a belly dancer. What if Happy Jack was talking about a once upon a time belly dancer who'd given it up to carry on more sedate? Many a soiled dove has married up and got religion over the years. But to any of their old admirers they'd still be called a whore."

The old-timer who'd seen folk come and go in Cairo nodded soberly and quietly replied, "I know of at least three ladies of our Christian Temperance Society who might have been a tad wilder in their younger days. But I've yet to hear tell of any former belly dancers walking straight and narrow here in Cairo and why would such a lady write to bounty hunters if she were expecting a romantic highwayman to show up with too much money to carry?"

Longarm shrugged and said, "The Irish sing a song about a gal named Sporting Jenny who double-crossed a romantic highwayman when he brought his gold to her for counting. If this does condense down to only one sneaky gal, more than one sneaky picture commences to emerge from the mist. How long were you planning on holding Boston Ferris, on what charge?"

The older lawman shrugged and decided, "Don't have to worry about habeas corpus for a full seventy-two hours and by then we'll be into the weekend, and any lawyer he might have will play hell getting any judge to issue one. So I reckon we can hold him at least into Monday and if you ask me, a bounty hunter riding out of Arkansas with a Kansas hunting permit sounds sneaky enough to hold on suspicion. Why do you ask? Are you saying we can't hold a suspicious stranger of suspicion until he starts to make more sense?"

Longarm replied, "I have no jurisdiction when it comes to Boston Ferris. I wouldn't be this far from Denver on a Nevada robbery if the postmaster general hadn't asked for me by name. Don't ever crack an unusual post office robbery if you don't want them pestering you every time the postal inspectors feel confused."

He turned back to the doorway to add, "That's what the post office dicks call a cold trail with an unknown belly dancer at the end of it. Confused. Hasn't anyone come forward to ask about Boston Ferris since you ran him in a good twenty-four hours ago?"

The town law answered simply, "Who did you have in mind? If that hired gun knows a soul in town by name he's yet to say so and somehow I just can't see the lady who sent for him coming by with a file baked in a cake for him, if she ever existed at all."

Longarm grimaced and said, "I wish you hadn't said that. A hired gun showing up to gun somebody *would* be inclined to throw some sand in our eyes. Let's go back in and ask to see that perfumed letter he got from his mystery lady."

Longarm moved with surprising grace for a man his size and so he suddenly wasn't standing where he'd been standing just before a rifle spanged in the distance and wood splinters exploded from the frame of the open door as Gandy Burgess hollered, "Jesus! Duck!"

The warning cry had come a tad late, but it was the intent that counted and he was mighty worried about his fellow lawman as that distant rifle fired again after he was safe inside. So he dove for his saddle to haul his Winchester from its boot and headed back the way he'd just come, telling the confused kid deputy to cover the damned doorway from behind the damned desk.

Then Chief Constable Burgess came in through that same doorway, alive and well albeit puzzled as he marveled, "They fired on us from the Central Pacific water tower, according to the drifting smoke over yonder. But there's nobody up on the nozzle platform now and I doubt they really aimed those last few shots at this worried child with serious intent or the least experience with a rifle gun!"

Longarm had been raised to be polite to his elders. So he never said he was dead certain they'd been aiming at him. He just chased the muzzle of his own rifle out into the lengthening shadows of late afternoon as he levered a round in its chamber and headed across to the railroad siding and that water tank looming against the cloudless sky. But after a long ass-puckering run across an open field of fire from on high he was hunkered behind a pile of lumber near the loading platform, noting not one of the hands spitting and whittling there, earlier, was anywhere in sight. So there went any hope of asking if anyone had seen who'd fired on them just now.

But what the hell, they'd told him they were sending him all the way west to Nevada to look for sneaky sons of bitches, hadn't they?

# Chapter 3

By the time the town law joined him behind that lumber with an old Spencer repeater, others were coming out on the far side of Front Street and nobody seemed to be shooting at any of them. So Longarm asked old Burgess to cover him as he made another dash in the open to the foot of the ladder leading up to the catwalk wrapped around the base of the redwood water tower serving the Cairo siding.

When he reached the platform he could smell gunsmoke lingering in the air. So the town law had likely been right about one aimed shot and some wilder shooting from a sneak departing in a hurry. Longarm moved around to the trackside, searching for spent brass until, sure enough, he found a still warm S&W .44-40 shell case under the big folded up nozzle they swung down to water the locomotive tenders. S&W made ammo for most every make of American small arms, and .44-40 was about as popular a round as they made because, like himself, most riders had long since noticed you could load a .44-40 six-gun and the most common chambering for the Winchester with the same brass.

A man could feel chagrined with his rifle magazine empty and dozens of pistol rounds left in his loops. Longarm knew his unknown attacker had fired from a rifle, likely a common-as-clay Winchester or Henry, because the same ammo sounded different, fired from a pistol, a carbine, or a rifle. Barrels of different lengths were tuned different.

Any other brass the mystery sniper had spent had landed down below in the trackside cinders and dirt. Longarm didn't care, seeing he'd figured a Henry or Winchester from that one spent shell. He moved on around the vertical redwood staves, hooped with steel tie-rods, to gaze soberly up and down Front Street with his own Winchester held at port-arms. The water tower wasn't tall as a steeple but neither was most of Cairo. So as long as he was watching for hostile intent he tried to memorize a more accurate mental map of the small town than you pictured right off at street level.

He could see at a glance they'd erected the water tower handy to the dusty bed of Skeliton Wash, running through a culvert under Front Street and the tracks, to fan out amid the sage flats to the southeast. The timber-laced earthen dam you didn't notice much at street level impounded a sky-blue sheet of stillwater betwixt those higher banks a quarter mile upslope, with the more serious aprons of the Trinity Range way farther off to the northwest.

It was going on five in the afternoon, with the cloudless sky a bowl of cobalt blue above. But the sun had already ducked behind the jagged outline of now blackening mountains. The Spanish word, *sierra*, meant saw toothed and surely fit most of the north-south ranges out this way. Most were what the geology professors described as "elongated fault blocks," meaning most of the same, from the High Sierra along the California Line to the Tuana Range closer to that Great Salt Desert of Utah Territory had been tilted up from a once-flat inland sea by some serious force of nature at about the same angles to form long gentle slopes to the west and steep jagged-ass and rocky slopes facing eastwards, with most of the exposed

20

mineral faces naturally more evident to that side. Cairo had somehow lucked out on Skeliton Creek. Like the way-bigger Truckee running down the eastern slope of the High Sierra, it likely commenced as springwater seeping through layered rocks from the more gentle and rained-on high country facing into the prevailing winds from the west. Longarm saw a big sheet-iron water main following the lay of the land betwixt one valve shack at the south end of the dam to where it vanished behind the roof tops across the way. He suspected a pump house off Front Street a ways to regulate which way Cairo's water ran underground. The railroad doubtless pumped locomotive water up where he and his Winchester were perched at the moment. You could pump a few gallons at a time, by wind or steam power, when you only had to water a few passing trains a day.

Most of the business buildings along Front Street were one- or two-story false-front frame. From as high as the water tower platform you could see the peaked or shed roofs behind the square facades facing the street. Nobody was really fooled by a false front. But even when you knew there was nothing but an attic behind what they'd gussied up to look like the front of a bigger building, the building still looked bigger and you could letter handsome signs above your doors and real windows under what appeared a wide, flat roof-line.

A two-story false-front structure across from the passenger loading platform up the track a piece was painted brick red despite its wood siding, and Longarm could see at a glance that the shuttered windows pretending to open from a third floor were fake. Above them, in black-trimmed yellow Gothic lettering, appeared the brag that he was gazing upon the one and original Sheppard's Hotel of Cairo. He suspected the one he'd read about in that other Cairo might be just a tad larger, and Boston Ferris had said there was only one hotel in town.

He spotted a couple of church spires and a bell tower

above the otherwise unremarkable rooftops and chimney pipes up the slope two city blocks or so from their furlong-long Front Street. There hardly seemed room for many belly dancers or train robbers to hide out in the tiny town. As Chief Constable Burgess joined him on the platform he declared, "No dust out amid the sagebrush all around. So our secret admirer never left town and where's that silver mine you used to brag on, hereabouts? I've been searching in vain for mine tips or tailing piles up the slope. I haven't been able to make any out with the light over yonder so tricky."

The old-timer who'd been there said, "You wouldn't see much more at high noon. The silver lode was typical for these parts. High grade as hell near the surface and bottoming out just about the time you'd sunk a serious shaft and even more development money into the son of a bitch. Some field geologist we hired told us Nevada silver salts are like that. Widespread, low-grade as far east as the Mormon Delta and concentrated here, there, and seldom serious by whatever cooked and heaved up all these mountainous ridges."

Longarm asked, "Wouldn't there still be a hole in the ground, with the mess you make mining, even a little ways down?"

The lawman-cum-liveryman who'd once owned a share in the Cairo Lode nodded wistfully and explained, "We live in changing times. We built that dam to impound Skeliton Wash with mine timbers and crushed rock from the tailings we'd piled up around the ore crushed. Then, as soon as a spur line of that Central Pacific found a customer for us, we dissassembled our stamping mill and sold it at a modest profit to yet another syndicate of silver suckers."

"What about the adit, itself?" asked Longarm.

The town law replied easily, "Covered over by my orders. Kids kept daring one another to explore the deserted drifts we'd removed the tracks and timbers from. I figured it was only a question of time so I nipped an expensive rescue effort in the bud by making sure none of the little shits would ever need to be rescued. Why do you ask? Were you aiming to search abandoned silver mines for belly dancers?"

Longarm shrugged and said, "My boss, Marshal Vail, calls it the process of eliminating. I'm trying to figure where that sniper *or* a belly dancer might *not* be before I start looking where they might be, see?"

The older lawman said, "Sure I do. I've done us some eliminating my ownself. Found a railroad hand down below who thinks he might have seen the rascal. Says he never saw anyone up here with a rifle, but as he came out of the dispatch shack to see what all them gunshots might mean he spied a slender cuss in blue denim run across the tracks to the southeast with a rifle gun."

Longarm swore softly and declared, "I wish you'd told me that sooner. How far could a body go on foot across the sage flats over yonder!"

Burgess followed as Longarm circled the platform to stare out across wide open range, with silvery-green and knee-high sagebrush offering a piss poor cover for anybody planning to get far from town, on foot or astride.

The local lawman decided, "If he's out there he's lying doggo in the sage, mayhaps awaiting nightfall?"

"When's the next train due?" asked Longarm. Then he said, "I have a better idea. Let's get on down from this fool water tower."

They did so, with Longarm leading the way, before the older lawman decided, "Webber, that dispatcher who told me about Little Boy Blue Denim, would be the one to ask about special runs. I do know the next regular eastbound won't be coming in before late this evening. Where are we headed in such a hurry? Webber's dispatch shack is up the other way!"

Longarm shook his head and forged on across the tracks, a siding and the single main line, as he explained,

"I want some light on the subject and those mountains to the west will have us all in deep shade any damn minute!"

He moved down the far embankment and then in line with the main line through the sagebrush and cheat until they reached the shallow expanse of sunbaked sand forming the braided bed of Skeliton Wash. Chief Constable Burgess gasped, "Son of a bitch! How did you know?" as they both stared down at the footprints leading across the smooth sand to the round opening of the culvert under the railroad right-of-way and Front Street beyond.

Longarm hunkered down to call, "I see you in there. Come out this instant with your hands held friendly and I won't have to empty this magazine of .44-40 up your hidey hole!"

When there came no answer, Longarm confided, "Elimination. We can assume that wasn't a belly dancer firing at us from the water tower and we agree our mysterious figure in blue denim never made it over the horizon on foot before we stared out across the flats for so much as a whiff of dust. We can eliminate him running back into town across the tracks and Front Street combined because nobody on our side saw him do so."

The man who lived there nodded soberly and decided, "He had to have known his way around town to know he'd have a clear shot at my office door from that water tower. He aimed that first shot, saw he'd missed, and scurried down the ladder, firing at the sky to keep us pinned down until he could dash across the tracks and into yonder culvert like the white rabbit Miss Alice chased into Wonderland!"

Longarm got back to his feet, deciding, "I doubt that culvert leads to Wonderland. Where might a white rabbit or a son of a bitch with a gun pop out at the other end?"

The older lawman replied without hesitation, "Same bed of this same wash. Far side of the Garland sisters' hat shop, facing Front Street with their front door and hanging over a bitty fenced-in back garth and the drop-off to the

24

wash out their kitchen door. When we run the culvert under Front Street we figured we might as well fill in a hundred feet of the wash and sell the results as business frontage."

Longarm was only half listening. He was already leading the way back across the tracks. As they crossed Front Street the town law pointed out a modest millinery establishment to explain, "Yonder's the hat shop owned by the Garland sisters."

Longarm replied, "I figured as much. How do we get to the far end of that culvert without having to go to either end of that tedious business block?"

Burgess decided, "We could cut through my corrals, over to the south a piece. Be faster if we just asked to cut through the hat shop, if you feel that lazy."

Longarm said he felt more in a hurry than lazy. The older lawman allowed he'd been funning and led the way into the millinery. A bell above the door tinkled and a mousy little thing in lavender and white checked calico came out of the back, smiling sweet and smelling even sweeter. Longarm decided the base of her French perfume had to be jasmine. She wore her brown hair severely bunned for a gal with such expensive tastes in stink-pretty.

Burgess introduced her to Longarm as Miss Fran and told her they had to cut through her establishment to the back garth.

She shook her head, sort of desperate, and declared, "I can't let you go through our private quarters. My sister, Jo, is, ah, in a state of *dishabille!*"

But the town law insisted it was important. So Fran Garland told them to hold their horses out front for a few seconds. Then she ducked through the drapery at the back of her shop to tend to such chores as she had in mind whilst old Gandy Burgess shifted from foot to foot like a schoolboy trying to hold in a piss.

Longarm felt just that impatient as the plainly pretty milliner took what felt more like a few days to come back out and tell them the coast was clear if they were going straight on through.

So they went straight through and tried not to notice the horse blanket tossed like a tent over the contents of a corner day bed as if to hide somebody head to toe. The sister on her feet didn't follow them out back, once Longarm warned her not to as he raised the muzzle of the Winchester he'd been aiming politely at the floor. So the older lawman who lived there was able to observe, as the two of them crossed a dinky expanse, mostly covered with flagstones, "Miss Jo, the elder sister, has been drinking hundred-proof medication for her female problems of late. You can see how how yonder back retaining wall overlooks the wash and dam above. We're standing right over the west end of that corrigated iron culvert."

Longarm allowed he'd suspected as much as the two of them moved on to the waist-high garden wall of cement-mortared freestone to peer over it, down to the sun-baked bed of Skeliton Wash.

There should have been footprints down yonder. There weren't any. The older lawman gasped, "Son of a bitch! He called your bluff! He was still in the culvert when you threatened to smoke it up and what if he's still there, now?"

Longarm soberly replied, "Only one way to find out. You stay here and cover this end of the culvert whilst I go back to check out the other. He may have doubled back on his trail like a sly fox. Or he may have gone to ground like a scared and not-so-sly fox. Do I cut another set of bootprints on the far side of the tracks? They may lead some damned place. If there's no new sign at all I'll assume he's still in the culvert and go on in after him. So be careful who you shoot in the head down below. But don't let the rascal get away!"

As he turned from the western field of fire to retrace his steps the older lawman gasped, "Hold on! You can't be serious, Longarm! That culvert ain't but four foot in

26

diameter! If you crawl up it to him he'll have you in a can't-miss field of fire!"

To which Longarm could only reply, "That works both ways. If he ain't up to a gunfight in such narrow quarters you'll have the drop on him as he pops out this end. If he has the hair on his chest to shoot it out down yonder in the dark, I have the same chance of winning as he has. So what do want, an egg in your beer?"

# Chapter 4

Longarm wasn't really as indifferent to his own hide as he sometimes sounded. But he'd learned long ago, at places such as Shiloh and Cold Harbor, that it didn't cost any more to sound like a man instead of a sissy when you were stuck with the same odds on dying, either way. So like many of the better gunfighters, he'd long since learned that a man willing to stare Mister Death in the face and just nod a howdy had a slight but important edge on the poor cuss who kept wondering if there might not be some way out of this fool situation as things got to the point of no-other-way.

Longarm was hoping like hell he'd find more sign on the far side of the tracks. But once he got there, to see those boot prints led into the east end of the culvert, period, he muttered, "Shit!" and hunkered down to one one side of the dark entrance and repeated his earlier offer. When he only heard echoes in reply to his final warning he sighed and held the Winchester away from him so he could lean his left hip and shoulder against the railroad ballast and risk only his hands and forearms while he emptied his magazine's fifteen rounds of .44-40 into the dark depths. Ricochets sure screamed eerily as they spanged back and forth betwixt corrugated iron.

Longarm reloaded but leaned the warm Winchester against the bank as he gathered some dried cheat to twist into crumbly sheaf. Cheat grass was not native to the Basin and Range Country. But you couldn't tell. It had crowded out and taken over from the slower growing native short grasses once it had followed the covered wagons west, hidden as fodder and bed straw amid more honest eastern or old-world grass stems.

They called it cheat grass because that's how it acted as it sprouted thick and green betwixt the sagebrush clumps after a rare but soaking rain. Buffalo, gramma, and other such short grass sprouted a tad later but more sincerely, with substantial stems that could nourish grazing critters after it had been sunburnt to tawny standing straw. But once a stem of cheat stopped growing and dried out, it dried out sincerely to offer little more nourishment that the promises of a false-hearted lover or a politician running for office.

Cheat grass sure burned swell, though. Old-timers said the sage flats out this way had been less barren betwixt rains in olden times before they had such regular gully-whopping grass fires in high summer. So when Longarm thumbnailed a waterproof match head and set his sheaf of cheat alight it burst into considerable flame and singed he hairs on the back of his hand as he lobbed it up the culvert as far as he could.

He figured anybody still alive in there might be tempted to fire on what should have looked like someone coming in at him with a torch light. But nothing happened.

Longarm considered that as he smoked down a three-for-a-nickel cheroot to give anybody in there time to sweat. Longarm considered blasting a few more rounds but upon reflection his bullets cost him almost as much as his tobacco and he sheepishly suspected he was stalling for time they didn't have to spare. The sun was long gone and the clear sky above was commencing to shift from cobalt blue to purple.

"I sure hope you're dead, you rascal!" Longarm muttered aloud as he took a deep breath, dropped to his knees on the sandy sill of the culvert exit, and followed the muzzle of his Winchester on in.

Nobody shot him, and vice versa, until he'd crawled close to a damned furlong on his hands and knees through the sand and trash-paved darkness toward a growing point of daylight at the far end.

He got there without meeting another soul, alive or dead. Near the far end he yelled, and when he heard Gandy Burgess yelling back he crawled the rest of the way out to stand up and turn 'round to stare up at the older lawman gazing down at him from eight or ten feet above.

When he asked if Burgess had seen anything, the local law replied, "Nope. Heard your rifle roaring down yonder and a couple of balls came out to skip dust spouts up the wash. Who were you aiming at?"

To which Longarm could only reply with a sheepish smile, "Nobody. I don't know how he did it, but he slickered us. I've followed the sign of gray foxes and Indian horse thieves into thin air in my time. Most white men just keep walking and leaving foot prints, till they get somewheres, or at least to hard ground."

Burgess asked if they could have been tracking an Indian. Longarm thought about that as he scaled the rough and slanted freestone wall to rejoin the older lawman. As he handed up his Winchester, Longarm decided, "You'd know better than me how many Indians you might have here in Cairo."

As he followed his rifle over the edge to dust off his tweed pants in the back garth of the Garland sisters the lawman who lived there allowed they were nigh fifty miles from the nearest Paiute agency but added, "We get wandering digger bands passing through now and again. Mostly when the pinyon trees are bearing over to the west or they get to hankering for jackrabbit in the greenup.

They don't bother us and we don't bother them as long as they keep going. We have us a few breeds and assimilates in the township, of course. Paiute can be stubborn as all get out when it comes to clinging to their culture. That's what Paiute call running around bare-ass, living on pine nuts, roots and lizards with an occasional rabbit for dessert. Culture."

Longarm said, "They call themselves the Ho Hada and you're right about the way they get around on foot out this way. Where might I find me one or more of your more gainfully employed local Indians?"

The town law said they had some Paiute hired help at Sheppard's Hotel if he was in a hurry. They were just digger gals who'd learned to sweep floors and make beds. The half-dozen buck Paiutes he knew of all worked for cattle spreads up and down the tracks and only got to town now and again."

Longarm observed he had to start thinking of hotel resevations in any case. So they went back inside, where the mousy Fran Garland herded them past her covered-up sister on the double and out the door opening on Front Street before she asked if there was anything else she could do for them.

Longarm didn't think it would be polite to tell a gal in calico what a natural man who hadn't had any since leaving Denver days back could do for him if she was really serious. So he asked if by any chance they had a cellar under the hat shop.

Gandy Burgess said, "I can answer that and the notion violates the laws of civic engineering and common sense. None of these . . . let's see, four and a half shops facing Front Street with their backs overlooking the wash to the west have cellars because there ain't room under this here hat shop and it wouldn't be safe for the ones to either side when it rains heavy and the overflow from the dam fills the wash to the west to the brim."

Fran Garland suppressed a shudder and added, "Jo and

31

I go to the hotel during weather like that. This whole stretch of Front Street acts like a dam in its own right and the water whooshing under us and out the far end carries on like a giant fire hose and makes the ground shake like jelly!"

Longarm ticked his hat brim to her and thanked her for eliminating a wild guess. As they strode away Burgess asked what that might have been. Longarm said, "Corrigated iron rusts, and rivets can be busted loose. But if there's no cellar walls to either side to tunnel into that vanishing Little Boy Blue of ours couldn't have escaped by such a route. I'd be obliged if I could leave my saddle and possibles over at your place for now. I want to check into the hotel with an excuse to go out more than once."

The older lawman nodded and said, "I follow your drift. But what might you be expecting to see as you pass through the lobby now and again for a bite to eat, something to drink, or mayhaps to gather up some baggage after things settle down a mite?"

Longarm replied, simply, "If I knew I could stay in my hired room and read *Captain Billy's Whizbang*. I don't know if you've noticed, but what sounded like a less complexicated chore keeps getting ever more confusing by the minute! They sent me to see if I could locate that belly dancing sweetheart of Happy Jack Henderson and here I am trying to make a lick of sense out of bounty hunters with no sensible reasons for being here and somebody else entire pegging shots at me for no good reason I can think of!"

Gandy Burgess started to make a dumb suggestion. Then he nodded to say, "He must have been after you. He'd have shot me for sure if I'd been his intended target. But why?"

Longarm didn't answer. The question didn't deserve one. The older lawman tagged along until they got to Sheppard's Hotel and went on in with him to introduce him to Miss Mabel Brookside, the no longer young but not bad looking owner and manager of the Sheppard. As long as a man considered henna rinse, an ample hourglass figure filling a brick-red shantung bodice, and the beginnings of a double chin not bad looking. After a couple of nights alone along the way she looked just fine.

Miss Mabel allowed they'd be proud to hire him a cool corner room with the crapper down the hall at six bits a day and never mentioned his lack of baggage, seeing the local law had introduced him as such a distinguished guest to Cairo. As he signed her register she dinged a desk bell and one of the Indians Burgess had mentioned came out from the back to take the key the white gal handed her.

It was only a *her* on second glance, since a long-haired Paiute of either persuasion looked as much like an Apache orphan in a shapeless white cotton blouse coming down to the bare knees.

The owner told her Indian maid to show Longarm up to room 222. He saw Gandy Burgess meant to linger at the desk a spell. So he allowed he'd see them both later and followed the short stubby Indian gal up the nearby stairwell with his rifle but no other baggage.

He was wondering how to gracefully ask a silent and sort of sullen-faced Paiute gal whether she had any kinsmen who dressed all in blue denim and played hide-and-go-seek with white lawmen when she unlocked the door to his corner room and threw it open with a sad little sob.

Longarm stepped inside and braced the rifle on its butt plate in one corner before he turned with a puzzled smile to ask, "What's the trouble, *skookumchuk*? Has somebody been treating you mean? Hear me, I ride for the Great Father if you have any complaints about any of us, a, *saltu*."

His limited grasp of her Uto-Aztec dialect seemed to bust a dam inside her round little head, and as tears ran down her smooth brown cheeks Longarm shut the hall door and took her in his arms to soothe, "It's going to be all right, *penat*. What's been going on, here? Have they

33

been working you without pay or making you sleep with some *saltu* you don't fancy?"

She burrowed her warm wet face into his vest as she sobbed, "*Ka!* Miss Mabel has been good to me. She pays me as much as she paid the black *saltu* maid who ran away with a Pullman porter and I *like* to sleep with *saltu*. They wash all over once a month whether they need to or not and they don't expect the woman to do all the work. I like that custom you call kiss, too. Don't you remember, Saltu Ka Saltu? Oh, what could I have done to make you scorn me so!"

Longarm had no idea. But some Ho speakers had dubbed him Saltu Ka Saltu in the past because of those Indian Ring agents left over from the Grant administration.

Old Sam Grant had doubtless meant well, but some of his back-room cronies had surely rid roughshod over little folk, red, white, black, or any other color as a damned fine general and a piss-poor president had set smoking and sipping on the back veranda of the White House.

As Longarm had modestly tried to tell his Ho Hada admirers, more than once, they owed their more recent changes of fortune to President Rutherford B. Hayes and his new secretary of the interior Schurz, or Little Four Eyes, than they might a mere deputy marshal. He'd known full well about the Indian ring when he'd first gone to work for a justice department run by another Grant apointee. But nobody had let him *do* anything about stolen reservation allotments, short measure, spoiled Indian beef, and such until Little Four Eyes had told them to go *git* the sons of bitches.

But, seeing few if any Indians really understood white customs, and vice versa, the Paiute, Horse Ute, Comanche, and other Ho speakers he'd helped out by running in their crooked agents had taken to calling him Saltu Ka Saltu or Stranger Who Is Not A Stranger, and the sobbing little thing he was holding in his arms at the moment seemed to know this, and have the advantage on him.

So he gently pried her loose to hold at arms length so he could stare down at her with a puzzled smile and cautiously ask, "Have we met somewheres before, *penat*?"

She sobbed, "You told me *penat* was *honey* in your tongue. You told I was pretty and that you would never forget me. But I see you have forgotten me and I feel so ashamed!"

Longarm tired, "Aw, don't feel that way, ma'am. I'm certain I'd remember meeting up with you in other surroundings if we were back in other surroundings. It's just that I've had a lot on my mind and wasn't expecting to meet up with any Ho Hada pals in this hotel, see?"

She brightened and said, "My heart dances around the dying coals of fire when I see that may be why you stared so coldly at me downstairs."

He said, "Aw, I wasn't staring cold at anybody. I just failed to recognize you in such tricky light, Miss.... What clan did you say you hailed from?"

"Sage Grouse, in your tongue!" she answered in a more cheerful tone as she whipped her one-piece cotton garment off over her head to face him naked as a jay in the fading light from the windows.

That fantastic figure was harder to forget than her pretty moon face had been. She was short as most diggers but built a lot more curvacious and he'd believed her the last time when she'd told him one of her grandfathers had been a California trader from the west slope of the High Sierra. So he beamed down at her to ask, "Is that really you, Miss Wapzewipe? I swear I didn't recognize you with clothes on!"

Wapzewipe scampered over to the bed to flop across the covers and roll on her back with her tawny thighs spread in welcome as she sort of pouted, "You don't have to explain, Saltu Ka Saltu. Take off your own clothes and prove to me that you still like me!"

# Chapter 5

As many a mountain man had noticed, and vice versa, Quill Indian gals, raised traditional, didn't feel much like their pale-faced counterparts up close and personal.

It wasn't a matter of anatomy. Men and women of all races came in all shapes and sizes, good, bad, and peculiar. So ladies of Indian blood living white as say, members of the Five Civilized Tribes or raised with white kids for some other reason tended to act a heap like white gals, aboard bedding they were accustomed to screwing on. But gals grown to womankind on furs or blankets spread on a way firmer surface learned positions that were easier on a poor gal's tail bone and spine. Men of any complexion found it easier on their own knees and elbows to lay on their backs with the gal squatting atop them when there were neither bedsprings nor much in the way of padding to take up the jolts, as things got passionate.

Little Wapzewipe had learned to like it on her back in bed with the man on top since last they'd tangled so delightsome. But as he let his fool duds land anywhere they wanted and mounted her once more after all those moons since Pyramid Lake, he found she still kissed as unusual, Lord love her sweet-smelling innards.

Kissing was an old-world invention the American Indian had never thought of before some Arawak maidens likely caught on to, fast, with the crew of the Santa Maria. Left to play slap and tickle without the white man's instruction, the different nations had rubbed noses, panted in one another's faces with open-mouthed admiration, or just yelled a lot. Longarm had taught Wapzewipe to kiss, or she said he had, a few summers back when he'd been riding herd on the few fish that could live in the brackish waters of the same. They'd been reserved for the local Paiute by the Bureau of Indian Affairs and he'd told those white poachers he'd arrested what he thought of any man who'd steal from digger Indians.

But as in the case of the way she moved her brown rump on a mattress, Wapzewipe was confused enough about kissing to offer some open-mouthed variety and unexpected tongue darts to what otherwise might have felt more like common courtesy to her friendly moon face. He suspected she might be a tad older than she looked at first glance. It was tougher to judge the age of some colored gals for the same reason. He didn't know whether white gals seemed to wrinkle sooner because they had thinner skin or whether it was just easier to judge the expressions and likely experience of one's own kind. As memories of their earlier grunts and groans came back to him, making her grunt some, dog style, Longarm recalled her name meant something like a lost soul and that she'd shyly confessed she'd been married up when her original band had been wiped out by Horse Utes and she'd been taken in by the Sage Grouse folk around Pyramid Lake. But she was built like a teenaged gal with some white blood to hourglass her tawny torso, as he couldn't help but notice as he admired the view from above, sliding in and out of her.

The view from below was as sassy, once they somehow wound up on the rug with her on top, hunkered on her bare heels to play stoop-tag in the asparagus patch, as old habits reasserted themselves in her passionate loins. The nice thing about that position was that the man got to play with the gal's bouncing breasts, albeit according to Wapzewipe and some other Indian gals he'd played with, Indian men paid less attention to tits than white men. Queen Victoria had known what she was doing when she forbade proper ladies to nurse in public or show a hint of cleavage below the collars of their buttoned-all-the-way bodices. But Indians gals said they didn't *mind* men admiring their bare tits. So things evened out and a good time was had by all.

It was too dark to rightly see what they were doing by the time they wound up back on the bedstead to share a smoke and catch their second winds. He assumed she'd led him astray upstairs as her last chore for the evening. But when he suggested they get dressed and go out for some supper Wapzewipe said, "We can't. You are *saltu*. I am Ho Hada. People will talk and I need this job. I would lose it if Miss Mabel knew I was up here in bed with you in secret. She has told me not to ever let her catch me in bed with a hotel guest again."

Longarm didn't care to know who she might have been in bed with to begin with. He'd been in bed with a certain widow woman up on Denver's Capitol Hill over the past weekend and sometimes it could be more comfortable for all concerned if you acted as if the two of you'd come out of the Garden of Eden, with the less said about others the better.

He knew she'd *tell* him how many other men she'd been with since Pyramid Lake, if he *asked* her. Her particular breed of Ho speaker had a more natural approach to the facts of life, growing up naked as they wandered the Basin and Range Country worried about such more important matters as their next meal or water fit to drink in a land where most streams ran down to salt flats. But when she passed the cheroot back to him in the dark and asked how many women he'd had since last she'd given him some, Longarm gripped the smoke in his teeth to reply in a desperately casual tone, "Can't think of anybody *better*. The only other gal I'm interested in tonight is the one they sent me out your way to serve with a summons. I don't know her name or what she looks like, albeit she can't be severely hideous. They say she's a belly dancer. That's a *saltu* gal, sort of, who dances snakey with her belly button exposed to public view as she wiggles it considerable. You'd tell me if you've noticed such unusual entertainment here in Cairo, wouldn't you?"

Wapzewipe snuggled closer and replied, "I would like to see a saltu woman dance like that. The only dancing *saltu* women I have ever seen had their bellies covered as they danced with *saltu* men. They did not wiggle anything. They seemed to skip around to fiddle music in those high-buttoned shoes they wear. Are you certain they said this belly button bouncer dances funny here in Cairo?"

"A holdup man told his followers he was coming here to meet her," Longarm exclaimed, going on to bring a gal who worked there up to date on his mission, confusing as they both found it.

The sharp-eyed Gandy Burgess had already told Longarm he and the locked-up Boston Ferris were the only strangers seen in town since the time of that post office robbery in Elko. Wapzewipe said they hadn't had any guests there at Sheppard's Hotel she hadn't recognized as local country folk in town for a spell or the traveling salesmen and railroad officials who stayed over regular when they were along that section of the Central Pacific.

Passing the cheroot back to her with a friendly feel, Longarm said, "I know more than one way to dance, my ownself. I generally lead the lady about in a two-step when they ain't calling a do-si-do or a reel. On the other hand I have been known to try for a fair fandango down Mexico way and somebody I knew from down yonder might describe me as a fandango dancer if they'd never watched me do-si-do."

Wapzepipe took the cheroot from her pouty lips to demand, "Why are you boasting to me about the Mexican women you have fucked?"

He chuckled and said, "I was bragging on the way I've *danced* with some. That Spanish flamenco heel clicking and hand clapping is unusual enough to leave a lasting impression on your average Anglo rider. So a poor but dishonest country boy who'd met up with a dance hall gal whilst she was belly dancing in the oriental or State Fair style might remember her as a belly dancing pal long after she'd switched to, say, that Sandwich Island hula-hula or, hell, a Spanish flamenco, see?"

Wapzewipe did but she couldn't steer him to any Cairo gals who'd danced professional in any manner in recent memory."

Longarm grimaced and considered, "Neither dance hall gals who dance nor the ones who go upstairs with the customers hanker to get old and gray at their trades. Happy Jack Henderson was older than those three saddle tramps he'd recruited over in the Mormon Delta. So there's no natural law forbidding a man who's rid the owlhoot trail quite a spell from having pals along it who might have worked at belly dancing when their bellies and the owlhoot trail were younger."

The Paiute gal who'd seen her world change some since she'd been wandering the sage flats bare-ass with a digging stick behind her bare-ass elders was able to follow Longarm's drift. She said, "I see what you mean. That *taibo*, Henderson, must have met some woman here in Cairo Township who *used to* dance with her belly."

Longarm knew enough Ho to grasp her not-too-subtle dismissal of the outlaw he was after. "Saltu" simply meant "stranger" and naturally applied to anyone, red or white, who wasn't a member in good standing of one's own extended Ho Hada kinship. "Taibo" was only used for white folk they despised, so it worked something like an Anglo calling a Mexican a Mex or a Greaser. He said, "By any name he sounds as missing. He told his pals he

40

meant to leave the proceeds from that robbery here in Cairo in the care of that mysterious belly dancer. On the other hand, to do so he'd have to get here with the money and give it to some Cairo gal whether she was dancing oriental or indulging in a Highland fling!"

"Have you tried it an easier way?" she asked, handing back the cheroot as she sat up in bed, adding, "You say he robbed that post office with younger men he'd invited to ride with him for the first time. What if he meant from the beginning to keep all the money for himself? He was not with them when they rode into that trap over in Battle Mountain, after he'd told them to go there. What if he never meant to leave all that money with anybody? What if the whole story about some dancing woman here in Cairo is a big pile of *kutsupah*?"

Longarm took a thoughtful drag on the cheroot, noting as usual that tobacco smoke didn't taste as good in the dark when you couldn't see it to blow thoughtful rings. He told her, "I considered that before I got here. They wanted me to ask around Cairo and see if there might be anything to the deathbed confessions, or ravings, of a gut-shot saddle tramp. Had I found nothing going on at all I'd have wired I'd found nothing going on and by this time my boss, Marshal Vail, would have wired back that I was to come on home."

He took another drag and confided, "I aim to wire him when I go out for that late supper you've made me miss, Lord love you. But I can't say nothing is going on. They're holding that bounty hunter in jail on suspicion of *something* and he swears he's here after holdup men."

He stubbed out what was left of the lit cheroot in an ashtray on the bed table when he noticed Wapzewipe had forked a chunky naked thigh across his bare lap, but continued, "After that I have even more to report. I told you how somebody pegged a rifle shot at me from that water tower and how we'd tracked him to that culvert. The one witness who might have caught a fleeting glance of the

41

cuss described him as kid-sized in blue denim. But I see they have you wearing more cotton than you used to and it occurred to me a Ho Hada dressed white might account for a clear trail that led into a rabbit hole and never came out."

Wapzewipe reached down to take the matter in hand and demurely rubbed the head of his semi-erection between the love-slicked lips of the yawning gulf betwixt her wide-spread thighs as she chuckled and said, "*Ai!* Our young men are good at laying false trails across a world infested with Horse Utes and cavalry officers out to make an easy name for themselves. I don't know too many Ho Hada this far south. But there are some working around Cairo Township, both as railroad section hands and riding for *saltu* cattle spreads. It is not true my people did not know how to ride in our shining times. We kept no ponies out on the open salt and sage flats because ponies need more fodder and water than we could find as we kept to the drier country our enemies avoided."

He felt himself rising to the occasion as he soothed, "I've told other saltu riders that Shoshoni and Comanche are just digger bands that wandered into range a horse can live on and naturally took to riding instead of walking, the way anyone with a lick of sense could be expected to. But let's get back to how anyone, red or white, might go about leaving clear footprints across crusty sand and somehow get out of that fool culvert without leaving other signs at either end!"

Wapzewipe settled down on his renewed enthusiasm and tried to work it harder with her muscular innards as she commenced to describe the ways, a good many ways, her band had left false trails across the wide open spaces to the east with keen-eyed Horse Utes busting a gut to read said sign.

But she hadn't gotten far, either way, before there came an imperious pounding on the door and a familiar female voice called through the thin paneling, "I know you're in there, Wapzewipe! And you ought to be ashamed of yourself, Deputy Long!"

Longarm tried to sound more sleepy than ashamed as he called back in a deliberatly befuddled voice, "Who's that knocking at my door and what are you ranting about? Can't a man catch forty winks around here without somebody waking him up, hysterical?"

Old Mabel Brookside from downstairs demanded, "What would any man be doing in bed at eight p.m. by himself? I know full well what you two are doing in there in bed and I'll have you know I don't run that sort of an establishment here!"

Longarm was sure glad he'd thrown the barrel bolt over the inside knob as he heard a pass-key turn in the lock before she commenced to rattle the bolted door considerable, demanding, "Come over here and unbolt this door this instant! I know she's in there with you!"

Wapzewipe had rolled off his pillar of desire to grope across the rug in the dark for her shimmy shirt as Longarm swung his bare feet to the floor, calling out, "I ain't dressed decent, ma'am. Seeing it was sort of stuffy in here, no offense, I turned in naked as a jay for my nap."

She kicked the door and insisted, "I don't care about that. I used to be in Vaudeville and there's nothing you could possible show me that I haven't seen before! Are you going to open up or do I have to get my hall porter and a fire ax?"

Longarm rose to gather his own duds from the rug and tossed them over the footrails of the bed as he suddenly noticed in the dim light that Wapzewipe was nowhere in sight. Figuring she'd rolled under the bed, Lord love her, he strode over to the door stark naked and threw the bolt as he warned, "You might have given me time to at least wrap a towel around me. But seeing you're so anxious, life is too short to spend this much of it arguing with a determined woman!"

Then he opened the door wide, exposing his full frontal

nudity in a state of semi-erection to the henna-rinsed landlady with the coal oil lantern in her hand.

The older woman swept her eyes up and down him to
calmly observe, "Not bad. But I see you only have one
of them and where are you trying to hide that Paiute pussy
who got you that hard, under the bed?"

# Chapter 6

What he'd just been up to was only a federal offense when you did it on a reservation, where the Bureau of Indian Affairs reserved the sole right to diddle Indians. So Longarm wasn't worried about his own job. But the pretty little Paiute had said she really needed her job here at Sheppard's Hotel. So he felt awkward as all get-out when the bossy white woman Wapzewipe worked for strode over by the rumpled bedstead, bent over to place her lantern on the floor, and got down on her hands and knees to peer under the bed.

Wapzewipe had slid off his old organ-grinder just as it was feeling up to the job and the broader behind of the landlady offered a new and tempting inspiration as her summerweight, rust, shantung skirting filled considerable with ass he'd never had. But he was braced for less pleasant excitement as he waited for her to haul poor Wapzewipe out into the lanternlight and give them both pure hell.

So he was more surprised than Mabel Brookside sounded as she crawfished back to stand up with her lantern in one hand and puzzled look on her face, declaring, "I don't know what to say! I was sure I heard you talking to somebody in here and would you please stop waving that thing at me, young sir?"

45

To which Longarm replied with a lewd grin, "It was your own great notion to barge in where it waves, ma'am. I reckon I must have been talking in my sleep because, as you can plainly see, I was having me a mighty romantic dream just now."

As she blushed and turned away he couldn't resist, "I don't suppose you or that Indian gal you were fussing about would care to make my dream come true? As you can see, you woke me up just as things were starting to feel swell!"

It worked. She chased her lantern out into the hall and slammed the door shut after her, plunging Longarm into darkness once again.

He waited until her footsteps faded down the second story hall before he quietly suggested, "You can come out and tell me how you did that, now, Miss Wapzewipe."

There came no answer. He moved over to the corner windows to gaze down on Front Street and the side alley leading around back to the stable and corral. Cairo, Nevada, was too small to have the street lighting they likely boasted in those other Cairos, whether on the Mississippi or the Nile. But windows and doorways down below spilled patches of lamplight out across the plank walks and alkali dust of Front Street. So he could see she wasn't fluttering like a nestling with a busted wing after such a drop. She'd either managed to land mighty graceful from a second-story window overlooking solid planking and packed earth, or, more likely, she'd swung by her arms like one of those gibbon apes along the rain gutter running back from the falsefront to another window opening on the side wall.

Longarm moved over to the corner washstand and sponged off with the help of a pitcher of tepid water, a shallow basin, and a braided string washrag as he murmured, "Thanks for eliminating that mystery, you pretty little Paiute! Whether that jasper in blue denim was one of you or one of us, I suspect I see how he did it. Planning

46

ahead and knowing that culvert better than us, he just pegged those shots and ran across the tracks to the east end of the passage clean under the tracks, main drag, and the shops fronting on the same. Then, just like yourself, he scaled that rough stone retaining wall to roll into the bitty back garth of one shop or another whilst everyone who might have noticed was out on the front walk, drawn by the sounds of gunplay!"

There were a few loose ends left. But nothing to compare with boot prints leading nowhere at all. So he got dressed and strapped on his sixgun to go back down and grab some supper before he took to asking any more questions up and down Front Street.

He left his Winchester in that corner, knowing from experience he was more likely to need his tweed frock coat before midnight than a long range weapon in town.

He knew the Western Union by the railroad stop would be open all night and Billy Vail could be such an old fuss about paying for extra wires, collect. So he resolved to hold off until he knew a mite more before he wired a progress report, at night letter rates. Nobody was going to be at the Denver Federal Building at that hour to read any wires before morning. Billy Vail had told his deputies not to have telegrams delivered direct to his home on Sherman Street because his wife tended to get excited when you woke her up at night.

He found a stand-up chili parlor wedged between the Western Union and a hardware shop across from the lockup and livery run by Gandy Burgess. The lonesome-looking fat gal in mint green working the stand-up counter facing the plank walk out front said she'd be proud to serve him pork chops smothered in chili con carne if he was man enough to consume such a supper. She stared in open admiration as he ordered a slice of mince pie for dessert with an extra mug of black coffee.

As she poured she wistfully remarked, "I wish I could eat that much and look so fit. This coffee was brewed to railroading specs, designed to keep a man awake a spell."

Longarm dryly observed, "I was planning on staying up this evening. My handle is Custis Long and I ride for the federal government as a deputy marshal."

She dimpled—it was easy to dimple when you had a weight problem—and said, "I know. They were talking about you when I carried some white bread and beans across the street for that hired gun they've been holding. They call me Bonnie MacDugal and I'll be off duty when we close at midnight."

Longarm smiled across the rim of his coffee mug at her and put the same back on the counter to remark, "I'll keep that in mind. But, no offense, I was hoping to scout up another Cairo gal this evening. Not to admire her more than present company, you understand. They want me to question her about a robbery over to Elko. I don't have a name to call her, yet. But they say she's a dancer. A belly dancer. A gal who shimmies and shakes in an oriental costume with her belly button and a good bit of midriff exposed to public view. I don't suppose you've served anyone like that across this counter since you've been working here . . . how long did you say it was?"

Bonnie MacDugal sighed, "Going on three years and I'm going out of my mind. I could tell you the tale of a foolish maiden who left her good home and kind parents to go chasing after the rainbow and a tin horn gambling man they called Ace. But you've no doubt heard it many a time in one version or another by now."

Longarm smiled in a brotherly fashion and replied, "I have indeed. What happened to old Ace? Did somebody gun him on you or did he just light out and leave you to get by as best a gal can in these parts?"

She sighed and said, "He left me for another up in Carson City. He told me I'd gotten too fat to support myself as a fancy gal and threw in the cruel suggestion I send home for money."

She blinked hard, wiped her eyes with the back of a

plump wrist, and added, "I wish somebody *had* gunned him. He deserved it and that might have given me an excuse to write home. It's not as shameful when a woman loses her man to gunplay. But how do you tell your mama she was right about the rascal all along?"

Longarm quietly suggested, "I'd start by writing, 'Dear Mama: You were right about the rascal all along.' Of course, you'd know better than me whether that might inspire your kind parents to forgive you or send you a box of poison chocolates. Could we talk about that other orphan of the storm, the one better known as a dancing gal, whether belly or some other wiggle waggle?"

The lardy waitress said they could. But when Longarm asked where in Cairo a dancing gal of any variety might be found she told him she'd seen two-step at the Granger balls and square dancing at church socials, there in Cairo. But confessed she couldn't say whether they had hoochy koochy dancers in the Fremont or smaller saloons further down Front Street because she wasn't the sort of gal who frequented saloons.

He was settling up with her when that kid deputy from the town lockup caught up with him to declare, "I've been looking all over for you since they told us at the hotel you'd gone out. Gandy wants you over to the Fremont. He's waiting out front with Nails Nolan and and Mike Rogers."

Longarm left a dime on the counter for Bonnie and trailed after the kid, who answered to Sam Hart if he'd remembered that right. On the catty-corner route to the biggest saloon in Cairo he naturally asked the kid what all the fuss was about.

Hart said, "Another stranger in town. Drinking alone in the Fremont as if waiting for somebody with his double action Remington .45 worn side-draw, low and tied down. Gandy said to mention he was wearing a blue denim jacket and jeans with a Texas crush to his charcoal gray hat."

49

Longarm asked, "How come? Ain't been any trains stopping since the one I got off this afternoon."

Deputy Hart replied, "He didn't come in by train. He rid in on a blue roan with a Henry rifle in its saddle boot. We know this because he stabled his mount at Gandy's livery. Said he'd rid into town from an outfit called the Rocking T. There ain't no outfit called the Rocking T for as far as anyone might ride a horse logical. Reckon he didn't know our chief constable owned the livery when he left his pony there with his saddle gun and a whopper about where they'd come from."

Longarm could make out Chief Constable Burgess and his younger deputies in the dim light as he and Hart drew nearer. Burgess and his boys were on the shaded plank walk in front of the shut-down hardware store next door to the Fremont. As he and Hart joined them he quietly asked if anyone knew what time the stanger drinking alone at the bar in the Fremont had ridden in from wherever.

Gandy Burgess dryly remarked, "I'm ahead of you, there. It's true he left his roan with us less than an hour ago. That don't prove he wasn't in town earlier this afternoon. Anybody slick enough to make it look as if he left bootprints leading to Wonderland would be slick enough to leave his mount tethered out of town a practical run on foot before he snuck in to pepper folk from water towers. In the meantime he's a stranger answering to the quick look that railroad dispatcher got of him, right?"

One of the local deputies said, "Hot damn, do a couple of us go in the back way whilst the others set up at both front windows and them swinging doors, we'll have him in a bodacious crossfire!"

Longarm shook his head and said, "Let's eat the apple a bite at a time and make sure he's not an innocent rider off a real Rocking T before we earnestly try to take him alive!"

Gandy Burgess allowed he was open to suggestions. So

Longarm said, "Let me move in ahead of you all. I ain't from here. So he's way less likely to know I'm the law and with any luck I ought to be able to get the drop on him before he finds out."

As Longarm drifted toward the nearest window of the Fremont Saloon the older lawman followed closely, trailed by his deputies until he told Nails Nolan and young Hart to circle around to cover the back exit. As he, Longarm, and the remaining Mike Rogers made it to the grimy glass spilling lamplight out into the darkness he asked Longarm what made him think the stanger knew *any* lawmen in town on sight.

Longarm explained, "If he's the little boy blue we're after he must have scouted the town before he fired from that water tower, bee-lined for that culvert, and scaled the retaining wall at the far end as if he knew the lay of the land and then some. Hold on. Let me get the lay of the land inside before I make my own next move."

He stood back from the grimy glass to regard the lone figure at the bar with interest. The man in blue denim and a Texican hat looked bigger than Longarm had been expecting. But after that things fell in place well enough. Longarm murmured to the others, "If he's wanted in other parts I don't recognize him. Stay out here and cover me whilst I mosey in, belly up to the bar beside him, and see if I can get anything out of him, peaceful."

The other lawmen agreed that seemed a good plan. Longarm couldn't see anything wrong with it as he moved along the walk to part the batwing doors and stride on in, not looking directly at the man bellied up to the bar, dead center. But the solitary drinker had been looking into the mirror of the back bar. So as Longarm casually approached, as if positioning himself a polite distance along the bar from the quiet man in blue denim, there came a sudden blur of motion as the mysterious stranger spun away from the bar to drop into a gunfighter's crouch and, worse yet, go for gun as he yelled a mighty mean thing about Longarm's poor old mother!

Longarm still had no idea who the cuss might be. But nobody moved his gun hand like so without considerable experience. And any experienced gunfighter knew that, given a head start, there was no way in hell a tied-down side-draw wasn't going to beat a cross-draw in a stand-up saloon fight.

# Chapter 7

So it got mighty noisy in the Fremont Saloon for a spell of two or three full seconds. Then, as the smoke cleared and the other lawmen charged in with their own guns drawn, they saw Longarm was still on his feet, which was more than the gunslick in blue denim could say. He lay sprawled along the base of the bar with one elbow hooked sort of casual over the brass rail and his tall Texas hat upside down in the sawdust beyond the nearest spitoon. His smoking sixgun lay in the same sawdust closer to Longarm's booted feet as he stared up pallid and confounded. The two shots he'd gotten off, too late, had drilled first into the floor and then the pressed tin ceiling. Then two sledgehammer blows had knocked him on his ass and turned his innards to cold jelly. So as he felt ever more numb he asked Longarm in a surprisingly conversational tone, "How the fuck did you do that, Longarm?"

Gandy Burgess stared as awestruck at the sixgun still in its holster on Longarm's left hip as he chimed in, "Yeah, how the fuck did you do that, old son?"

Longarm ignored him to hunker down and tell the man he'd just now killed, "I can see by your Stetson that you were from Texas. I see by the tailored grips on your shooting iron and a holster lined with patent leather that you

53

were a gunslick. But after that you have the advantage on me. Do I know you from somewheres, friend?"

The dying man smiled wearily and replied, "Don't say you didn't recognize me. Tell me how you killed me without ever drawing your fucking six-gun!"

Longarm replied firmly but not unkindly, "You first. Who might you be and what brought you here to this Basin and Range Country? Who told you to peg that rifle shot at me this afternoon? Or was that your own grand notion?"

The man he'd downed didn't answer for a held breath or more and for a moment Longarm doubted he was ever going to. Then, with his eyes shut, the Texas gunslick muttered, "I used to be Jed Walters and our homespread was the Bar Eleven on the Brazos. My daddy would be Big Jed Walters and I'd be obliged if you'd see he gets his watch I carried off that time he whupped me once too often. You were fixing to tell me how you killed me, Longarm."

Longarm held out his big right fist and opened it to expose his small but deadly double-derringer as he laconically observed, "When you're moving in on a sinister stranger packing side-draw, and you're packing your six-gun side-draw and your derringer in your vest. You'd have to be a total fool to depend on your six-gun."

It wasn't clear whether Jed Walters had heard or not. His eyes were half open, now, but he didn't seem to be breathing.

As Longarm pocketed his derringer and felt for a pulse, old Gandy Burgess quietly observed, "Remind me never to pick a fight with you, Longarm. You're downright *sneaky*! That name, Jed Walters, sounds like I ought to remember it better."

Longarm got back to his feet with a grimace of distaste to reply, "We both missed recalling him, at first, for the same reason. It was six or eight years ago, just about the time I was giving up the joys of punching cows for slightly higher pay when Walters, there, gunned a young cowboy in Ellsworth under the mistaken impression he was a wanted outlaw."

The older lawman grinned down at the body along the base of the bar to brightly exclaim, "Why, sure! I read about that killing in The Grand Central Hotel in Ellsworth. They wanted to hang somebody for it. But Walters, here, got off with five for manslaughter on account he was packing a bounty hunter's license and could claim it as a natural mistake!"

By this time the deputies from out back had crowded in with some townsmen from outside. So Longarm suggested they leave everything but that watch Walters had mentioned to Gandy's deputies. As he hunkered back down to feel for and find the gold-washed watch on a rabbit's foot fob, the older lawman asked where they'd be headed next.

Getting back to his feet and pocketing the watch, Longarm explained, "I'd like to gather up those possibles I left with you and as long as I'm about it I thought I'd ask that bounty hunter you're holding what he has to say about this bounty hunter I just had to shoot."

But when they got over to the jail to ask him, Boston Ferris swore he knew nothing about the late Jed Walters, save that Ferris, too, had heard Walters was a trigger-happy fool nobody with a lick of sense would ever hire. When Ferris said they'd never met, Longarm told him, "He seemed to have known *me* by rep as well. You have a cast-iron alibi for any and all attempts on my life by that other hired gun. So why don't you do us both a favor and tell us who really hired you and your own skills, here in Cairo Township."

Ferris said, "I told you. I got a letter in a womanly hand nobody never signed. She never wrote she wanted me to gun anybody for her. She wrote that once I got here she'd point out a wanted man for half the bounty on his hide. She never mentioned writing to any other bounty hunter, if she wrote to any at all."

Longarm and Gandy Burgess exchanged thoughtful glances. The older lawman nodded and said, "It's starting to look like somebody surely wants somebody here in Cairo fed to the worms. Walters was on record as a shoot-first natural killer. This one may or may not have as much common sense as he'd have us believe. Have you ever noticed how sweet and reasonable they all sound as soon as you get them ahint the bars?"

Longarm asked Ferris again to be sweet and reasonable, adding, "It ought to have occurred to you by this time that your perfumed letter writer could have been out to use both you and Jed Walters as dupes. There's no evidence at all that any members of that James-Younger gang are anywheres in Nevada and did she tell you she'd written to another gun for hire, or vice versa?"

Boston Ferris went over to the bunk and sat down as he replied in as calm a tone, "To tell the pure truth I don't give a shit. I know my rights and you all know I ain't done nothing you can hold me on for more than seventy-two hours."

Gandy Burgess said, "We could let you out sooner if you showed a less surly attitude, old son."

Ferris shrugged and said, "Fuck you. I don't have to kiss ass to get out of here, come Monday at the latest. I have friends who know where I went and by now they're already wondering how come I never wired 'em from Cairo. Once they tell a lawyer we know, if they ain't already, you'll be in a whole lot of trouble if you don't turn me loose with a sincere apology, hear?"

Longarm tried, "Who might these friends be and how do we get in touch with them, Boston?"

Ferris snorted, "Fuck you, too. They ain't done nothing, neither, and I guess I know how this game is played as well as you country boys!"

Longarm motioned with his head and they left the sullen prisoner to sulk alone. He could have heard anything important they said inside. So Gandy waited until they were outside, with Longarm's army saddle and possibles braced on the taller lawman's hip, before he demanded, "All right. What are we supposed to do with Ferris, now?"

Longarm said, "Hold him. For as long as you can. It's tougher to tie down a loose cannon once it gets to rolling all over the deck and if by any chance he was telling the truth about somebody here in Cairo sending for him, you can bet the farm that she, he or it ain't about to come forward to contact Ferris if you cut him loose."

The older lawman grimaced and muttered, "Shit. There went a great notion! I was going to suggest letting him go but ordering him to stay in town whilst we kept an eye on him. But I follow your drift and no matter what that letter writer had planned . . . Hold on! I just now thought of something!"

Longarm nodded and asked, "You mean what if somebody wrote to the late Jed Walters after you and your boys had picked up the first hired gun recruited by mail?"

The old lawman sighed wistfully and said, "Aw, you're no fun."

Longarm said, "It won't work. You spotted and arrested Ferris just about forty-eight hours ago. Even if someone sent a wire instead of a perfumed letter to a Texas killer, there's no way Walters could have made it here by this afternoon by rail, and leave us not forget he rode in from at least the next rail stop up or down the line on that blue roan you still have in your livery next door."

The chief constable-cum-livery owner brightened and said, "By gum, I'd forgot that pony and the saddle he left in our tack room. What's say we have us a look!"

So Longarm shifted his own saddle to his left shoulder and tagged along as the older lawman awkwardly confided, "I hope you understand I got to wire the county coroner about you shooting Walters, whether I'd care to or not?"

Longarm dryly replied, "Aw, hell, you mean I don't get to just gun a man, kiss a gal, and be on my merry way like Wild Bill in one of those Ned Buntline magazines? Where are they likely to hold the damn inquest, up in Lovelock or down to Fallon?"

The lawman who lived there said, "Fallon is the current county seat, and the Paiute Agency's there as well. But you won't be summoned down to Fallon as long as you don't make a *habit* of shooting folk here in Cairo. Doc Greenberg, our druggist here in Cairo, acts as a deputy coroner on such local occasions as arise. Doc's all right and it's an open and shut justifiable with me and Mike Rogers witnessing it through a front window whether the saloon help's willing to say they saw shit or not. Don't it beat all how Mahoney behind the bar can move with that game leg when he smells trouble in the air?"

Longarm smiled thinly and said, "Old barkeeps get to where they can move pretty good. That's how they get to be old barkeeps."

Gandy led the way into his livery stable and struck a match as he said, "Tack room's over to our left. I've noticed how wild a saloon fight can get. There's something about the mixture of strong spirits and gunpowder as can take years off a man's life. Which saloon fight would you call the wildest, betwixt say the General Massacre of '77 held in Tuttle's Saloon at Newton or that more recent showdown in the Dodge City Longbranch betwixt Levi Richardson and Cockeyed Frank?"

Longarm smiled thinly and said, "The Tuttle Saloon fight, hands down and until such time as they wind up with nine men dead on the floor as the smoke clears away. That more widely reported shootout in the Longbranch only resulted in one dead body despite all the gunsmoke occasioned by eleven shots at point-blank range. Richardson just emptied his wheel in most every direction, trying to fan his sixgun the way they keep saying you can in those Ned Buntline yarns. Cockeyed Frank Loving got off to a slower start but kept aiming at the fanning Richardson until he'd set his victim's shirt on fire and left him smoldering, dead, under a pool table. But wild as their gunplay must have seemed to others in a crowded saloon on a Saturday night, the earlier gunplay in Newton has the one in Dodge beat by a mile, or at least eight fatalities."

Gandy Burgess lit a wall candle by the tack room door and they went inside to investigate the late Jed Walters' center-fire dally, draped over a saddle rack. There wasn't much to investigate. Walters hadn't lashed a bedroll across the saddlebags. As Burgess hauled the Henry rifle from its boot, Longarm found a bar of soap and a change of socks in one saddlebag, along with a livery stable receipt lest anyone accuse a man traveling under his own name of stealing that blue roan out back.

Longarm moved closer to the candlelight to make sure before he decided, "This says he hired that mount up in Lovelock this morning and that sure cuts the baloney *thin*."

The local lawman replied, "Well, he could have made it down here from Lovelock by this afternoon, pushing his mount cavalry style."

Longarm handed the receipt over with a dubious frown, saying, "He wasn't mounted on a cavalry horse. He was riding a livery nag in hot dry country. Saying he could have made more than thirty miles in the time that nine a.m. checkout leaves him, how do you account for a stranger to these parts learning so much about your town in such time as he'd have had before he fired on us from your water tower, scooted under that culvert, and scaled a retaining wall you can't see from out along Front Street?"

"Are you suggesting that little boy blue the railroad dispatcher spotted might not have been the little boy blue you just now shot?"

Longarm nodded soberly and said, "That works better

than a stranger in a strange land moving around slicker and sooner than he'd have any right to. Like that old Henry rifle you're holding, blue denim tends to sell cheap and plentiful. I often wear it myself, traveling far and dusty in warm weather, and I noticed right off, back at the saloon, how the stranger at the bar was too chunky to describe as slender."

The older lawman sighed, "Aw, turds in the milk bucket, this is all too complexicated by half, even if we had the least notion where Frank, Jesse, or your belly dancer might be currently residing in Cairo Township!"

Longarm hefted his own saddle and said, "Ain't after Frank or Jesse. Ain't even out to arrest that belly dancer if she wants to tell me where I might find Happy Jack Henderson or the money he robbed. Meanwhile I'd as soon tote this load and be shed of it for now."

There being no objection they parted friendly and Longarm toted his McClellan along the shadowy walk to the nearby hotel. Everything seemed nearby in Cairo.

An old geezer Longarm didn't know was dozing at the key desk in the lobby. Like most experienced travelers, Longarm hung on to his hotel keys until it came time to check out. So he had no call to wake the night clerk, and that was why they seldom minded when a paid-up guest hung on to his keys.

He let himself into his corner room, draped the loaded-up saddle over the rails of his hired bedstead, and slid his Winchester back in its saddle boot before he turned to go back down and send that night wire to his home office in Denver.

Before he could reach the hall door someone was tapping gentle as a raven on it. So he drew his .44-40 and opened it, hoping it might be Wapzewipe so's he could ask her how she'd vanished into thin air.

It wasn't the little dark Paiute gal. A taller white vision of pure delight was standing there in a sky-blue riding habit that matched her wide set eyes, with her fresh-pulled taffy hair pinned up atop her fine-boned head as she gazed up at him imploringly.

With some effort Longarm managed not to stammer as he ticked his hat brim to her and assured her he was at her service.

To which she demurely replied in a contralto voice, "Thank the Lord! I've been waiting for you down the hall for hours and I feared we were done-for before they told me you were in town!"

# Chapter 8

His uninvited but hardly unwelcome guest introduced herself as a Theresa Bishop of the B Bar B and confided that her friends called her Tex. He said he'd noticed her Gulf Coast accent and invited her in.

She said, "We'd better talk in my room. Miss Mabel, the owner, has been known to wander her halls and then gossip about unwed women sharing rooms with gentlemen guests."

So Longarm holstered his sixgun and allowed he'd be proud to go to her own room with her, if that was what she had a mind for.

As he followed her along the dimly lit second story hallway he knew she was greening him, even as he admired her rear view. For anyone could see that a landlady who'd gossip about a shemale up in a man's room could make it sound as bad or worse if she caught a man in a single occupancy hired by a woman.

So things were looking up as she led him waggle-bottomed into another room at the far corner of the hotel, set up mirror image like his own. But a man who kissed a maiden in distress was well advised to find out how many dragons she wanted slain before he obligated his fool self to slaying any. So he doffed his hat but kept his hands to himself as she sort of leaned against him to shut her own door behind him.

That scented candle aglow on her bed table in place of the lamp the hotel supplied could be read romantical as well. But she seemed clean-cut for a hooker and he'd seldom had one of them ask him to save her from a dragon before she got around to asking for money.

Tex Bishop sat on the bed covers and patted a space beside her blue skirted bottom as she elaborated, "I've been to Chief Constable Burgess about it. He agrees with Buddy and Dutch that I'm putting two and two together to get a dozen."

Longarm remained prudently on his feet as he soberly asked, "Buddy? Dutch?"

She explained, "Buddy, or Luke Bishop would be my kid brother. I hung the nickname on him when were were kids and it stuck when he grew up sort of baby-faced and, well, sort of boyish. Dutch Krinker is our foreman. The name I write on his paycheck is Peter Krinker. He's older than Buddy and me and tends to act as if he were a Dutch uncle now and again. We sort of inherited Dutch from our late mama. We lost our dad to the The Cause at the Battle of Chattanooga. General Hood lost a heap of Texas riders at Chattanooga and Mama couldn't abide the Damn Yankee Reconstruction. So here we are out Nevada way with contract to sell Indian beef to the same Damn Yankee B.I.A.!"

Longarm gently but firmly pointed out, "The War Betwixt the States has been over a spell and you surely don't expect a man who rides for the present government to get you out of an Indian beef deal?"

She shook her blond head to exclaim, "Lord, no, we'd starve trying to ship sage-fed longhorn beef to the eastern market and, to give the devil his due, the B.I.A. pays a fair price to feed Paiutes. Our homespead in a well-watered fold of the hills west of Cairo is unlikely to come under attack. Mama had our main house and outbuildings built of thick freestone with stabilized earth mortar when we first came out here after the war. Mama had lost her first husband to Comanche back before she met up with our dad. After that, aside from Dutch himself, we have four ranch hands backing his play if they come in on us to get at Buddy, and Dutch alone, is a man to be reckoned with!"

Longarm knew stabilized earth was plain country mud instead of sand and pebbles mixed with Portland cement. He could picture stone walls mortared with the waterproof but softer mortar soaking up bullets if it had to, and five men and a boy ought to be able to hold a small army at bay. So something didn't add up and he told her so, saying, "I seem to be missing something, Miss Tex. First you say you need me to save you from somebody and then you say you live in a private fort with a tough ramrod and four grown men to back his play? Who were you expecting to ride out to your B Bar B, Victorio? I know they say he's off the reservation with four hundred bronco Apache this summer, but the last I heard of them they were raiding along the border, way off to the east of Apache Pass!"

She sort of sobbed, "You sound like all the others and I was hoping you'd be less ready to leap at conclusions! Chief Constable Burgess *told me* they're holding one hired gun down the way in his lockup and I was in town this evening when you gunned that other professional in the Fremont Saloon! Can't you see that makes *two* hired guns the witch has sent for?"

Longarm quietly replied, "Might be three, if the one pegging shots from the water tower, earlier, wasn't a local boy with his own ax to grind. Why don't you tell me who this witch you suspect of sending for hired guns might be?"

She replied without hesitation, "I don't know her real name. She said they called her Calico in her Virginia City days and that was what my poor simple Buddy called her until I made him see the light."

Longarm said, "I'm commencing to see some, too. Are you saying your kid brother is involved with a . . . lady you don't approve of?"

The gal called Tex nodded primly and replied, "*Lady* is not the word I would use to describe Calico O'Connor. She bragged right out that she was known thoughout the mining country as an honest faro dealer and she was far too old for Buddy, even had she worn less war paint! The crazy Gypsy witch must be at least thirty!"

Longarm managed not to smile, it wasn't easy, as he soberly assured her, "That does sound sort of ancient. Did this adventurous wandering gal brag on any *dancing* she might have indulged in along the way and how come you say she's a Gypsy if her last name is O'Connor?"

Tex Bishop wrinkled her pert nose and said, "She told Buddy she was from the clan of O'Connor Don and would have been a queen if Strongbow hadn't stolen the Hill of Tara or some such nonsense. Buddy was more impressed than me when he told us about her out to the B Bar B. She told him herself she was some sort of Irish Gypsy."

Longarm nodded in sudden understanding and said, "Some Irish folk I know tell me the folk of whom you speak ain't Gypsies to the real Gypsies or *Rom*. Some call 'em Irish Tinkers, or The Travelers. They have no written history because few of 'em can read or write. But it seems they took to wandering like homeless Gypsies in the same sort of carts way back when they got evicted by new landlords crowding in from other parts. What might this crone who describes herself as a Gypsy look like? Could she pass herself off as an A-Rab or Turk? I have a reason for asking."

The blonde on the bed shrugged and decided, "I reckon. She's black-eyed and black-headed. It's hard to judge her natural complexion under all that war paint she smears on. She smokes in public, too!"

Longarm asked, "Why do you reckon she's sent away for hired guns and just where might she be found this evening?"

Tex Bishop wrinkled her pert nose and declared, "If I knew where she was holed up around here I'd track her down myself and snatch her bald headed! I suspect Buddy must have told her how I used to be able to whup him with my fists when we were little. She was shacked up with Buddy in this very hotel until Miss Mabel threw them out. After that they hired a shack up the slope by the dam until I found out about it. I caught her alone up there this spring, when Buddy and the others were rounding up our herd, and we had a mighty ugly scene. She told me she and Buddy were in love and that he'd promised to marry up with her as soon as he came of age. I offered her a fair choice. She could accept my kind offer of some traveling money and be on her way, or I'd have the law on her for messing with an innocent young boy!"

Longarm cocked a brow and asked, "How old did you say your kid brother was, Miss Tex?"

She replied with indignation, "Seventeen going on twelve. I doubt he knew why boys and girls were different until that painted witch woman robbed him of his innocence. Lord knows what might have become of Buddy if I hadn't stepped in to protect him!"

"You likely saved him from a fate worse than death," Longarm said dryly, adding, "Get to the part about hired guns. Did Calico O'Connor threaten you or your kid brother when you told her to leave him be?"

She said, "Not in so many words. As a matter of fact she laughed at me, dirty, and implied I had unnatural feelings for a growing boy. That's what she called Buddy, a growing boy. Then, after she took my money, she stared at me Apache-mean and told me to enjoy my handsome baby brother while I still had him."

Longarm nodded thoughtfully and said, "Some knock-around gals can take it hard when us decent folk run them out of town. But did she threaten you or your kid brother direct? Or might she have meant it gets tougher to boss a growing boy about after he's grown all the way up?"

She sighed and said, "You sound just like Dutch Krinker and Chief Constable Burgess! They both seemed to think Buddy and that wandering faro dealer would have broken up natural, once he'd had his fill with her or she'd gotten a better offer from some older and flashier tin horn. You men all stick together when it comes to one of your own kind getting fresh with girls!"

"That's the simple truth," Longarm confessed, adding, "I'd like to help. I'd like to have a word with any oriental-looking gals in these parts if they were still in these parts. But seeing you paid her off and ran her off . . ."

Tex Bishop unbuttoned the bodice of her riding habit to reach for something hidden for safekeeping betwixt her firm young breasts as she cut in, "Read this if you think I'm just being a flighty female!"

So he did. The perfumed note, written in purple ink on pale lavender paper, read, "YOUR PRECIOUS BABY BROTHER'S DAYS ARE NUMBERED. YOU'D BETTER BED HIM SOON IF YOU'VE A MIND TO!"

"That's no way to write to a lady," Longarm decided, adding, "May I keep this as evidence, ma'am? That Boston Ferris they're holding just down the way claims he came here to Cairo in reply to a perfumed note in a woman's hand. He hasn't been able to produce it. I'd like to show this to him and see if it's at all possible he was telling the truth!"

She told him to keep the evidence. As he was putting it away in a vest pocket he explained how Ferris had claimed the note *he'd* been sent had made no mention of any Luke or Buddy Bishop. She said she'd never heard of anybody named James or Younger moving into the township lately. She said, "There's an Indian agent named James down to the Paiute Agency betwixt Fallon and

Carson Lake. I don't know why any bounty hunter would care about *him*, though."

Longarm said, "Neither do I. Why don't I run back down to the lockup with this note before it gets too late? If Boston Ferris tells us it's the same handwriting, your worries about your baby brother might make more sense. Albeit somebody sure seems to be beating about the bush with coy notes and conflicting stories! Will you be here when I get back in, say, an hour or so?"

She hesitated, then shook her head and said, "I have to mount up and ride back to our homespread lest I get in after midnight!"

He asked, "What happens after midnight? Does your kid brother turn you back to Cinderella?"

She sighed and said, "That'll be the day. But since Mom died, Dutch Krinker has been acting more and more as if he really was my uncle and it's just as easy to get home at a reasonable hour."

He allowed he understood and left her hired room with the mystery note, not sure he really understood a gal old enough to ride to town unescorted and hire hotel rooms on her own being so worried about a man who *worked* for her.

She'd said she paid Dutch Krinker by check, meaning they had her down as the responsible manager of an established stock spread and her own affairs. But old family retainers did tend to get the Indian sign on family members they'd helped raise. They said Queen Victoria had a Scotch butler who bossed her around like he was man of the house and there'd been mighty spiteful gossip about just how he served Her Majesty late at night after all the other palace help was downstairs.

But Billy Vail hadn't sent him all that way to worry about pushy hired help or even hired guns unless he could tie Jed Walters, Boston Ferris, and the child-molesting Calico O'Connor into Happy Jack Henderson and that belly dancer he'd said he'd be meeting in these parts.

As he headed down the dark stairwell he muttered, "You're looking to see tigers in the roses. Patterns in the wallpaper nobody ever put there on purpose. There's nothing saying Calico O'Connor ever exposed her belly button, in public, and the country is infested with more gunslicks than Happy Jack Henderson. So let's keep it in mind that he's the gunslick, and the *only* gunslick, they sent you after out this way! So let's start by seeing if he can be eliminated from this other shit about spiteful fussing over a young stud."

He got to the foot of the stairs and would have crossed the lobby if his landlady, Mabel Brookside, hadn't been standing there with her hands on her hips. She said, "I want to have a word with you, Deputy Long! In private, if you don't mind!"

That seemed obvious. She wasn't wearing that rust red day-dress at the moment. Her bathrobe of brick red Turkish toweling hung open just enough to let a man see she wasn't a natural redhead under all that henna rinse.

She said, "Come with me!" and so he followed, repressing a grin as he soberly replied, "If that's your pleasure, ma'am!"

She ushered him into a candlelit chamber that smelled of sandalwood incense and bolted the door after them as she turned to ask in a conversational tone, "All right, just what do you do to them, you brute? That Paiute maid may be no better than she ought to be but I had Tex Bishop down as a nice girl and so what's your secret?"

Longarm would have assured the older gal he hadn't even held hands with that prim blonde upstairs. But the henna-rinsed woman of a certain age was suddenly all over him, having shucked her bathrobe like snake skin as she backed him to the bed, pleading, "Never mind *telling* me how you get that swamping love-sausage in them! *Show* me what you can do with it! For it's been so long, and you're hung so fine I've been waiting since you left and I should fire Pop Withers for letting you get past him and into that other gal before I knew you'd come back!"

As she snatched off his hat to scale it across the room Longarm tried not to land across the bed atop her with all his weight as he laughed, "Don't fire the poor old cuss, Miss Mabel. I ain't done anything to any other ladies, recent!"

She growled, "Prove it!" and then her growl turned to a purr as she ran her hand inside his fly to marvel, "Good heavens! Is all this for little old me?"

# Chapter 9

A man who packed a gun for a living had at least two good worries for staying single. There was the worry about leaving a young wife in widows weeds. Then there was the worry about missing out on all the swell surprises a gent with a curious nature and a clear conscience encountered in the line of duty.

He was sure Billy Vail would understand it was his duty to question Mabel Brookside, in depth, as a witness who could make or break the tale Tex Bishop had just told him upstairs, with her thighs a whole lot closer together. But before he questioned the landlady said to have thrown Buddy Bishop and Calico O'Connor out of this very hotel, he thought he ought to try and get on the good side of her first.

She seemed to like him best on her insides, once he'd shucked his own duds and had her moaning that she wasn't used to that position as he got her used to two pillows under her Junoesque rump with one of his elbows hooked under either of her wide-spread knees. It sure beat all how different two gals could look in that position without at least one of 'em being ugly. But the contrast betwixt the bigger and more mature-looking white woman with the little Indian gal he'd had earlier that evening sure in-

71

spired some exploration by his old organ-grinder, and, seeing Wapzewipe had made him come more than once, earlier, he was able to hold back as the hard-up and horny landlady went deliciously stark-staring mad under him. He'd have never lasted until she came if it hadn't been for good old Wapzewipe. For though the perky little Paiute had been grand in bed, her boss lady was more desperate to come and once she had, she sobbed, "Oh, Dear God I'd forgotten how good the real thing feels. Don't stop! Don't ever stop! It's been so long since I've had anything that long in me and I just can't get enough of it!"

Since he'd had enough, earlier, and she was moving her bigger hips as if they were steam powered, Longarm found it possible to just post in the saddle as she did all the work and complimented him again and again on his endurance until she came again. Then he had to take over, and she took that as a compliment and went out of her mind some more.

Once he'd come himself, enjoying it more than he'd expected toward the end of his wind, the older woman sobbed, "Oh, that was wonderful! But whatever must you think of me after the way I fussed at you upstairs earlier?"

Longarm kissed the softness where her throat met her collar bone and gallantly lied, "I'd forgot about that. You woke me from a nap and likely we were both confused. But for the record I wasn't even holding hands with Miss Tex, just now."

She hugged him tighter with her thighs and said, "I'm glad. They do say Theresa Bishop's still a maiden and if she isn't she's mighty discreet. She's never had a man in her room the other times she's stayed here. But having heard your reputation and seen what you had to offer, I had to know for certain. I hope you don't think I'm in the habit of fornicating with our male guests, Deputy Long."

He nuzzled her some more and said, "My friends call

me Custis, you friendly little thing. I wasn't planning on screwing you this evening, either. These things just happen and ain't that fortunate?"

She laughed despite herself and said, "I know you think I'm just as silly as that silly Jo Garland who heads up the Cairo chapter of the Women's Christian Temperance Union and drinks like a fish. But I really try to avoid getting mixed up with men, these days, and there are sound business reasons for running a hotel respectable!"

He shifted his weight to a more comfortable position without taking it out as he assured her he understood about running a respectable hotel and decided, "You figure what's good for the goose is sauce for the gander. So you don't allow no slap and tickle here and try to set an example, right?"

She sighed and began to move her hips under him again as she confided, "There's more to it than that. Now and again I do get to feeling left out and when I do let myself go, as you may have noticed, I try to make up for my respectable widowhood by getting downright sluttish as long as I can rut this dirty *discreetly*."

He began to move in time with her, hoping he was up to the chore, as she explained, "I knew I could get away with this with you, Custis. Another old vaudeville trouper they call Trixie bragged on a weekend with the famous Longarm in Omaha."

He thrust into her thoughtfully and replied, "Never heard of her."

The henna-rinsed Mabel dug her nails in his rump and gushed, "Trixie told me you don't kiss and tell! That's why I felt so jealous when I thought you might be fooling with that sassy maid of mine, and why I had to come down here and strum my own banjo this evening after I'd seen you were hung as nicely as Trixie boasted."

He repeated that he had no idea who they were talking about as he took advantage of the contrast bewixt the Junoesque Mabel he was on top of and that long-bones skinny brunette, Trixie Masters, who'd liked to get on top.

It still took him longer than usual to get over the crest with his henna-rinsed landlady, and he suspected she was starting to show off a mite, too, by the time she came again, or said she had.

Then she broke the spell by asking if he'd really made Trixie come eight times in one night. As if any man could answer any such a fool question. So he answered, truthfully, "I'd much rather gossip about ladies here in Cairo. That mission to Nebraska was another mission entire."

He gently withdrew from her and rolled over to fumble a cheroot from the vest that had somehow wound up on the rug. He lit it from her bedside candle and rolled back to take her in his free arm as he continued, "Gandy Burgess told me about that one Garland sister with a drinking problem. I found Tex Bishop proper enough up in her room. She invited me in to say she was worried about a gal you threw out of your hotel with Buddy Bishop a spell back?"

The stark naked landlady who ran such a respectable hotel made a wry face and replied, "Oh, you mean that Irish Gypsy wench they call Calico. I had to put a stop to such goings on. Buddy Bishop is just a kid, and that gold-digging Jezebel is as old as I am, if you want to compliment her on not looking her age! I told her what I thought of her cradle robbing when I sent her on her way! I understand the poor innocent Bishop boy rented a bungalow for her up the slope and down-wind from the railroad siding."

Longarm nodded thoughtfully and silently offered her a drag on his lit cheroot as he dryly observed, "I can't say how innocent the two of them were acting before his big sister put an end to their May and September romance. It wouldn't matter to me if I could dismiss some hard feelings as a local family matter. But Miss Tex says she got a threat in writing from Calico O'Connor, we have a known hired gun in jail who claims he was invited here by some mystery woman writing him on perfumed paper, and I just this evening shot it out with yet another known gun for hire."

Mabel said, "We heard about your fight in the Fremont. So doesn't that mean *you're* included in Calico's death threats, whether you wanted to be or not?"

He grimaced and grudgingly conceded, "It does if I can establish Calico O'Connor as the one who invited Boston Ferris here to Cairo on perfumed paper. I understand she brags on dealing faro over in Virginia City?"

The lush landlady snuggled against him, sniffed and said, "They tell me Buddy Bishop picked her up down in Fallon this spring when he tagged along to the Indian Agency with the B Bar B beef delivery. There's no saying what she'd been up to down yonder. She didn't work at anything but Buddy Bishop, once she followed him back to Cairo."

Longarm blew a thoughtful smoke ring and replied, "So his sister told me. To tell the truth, if it wasn't for those perfumed letters, I'd be more inclined to picture this over-the-hill drifting gal as what they call an opportunist. That's somebody too lazy to work, an opportunist."

He blew another smoke ring and added, "I'm out here looking for a gal with a rep for bending the rules on short notice. But the one they want me to track down is said to be a belly dancer, not a faro dealer. Miss Tex tells me Calico O'Connor looks sort of oriental. Your turn."

Mabel Brookside thought before she decided. "She looks more as if she could use a bath, to me. I haven't heard of anybody dancing all that exotic west of the Rockies since Lola Montez cashed in her chips in Brooklyn, York State, a few years back. But wasn't *she* supposed to be an Irish Gypsy?"

Longarm started to say the famous spider dancer of the gold fields had been before his time. But, keeping in mind that the lady in bed with him had a few years on him, he only replied, "Born in Ireland, leastways. Her real name was Rosanna Gilbert. But lots of Irish gals have black hair and flashing eyes. So could we stick to Calico O'Connor? No offense, but I just can't see anybody hiding the swag from a recent hold-up with an Oriental dancer who died aback in '61!"

The henna-rinsed Mabel shrugged her bare shoulders and allowed she'd only heard about the spider-dancing Lola from her elders. She repeated her assurance she didn't know of any belly dancers out her way and she'd already told him she'd once toured in Vaudeville.

He said, "Well, it's getting on, but it ain't too late to run over to the lockup and show the death threat sent to Miss Tex to Boston Ferris. Do you reckon you could keep the home fires burning here for say half an hour?"

She hesitated, then softly replied, "Custis, I'm going to say something that may make you hate me."

To which he replied in an understanding tone, "Hate's a strong word betwixt ships that pass in the night, honey. Why not leave it at that-was-nice-and-maybe-I'll-see-you-in-church?"

She sighed and said, "I'd better start at the beginning. I was married, more than once, before I met my last husband, the late Ben Brookside."

Longarm kissed the part in her henna-rinsed hair and told her she didn't have to explain.

She said, "I want to. I doubt anyone but another widow would know what I'm talking about. But I don't want you to remember me as a silly old slut. So I have to try."

He didn't answer as he took another drag on the cheroot.

She said, "When you say you married a drunk you don't really need to tell the rest of the story. When you say you married a gambling man you don't need to tell the rest of the story. When you say your husband beat you, you don't have to explain why you left him."

Longarm asked which bad habit the late Ben Brookside had been most prone to.

His widow sighed and said, "None of them. The last time I married I got it right. Ben was kind and gentle and a good provider. He'd made out modestly well as a prospector and bought this hotel here in Cairo when he felt ready to settle down. I didn't know it when I married up with him, but I suspect Ben knew he'd strained his poor heart chasing color all over the Basin and Range Country until he finally found some. He seemed healthy enough at first and I don't mind saying we had a few years that made up for a lot of tears on my pillow with other men. But then Ben took sick and took his time dying, and so our last few years together were pure hell. He said he was sorry to be such a burden and to the end he was sweet and gentle, but he naturally wasn't up to the efforts of a natural man and I'd taken to strumming my own banjo long before he died—one evening as the sun was setting."

Longarm didn't say anything. He knew what it felt like when they'd buried Roping Sally up Montana way that time. But he doubted she wanted to hear about other women, or the sorrows of other folk at all.

She said, "For a long time after Ben died I didn't want to feel anything but my own skilled fingers down there. I still go months at a time without any need to complicate my life with all the other bullshit that seems to go with screwing other people. Wouldn't it be grand if we could just rub a magic lamp and have a magic lover pop out to screw us blind and then go back in his damned lamp and let us get on with our chores?"

Longarm laughed at the picture and replied, "It surely would. But I've noticed how you have to spend hours feeding and entertaining a pal for every minute you get to bounce in bed with them. I think they call the less exciting parts romance. I won't bring you any flowers, books, or candy when I come back from the lockup and mayhaps Western Union if you don't cotton to such mush."

She snuggled closer and sighed. "I wouldn't mind flowers, books, and candy. But on the very few occasions I've taken lovers since my husband died they've wanted to move in with me and help me manage this hotel and the modest bank account Ben left me. A woman loses the right to manage her own affairs when she weds a lord and master in Nevada!"

He nodded in sudden understanding and said, "Most other states as well. That's one of the things Miss Virgina, Woodhull was harping on when she tried to run for president that time. You're saying you'd as soon spend your golden years in the company of your own familiar fingers than give up your freedom for a few hours worth of the real thing in exchange for keeping house for yet another man?"

She sighed and asked, "To what end? Three out of four human beings are not worth marrying up with and when and if you *do* find the right one they're just going to *die* on you, unless you die on them, first."

He patted her bare shoulder with one hand and got rid of his smoke with the other as he dryly remarked, "They don't put that down in the fairy-tale books we read askids. Do you reckon Prince Charming left Cinderella for a younger gal in time, or just got old and died on her in that castle in the sky?"

As he held her closer she said, "Please don't, Custis. You've left me satisfied and, if the truth be known, a little sore down there. I haven't been getting as much of the real thing as I suspect you must be used to. So I doubt I'll need any for the next few nights!"

He said, "I won't be here more than a few more nights. So we'll say no more about it unless and until you change your mind."

Then he got dressed and got out of there before she could change her mind. Next to that bullshit with flowers, books, and candy, a gal who blew hot and cold betwixt her legs could be tedious as hell.

# Chapter 10

Longarm wasn't surprised to find Boston Ferris not only awake but pacing his patent cell with his fringed buckskin jacket and whipcord pants back on. Nights were restless behind bars, even when things didn't cool off as much after dark.

Longarm treated the hired gun to a cheroot and asked him to take a look at the threatening letter Tex Bishop had received.

Holding it up to the lamplight through the bars, Boston Ferris told Longarm, "Different paper. Same purple ink in the same hand, though. Is this supposed to prove something? I told you I never met the lady as wrote any of this shit!"

Longarm took the evidence back and put it away as he explained to the puzzled prisoner, "A lady I have met says she knows the woman as wrote to her. Do you know Miss Theresa Bishop or her kid brother, Luke, better known as Buddy?"

Ferris sounded sincerely puzzled as he replied, "Nope. Why should I? What have they got to do with me or that belly dancer you keep after me about?"

Longarm said, "Maybe nothing. I'd have no reason to suspect the gal who seems to have written to both you and Miss Bishop knew anything at all about the case I'm on if somebody hadn't pegged a shot at me early on and another gent in your line of work hadn't slapped leather on me just this evening."

Ferris nodded soberly and said, "I've already said all I know about your shootout in the saloon down the way. I only knew Jed Walters by rep. Some said he was pretty good with a gun. Others said he was a trigger-happy asshole. I reckon you just proved their point. But I don't know why he came to Cairo or what could have possessed him to draw on you after they'd just let him out of prison."

"I can answer that," Chief Constable Gandy Burgess said as he came back to join them with a know-it-all expression.

He said, "Doc Greenberg won't be holding a full inquest. The county only wants a pro forma deposition from you, me, and Mike Rogers on the last dumb move by Jed Walters. They know he would have drawn on you and how come. He was wanted, federal, on the recent gunning of an Indian agent. The Indians never paid him to kill their agent. It was the trading post operator the victim had justly accused of double billing and short measure. He made a full confession implicating Jed Walters when they followed up on the charges over in Utah Territory."

Longarm sighed and muttered, "Shit! That means Walters could have thought I'd been sent after him. He called me by name. So he must have known me on sight. I do wish owlhoot riders wouldn't point us out to one another in smoke-filled saloons."

Burgess shrugged and said, "I thought you'd be pleased not having to sit through a formal inquest."

Longarm explained, "That ain't the part that pisses me. What pisses me is that there's no proof anybody inviting hired guns out your way by mail pointed me out in particular! So I'm back where I started as far as Calico O'Connor being that mysterious belly dancer or just a woman scorned with her own ax to grind! I ain't allowed to arrest promiscuous pussy on local charges. *You'd* be the one with jurisdiction if that Calico gal was mean to Miss Tex or her kid brother, right?"

The older lawman grimaced and said, "If there was anything serious to the Bishop girl's charges. She wanted me to arrest Calico just for taking a growing boy home to raise. Then she came to us with a wild tale of death threats in the mail and . . ."

Longarm handed him the note he'd fished out of his vest pocket and said, "You'd better read this. Boston, here, says it's written in the same hand as the note he said he'd gotten about some member of the James-Younger gang hiding out here in Cairo Township."

Burgess held the paper up to the light and scanned the feminine handwriting before he decided, "This ain't friendly at all. But who's to say who sent it? It wasn't signed, by Calico or anybody else."

Longarm said, "Boston, here, says the note to him wasn't signed, either. But whilst any woman in town could have written that note, who but the older gal she ran out of town would have cause to warn Miss Tex Bishop she was in a whole lot of trouble? Who else but the gal who wrote this note would write another in the same hand to Boston, here, and mayhaps the late Jed Walters for all we know?"

Burgess pointed out, "It wasn't Miss Tex that Walters aimed at, first from the water tower and later the same evening in the Freemont!"

Longarm shrugged and said, "He'd just ridden into town. He was on the run from a federal warrant. He spotted a federal deputy here in Cairo and added one and one to get three. I try to avoid that. So I have to keep an open mind about some loose ends I'm still trying to tie together. But who's to say Walters wasn't having shithouse luck this afternoon as he shinnied up the only nearby high point to peg a shot at me and just ran for the nearest hole in the ground with the natural instincts of a rat? It *looked* as if we were dealing with a man who knew his way around Cairo better than a stranger should have. But who's to say that wasn't the way things went?"

"Me," said Boston Ferris from behind his bars, adding with a superior look, "You boys may think you know it all, but I track down wanted men for a living and didn't I just hear Jed Walters was wanted, federal, on a recent warrant?"

Gandy Burgess said, "Of course you did. I just said so. Make your point."

The bounty hunter said, "If Jed Walters knew a federal lawman was in town, he'd taken a potshot at him in town and missed, what in blue blazes was he doing in town, bellied up to the bar in the most likely saloon you'd expect him to be in when you saw him there? I never got to see it. But from what I hear, he was caught by surprise and acted the fool when Longarm, here, walked in on him. So I ask you, does that sound like a man on the run who'd already pegged a shot at Longarm, and run?"

The two lawmen outside his cell exchanged thoughtful looks. Longarm said, "I don't like him, neither. But fair is fair and he just made some sense."

Boston Ferris pressed his luck with, "You know it couldn't have been me. You know I know I'd never get away with gunning anybody here in Cairo, now. So what say you turn me loose and see whether that Calico gal or anybody else contacts me to say what the hell she really wants!"

Burgess murmured, "Longarm?"

The federal lawman shrugged and said, "Local disputes over the virtue of horny young stockmen is a local problem. But I'd sure like to ask your Miss Calico if she ever trifled with the virtue of Happy Jack Henderson or worked as a belly dancer when she wasn't dealing faro or seducing somewhat younger riders. So do you reckon she's here in town to contact anybody about anything?"

The town law shook his head and flatly replied, "Not if she ain't hiding under a bed in some house of ill repute my boys and me don't know about. You have to understand the gal they call Calico is flashy for a town of any size and the folk here in Cairo don't see much flash. Miss Calico is built bodacious and shows more ankle than most under flouncy skirts worn Rainy Suzie. After that she seems to dye her hair with blue ink, she wears almost as much war paint as a Horse Ute, and she jingle-jangles her bangles and beads when she struts her stuff."

From his cell Boston Ferris said, "I'd sure like to jingle-jangle her if she's lured me all this way with a big fib about bounty money! Turn me loose and I'll be proud to bring her in, myself, when and if she approaches me!"

Gandy Burgess motioned silently with his eyes and told Ferris to hold the thought. He waited until he and Longarm were out on the front walk in the dark before he asked, "What do you think? What can we lose by trusting him a tad?"

Longarm said, "Him. He ain't going anywhere as long as he's locked up. With Walters dead that leaves us one loose cannon on the deck or mayhaps none at all to worry about. If our little boy blue from up on the water tower makes another move we'll know there were three of 'em. If you let Boston out and he gives you the slip, we won't know shit for certain. But, like I said, you're the law here in Cairo."

The older lawman nodded and said, "It won't hurt to keep Boston on ice for the full seventy-two. Meanwhile, I'll have my boys turn over some wet rocks to see if that Calico gal could be shacked up here in town with somebody else. She sure ain't been out on the streets or even to an outhouse in broad day since Miss Tex ran her off, weeks ago. Like I said, she stands out in a crowd and Cairo ain't a crowded city."

They shook on it and Longarm went to the Western Union to wire that progress report at night letter rates.

Then, seeing that chili joint had just closed for the night, he ambled over to the Fremont to see if they'd serve him a sandwich with his nightcap.

They could. The place was nigh empty but they were still talking about his earlier visit and he saw they'd spread fresh sawdust on the floor boards they'd mopped with plenty of cold water and vinegar. So he sat at a corner table with his back to the angled walls and a beer in front of him whilst he waited for them to build him a ham on rye in the back. He didn't want to order more than one beer before he turned in, so he lit a cheroot to let the suds set as he waited.

The same barkeep who'd run and hid during his past two visits came over with his ham on rye and some peanuts, allowing the peanuts were on the house and he hoped Longarm understood the shyness of a married man with kids at home to feed.

Longarm assured him he hardly ever asked a barkeep to back his play in a saloon fight and dug into the ham on rye. He hadn't known how hungry he was until then. It went down sudden and he was considering another when a tall drink of water wearing chinked chaps and a brace of Remington .45s came through the batwing doors under a tall white Texas hat to head right for Longarm's table with a thoughtful frown.

He stopped to loom some at point-blank range as he quietly announced, "I'm looking for Miss Theresa Bishop. I undersand she rode into town in search of you, if you'd be Deputy Long from Denver."

Longarm nodded and replied, "Set down and take a load off, whether you'd be Dutch Krinker or one of her other riders. Miss Tex found me at Sheppard's Hotel, earlier this evening. She said she'd be riding home before midnight and, as you can see, it's after midnight. Your turn."

The man, who was as tall but somewhat older and heavier than Longarm, told him, "I would bet Dutch Krinker and Miss Tex never came home this evening. What have you got to say about that?"

To which Longarm could only reply, "Nothing. I haven't seen her since just after sundown. Are you sure you didn't pass her on the range in the dark? What time did you start worrying about her getting home? It's barely after midnight, now. How long might it take you to ride in or out from the B Bar B?"

The ramrod of the B Bar B said, "I'm the one asking the questions, here. We've heard about you and the ladies, Longarm. I warned little Tex about meeting up with you alone!"

Longarm got slowly to his own feet as he quietly replied, "I said we met up earlier at Sheppard's Hotel. We talked about some problems she had for just a few minutes. That was the sum total of our meeting, and I don't like to be called a liar or worse, friend."

Dutch Krinker demanded, "What were the two of you talking about if it was all that innocent?"

Longarm said, "A man who repeats a private conversation with a lady is worse than a liar. When you see your boss lady, feel free to ask her what we talked about and if she wants you to know I'm sure she'll tell you. I will tell you nobody was low rating you, personal, and if she never came home, or avoided you on the trail, she had reasons of her own I don't know beans about. I know you're going to find this hard to believe, Dutch, but I hardly ever lie when the truth is in my favor, and the pure truth of the matter is that I just don't know where Miss Tex went after our short chaste conversation up the way."

Dutch Krinker declared, "I know what she wanted to talk to you about. She showed me that fool note from that sporting gal her kid brother met down Fallon way."

Longarm shrugged and quietly replied, "That's for her to say the next time you talk to her. But I'm commencing to see why a damsel in distress might not turn to a family retainer who calls her a fool."

Dutch Krinker protested, "I never said Miss Tex was a fool. I said Calico O'Connor was a fool for threatening folk in her own hand in black and white or, all right, purple ink. I told Miss Tex to just have the county law on the cradle-robbing vixen. I don't know why she thought she needed a federal lawman, said to have an eye for the gals, instead of old Gandy or, hell, the county sheriff if Gandy wouldn't do anything about the spiteful slut!"

Longarm said, "When you're right you're right. I'm not at liberty to repeat a privileged conversation with a lady. But if you were to ask me what you ought to do about a cradle-robbing gal inclined to write nasty letters, I'd tell you you ought to take the matter up with your local lawmen because screwing young white boys is not a federal offense."

The big ramrod cocked a brow to quietly ask, "What about screwing young white gals, as some say you're inclined to?"

Longarm took a deep breath, let half of it out so his voice would remain level, and quietly replied, "I'm fixing to say this one more time. I have neither done nor said one thing to or about your boss lady that any man with a lick of sense would take as the least bit improper. If that ain't good enough for you, fill your gun hand or, if you'd rather, take off your guns and let's take this discussion to fist city, you tedious cuss!"

Dutch Krinker had doubtless heard about the smell of vinegar in the Fremont that night. For he suddenly looked sort of uncertain and declared, "Hold on. I never said I was looking for a fight with you, Deputy Long!"

Longarm said, "You mean you were looking to see if you could get me to crawfish. So now that we've established that I won't be bullied why don't we see if we can find out whatever happened to Miss Tex? It is after midnight and she did say she aimed to be home before then."

# Chapter 11

Dutch Krinker allowed now that he'd decided not to bluster at a man who wasn't impressed by him, that he knew more about finding stray cattle than independent young women who were likey tired of his avuncular ways. Instead of running around in circles in a town that was bedded down for the night, once they'd established at the hotel that she'd checked out early, as she'd said she aimed to, the more professional manhunter simply led the worried ramrod down to the livery stable to ask the night man on duty whether they still had Miss Bishop's pony.

The night man told them Tex Bishop had rid off on it just before midnight. So Longarm turned to Krinker to say, "There you go. She'd implied you riders out to the B Bar B were worrywarts. Instead of waiting for her to get home around midnight, you headed in well before midnight and missed her in the dark."

"How come?" Dutch demanded, insisting, "I left the B Bar B about the time she'd have been leaving town. How come we never met up on the trail?"

Longarm shrugged and replied, "Maybe she didn't want you to meet up on the trail. Am I safe in assuming there's a lot of open sage flats betwixt here and your homespread in the foothills to the west?"

When Krinker replied there was only the one well-traveled wagon trace, Longarm volunteered, "If she knew she was getting home a tad late, and expected you to be worried, she may aimed to save some fuss by riding wide. It may be to your credit that you worry some about kids you helped raise but, no offense Dutch, you're sort of bossy for hired help. How long have you rid for the Bishops? Miss Tex said you all moved out here after the war. She and her kid brother would have been sort of young then, right?"

Dutch Krinker wistfully replied, "Seems like yesterday, but Buddy was an infant and little Theresa was a bitty tyke in pigtails when Miss Edna, the widow Bishop, allowed she'd had enough of the reconstruction and asked me and the Vargas brothers if we'd help her start over out here where nobody cared which side you'd been on. I know Miss Edna's long gone and her daughter's a woman grown in her own right, for she tells me so, sort of shrill, now and again. But she ain't half as wordly as she likes to think she is and she needs to be looked after, the way I always looked after her mama, Miss Edna."

There was no decent way a gent could ask another just how well he might have looked after the widow Bishop. Old Mabel, back at the hotel, had explained how a widow might treasure her independence and still feel horny as hell now and again. But Dutch didn't strike Longarm as a man who could screw a boss lady discreetly and leave her in charge. Longarm wasn't as annoyed with the naturally bossy cuss, now that Dutch had stopped trying to boss him, but he knew the breed, and men like Dutch Krinker just couldn't feel equal to other men or women. He only felt comfortable at your feet or at your throat. So the widow Bishop had likely found him a great help to her, kept in his place, and if Miss Tex found him a pushy old fuss, she seemed to know how to handle him and he'd likely use those Remingtons on anybody he thought a danger to her. The only trouble was, he didn't seem too bright when it came to looking out for her best interests. She didn't need a bossy old hired hand to protect her virtue. She was looking for somebody to help her out with that spiteful older woman.

As Dutch Krinker led his own pony out of the livery and mounted up to run home and give his young boss lady a lecture on riding alone in the dark, Longarm got to wishing the wayward Calico O'Connor worked better as that mysterious belly dancer.

But by the time he got back up to the Sheppard Hotel, mulling over the pros and cons in his head along the way, he had to admit Calico O'Connor worked better as a cradle-robbing pest, even a dangerous cradle-robbing pest, with eyes on the prize of the B Bar B, than the doxy of a serious owlhoot rider and a receiver of stolen goods. For everyone said the wayward Calico had been run out of town before the robbery over in Elko and why would Happy Jack trust an older woman who shacked up with young boys to guard his swag?

Speculating on Happy Jack not knowing was to suppose a professional criminal trusted women he knew next to nothing about. Everyone Longarm had asked in Cairo had known about Calico's scandalous affair with a teen-aged boy. And after that nobody seemed to think Calico O'Connor had ever been a belly dancer. She was known far and wide as a faro-dealing gal of advanced years and sluttish ways. So she didn't work so good as a belly dancer entrusted with twelve thousand stolen dollars and, son of a bitch, he'd forgotten to ask Tex Bishop how much she'd given Calico O'Connor to go away and leave her baby brother's little tassle alone!

"Forget it!" he sternly told himself, out loud, as he turned into the Sheppard Hotel, nodded to the now-awake but sleepy-eyed night man, and went upstairs to his hired room.

Once there he lit the bed lamp, bolted the door, and got undressed to see what it felt like in that bed all by himself.

He'd had a rougher day than most. But in spite of that, or mayhaps because of it, he was way too wound up to even trim the lamp. So he took his travel orders from a saddlebag to read over the deathbed statement of that young outlaw who'd died in Battle Mountain, pissing and moaning about belly dancers in Cairo.

The transcribed shorthand of a court reporter read about the same as Longarm remembered reading it more than once on the train, as he'd wondered what they'd left out.

Longarm was experienced enough to know how tough it was to take down a deposition word for word, even when the witness making the statement was cold sober and talking slow instead of gutshot and full of opiates. Few if any real folk talked as stenographers were taught to write, with the words spelled out in full and punctuated the way they were supposed to be but seldom were in natural speech.

As he scanned the disjointed but correct grammar credited to the dying outlaw in Battle Mountain, Longarm could picture the lawmen up that way asking a drugged and frightened kid in his final agony to repeat that last remark about Happy Jack Henderson leaving the money for safekeeping with someone the kid agreed each time, in one groan or another, his leader had described as a belly dancer.

After that the late Tim Coleman had described the mystery woman as Henderson's gal, some other pal's gal, or just some old whore Henderson was certain they could trust with their swag. When some lawman in the room had pressed Coleman on that, the dying man had confided that he and his pals had asked Henderson the same question and that the older and harder Henderson had laughed sarcastic and assured them there was no way in hell his belly dancer was going to ride off from Cairo with toad squat. Longarm was as puzzled as those other lawmen by the meaning of that smug assurance. They'd have told him if they'd had a belly dancer or any other shemale prisoner

90

under lock and key in Cairo. So Henderson had likely meant the gal he knew there was tied up in town some other way.

He set the typed pages aside, muttering, "Calico O'Connor wasn't stuck here in Cairo. Buddy Bishop brought her here from a day's ride south and his big sister paid her off and ran her out of town."

Of course, he thoughtfully warned himself, that didn't mean they could be certain Calico hadn't come back. She'd said in her note to Boston Ferris she'd be getting in touch with him once he got into Cairo to lead him to . . . Yeah, that had likely been a big fib, meant to lure the bounty hunter to town. But she'd still had some reason for luring Ferris and likely that other hired gun, Jed Walters, here to Cairo. And Happy Jack Henderson had said he'd be meeting some gal who sounded just as wild in the same dinky jerkwater!

He reached a naked arm out to trim the lamp as he cussed that shorthand stenographer in Battle Mountain for having guessed at meanings their dying prisoner might not have meant. For Calico worked swell until you tripped over that part about her being tied down tight and trustworthy in Cairo Township. A wayward slut who wrote invites to hired guns and likely had at least one of them peg shots at the one federal lawman looking for Happy Jack and his belly dancer made a lot more sense than *two* mad-dog vicious badgirls in a town this size!

Longarm knew he wasn't likely to come up with anything he could be sure of, whether he got a night's sleep or not. So he lay back and shut his eyes, listening to a night bird call his name in the distance, more than once, before he opened his eyes with a frown to ask, "What the hell?"

He'd never heard a night bird call his name so clear. The NaDéné allowed that when a man heard an owl or other night bird calling his name it meant his days were numbered.

For all their reputation as night raiders the NaDéné, as the folk described as Navajo or Apache called themselves, were scared shitless of the dark. An unexpected owl hoot could get them to call off a raid, and they suspected every shifting shadow in the moonlight of being a *chindi* or an evil spirit so awful that none of them could describe it because nobody who ever saw a *chindi* lived to tell about it.

The half-moon was beaming through an east-facing corner window as damned if he didn't hear a high-pitched voice softly calling from out in the moonlight, "Custis! Custis Long! Are you yonder?"

It didn't sound like an owl when you propped yourself up on one elbow. Old Mabel knew he was up here and little Wapzewipe knew enough to knock on his damned door if she was feeling lonesome.

Nobody else in town made any more sense. It was well after midnight but there was a gent at the desk downstairs to ask such questions and it wasn't as if he was Miss Juliet, forbidden to meet Romeo late at night on some balcony.

He tossed the covers aside and swung his bare feet to the rug as he muttered, "Romeo, Romeo, wherefore art thou, you loco son of a bitch?"

He rose to totter over to the damned window and find out who was out there. Then he had a better notion and moved around to draw his Winchester from its saddle boot and poke the barrel inside a pillow case so the pillow, itself, would hang down from the rifle barrel like a sort of fat white flag, or a blur of something in the pale moonlight.

His ruse worked alarmingly well. He'd no sooner positioned the pillow chest-high at the window, keeping his real chest and the rest of him out of line to one side, when another rifle spanged in the night to shatter glass just above where a dumber man's head would have been!

Then another shot took out another pane of the raised sash!

Whipping the Winchester's muzzle to rid it of that pillow, Longarm swung it around to aim it outside, offhand, with one eye peering cautiously around the jam. But he didn't fire his own weapon as he waited for his unseen foe to show him some muzzle flash.

There came none. No responsible adult was about to fire blind potshots out at a sleeping town filled with innocent men, women, and children. So he held his fire and a heap of sleeping men, women, and children seemed to be waking up, from the sounds of all those doors and windows opening as lamps winked on in many a window out yonder.

There came a not-so-gentle rapping on his chamber door and he heard old Mabel Brookside calling his name in a far less owlish tone from out in the hall.

He called back, "Go downstairs and send for the law! I seem to be under fire, here! I'll pay for the glass they just took out of one window. But I want you out of their line of fire before it occurs to them they can fire at will through pine siding, no offense!"

His unusually friendly landlady called back, "What about you? Why don't you get downstairs to safety along with the rest of us?"

He insisted, "I can't shoot back at anybody I can't see! Those first two shots went high. If they fire a third they're as likely to miss and I'll have a muzzle flash to shoot back at. So get going! I ain't got time to lecture on basic infantry tactics!"

He heard her footsteps fading down the hall. That was about the most important thing he heard until old Gandy Burgess was calling out to him from the street down below, "Longarm? What's going on up this way? I got Sam Hart and Mike Rogers down here with me. Who might we be after?"

Longarm called down, "Beats the liver and lights out

of me. Somebody called me to this window and once I got here, let fly with what sounded like a rifle. Hold your horses and I'll be down to join you as soon as I can get my duds and boots back on!"

Suiting actions to his words, Longarm was soon fully dressed and strapping his sixgun on under his frock coat, seeing things had cooled off outside since sundown.

He carried his Winchester downstairs with him as well and met the town law and his two deputies as they were coming into the lobby.

Longarm started to point out that nobody had been firing at him from the lobby of Sheppard's Hotel. But he'd noticed standing by that open window in his birthday suit that his unseen admirer had seemed content with just two shots and it was more comfortable indoors, now.

So Longarm led the way to a corner where the four of them could sit around a dinky round table as he brought the other lawmen up to date, not having a whole lot to tell them as he ran out of guesses.

Gandy Burgess decided, "One thing seems certain. Somebody here in Cairo is afraid that you and you alone might have the key to whatever in blue blazes they're trying to hide! But what might that be?"

Longarm shrugged and pointed out that the minute he knew it would hardly be hidden.

Mabel Brookside came out fully dressed with four cups of coffee and some sponge cake on a German silver platter. She placed it on that bitty lobby table and allowed they only had to holler if they wanted anything else. Then she left them be to go on talking.

As she left, Chief Constable Burgess smiled fondly after her to remark, "That's one fine lady and a credit to Cairo Township. It's a shame she ain't been able to find another man that suits her since her husband passed away. More than one man here in Cairo has been willing to take her under his wing. But Miss Mabel seems to prefer to devote all her time and efforts into running this swell hotel."

To which Longarm soberly replied, "Some widow women are like that."

It hadn't been easy to say that without smiling.

# Chapter 12

After things settled down again Longarm got back into bed before three in the morning alone. It didn't hurt him, but he slept until a train whistle woke him up around nine. He wasn't sure where he wanted to start that morning in any case.

That fat gal, Bonnie, at the beanery, served him eggs over chili with a pouty expression, black coffee, and a slab of custard pie. She tried to hold her tongue, but before he left she asked him who he'd been fighting over at Sheppard's Hotel the night before.

He smiled wearily and replied, "Rifle shots do carry, after midnight. But it was my understanding they don't allow no fighting over women at Sheppard's Hotel. I got the impression the Widow Brookside runs a sort of prim place."

The waitress from Cairo scoffed, "You must be a sound sleeper, then. I hear they make a handsome profit renting the same beds more than once a night. Tex Bishop caught her bitty kid brother in Sheppard's Hotel with an old bawd of thirty or more! They called her Calico and allowed she'd been a dance hall gal until her poor old legs gave out!"

Longarm smiled thinly and mused aloud, "It sure beats

96

all how a jar of olives busted on the walk at one end of the street can turn into a wagonload of watermelons overturning by the time you hear of it down to the other. I was told the hotel management threw Miss Calico out for inviting male guests to her single occupancy and that she'd been a faro dealer, not a dancer, over in Virginia City."

The waitress shrugged her well-padded shoulders and allowed she could have heard wrong.

Longarm ordered another coffee and suggested, "Let's study on that. I ain't as concerned about the morals of a wandering woman described as exotic in appearance as I am her apparent means of support. I've been trying to locate a possible shemale witness described as an oriental style belly dancer. A gal known to dance one way might well be capable of dancing another and you'd only have to belly dance now and again to be recalled as a belly dancer by an old admirer."

Bonnie MacDugal allowed she had no idea what he was talking about.

He said, "That's all right. I know what I'm talking about. Do you know this dealing or dancing Calico O'Connor to howdy, Miss Bonnie?"

The waitress nodded and said, "She and that young boy she was messing with came by for a bite now and again. She didn't seem to think much of me, neither. Her teenaged escort, young Luke Bishop off the B Bar B, ordered for the both of them. She just sat there looking smug, as if *she* was the fat old cat around here!"

"She might have been embarrassed." Longarm pointed out, adding, "She could have thought you were looking down on her as a pathetic older woman who couldn't get grown men to buy her chili for her. They tell me the Bishop kid picked her up down around the Paiute Agency and got her to come to Cairo to be *his* play pretty. I reckon he couldn't get you more grown-up single gals in Cairo to take him serious."

The fat but otherwise not-bad Bonnie laughed scornfully and told him, "You reckoned that right! He's a spoiled rich kid who shows up with flowers, so they say, but he can't be more than sixteen or so, soaking wet, and his parents ought to be more strict with him!"

Longarm said, "Such elders as he has say they've tried. But how do you control a teenager with pocket jingle and his own ponies when he's just found out why ladies and gents are built so different? I heard that after they were evicted from the hotel they shacked up some other place in town for a spell. What did you hear, Miss Bonnie?"

She made a wry face and protested, "I don't keep tabs on dirty old women and naughty children. Somebody did say Calico had been run out of town a few weeks or months ago. All I can say for sure is that she hasn't been by for chili of late. But I have seen the Bishop boy and some younger and darker gal around town. I suspect she's a Mex, or a breed. He hasn't brought her by for any chili. I reckon he's afraid I'd laugh."

Longarm sighed and said, "I worried about folk laughing at me when me and this cruel world were younger. The important part of the small-town scandal, to me and my Uncle Sam, is that Calico O'Connor could have been set up in Cairo with what appeared a permanent address when another gent called Happy Jack rode through on his way to the Mormon Delta to meet up with some others adrift along the owlhoot trail."

The waitress stared goggle-eyed at him to ask, "Do you mean to say you suspect that dirty old woman messed with grown outlaws as well as spoiled rich kids?"

Longarm thoughtfully replied, "A lady getting on in years after a checkered career dealing or dancing might want to keep in touch with all the men willing to remember her. Talking to you this morning has sure been interesting, Miss Bonnie."

To which she demurely replied, "I still get off at midnight, if you'd care to interview me in depth."

So he laughed, left a whole quarter from his change on the counter, and ambled over to the general store, where, as was usual in a town the size of Cairo, they had the local post office set up in the back.

The little old lady who doubled as postmistress when she wasn't way busier running a store, said she'd heard the gossip about that older woman and the Bishop boy, but couldn't offer Longarm a mailing address for their love nest in town. She explained she had neither the staff nor the time to mess with mail deliveries to private residences. She waved at the racks of cubby holes inside the brass cage set up along a rear wall and explained how local folk who got much mail were free to hire their own slots by the month whilst anything else sent "COGP Cairo, Nevada," were just held in the general delivery bin 'til somebody came to the cage and asked if they had any mail.

After that she didn't recall either the Bishop boy or anybody called O'Connor hiring a private pigeon hole or asking about general delivery. She said they did have a pigeon hole for the B Bar B, along with other spreads and homesteads within easy riding. But she said Dutch Krinker or one of the other grown riders from out yonder usually picked up for their boss lady, Miss Tex.

Longarm thanked her and tried Western Union. The consumptive gray-haired gent in charge there didn't recall handling wires to or from the mysterious Calico, either. So what was left?

Out on the walk, lighting a thoughtful cheroot in such shade as there was by late morning, Longarm told himself, "Let's say Happy Jack came through one evening whilst junior was out to the B Bar B doing his homework. Would Calico have told an old flame she was shacked up with a schoolboy after she met up with Happy Jack in more grown-up surroundings? Not if he was just passing through and she felt like a change. A heap of married women take such chances whilst their husbands are at work in town. So then let's say she sent Happy Jack on his way, all screwed and blewed, under the assumption he had a gal in Cairo with a more permanent address than his own?"

He started strolling toward the livery as he pictured a desperado on the run dropping off the train, over yonder, and legging it on to a bungalow for hire where he'd expected to find a candle burning in the window for him? They were talking a time span of weeks, here.

Longarm muttered, half aloud, "He wouldn't have known whether he ought to shit or go blind. But he must have done something smarter or we'd have heard of him and all that money by now."

He got to the livery and as luck would have it, found old Gandy Burgess supervising his hostlers as they tended a bronc with a split hoof out back.

When the livery man-cum-town law asked what he was there for, Longarm said, "Eliminating. To begin with, could you give me the street address of that bungalow here in town the Bishop boy and that Calico gal were using as a love nest?"

Burgess said, "Sure I can. I writ the number down when I gave the the kid hell for carrying on so scandalous. There's lots of them cabins built for railroaders who bought better or moved away, depending on whether they were promoted or fired. I got that exact address in my desk if you'd care to wait till we get this poor pony back together. Damn fool as hired it, yesterday, never noticed they'd throwed a shoe and rid her across the rail yards at a trot!"

Longarm nodded soberly and said, "Some riders are careless with mounts they don't own. That address in town can wait. I need to hire another mount to ride out to the B Bar B. What'll it cost our dear old Uncle Sam?"

The part-time lawman said, "Nothing, in the name of the law. Is it in the name of the law?"

Longarm said, "It is. Boston Ferris wasn't able to produce that letter writ in the same hand as the one Miss Tex got. She's let me hang on to her sample. But she wasn't packing the envelope it came in and your postmistress just now told me she can't recall anyone like Calico posting mail here in Cairo."

The older lawman brightened and pointed out, "If Tex Bishop can show you a post-marked envelope from somewhere else you might be able to locate that Calico gal before she occasions more trouble!"

Longarm nodded but said, "If Miss Tex kept that envelope and if Calico is really the cause of so much trouble. If is a big word."

Gandy said, "I know. If the dog hadn't stopped to shit it might have caught the rabbit, and if you do catch up with Calico she still might not be that belly dancer you're after. What if she just asked some trouble she sent away for to kill you for her, as long as you were both in town? Have you considered a wandering crazy lady you've yet to lay eyes on could have some personal grudge against you as well as Tex Bishop? Didn't I hear something about you cracking a case over in Virginia City a spell back?"

Longarm said, "You did, and Virginia, as they call it, ain't all that far from here. Meanwhile I'll go fetch my saddle whilst you decide on what you want me to ride out to the B Bar B."

Gandy pointed out, "We have plenty of saddles for hire in our tack room."

But Longarm dryly inquired, "With a Winchester I've zeroed in to suit my own eye? The hotel's just a jump and a skip up the street and my ass has gotten used to its personal acquaintance with old General McClellan."

Burgess didn't argue. So Longarm was free to amble on up to his hotel for his own saddle and saddle gun. Upstairs, he saw someone had already repaired the damage to that one window. As he turned to go back down with the McClellan little Wapzewipe popped in, wearing her thin cotton outfit, to ask him if there was anything she could do for him as she hoisted her skimpy skirt sassy.

He laughed and said, "Ain't got the time, albeit I can't say I ain't tempted. How did you escape yesterday? Hand-over-hand along the rain gutter?"

She modestly replied, "I learned to dart for cover like a lizard before I had asked or learned why the Horse Utes hunted us as if we were rabbits. They never seemed to want to eat us or even fuck us. Do you know why Horse Utes have always been so cruel to us, Custis?"

He soberly replied, "Horse Utes are human beings and being cruel to weaker folk comes natural to most human beings. If your folk had been mounted up and armed with trade rifles the Horse Utes might not have pestered you all. They might have invited you to ride along with them to raid some other pedestrians armed with digging sticks."

She tagged along to the head of the stairs but didn't follow him down to the lobby. He saw why when old Mabel calmly smiled at him from behind the desk and asked in a businesslike tone if he was checking out.

He told her he was only going for a ride and meant to be back by that afternoon if anybody asked for him. He couldn't tell whether the news cheered her up or not. The McClellan saddle was commencing to feel heavy by the time he toted it down to the livery in the noonday heat. He paused under the awning in front of the hat shop run by the Garland sisters and peeled off his frock coat to lash it behind the cantle. A pale face was peeking out at him through the crepe paper drapes behind their show window. So he ticked his hat brim to it and moved on, reflecting as he often did when he noticed the weight of a loaded-up McClellan, on its inventor, General George B. Mc-Clellan of the Army of the Potomac, a man who'd have gone down in history as a military genius if they hadn't asked him to command troops during a time of war.

As both a West Point grad and instructor whose active service up to '57 had been as an army engineer and military observer in the old world, General George had introduced some fine notions to the U.S. Army, including an improvement on a Hungarian saddle some now held to be the best cavalry saddle in the world. Possessed of a keen mind and an appetite for sensible nit-picking, Mc-Clellan had been called back to the colors after a hitch as a railroad vice president in '61 and placed in command of the Army of the Potomac, which he had then organized into a fine spit-and-polish outfit with high morale because everyone got fed and paid on time under "Little Mac" McCellan, who couldn't do shit with it, because he knew everything there was to know about military science but how to *fight*!

He'd still invented a swell saddle, though, and Longarm kept one on hand for occasions such as this because it was easier on a horse and covered with brass fittings you could lash all sorts of shit to.

At the livery he found they'd readied a cordovan barb gelding for him with the Spanish bridle it was broken to. So as a Mex hostler saddled it for him, Longarm asked Gandy Burgess for directions to the B Bar B.

The local lawman pointed out a skinny kid in blue denim leading a brown and white paint out front as he replied, "It ain't far or hard to find. But why don't you ride on out with the kid there?"

Longarm nodded and said, "Suits me, if he knows the way. Does he ride for the B Bar B?"

Gandy Burgess replied, "Not exactly. The B Bar B could be said to ride for him. Him and his big sister. That's young Buddy Bishop, the kid brother Miss Tex seems so worried about."

# Chapter 13

Longarm could see why after Gandy got the kid over to introduce them. Longarm had looked older and been way bigger at fourteen. They got off to a swell start when Buddy Bishop asked, "How come you don't have a saddle horn on that saddle? How can you rope cows when you don't have a saddle horn?"

Longarm said, "I can't. So I don't even try. Cavalry troopers don't rope cows much, either, and this here's a cavalry saddle. Could we talk about saddles along the way, Buddy? I aimed to be back here in town by supper time. So we'd best get going, if we're going."

The kid shrugged and turned to mount up. So Longarm nodded at the thinly smiling Gandy Burgess and forked himself aboard the cordovan barb, suggesting Bishop take the lead.

The kid did so but reined in as soon as they were on a westbound crossway to say, "There's room along the wagon trace to ride side by side and I don't know about you, but I'd as soon talk along the trail as stare up the asshole of a shitting pony."

Longarm laughed and fell in beside the young cuss. Like most grazing critters, horses did shit, in bulk, with monotonous regularity, and an awkward social convention of the Victorian era called for properly brought up young ladies to just go on flirting and fluttering as they rode to or from the ball behind a team of almost constantly farting and shitting carriage horses. Longarm was hankering to question the squirt some in any case.

Like most smooth talkers, Longarm didn't press harder than he had to and encouraged a suspect to open up by not asking the important questions until he had the bullshit flowing. But the trouble with Buddy Bishop was that he seemed either hard of hearing, just plain in love with the sound of his own voice, or clever enough to play dumb. Bishop, a man with a lot to hide, who behind the mask of a stupid bullshit artist, was one son of a bitch to question.

But as they rode out of town together toward the Trinities in the middle distance, Longarm began to accept the kid as a self-conscious teenager, small for his age, mayhaps in more ways than one. For he did carry on about having spent the night in town with a wild woman who'd made him take off all his duds. Longarm wasn't ready to press him about the older Calico, yet. So when the squirt let it slip that he'd been playing slap and tickle with the daughter of a railroad Mex who was working way down the line, as that waitress had already said, Longarm said some gals liked it better buck naked and changed the topic to how far the B Bar B might be.

By now they had sagebrush, rabbit bush, and green tumbleweed out to either side. Tumbleweed or Russian thistle didn't turn straw-colored and bound across the range in the wind until it had taken time to grow up and set seeds. During its early spring growth, stock could graze on tumbleweed if there wasn't anything better. Toward the end, before it busted off at the root-crown to start tumbling and sowing its seeds, it got tough and prickled enough to be pesky. One mostly saw the introduced tumbleweed along roadsides, railroad banks, city lots, or, more ominously, on overgrazed range. Neither tumbleweed nor mesquite thrived on sensibly grazed range where the roots of native grasses guarded their thick sod from intrusive weeds. So Longarm was keeping tally on the occasional cow he saw grazing or lazing off to either side as the sun commenced to beat down even hotter. Brands were tough to make out at any distance in shimmering air. So he casually asked his young guide whose beef grazed out yonder and that served to get him off the subject of naked Mex gals.

Buddy expansively explained, "Half of what you might see this close to the tracks could be Diamond H or Circle Slash. But most all the range stock betwixt here and the Trinity divide carries our own B Bar B. This here's open range, so we can't ask tidy neighbors not to graze it betwixt roundups, when we cut and tally the consolidated herd closer to the tracks."

Longarm modestly remarked he knew how you rounded up range cattle in cooperation with the neighbors, spring and fall, but refrained from adding he'd ridden the Goodnight Loving Trail and played poker with the Thompson brothers in the Devil's Addition of Abeline before the A.T.&S.F. laid tracks further south to save the cattle industry a whole lot of herding just as poor old Marshal Tom Smith had that Devil's Addition halfway tamed.

He let the kid who seemed to know it all go on and on about how you raised beef out west. Longarm didn't want to discourage him by topping his brag on the swamping B Bar B herd by mentioning what the seriously real McCoy, Joseph McCoy from Chicago, had called a brag of cows. The real McCoy had shipped three hundred thousand head of Texas longhorns to the meat packers of Chicago in 1870 alone. But when Buddy Bishop said they sold B Bar B beef in three figure lots to the B.I.A. Longarm allowed that sounded like a fair-sized operation for Nevada.

That got the kid wound up about the history of his homespread. So Longarm listened with more interest as he was mostly offered a history of the small Bishop outfit and their thriving herd.

Miss Tex had already told Longarm their dad had been killed in the war. Young Buddy bragged a lot on that, considering he'd been a babe in arms who couldn't possibly remember a young family man who'd fought and died for a lost cause that, for a West Texas cattleman, might have seemed sort of pointless as he breathed his last.

Buddy Bishop recalled their widowed mother proudly and seemed more impressed with their ramrod, Uncle Dutch, than his big sister. Longarm let the kid drone on about how Dutch Krinker had been such a pillar of strength as they'd had to start all over, further west, and how Uncle Dutch had taught both Bishop kids all they knew about working cows and running a spread as a business. Young Buddy said, and Longarm knew he was right, that heaps of folk who came west to homestead or graze went broke before they ever saw any profit. For there was more to raising crops or stock in the wide open spaces than simply getting either to grow. Once you had the fickle weather, grasshoppers, and mean neighbors licked, you still had to get your produce or stock to market. For without somebody to buy what you'd raised you just had an oversized garden or a whole herd of pets!

Longarm listened with a cocked brow as Buddy Bishop went on and on about the slick business methods of a man who hadn't struck a current lawman and former stockman as all that bright. But he had to allow that any foreman who could start from little more than scratch in a well-watered but uninhabited hollow to build up a comfortable homespread and an ever-growing herd of a thousand or more with a handful of Mex help and the modest inheritance of a war widow was a man who'd done something impressive.

Longarm casually asked if the kid recalled how much breeding stock they'd driven out this way from Texas.

Buddy admitted he hadn't known much that was going on at the time, but added, "I know from hearing Mom and Sis talking about it, not long before Mom died of that cancer she'd carried quite a spell. She told Sis to listen to Uncle Dutch when she couldn't be there to tell us what to do, her ownself. She said Peter, as she called him, was way smarter than he might seem and that he'd performed miracles for us all, more than once. Sis didn't think Uncle Dutch was smarter than herself. But Mom warned her that until such time as she could wrangle bank loans with little or no collateral, or keep a herd alive through a hard winter and save the spring calves, she'd best let Uncle Dutch run things as he saw fit."

Longarm chose his words carefully before he tried, "I met old Dutch Krinker back in town last night. He seemed worried about both you and your sister for some reason. I can't recall him saying why."

Buddy Bishop laughed and said, "We heard about your shootout with that hired gun, earlier. Do you reckon there could be anything to my sister's suspicion that this . . . gal we used to know might have set out to do us dirt with hired guns?"

Longarm reached for a smoke as he cautiously replied, "Don't know. Why don't you tell me about her?"

He reined closer to reach out a cheroot to the teenager as he waited. Buddy Bishop held out until they'd both lit up before he said in a sheepish voice, "Her name was Calico and she gave me the first blow job I ever had, down by the Carson Lake. I mean, that gal was old as hell. Thirty at least. But, man, that was the first real woman this child had ever had and, next to Calico, all the earlier slap and tickle I'd had with younger gals was hardly hotter than jerking off!"

"What about your most recent conquest, the railroad man's daughter?" Longarm asked.

The beardless youth smiled smuggly enough to deserve a slapping and confided, "Thanks to old Calico, I know enough now to break a younger gal in right. Did you know most gals would rather have you lick their pussy than suck their tits?"

"I've heard as much," said Longarm, adding, "I hope you're taking no chances with that railroader's young daughter?"

The kid smugly patted the one-piece walnut grip of his double-action Starr .36 five-shooter as he replied, "A man's always taking a chance when he beds a woman of any age. But I reckon I can handle the old Mex if he finds out about us and flies off the handle."

Longarm tried to hide his disgust, which wasn't easy, as he replied, "I reckon he'll know better than to buck an Anglo with a whole outfit to back his play and come after you if you beat him. Your sister, Miss Tex, seems more worried about your earlier adventures with that older gal."

Buddy Bishop sighed and said, "I know. She showed me a poison pen letter Calico wrote her. I don't know what could have got into the poor old slut. I never did nothing to her she didn't suggest to start out with. I never would have come up with half those wild notions on my own. Before I met up with Calico down by the Indian Agency I thought a man had gone all the way as soon as he stuck it in her, face-to-face with his shirt and her bodice in place. I like to blushed myself to death the first time Calico showed me everything she had, by lamplight, and asked to see mine!"

"She seems to have cottoned to you, some," Longarm pointed out, to add, "Some women have been known to get peculiar over a man, once they took it in their head that they'd found what they'd been waiting for, all those years."

The kid snorted, "That's what Sis thinks! I couldn't offer her as much detail about me and old Calico. But I told her it was Calico, not me, who said we were through, just like that, after I'd rid all the way to town with a ferocious hard-on. She said she had to pack and catch a train. So she wouldn't even give me a quick one that afternoon. If anyone was sore about us busting up, it was me. I suspected at the time she had some other cuss lined up for later in the day and didn't want to have to get cleaned up again for him. She was surely clean for a gal who took it every which way. She told me lots of older gals who liked it lots of ways had to keep their privates tidy, between times, lest they wind up with all sorts of itchy crud where the sun never shines."

Longarm allowed he'd heard that, too, as they topped a rise and he spied rooftops of corrugated iron beyond the next one. A grassy slope rose behind the layout to slabs of jagged-ass rimrocks above. Longarm asked if that was the B Bar B they were coming into. The rider who'd grown up there replied, expansively, "It's all ours, a furlong either way we pay taxes on, with the open range ours to graze all around because we have the only water for over three miles in any direction."

Longarm allowed he was impressed. The Widow Bishop, or more likely her ramrod, Dutch, had sewn up a whole township's worth of grazing by grabbing the water rights for a six-by-six mile expanse of fair to middling range. They had no need for fencing as long as they had water for their cows to come home to. Three miles or an hour's walk either coming or going would keep your average cow closer in than three full miles as long as there was enough grass. As they rode on he saw cows, a heap of cows, but not too many for the sagebrush, cheat, and even some gramma and bunch grass all around. So by the time they rode into the dooryard, where chained hounds bayed and some Mex kids ran out to meet them, Longarm had grudgingly decided he might have misjudged Dutch Krinker as a blustering windbag.

As they reined in out front of the metal-roofed and stone-walled main house, Dutch Krinker was first out of the house, followed by the way smaller and prettier Tex

Bishop and an older Mex woman, who was as likely her housekeeper.

Dutch Krinker nodded at Longarm but scowled like hell at his young guide to roar, "Where in thunder did you spend the night, Buddy? We looked high and low for you before we gave up. But you weren't at the hotel, in any of the saloons, or that bungalow where you used to hang out with that honky-tonk dancer!"

Buddy dismounted, ears burning, and handed his reins to a Mex kid as he protested, "Aw, come on, Uncle Dutch. You used to be a sporting man when you were younger. I was only acting natural."

Dutch Krinker snapped, "I never acted natural with the only child of a section strawboss, you fool kid! Do you expect me and our own boys to fight it out with old Hernan Ramos and two dozen grown men who wrestle steel for a living, just so you can play Don Juan?"

As Longarm dismounted he heard Buddy pout, "Aw, mush, we carry guns if them Greasers start up with us!"

Longarm handed his own reins to the sullenly silent Mexican youth who'd come forward to help. Longarm had met up with assholes who made cracks about niggers while their household help was serving juleps on the veranda, too. It sure was a shame he'd likely have to run Calico O'Connor in before she could make good on her threats against the kid. Longarm was commencing to see how any adult he'd ever met might want to have him taken down a peg.

As he strode around his cordovan toward the front veranda, Dutch Krinker headed him off to softly say, "I'd as soon you didn't mention our conversation in the Fremont Saloon last night."

Longarm calmly replied, "Did we have a conversation in a saloon last night? It seems to have slipped my mind, what with all the other conversations and . . . by the way, where were you just after midnight? I have a good reason for asking."

Dutch Krinker easily replied, "I was out here, of course. I told you in town where I was headed. You can ask Miss Tex. She was here when I rid in. What's this all about, Deputy Long?"

Longarm said, "Just eliminating. Somebody else who didn't cotton to me all that much took a few shots at me in town, late last night."

# Chapter 14

Tex Bishop demanded everyone have sangria and nachos if they found it too hot inside for coffee and cake. She went to fetch the envelope that went with that threatening letter whilst the older housekeeper served the two men and boy.

Once she had, Longarm fished out the folded letter to place it in the envelope as he casually compared the paper and purple ink. The stamped envelope was postmarked from up the line in Lovelock, which was a hard day by horse or a fairly short haul by rail. That explained how come the Cairo postmistress couldn't recall anyone posting it from the back of her general store. When he asked Tex how she might have come by it, Dutch Krinker volunteered, "I likely brung it back from town with the rest of the mail we got that day. I drop by the post office when I'm in town or send one of the hands in at least twice a week. Most of the mail Miss Theresa gets is business mail, so we like to see she gets it. I don't recall that envelope in particular. So I reckon it must have been mixed in with the others."

Before Longarm could answer, Buddy Bishop smiled uncertainly at his big sister to remark, "You told us you feared old Calico was lurking around Cairo after she'd

113

agreed to go someplace else. If she's up in Lovelock she *went* someplace else!"

"Why did she send that letter if she planned on staying away?" his sister demanded.

Dutch Krinker opined, "She must be lovesick loco no matter where she may be! Makes no sense to write threatening letters if you don't mean any harm to anybody!"

Dutch turned to Longarm, who was seated closer to Tex on the horsehair sofa, to ask, "Would you want to warn somebody in advance that you were after them if you were really after them, Lawman?"

Longarm shook his head to answer, "Nope. But as you were just kind enough to point out, I'm a lawman, not a lovesick lunatic. It ain't true that folk threatening suicide or murder never really mean it. Any lawman can tally many such sad outcomes. Folk ranting and raving about killing themselves, somebody else, or both ain't playing with a full deck. If they were thinking straight they wouldn't be raving and ranting. So whether Calico O'Connor or somebody else, feeling upset as all hell, posted this love letter or not, somebody sure set out to shoot somebody, namely me, more than once."

As he put the envelope away Longarm added, "Last night I showed just the unsigned innards of all this to that hired gun, Boston Ferris. He said it seemed to be from the same someone who wrote him an invite to some gunplay in Cairo. The late Jed Walters can't tell us what brought him and his gun for hire to Cairo. But something did and after he was dead, with Boston Ferris locked up for the night, somebody else called me to my window at Sheppard's Hotel and pegged more lead at me."

Young Buddy Bishop looked up from the pitcher of sangria he was refilling his own glass with to say, "Hold on. I'm still missing something, here. I've told you all I couldn't see poor old Calico hurting anybody, with a gun, and if she's after me, or anyone else out here, how come she'd want *you* shot, Longarm? Have you ever laid eyes on old Calico?"

Longarm quietly replied, "Not yet," as the avuncular Dutch Krinker murmured, "Out of the babble of babes. How do you account for at least three serious attempts on your life if somebody is after anyone on the B Bar B?"

Longarm said, "I can't. I mean to ask about that as soon as I catch up with Miss Calico or whoever else might be behind this shell game."

Tex Bishop asked what he meant by a shell game. Gals didn't ride into a cow town after a long trail drive to let off some steam and blow their accumulated wages on drinking, whoring, and gambling. So Longarm explained, "When a slicker don't want his mark to guess which walnut shell he may have hidden a pea under, he moves 'em around all razzle-dazzle and, can he manage it with a shill or more, he distracts the mark's eyes from the shells entire! Stage magicians call this ploy a misdirection. I was told all this by a traveling show magician of the shemale persuasion, one time."

The distractingly pretty Tex arched a brow at him to remark, "I'm sure she remembers you fondly. Do you mean to imply all these wild threats and even sending away for known gunmen could have been planned by someone other than Calico O'Connor just to get at you?"

To which Longarm modestly replied, "The thought does cross one's mind the second or third time someone tries to kill one!"

But Tex said, "You're forgetting something. Nobody could have sent death threats to us or recruiting letters out to those hired guns well ahead of your arrival if you were the intended target!"

"Then why am I the target they keep trying to hit?" asked Longarm as he got to his feet, adding, "I doubt I'm likely to learn why, out here, no offense. So I thank you for this fine sangria, and with your permit I'd better get it on down the road."

Hearing no objection, he turned to Dutch Krinker to ask where they might have gone with his livery nag.

The tall ramrod rose to his own feet to set his glass aside and say, "You'd better let us fix you up with a fresh mount, as hot as it is on the trail right now."

As they strode outside together Longarm pointed out it was less than two hours into town from the B Bar B. But the man who ran the spread insisted, "We do this all the time and old Gandy won't mind. We'll send you back to his livery with a bronc from our remuda and the next time I ride in I'll ride that rested up cordovan barb in one way, and the rested-up bronc we're lending you the other, see?"

Longarm allowed the notion would be easier on both mounts when you studied on it. So they went on around to the stable and a few minutes later Longarm was riding back to town aboard his own saddle on a bay mare with a white blaze and stockings.

He was glad he'd accepted Krinker's offer by the time they got in. He'd been right about it being a fairly short ride and Dutch had been right about how hot it could get out on the sage flats of an afternoon.

The Bishops weren't the only southwesterners who had settled in Nevada since the war. But enough of the earlier Anglo settlers had been from north of Tennessee to keep Nevada and its silver on the Union side. So, like other North Range folk, those of Nevada sneered at the southwest customs of *la siesta* as a lazy Mex notion, and things stayed open during the hotter hours of the day and shut down after sunset, just when any Mex could tell you things were cool enough to open for business again.

But when in Rome you had to ride Roman style. So Longarm rode the lathered cowpony in to find old Gandy Burgess in the tack room of his livery, saddle-soaping some harness in his undershirt as a good excuse for splashing in water at that hour.

There being no call for toting a bay mare as well as a saddle back to the tack room, Longarm explained about

the swap of mounts to the older man as he draped his sun-
baked McClellan over a sawhorse.

When the owner said they did that a heap, Longarm
said, "That blue roan the late Jed Walters rode in on don't
seem to be with us today."

Gandy wiped his sweaty brow with the back of a wet
forearm as he replied, "That's on account we hired it to
another customer, bound for Fallon with no trains headed
that way until late tonight."

Longarm replied, "It's your own beeswax, but didn't
that blue roan belong to a livery in Lovelock, up the *other*
way?"

The town law, acting in his capacity as a livery man,
splashed some more water down the front of him and
cheerfully explained, "That's the truth. You got to use
common sense in the livery trade. When a customer hires
a mount to ride somewhere they're generally out to *ride*
somewhere. So livery nags are a lot like beer bottles, boxcars and such. They carry whatever they're loaded with
to where they get emptied. Then they're used to carry
something somewheres else. That livery up in Lovelock
may or may not ever see that blue roan they hired out
again. But since they took a deposit on it, and I wired
that ten bucks to them before I demanded my own deposit
from the man on his way to Fallon, they don't give a shit.
Sooner or later somebody is sure to leave as good a pony
from *this* livery up in Lovelock. So as long nothing is lost
for keeps—"

"Like empty beer bottles or boxcars." Longarm agreed,
asking if the older lawman had found that street address
where Buddy Bishop had been shacked up with the mysterious Calico O'Connor.

Reverting to his role as the town law, Burgess muttered,
"Shit, I have to put my hat, shirt, and gunbelt on if you
want me to tag along."

As he straighted up from his soapy washtub he added,
"I had some of my boys look things over, earlier this morn-

117

ing. The Swedish family as lives there now were sporting about search warrants. They might not have known about search warrants. I'd have told you right off if my boys had found doodly shit in or about the premises. But if you'd like another look-see . . ."

Longarm asked how long the newcomers had been staying at the abandoned love nest of the Bishop boy and his over-the-hill love goddess. When Burgess worked it out as the better part of a month Longarm said, "Makes no sense to pester them, then. If Calico is really that belly dancer Happy Jack mentioned he *might* have met up with her there on his way through to the Mormon Delta. He *might* have thought she was still there when he told his followers he'd be leaving their swag with a belly dancer in Cairo for safekeeping. But he'd have never left anything with anyone else when and if he got back here, only to discover Calico had been run out of town!"

The local lawman nodded and opined, "We'd have noticed. We asked them Swedes if anyone answering to Happy Jack's wanted fliers had come by, with or without a package. They said he hadn't and ain't we talking about a fair-sized package? How much would twelve thousand silver dollars weigh?"

Longarm grimaced and said, "Around seven hundred and fifty pounds. But according to the postmaster general's office they rode off with a mixture of paper, gold, and silver weighing less than half that. Say roughly three hundred pounds, including the canvas sacks."

Burgess whistled and allowed that was still a heavy load for one horse and rider to carry very far.

Longarm said, "He might have been leading a pack pony. It's even possible he rode down by rail with the money in a big old Saratoga. And he'd have surely moved on, desperate, when he got here one way or another to find her gone. Unless she'd left a forwarding address."

Gandy Burgess brightened and said, "Hot damn, what if they'd been keeping in touch by wire, all the time?"

Longarm grimaced and replied, "I just said that. But it leaves one loose end. Why would Happy Jack tell his pals he was leaving the loot here in Cairo with his belly dancer if they'd been keeping in touch and she'd already told him she'd been run out of Cairo?"

Burgess decided, "We're back to another belly dancing gal at some other address entire. What if Calico never belly danced in her life and wasn't ever the Cairo gal Happy Jack had in mind?"

Longarm sighed and said, "I wish you hadn't just said that. But I fear somebody had to. A lovesick older woman messing with that Bishop boy and writing spiteful letters could be eliminated from my federal mission, easy, if it wasn't for all them rifle rounds whizzing past my head! If Happy Jack left his swag with some other gals entire he'd be long gone and she'd have no call to draw attention to herself with hateful mail and repeated attempts on a federal lawman's life!"

The town law started to say something dumb. Then he nodded and had to allow, "Nobody's pegged one shot at me or my deputies. Nobody has made a serious attempt against Buddy Bishop or anybody else off the B Bar B. I follow your drift. It's almost as if somebody was out to make us look for that dirty old woman from Virginia City instead of somebody such as a *real* belly dancer sitting on all that real motive!"

Longarm nodded and confided, "That works better than an old pro like Happy Jack Henderson entrusting twelve thousand heavy dollars to a cradle-robbing madwoman. Miss Tex tells me she gave her kid brother's elderly sweetheart a little money and a stern warning about having the law on her if she didn't vamoose. It remains to be seen if she really left for Lovelock to post crazy letters from there. I understand the Bishop boy has taken up with another lover since his big sister ran old Calico off?"

The town law didn't seem excited as he nodded and

replied, "Conchita Ramos. Pretty little Mex gal who might have been lonely because most of the other young studs around the township have more sense. Or less pocket jingle. I told Miss Tex she was wasting her time trying to keep that fool kid brother off the primrose path at his age, given the simple arithmetic that her kid brother is twice as rich as well as twice as horny as most boys his age. I've warned the two of them, to no avail. He will sashay around town with that sassy Mex gal as if her dear old dad was dead instead of away from home a lot."

The town law grimaced and added, "Maybe old Ramos don't really care, if the truth be known, as long as the rich kid doesn't rut with his daughter in front of him and everybody else. Thanks to his sharing in the profits of the B Bar B as an equal heir, young Buddy has been able to spoil gals almost as much as he spoils his fool self. I know that gal called Calico was milking him for more than any grown man would thought she was worth. Since his sister got rid of her, Buddy's been spoiling Conchita Ramos rotten with high button shoes and high fashion hats that look comical as all get-out on a gal raised barefoot in a cotton blouse and fandango skirts."

Longarm almost let that pass over him. Then he frowned thoughtfully and asked, "Might you be implying Buddy Bishop might know his way around that hat shop, astraddle that culvert I chased a mysterious figure in blue denim into yesterday?"

Gandy Burgess nodded absently, blinked, and demanded, "Jesus H. Christ, are you saying that might have been young Buddy Bishop up on the water tower with that rifle yesterday?"

Longarm shook his head and explained, "I ain't saying who it was, yet. I'm still working on who it *could* have been and whilst I can eliminate you and a whole heap of other gents, I'd best get cracking if I mean to eliminate a slender figure in blue denim with no alibi as I can see, so far!"

Burgess said, "All right, he was in town yesterday, and all last night, to hear him admit his ownself. But why in God's name would an innocent kid with a lick of sense be out to do you dirty?"

Longarm quietly replied, "He wouldn't, providing he's innocent, or providing he ain't crazy. Somebody has sure been acting crazy as all get-out around here!"

# Chapter 15

Longarm decided to leave his saddle in the livery tack room for the time being. Somebody who didn't seem to like him knew he'd been staying at Sheppard's Hotel. But a well-kept Winchester '73 could be a mortal temptation to a growing stable boy or another customer passing through. So he carried his saddle gun off with him as he headed first to Western Union to see if there were any messages for himself. He'd asked them to wire him care of Western Union instead of the hotel because he'd learned in the past on other missions how a man might need to change his local address all of a sudden.

There was a longer-than-usual message from old Billy Vail, sent day-letter rates, earlier that morning. Like night-letter rates, the telegraph monopoly offered slower and cheaper service at what they called day-or-night-letter rates because they could poke along the wires in their own good time, a dot or a dash now and again, when the lines weren't in use for straight telegrams at a nickel a word.

As Longarm scanned Billy's day letter with his rifle cradled over an elbow he saw why his boss had felt no great urgency. Old Billy said he'd been thinking things over and opined, seeing his man in the field hadn't cut the trails of Happy Jack *or* his belly dancer, it was time to pack it in and head on home where he could make himself more useful around the federal building.

Vail pointed out, and Longarm couldn't dispute it, that no outlaw with a lick of sense would stay in Cairo long enough to matter, if he'd ever headed for Cairo at all. Happy Jack had surely known his own followers had been taken by the law after he'd told them about his belly dancing doxy down the line in Cairo. Whether he'd headed on a horse or by rail he'd have known a telegraph message from Battle Mountain could beat him there by hours. After that, Billy had decided, the suspect Longarm had described as Calico O'Connor didn't work worth a tinker's dam as the belly dancer, active or retired, a grown up crook would trust to guard twelve thousand dollars or, for that matter, his spare socks if he really valued them.

Vail said he'd wired lawmen all around the Great Basin from Tahoe to The Great Salt Lake about both belly dancers and dirty old women called Calico who dealt faro when they weren't taking advantage of young boys. Vail went on to report that there *had* been a lady known as Princess Fatima, nee Kathleen Maguire, billed as an oriental dancer out that way during the Bonanza Days of the Comstock Lode. But she had come down with the consumption, likely from dancing in drafty false-fronts with all that hide exposed, and died in '74 aboard a train on her way home to Chicago. They did have her down as intimate with a road agent known as Slippery Dick Hanks, but he'd been killed by a railroad dick trying to stop the Union Pacific Flier up in the South Pass Country a couple of summers back. The same sources had described old Calico O'Connor, or at least a vagrant barfly called Calico, as just a friendly old drab willing to deal faro for the house for drinking during those times of the month she couldn't expect a man to pay for her more usual services. She had no record as a receiver of stolen goods or for managing hideouts to hole up in along the owlhoot trail. And so why, Billy Vail demanded, had Longarm been wasting his time and the taxpayer's money searching for a cradle-robbing slut Happy Jack would hardly wipe his feet on?

It was a fair question. Setting his rifle aside on the counter and using one of their stub pencils and a yellow telegram pad, Longarm kept it short and simple as he could, explaining how hard somebody there in Cairo seemed to be trying to keep him from asking the gal they called Calico what she might or might not know about all the gunplay in and about Cairo Township. Longarm cheerfully agreed with his boss that Calico O'Connor might not be the belly dancer Happy Jack had told his followers about. Longarm brought his boss up to date on the hate mail postmarked from Lovelock up the line. He agreed it made more sense to assume a discarded drab was at feud with a local cattle spread for personal reasons no federal agent had jurisdiction over. Then he wrote that he meant to sneak up to Lovelock, see if Calico was yonder, and just *ask* her if, and if so why, she'd sent her hired guns after *him* instead of Tex or Buddy Bishop, seeing he'd neither used and abused her ass, nor run it out of town.

Directing the telegraph clerk to wire his message as a night letter, Longarm headed next for the nearby hat shop run by the Garland gals.

As his eyes adjusted to the light indoors, Longarm thought at first he was talking to the severely pretty Fran Garland he'd been introduced to the day before. Then he saw this one stood a tad taller, wore her darker hair less neat, and smelled of sloe gin at conversational range. So he wasn't surprised when she said she was Jo Garland, at the helm of their business whilst her sister, Fran, was off trying to wrangle a business loan.

Longarm explained he was there to ask about Buddy Bishop. Before he could say why, Jo Garland stared at him goggle-eyed to sort of sob, "I was . . . lying down when somebody shot at you and Gandy Burgess from across the way. So I never laid eyes on anybody crossing our backyard with a rifle. But Fran would have told me if it had been Buddy Bishop and she never!"

Longarm kept a poker face and calmy inquired, "What did your sister say the slender cuss in blue denim looked like, Miss Jo?"

The milliner who seemed to drink more and see less shook her head as if to clear it and replied, "She didn't say. She said she didn't want to talk about it."

A more sober and downright chilly voice from behind Longarm softly remarked, "You'd best lie down and sleep that off, Josephine. I fear that you've gotten things turned about in your gin-soaked mind again!"

Longarm turned to nod politely and say, "I was hoping you'd come back, Miss Fran. I didn't hear the bell you have over your door when you came in, just now."

Fran Garland calmly replied, "It only rings when I want it to. I saw from out front you were questioning Josephine, here, and . . . I told you to go lie down, Josephine!"

Jo Garland sobbed, "What have I done? Why is everyone so mean to me?"

Then she left the room. Longarm absently wondered where their bedroom might be in such a dinky frame structure, taken up for the most part with a small enough hat shop.

Turning to face him with her little fists on her hips, Fran Garland said, "All right. Let's have it out. I was not lying to you and Chief Constable Burgess yesterday when I said I dashed out front when I heard all that gunfire. So I did not see anybody, slim, fat, in blue denim, or red underwear out back with a gun or a fire ax. I made the mistake of telling my sister when she finally woke up that you lawmen were searching for a slender figure in blue denim who might have been out back. I warned her to keep an eye out for him. As you must have just noticed, Josephine tends not to listen too carefully."

Longarm was trying for a poker face. She may have

read no expression at all as an expression of doubt. She sighed and demanded, "If I *had* seen anything, and wanted to keep it from the law, do you think I'd confide it to a hopeless drunk?"

Longarm soberly shook his head and said, "I never came to ask either of you whether you were harboring criminals, Ma'am. I wanted to ask about the ladies' hats you ladies deal in. I was told young Buddy Bishop buys such hats from you now and again. Not for himself, but for ladies he admires?"

Fran Garland looked relieved but a mite disgusted as she nodded and replied, "We have no choice. It's not as if we were dealing in hard liquor or French postcards, and Lord knows we need the trade."

She sighed and added, "I do wish his old bags and wicked children wouldn't tell anyone where they got their new hats, though. Neither that spoiled brat nor his working-class drabs have any taste at all, and a barefoot Mexican girl looks so silly in a fashionable straw boater with a veil!"

Longarm smiled at the picture and said, "I understand he bought his Conchita some high buttons later. I was told he'd eaten in public at the chili joint with that older Irish woman they called Calico. Might he have bought a hat or more for *her* whilst they were still, ah—"

"Shacked up is the word you're groping for," said the prim-looking milliner without batting an eye. She nodded and said, "It was quite a small-town scandal while it lasted. I understand his family bought her off. I haven't seen her along Front Street for some time. During their May and September romance he brought her in here more than once. I suspect the uncouth *muc na seantigh* enjoyed being waited upon by her betters!"

Longarm felt no call to ask whether a lady who cussed a social inferior out in the Gaelic might be Irish. Thanks to another lace-curtain Irish lady in Denver, he knew the milliner had referred to her unwelcome customer as a pig

126

from a really old house, or a shanty pig. He didn't see how the Garland gals being Irish might mean much. But filed it away in the back of his mind for now.

Fran Garland couldn't recall Buddy Bishop buying hats for anyone more recent than Conchita Ramos, and when he described Happy Jack to her she allowed she'd recall a hatchet-faced stranger who looked so bitter and mean that his pals all called him Happy Jack. When she told him she hadn't met any strangers in town of late, save for himself, Longarm ticked his hat brim to her and left with his mind in a whirl and his Winchester aimed politely at the ground. You had to be sort of careful about swinging a gun muzzle around in public, even in broad-ass daylight, and the light was getting tricky as the sun once more hid out behind the Trinities by late afternoon.

Longarm was glad the light was getting tricky as he ordered an early supper off Miss Bonnie at the chili joint and consulted a railroad timetable in the gathering gloom.

As the pleasantly fat waitress fed him a ham steak and home fries for a change she asked in a sort of worried tone if he was fixing to catch the evening eastbound combination.

"Not hardly," he lied. "I'm just fixing to see if another lawman I sent for gets off when it rolls in from the West Coast. I would have more baggage with me if I was fixing to catch a train. But as you can plainly see, I left my McClellan and saddlebags over to the livery."

He didn't know whether a waitress who served lots of stand-up suppers might or might not pass such misdirection on. But he sure didn't want her telling anyone in Cairo he was sneaking up to the bigger rail stop at Lovelock under cover of the gathering dusk.

The timetable he'd asked for coming west from Ogden, where you changed from the Union Pacific to the Central Pacific, said he could catch a westbound freight back down from Lovelock later that same evening if he drew a blank in Lovelock. The distance by crow, either way, was around forty miles. Better than a day's usual ride for the U.S. Cavalry, but little more than an hour by rail along the transcontinental tracks of the Central Pacific if you caught a wayfreight as had to clear the main line for the varnish and through-freight now and again.

As he polished off his devil's food cake Bonnie wistfully suggested he and his pal from the West Coast would likely want to talk in private, later that night.

Longarm surprised her by smiling at her sort of sly and replying that he might bring his pal back for a late snack, or mayhaps come by for one of his own, around closing time.

Then he left before she could pin him down to a promise he wasn't sure he wanted to make. A man had to leave his options open when some bastard with a rifle might expect him to spend another night in that same hotel room. On the other hand, he might get lucky up the line in Lovelock. So he moseyed over by the tracks to light up and loiter in the darker shadows of the water tower as a million years went by and then at last he spied the headlamp of a powersome Baldwin 4-6-2 puffing, thirsty, up from the southwest.

Being a combination, with passenger varnish up front and express freight to the rear, the evening train was made for a man out to bum a short ride on the sly. They let him ride in the caboose with the crew instead of up front where most anybody might have spotted him.

He rode the short way smoking on the platform of the caboose as the sky above got seriously dark. The half-moon rose from the east to paint first some sage flats and then some miles of barren salty sinks until, in no time at all, he got off at Lovelock with a wave of thanks to the boss brakeman, just as the town was coming back to life after everyone had gone home for supper.

Lovelock was a jerkwater set deep in the depths of what had once been a mighty inland sea. But Longarm didn't care. He wasn't there to study geology. There was no return address on the envelope Tex Bishop had given him. But seeing it had been postmarked in Lovelock, Longarm carried it to their post office, in this case set up as a regular one in a small frame structure near the tracks, only to find it closed for the night. So he tried his luck at a saloon next door, figuring anybody who picked up mail at the one place was likely to frequent the other, seeing he'd been told she was a barfly.

He'd figured right. It only cost him the price of a needled beer to have the barkeep call across the room to some regulars playing checkers, "Might either of you boys know where that Irish gal they call Calico could be found at this hour?"

A grizzled old gent who really needed a new hat looked up to reply. "Sure I do. Hired cabin on the other side of the tracks, just north of the loading chutes. She's been there two weeks or more, staying with a surly cuss you want to stay away from."

Longarm chose his words carefully before he said, "I ain't playing the nosey parker for no good reason. I'm the law. Federal. So I have just cause to ask directions to Miss Calico and a surly cuss we hoped she might be keeping company with."

The old-timer rose to his feet, saying, "Buy me a drink and I'll be proud to show you the way."

Then he said, "Don't ask me to go in with you, though. That hairpin she's shacked up with looks mean as hell!"

# Chapter 16

Longarm and his Winchester followed the old checker player across the once-more-empty rail yard and along a moonlit cinder path to see a domino row of identical balloon frame cabins up ahead. There were lights in some of the windows. Others stared back at them as dark as the eyes of skulls. The old-timer explained how another old geezer he played checkers with on occasion had bought the cabins cheap from the Central Pacific after the construction crews they'd been built to house had finished building Lovelock and moved on. Longarm asked the old-timer which cabin Calico and her male companion might be shacked up in. The old-timer pointed out a darkened one, near their end, and allowed he had to get back to his checker game. So Longarm pressed on alone, crunching softly as he could in the softer bare soil off the cinder path.

Knowing he'd be expecting the law to come to the front door if he was hiding out from the law in a one-room cabin, Longarm swung wide across the bare alkali bed of the Humboldt Sink to circle the first couple of cabins and approach the one that mattered from what he hoped might be an unexpected direction.

The first cabin he passed was lamplit inside and since

its rear window faced the nothing-much of wide open alkali there were no window shades, and the young gal undressing for bed doubtless thought nobody but the goofy-looking young gent on the bed in his birthday suit was admiring her swell tits.

Longarm was tempted to stay put and see if they trimmed the lamp when she got into bed with that other gent. But he hadn't ridden up that way to play Peeping Tom. So he moved on, ignoring the groans of passion coming from another rear window, blacked out but open to the evening breezes off the alkali flats.

Then he'd made it to the cabin Calico and her unknown companion had hired. That rear window was shut, with nary a gleam of lit tobacco to indicate anyone might still be up, inside.

"Folk sure turn in early, here in Lovelock," Longarm muttered to his rifle barrel as he followed it around a corner of the dark cabin. He quietly pressed an ear to the shiplap siding, to hear nothing at all from inside. It was just after nine p.m. It made sense to go to bed that early with a view to fornication. Honest farm folk turned in that early when they had some cows to milk or rows to hoe in the cold gray dawn. That old-timer hadn't been able to say whether the mean-faced cuss Calico was entertaining had a job he had to go to. Calico was said to work as seldom as possible at anything but pure sluttery. So how come he didn't hear anything at all going on in there?

Trying to sneak in through a window of a blacked-out residence with moonlight behind you was just begging for a bullet in your brainless skull. Knocking on the front door of an owlhoot rider in residence could be almost as suicidal. So Longarm eased around to the door with his rifle held like a pistol in his gun hand whilst he gingerly tried to silently twist the knob with his left.

To his surprise the knob turned freely. The door wasn't locked. But when the latch clicked loud as a chirping cricket near the end of his twist, Longarm kicked the door open to charge inside and crab sideways along the wall, braced for blind shooting as he forced himself to consider innocent bystanders in the scary blackness and risk shouting, "I see you there! Reach for the rafters or I swear I'll shoot!"

There came no answer. The moon was on the far side. But some stray streetlight from the settlement across the tracks sent a feeble shaft of bare visibility across the dusty floorboard as far as an empty bedstead, with nothing covering the bare mattress.

Longarm hunkered in one corner as he thought about that for a spell. It was possible someone in another corner was just waiting like a spider in its web to see if he was dumb enough to strike a light. It was just as likely the loving couple was out getting drunk somewhere else.

As if to underscore that notion, he heard two sets of footsteps along the cinder path out front and braced himself to hear somebody mention that wide open door to his left. Then he heard that same old-timer who'd shown him the way calling, "You in there, Deputy Long?"

Longarm called back, "I am. I just can't say if I'm alone!"

Another voice called, "If you're looking for that Shanty Irish gal and her worthless bum, you are. I throwed them out the day before yesterday. I'm a live-and-let-live cuss. I know how it is to be down on one's luck, but Jesus H. Christ, I can't let tenants stiff me on the rent indefinite!"

Longarm moved out on the cinder path to join the two old checker-playing pals in the moonlight. The one who'd led him there in the first place said, "I told Will, here, when he came in that saloon for a nightcap. When he told me the folk you were looking for were long gone I figured we'd better let you know."

Longarm nodded soberly and said, "That's another drink I owe the both of you. Let's talk about it on the way back. I have another train to catch if that Juliet and her Romeo ain't here in Lovelock!"

The old-timer who hired cabins to the transient trade assured him, "They ain't. They owe me for two weeks rent and I've asked around town for the deadbeat drunks. They might have headed out Californee way. Somebody told me he'd seen them boarding a westbound the same day I ordered them to pay up or get out."

Longarm felt no call to point out that you got to Cairo before you got to the West Coast when you caught a train headed down toward the Truckee. They doubtless knew this, whether it was any of their beeswax or not.

Back at the saloon, he stood both old-timers to bourbon and beer boilermakers as he sounded Calico's recent landlord out about her stay there in Lovelock. He said she'd shown up clean and prosperous enough but appeared to run low on money and soap once that mean-eyed jasper of forty or so had moved in with her. Neither of them could say when or where a sort of Gypsy-looking gal who admired young boys down in Cairo might have picked up an older man to shack up with in Lovelock. The trouble with all the descriptions Longarm had on Happy Jack was that he was a big mean bastard in his late thirties or early forties with no distinguishing features save for a sort of hatchet face worn with a perpetual scowl. The landlord who'd evicted *somebody* allowed the gal described as a possible Irish Gypsy in her thirties with a drinker's nose. Her drinking companion hadn't struck their landlord as all that big. He told Longarm. "Not as big as you, least ways. But he sure stared mean at you when you asked if he ever meant to pay the rent and I reckon you could say his face was more narrow than wide, if that's what you mean by a hatchet face."

Longarm decided to leave that an open question for the time being. The older man who hired out cabins was a tad above average in height. Like most lawmen, Longarm knew a witness tended to describe a suspect as tall or short, depending on how tall or short said witness might be. Hatchet face was a sort of fuzzy term as well, depending a heap on the standards of beauty held by the witness describing a mean-faced outlaw he or she could hardly admire. Longarm had heard the very same gent described as distinguished or senile, depending on who you asked about a somewhat older cuss.

The cross-country varnish his timetable had down for its pause there just after ten showed up on schedule, to jerk water, not to take on local passengers. But the conductor said it was no skin off his nose and allowed Longarm to ride free in the club car as far as Cairo, if he was willing to hit the cinders running. The conductor, being in charge of the train, said he could slow it down on its way through Cairo, but he couldn't authorize an unscheduled stop there. Longarm said he understood and that the rules fit right into his own plans for the evening.

Steam locomotives only had to stop for boiler water when they needed some, and so a passenger varnish only had to jerk water every hundred miles or so, unlike an engine hauling heavy freight and thus having to stop at every dinky watering stop such as Cairo. Longarm was counting on nobody in Cairo paying much attention as a westbound passenger varnish passed on through, late at night.

It worked; the friendly conductor slowed his flier to less than fifteen miles an hour as they approached the dangers of the Cairo siding in the dark, and so when Longarm hit the trackside ballast at a dead run he didn't fall until he'd slowed down a mite, and when he did he landed on one shoulder in soft dirt to fetch up seated in a clump of springy rabbitbush instead of prickly tumbleweed. So as the tail lanterns of the passenger train faded off to the southwest Longarm found his hat, dusted his tweed and sailcloth off with it, and trudged on into town to find that chili joint still open, with Miss Bonnie looking sort of anxious.

When he bellied up to her counter with his Winchester and said he could sure use some coffee and a bite of

134

solid grub, the waitress, who looked as if she'd seldom gone hungry in her time, glanced around as if to make certain nobody else was coming before she leaned across the counter, an inspiring sight, to whisper, "The cook's already cleaning up in back and I can feed you better, free, if you'd care to walk me home in just a few minutes."

So Longarm allowed he'd be proud to and wanted to hug himself for timing things so tight. Not a soul in Cairo knew he'd been up to the bigger Lovelock and back. Only Bonnie, her sweet fat self, was likely to know he wasn't likely to spend another night at Sheppard's Hotel, Lord willing and he was reading Bonnie's smoke signals right.

That was something to study on as she ducked in the back a few moments to come back without her mint-green uniform and white apron to explain the kitchen help got to finish closing up.

As she took his elbow on the side away from his cradled Winchester he asked in a desperately casual tone whether there'd be anyone else at her place to sup with them.

She laughed and snuggled closer in the moonlight to reply, "That would be silly. Why would a girl invite a gentleman caller to join her for a midnight . . . snack, if she had somebody waiting at home for her? Why are you still carrying that rifle, Custis? Were you worried about meeting a stern father with a shotgun?"

Longarm grimaced at the notion and explained, "I had a rifle like this one stolen on me, back when I was a more trusting soul."

She said it was reassuring for a gal who worked late to have an armed escort, and as they strode alongside the C.P.R.R. right-of-way in the moonlight Bonnie explained how she, too, had rented a trackside cabin built a few years back for married-up railroad workers. As if to get it out of the way before he asked, she added she'd been raised on a potato croft in Nova Scotia and married young

135

to get away from such stern surroundings and learn to speak proper English.

He said he'd noticed she's lost any brogue that went with her Mac and she said, "Bite your tongue!" in mock anger. Then he got a lecture on the fine distinctions between Highland Scots and Irish, starting with their different ways of saying Gaelic, with Irish pronouncing it "Gay Lick" and highlanders more like "Gallic." Bonnie said lowlanders didn't have to worry about a lingo they'd never spoken to begin with in spite of the awful things they did to the Queen's English in their northern dialect of the same.

By this time they'd made it to her cabin, and he was just as glad when she switched the topic to midnight snacks. She naturally had no way of heating up her coal-fired stove in less than half an hour. So she kept a pitcher of iced tea, or cool tea, leastways, in her ice box, with cold cuts, cheese and such, to save her from starvation when she got home from working twelve hours serving food. He said a cheese and salami sandwich with anything wet would suit him fine and idly asked how come the place where she worked stayed open so late in a town too small to rate its own bank, courthouse, or public library.

Bonnie got out the makings and built them man-sized sandwiches with thickly sliced rye bread as she explained how many a rider in town off a cowspread worked up an appetite by the time he was ready to ride off across the sage flats after an evening at a card house, the Fremont, or places of lower repute she wasn't supposed to know about.

As she poured sort of tepid iced tea, the well-traveled gal from Nova Scotia mused, half to herself, "I considered taking up that way of life when I beat the crap out of a husband who'd hit me and headed west to fend for myself. Lord knows those painted tarts get to wear the latest Paris hats, and they don't spend a tenth of the time I do working on my *feet* for a lot less money. But I fear I like men too much to take advantage of them that way."

Longarm didn't ask for further explanations as he sat down at her small table against a rear wall to dig in whilst she left her own plate and glass across from him to move off to the less brightly lit side of the one room, closer to the brass bedstead, as she suggested he might be more comfortable if he hung his hat and gunbelt over that rifle he'd leaned against the wall by the door.

So Longarm rose to do so and, in turning, noticed his gracious hostess had already draped her street duds over the foot of the bed and seemed to be shucking her pale pink chemise off over her head, as calmly as if they'd met before.

But if there was one thing Longarm was sure of, as he stared her way thunderghasted, was that he'd never beheld a naked body quite like the one she had on sudden display, glowing pinker than her chemise as she let down her pinned up chestnut hair to demurely confess, "We full-figured girls have a time finding clothes to fit us properly. But I find I don't look that fat to my friends in my birthday garb and, well, you do want to be my friend, don't you, Custis?"

He had to allow he surely did as she stood there bold as brass in just her black lisle stockings and high buttons with her long hair hanging to her waist but not really hiding anything. For whilst Bonnie MacDugal was still downright fat above and below said waist, her waist without a corset couldn't have been thirty inches around, and the hourglass effect was spectacular.

As he stood there trying to decide what he ought to say next, Bonnie demurely suggested, "Why don't you hang everything up, while you're at it, and show me just how friendly you feel about me right now!"

# Chapter 17

A nice thing about big butts was that you didn't need to put a pillow under a gal with an ass like Bonnie's to position her point of entry just right. In her case this seemed a vital consideration. For in spite of her bold approach to making new friends, and in spite of her saying she'd been married up at least once, she was tight betwixt her massive thighs.

But once Longarm had worked his old organ grinder all the way into her hot little velvet trap, he never doubted her brag that she'd beat the crap out of another grown man who'd displeased her. For he hardly had to do any of the work as the doubtless bored and lonely waitress treated him to some hard riding in her love saddle, jumping them over some fences as she moaned and groaned that she was coming, but kept on jumping fences as she tried to bite his cock off with her old ring dang doo whilst he held politely back.

So a swell time was had by all as the two of them illustrated what a kindly old philosopher had once defined as passion, doubtless in French. He'd dryly remarked, or warned, that a really exciting fuck consisted of a woman trying to come with a man who was trying not to.

But while it lasted until they were both slickery with

sweat and he was sliding all over her big firm tits on his own bare chest whilst his forehead dripped in her face, she managed to come at last, and when he let himself go he could feel it all the way down to his curled-under toes, and it hardly seemed he'd ever want to look at a woman again.

But he was too romantic, himself, to just roll off her and leave, even if he'd had another place to hide out for the night. So he just rolled far enough to grope for a cheroot as Bonnie got up, looking even more like a bare-ass hour glass from the rear, to fetch them some more iced tea.

It sure beat all how interesting those big sweat-slicked tits looked on the way back, over a tray of refreshments, now that he was getting his breath back. He held off on lighting up, seeing the evening seemed young, even though it was past midnight.

As the two of them picnicked naked atop the bed covers, Bonnie asked in a desperately casual voice how long he figured to be in Cairo.

He answered, truthfully, "I can't say. They want me to head on back to my home office in Denver as of now. I don't know how long it might take me to tie up just a few loose ends in these parts. On the face of it, the armed robber and his doxy I was sent out here to look for may be long gone. I was sent on no more than the confused deathbed ravings of another crook who might have had things wrong. The ones they sent me after may have never been through town at all. But *somebody* sure has pegged more than one shot at me in these parts, and, call me nosy if you will, I'd like to know why before I call it a day out here."

Bonnie purred, "Let's call it a few more nights. I have to work in the daytime. I don't mind coming home alone, most nights. After being raised strict and waiting hand and foot on the cruel thing who said he wanted to take me away from a life of household chores I've grown fond of living alone as I damned well fancy. The nicest man or woman any of us can hope to meet has ways of their own you have to meet at least half way, and I mind the first time I felt really *free* was one night, a few weeks after I'd left my husband for good reason, when it suddenly occurred to me how swell it felt to be planning on supper and not having to wonder whether I ought to bake beans or fry some pork chops because I was the only one I had to please!"

Longarm washed down the last of his second sandwich with some tepid tea he'd have made different if he was in his own furnished digs in Denver and said, "I was talking, recent, to a widow woman who told me she'd gotten used to living alone, if only it wasn't for going without a little slap and tickle now and again."

Bonnie smiled wistfully and confessed, "I'd sound foolish telling *you* I didn't enjoy getting laid, a lot, but do you think it's fair that a poor girl is supposed to cook and sew and clean up after a man all day just for fifteen minutes of pleasure after sundown, if she's lucky and he doesn't play poker after work a lot?"

Longarm lifted the chimney of her table lamp to light that cheroot before he soothed, "I'm sure we can manage more than fifteen minutes if you'll allow me to get my second wind. But I follow your drift and I admire a lady who sees things much the same as a knockaround gent. I usually tell you sweet young things I ain't ready to settle down because I carry a badge and get shot at a lot, as you may have noticed since I first came to your fair city. But to tell the pure truth, and you must know how good that feels at times like these, I have noticed myself how much you have to reset your sights to suit the aims of others if you want to get along with them."

Bonnie said, "You might not have met up with that hired gun in the Fremont if you'd been home at a respectable hour with a wife and all."

He handed her the lit cheroot as he replied, "I just said

that. I like to shoot pool or mayhaps chase after the sounds of a fire engine after dark as well. But as you just remarked about choosing to have pork or beans, it's the little picky things you have to worry about, or at least keep in mind, in exchange for those few minutes of slap and tickle. I have this . . . friend back in Denver who expects me to escort her to the infernal opera when it's in town, and two hours of Herr Richard Wagner can't begin to compensate a man for a shorter spell of hugging and kissing. I know you're supposed to admire Herr Wagner's High Dutch caterwauling if you were brung up hightoned, but nobody ever sang like that in West-by-God-Virginia, and on top of that, you ladies, no offense, get offended as all get-out if a man forgets your birthday or the anniversary of the first time he got in bed with you. So, yep, riding the trail to nowheres alone has a lot to be said for it, as long as you ain't feeling horny."

Bonnie sat up to remove the tray from the covers between them as she demurely remarked she was starting to feel horny again.

Longarm said, "I aim to please, and you did say the last time that you thirsted for variety. So, seeing we're both speaking so frankly, and seeing these cheroots sell three-for-a-nickel, I know one position allowing me to finish my smoke whilst I attempt to satisfy your own cravings."

She told him he was awful, but laughed like a good sport when Longarm positioned her awesome form on her hands and knees across the mattress, so he could grip the cheroot in his grin, grip a great big cheek in each hand, and part them like the Red Sea to admit his renewed interest and feel it getting harder as he shoved it on over into the Promised Land.

Bonnie lowered her face to the bedding to chew some on the patchwork comforter as she arched her spine to take it even deeper and reached down bewixt her thick thighs to play catch with his bouncing balls. As she did so she crooned, "Oh, promise you'll stay in Cairo at least over the weekend whether you catch that other couple or not!"

He'd suggested dogstyle in part because, as he'd noticed after the opera with that Junoesque society widow in Denver, a man who really enjoyed the company of women could chat with them as well as smoke in that position, feet planted firmly on the rug and body erect to breathe as freely as if he was just walking fast uphill. So he told her how he and their coroner were inclined to suspect that gunplay over in the Fremont had been a possible misunderstanding betwixt an innocent lawman and a hired gun with a guilty conscience.

He said, "Somebody with a spiteful nature may have sent for the late Jed Walters. We're still working on why. Your town law is holding that Boston Ferris you've been feeding from your chili joint on suspicion because he keeps telling us somebody surely sent for him. But he can't or won't show us that invite. He says—he can't prove—he was invited out your way to collect a bounty on a wanted outlaw. He says the invite to him seems to have been extended in the same womanly hand as appears on a death threat to the B Bar B extended from up the line in Lovelock."

Bonnie answered, "Faster, a little more to your right and, ooh, that feels just right, and I heard some of the town deputies talking about that greasy old gold digger young Buddy Bishop brought by our place to be served, more than once."

Her voice got more low as she purred, "I bet they couldn't do it half so fine in this position. He's not a full-grown man, and she's said to have a gash like the Grand Canyon!"

Longarm didn't miss a beat but stared down thoughtfully as he tried to picture her fantasy, asking, "Oh? Am I to understand Miss Calico had been . . . examined by other gents around town?"

Bonnie shrugged her naked shoulders, an inspiring

sight from where he was standing, and said, "I only know what I overheard when cowhands were snickering behind both our backs. But from remarks made about a spoiled rich kid paying through the nose for what could be had for a beer, I got the impression she'd been passed around before that boy took up with her down in Fallon. Some even said she'd been passed around like a peace pipe by prosperous Paiutes off their agency down yonder. I can see why Tex Bishop paid her off to leave her little brother be. The old bawd has no shame at all, and Lord knows who a man might be going seconds to since the last time she ever bathed, if such an event has occurred in recorded history!"

Longarm grimaced, thrusted, and observed, "The more I hear of this mysterious Calico O'Connor the less I feel I'd ever trust her with hot money from a post office robbery! I don't want to go into how I know. But I did find out she was evicted from a cabin much like this one, up in Lovelock, for not paying the rent. You wouldn't care to tell a federal lawman what you pay a week for this place, would you?"

She said, "A little to the left, now. I don't pay by the week. I pay Miss Tex twelve dollars a month, and how did you find out Calico got evicted up in Lovelock? Have you been sending wires all around?"

He said, "I've sent a heap of wires. Aim to send more out California way and all the way east to Cheyenne. Did you just imply Miss Theresa Bishop of the B Bar B was your landlady, here in town?"

The waitress who usually preferred to live alone replied, "Sure I do. The Bishops own half the town as well as the best cattle spread for many a mile. Didn't you know that?"

He said, "I do now. I can see how an older woman with a drinking problem and social climbing aspirations might find Buddy Bishop the boy of her dreams next to a rider of the owlhoot trail who dropped in on her now and again. But after that the whole convolution falls apart, and I just can't get old Calico to fit as either the doxy of an outlaw who just rode off with twelve thousand dollars or just a woman scorned causing other trouble on her own. Would you care to turn over, now, so's we can finish more romantical?"

The astoundingly curvacious Bonnie would and did, to enjoy it feeling more relaxed with her arms and legs wrapped around an old pal whilst a now more familiar love tool tickled her fancy.

Longarm meant it when he kissed her tenderly and shot his wad in her some more. As they lay there limply entwined, with him gasping for his second wind, Bonnie calmly asked, "Why doesn't Calico O'Connor work as the mastermind behind all this recent skulduggery in Cairo?"

Longarm shifted his hips betwixt her thighs to soak it in a more comfortable position as he explained, "To begin with, she was down in Fallon when Buddy Bishop first met up with her, and more recently she'd been shacked up in Lovelock with another older gent. So that makes for tight timing if she met up with the infamous Happy Jack Henderson in the short time she was here in Cairo, shacked up with that rich kid."

Bonnie asked, "Would a woman shacked up with any other man be sending mean letters to the B Bar B?"

Longarm replied, "That part's possible. A gal can go on hating in the company of someone friendlier. But I can't see her newfound love up Lovelock way as a man hiding out with twelve thousand dollars, a good part of it in silver and gold coinage as can't be traced."

Bonnie suggested, "Maybe they were fixing to move on and so they were just too tight to pay their rent. Or maybe they wanted you and everyone else to think they were broke. You've been looking for *rich* crooks, right?"

He kissed her some more and sighed, "See what I mean? You can fit the shoe more ways than once when you ain't sure who you're trying it on in the dark!"

She said she was glad he had no idea how long he'd

be out her way and suggested he let her get on top if he was feeling tired.

So he did and they wound up finishing romantical that time as well before the hard-up waitress allowed she'd had enough for the time being and he got to sleep a few winks.

Then it was morning and he had to service her some more, seeing how she woke him up so friendly with a French lesson. Then she rustled up an uncooked but tasty breakfast and told him to laze about and leave later on, giving her time to set up an alibi neighborhood gossip would have a time shaking.

So he took his own good time washing up and getting dressed after Bonnie left for work in a fresh dress, smelling of soap, water, and violet cologne. Then he put on his Stetson and six-gun, picked up his saddle gun and stepped out in the morning sunlight to lock her door with the key she'd left him, nodding pleasant to the old biddy weeding out front of her own cabin, and pocketing the key to say, "Miss Bonnie said there were rats in her walls."

Then he strode on without saying whether he'd found any or not. He headed into town as they'd agreed to drop her key off where she worked as she served him his morning coffee.

Before he could get there he met up with old Gandy Burgess, looking fit to bust.

"Where have you been?" The town law demanded, "We've been hunting high and low all over town for you!"

"Well, you found me," Longarm replied, adding, "What's up? I didn't hear any more gunplay last night, wherever I was."

Burgess said, "I hope she was pretty. We didn't have any gunplay. I'd have known what to do about gunplay. But we got a pure hot potato this morning and I just don't know what in blue blazes I'm expected to do with it!"

# Chapter 18

Longarm said, "I was fixing to have me a cup of wake-up at the chili joint. Could I buy you a cup while you tell me about it?"

Gandy Burgess couldn't wait until they'd made it to where Bonnie was waiting for her key. He said, "Another letter in that same purple ink came in with the morning mail train. Addressed to Buddy Bishop, personal, this time. I wanted to talk to you about it before I sent a rider out to the B Bar B with it."

By this time they'd made it to the chili joint to belly up to the counter. Bonnie stood behind it smiling as if butter wouldn't melt in her mouth. She said, "Morning, Gandy. Morning, Deputy Long. You look a little peaked this morning. Did you have a rough night?"

Longarm managed not to grin like a shit-eating dog as he soberly replied, "It wasn't so bad, Miss Bonnie. But I could use a cup of joe, strong and black."

Chief Constable Burgess said he'd just have coffee, himself, since he'd et breakfast recent, at home. While the amazingly buxom waitress served them, Gandy took out the sealed envelope addressed to "Master Luke Bishop of the B Bar B in care of Cairo General Delivery, as the local general store could be described.

The town law told Longarm, "You can see it's in the same hand and postmarked Lovelock like that other one Miss Tex showed us. Figuring better than three miles out to the Bishop spread and three miles back I don't see how we'd know what this one says before noon!"

Longarm nodded and suggested, "Why don't you open it, then?"

"Ain't that against the law?" asked the older lawman.

To which Longarm replied, "It is. Who's likely to press charges? Miss Tex *wanted* us to read that last death threat, as I recall."

So Gandy Burgess slit the tinted envelope with his pocket knife and took out yet another note and, this time, a U.S. Treasury silver certificate.

He whistled and marveled, "Great day in the morning if this don't look like a hundred dollar bill! Do you reckon it's real?"

Longarm held the treasury note to up to the light and decided, "It looks real. What does the note included with it say?"

The town law read aloud, "You poor, pathetic sissy boy: You could have chosen to stay friends with me. But you chose to make an enemy of me instead. So be it. I enclose simple proof that your snotty big sister was wrong about my being after no more than money. As you can plainly see, I have plenty of money. So spend this token of my undying hatred on your little Mexican slut or shove it up your ass, for all I care, in the time you have left."

Gandy added, "That's all she wrote. There's no signature. But there ain't no mystery about who sent it, right?"

Longarm said, "Yes there is. Calico O'Connor got run out of Lovelock days ago. Before that she was keeping company with another swain. A grown man in this case. I was given to understand they'd last been seen aboard a westbound train and what's the date on that postmark?"

Burgess turned the envelope over and replied, "So that's where you were last night. This envelope was postmarked yesterday in Lovelock. So what if they told you about another gal entire who just looked like Calico O'Connor?"

Longarm swallowed a thoughtful sip of black coffee before he came back with, "How many gals called Calico and described as sort of Irish Gypsy in appearance might you encounter on an average out this way?"

The town law grimaced and tried, "What if we've all been guessing wrong about the authorship of this hate mail? What if some other gal wrote 'em? Wouldn't that let Buddy Bishop's old drab off the hook?"

Longarm sipped more joe and decided, "It would. I could dismiss her as Happy Jack's belly dancer as well, if I bought her being no more than a dirty old woman with a drinking problem. But after that we're stuck with some *other* woman writing spiteful, assuming it's another woman!"

Burgess brightened and said, "By gum, a man *could* use purple ink in a sissy way if he had a mind to, and a mastermind with some other dirty motive would have known about old Calico and the Bishop boy. But what motive do you reckon the troublemaker might really have?"

Longarm sighed and replied, "I wish you hadn't asked that. Don't you expect a westbound combination stopping here before noon today?"

The local lawman nodded and said, "We do. They'll be dropping the freight cars off in Utah Territory and hooking the varnish up to the eastbound U.P. flier they make up in Ogden. Why do you ask? I hope you ain't aiming to light out on us, *now*!"

Longarm pretended not to notice the stricken look Bonnie threw at him across her counter. He said soothingly, to old Gandy, "Not hardly. But if Boston Ferris was willing to get aboard and get out of Nevada entire that would be another befuddlement eliminated from the board. I know you could hold him till Monday if you wanted to.

But why would you want to? Boston ain't wanted any-wheres and he hasn't been a bit of help to us in that patent cell."

The town law holding Ferris on suspicion looked un-decided as he replied, "We got to turn him loose sooner or later. But what if he tries to pull something sneaky as soon as I let him out?"

Longarm felt no call to answer a question like that.

Old Gandy grinned sheepishly and said, "I follow your drift. Let's go tell him he has a train to catch."

As he turned away Longarm left Bonnie's key in his empty mug along with the change he'd spread out by the saucer. She murmured, "Call again whenever you're ready for some more."

He didn't answer as he hurried to catch up with the older town law. The lockup next to Gandy's livery wasn't far. So they heard the alarm triangle loud and clear as soon as someone proceeded to whack it with a steel poker.

Dog-trotting across Front Street, Gandy Burgess called ahead of them, "We hear you, damn your eyes! Cut that wanging and tell us in plain English what's going on!"

"We got us a killing!" wailed the kid deputy on the front walk of the Gandy's constabulary as Tex Bishop dashed out from the livery next door, sobbing, "Thank God you're both here! It's poor Uncle Peter! Someone shot him in the back, right in front of me, as we were riding into town just now!"

"Dutch Krinker was the one they hit?" marveled Gandy Burgess as the honey blonde ran over to them red-eyed in her half-open bodice and blue riding skirt. Longarm asked where her ramrod was and whether she was certain Dutch was dead.

Tex threw herself against Longarm to sob, "I left him just a mile or less outside of town. His pony bolted and ran on ahead to your own corral; it was that cordovan barb you hired yesterday, Custis."

Longarm said, "We all know horses head for their own

stables after they've run off a bolt. Are you certain Dutch lies dead out yonder?"

She sniffed, "I know you think I'm just a girl, but give me credit for *some* grit! I rolled out of my own saddle and hit the dirt when a rifle spanged from off in the sage and poor Uncle Peter gasped a warning and fell from the far side of his livery mount. As you see, I wasn't wearing a revolver, and like a fool I'd left my own saddle gun way in the middle of the air while I tried to dig my way to China between two clumps of sagebrush. But then I heard the killer riding off, I'm sure I only heard one set of hooves, and so I crawled over to where poor Uncle Peter was breathing his last and there was nothing I could do for him. I held his head in my lap and begged him not to die until I could see by the way he was staring at nothing that he had. I had an awful time catching my own spooked pony and I like to chased it halfway into town before I caught it. So can't we go back out yonder with a wagon for the poor old dear's remains?"

Longarm gently disengaged from her as he gently but firmly told her they'd be scouting for sign as well. She shook her head as if to clear it and said, "That's right! I fear I've been too excited to think that clearly! The killer *should* have left a trail for us to follow and when we catch up with him . . ."

Gandy Burgess gently pointed out, "You'd best let the law deal with him, if it's a him. You got another hateful letter from Lovelock, Miss Tex. Me and Longarm, here, took the liberty of opening it."

She said she didn't mind as Gandy handed it to her, ordering his alarm triangle hand to go inside the livery and tell them they wanted fresh mounts saddled ready to go, along with a team hitched to one of their buckboards.

Gandy explained to the distraught girl that he needed to have a word inside with Boston Ferris before they could light out for the scene of the crime.

She waited on the front walk with Longarm, reading

the note from Lovelock as the town law went inside to turn Boston Ferris loose.

Longarm let her finish it before he said, "That hundred-dollar bill might have been a serious mistake. I'm still working on whether it was meant for you or me."

She looked up at him with a puzzled frown to point out, "This note is addressed to my kid brother. I shant repeat what it suggest he do with the money. But wasn't this treasury note intended to taunt *him*, not you or me?"

Longarm soberly replied, "I'm still working on that. They didn't send me all this way to catch a dirty old woman messing with young stockmen or even backshooting the foreman of a local stock spread, no offense. I was sent to see if I could cut the trail of a gang leader who'd robbed a federal post office of twelve thousand dollars and, like those rifle shots across my bow, that rare and wonderous sample of paper money, *traceable* paper money, seems designed to attract my notice the way a red herring dragged across the train of a fox is designed to throw the foxhounds off the scent."

The red-eyed blonde said, "It was poor Uncle Peter, not you, they just now shot in the back!"

He nodded and pointed out, "The first time they aimed at him, the way you tell it. They might have missed me once by accident. To miss me twice, with as clear a field of fire and me standing still on my feet instead of swaying in the saddle aboard that livery mount—"

"A cordovan barb livery mount you rode out to the B Bar B!" she cut in, adding, "That just now came to me! Uncle Peter was about your height, mounted on a pony you'd been seen riding out of town aboard!"

Longarm thought and conceded, "It's possible the third time was a charm if they thought that was me they were shooting at. Makes as much sense as poor old Dutch being the intended victim."

She nodded but said, "I don't see why anyone would want to shoot at either you or Uncle Peter. Neither of you did any harm to Calico and . . . What was that about you being able to trace this paper money?"

He took the note from her and said, "I'd better hold this evidence. I know it was sent to your kid brother, but it never came out of his pocket or your own, and as soon as I get the chance I mean to send some wires about it."

Gandy Burgess and two kid deputies came out to join them. The older lawman declared, "They're getting Ferris squared away in there. I have warned him to go straight to that cross-country train and get aboard it when it stops for water. Let's all go 'round to the corral and see if they have us set to ride."

As they followed him, Tex Bishop asked, "Who are you expecting to help you with that money meant for my brother?"

Longarm replied, "I thought you read the sender's suggested use for the same. That postmaster in Elko wouldn't have had a bill this size to pay off money orders from other post offices. He'd have only had it in his till if somebody used it to buy a money order sent *from* Elko. So it's my fervent hope a clerk having such a whopper handed to him would have written down and kept a record of its serial number."

"I never thought of that." She nodded, adding, "They do number each and every treasury note, don't they? But what if they don't have that one on record, over in Elko?"

He said, "I'll assume they kept sloppy books, or the money came from somewhere else. It seems *likely* a knockabout gal with a willing nature but no visible means of support would have come by three months' worth of day wages in a shady fashion. But for all I can prove, here and now, her new boyfriend could have robbed another post office or, more likely, a bank. Banks are more likely to have hundred dollar treasury notes on hand than your average post office."

As they rejoined old Gandy by a hitched-up buckboard out back of his livery, they heard a whoop, and young

Buddy Bishop came tearing to join them at a dead run, looking wild-eyed and hysterical.

He yelled, "I just heard, Sis! Is it true that bitch just shot our poor old Uncle Pete in the back?"

Tex nodded. But Longarm warned, "We don't know who shot him yet."

Gandy Burgess chimed in with, "We're headed out to see if we can find out, and where did you say you've been all this time, Buddy?"

The kid looked away and allowed he'd ridden into town the night before and sort of hung about with a pal.

When the town law pointedly asked the name of this friend who'd be able to vouch for that, Tex Bishop leapt to her kid brother's defense, saying, "Don't be so thickheaded, Gandy. We all know who he spent the night with, and haven't we got enough trouble without you roiling up a bunch of Mexicans?"

As the older lawman hesitated, Longarm pointed out, "It wouldn't prove anything one way or the other, and Miss Tex is right about leaving things be when you can't check an alibi one way or the other."

The older lawman demanded, "Why can't I check his alibi with that Ramos gal, seeing she ought to know whether he was with her last night or off somewheres else he don't want us to know about?"

Then he paused, grinned like a kid who'd just wet his pants, and decided, "I follow your drift. She'd hardly say anything to get him in trouble and we sure don't want it a matter of public record that a suspect spent the night with her. Not when her daddy gets back from down around Carson Lake with all them other Mexicans."

# Chapter 19

They rode out most of the way in a bunch. Then Longarm declared he'd take the point and nobody saw fit to argue. They were all range savvy enough to know it was tougher to cut sign after others had rid over the same ground.

It wasn't possible to make sense of the overabundant disturbances along the well-traveled wagon trace, itself. So Longarm didn't try until he spied carrion crows tossing one another in the air up ahead. As he rode in he fired a pistol shot over the feeding crows to break up their party. He didn't aim to hit one. The Paiute said Taiowa the creator had made Crow to tidy, to keep their gathering grounds clean, and they mostly fed on dead jackrabbit and fallen range stock. But he sure wished carrion crows wouldn't start with the eyes as he rode on in to gaze soberly down on what they'd left of Dutch Krinker's face.

Longarm dismounted to rummage Krinker's hat from a nearby clump of green tumbleweed and place it over the dead man's ravaged features. The only thing to be said for the crows getting to a dead man first was that you sure didn't have to feel for any pulse.

Not knowing the livery bay he'd ridden out on all that well, Longarm tethered it to a trailside sagebrush to start from the body, sprawled just off the right-of-way on the south side, and circle out on foot with his Winchester at port and his eyes aimed mostly down. Mostly because he was searching for sign and not every step of the way because a killer with another gun had been out this way right recent.

The dry country further south was covered with caliche, or desert pavement, where nothing was growing. Such dry gray crust recorded a hoof or boot print as if it was brittle, clean-breaking cardboard. But this far north the dry range extending from border to border in the windshadow of the coastal ranges tended to stay dry, but plain old dirt, overgrown with more summer-killed grass the color of a welcome mat than bare soil. So Longarm couldn't tell whether the occasional scuffs and depressions he spotted had been made recent by the killer of Dutch Krinker or since the last rain by any of the B Bar B beef grazing all around.

He circled the scene of the crime completely and spiraled in without much luck to find the others had moved in around the murdered ramrod. Longarm didn't comment when he saw they were wrapping the body in a wagon tarp to load it aboard the buckboard. Their deputy coroner in town was as likely as anyone to notice anything more unusual than that little hole in Henderson's back lining up with the bigger one in the center of his torn-open shirt.

"Find anything?" asked Gandy Burgess as Longarm walked out of the sage to join them on the wagon trace.

"Not even a spent shell," said Longarm in a disgusted tone, adding, "That low chaparral all around is higher than it looks from horseback on this wagon trace. So the killer might have just hunkered down in the same at some distance, let Dutch and Miss Tex, here, ride on by, and just rose high enough to fire and flatten out."

The local law nodded and said, "That ties in with the notion the killer might have thought he was aiming at someone else. If someone in town knew you'd ridden out to the B Bar B on that cordovan barb, and then he spied

Miss Tex riding back from there with a tall man on a cordovan barb—"

"I'll buy that if you'd care to offer me a *motive*," Longarm said.

Two deputies were lifting the bulky body up to the wagon bed as Gandy Burgess stared at it morosely and replied, "What are you talking about? Didn't they try to kill you three times before they got lucky with poor old Dutch, yonder?"

Longarm nodded, but insisted, "Why? That confusion with the late Jed Walters in the Fremont could add up to a gunslick with a recent killing on his conscience meeting a known lawman, unexpected. But try as I may I can't come up with any sensible reason for anyone else in these parts to be after *me*. If we take the notion of a woman scorned sending hate mail and hundred dollar notes to the B Bar B at face value, old Dutch was running it for these Bishop heirs, Miss Tex and Buddy. So Calico O'Connor, if that's who's been tossing serious money around after she couldn't pay her rent, has no blamed reason to be after me, or to even know I was headed out this way!"

Gandy Burgess frowned thoughtfully and decided, "That's true. Such untidy family matters don't come under federal jurisdiction, even when they turn deadly! Are you saying this backshooting out here ain't none of your beeswax, Uncle Sam?"

Longarm hesitated, then said, "I'm making it my beeswax, seeing the killer might have possibly been out to murder a federal rider. I just can't picture the dirty old woman known as Calico as the devious mastermind of all this crap. Sorry, Miss Tex."

The pretty young blonde demurely replied, "Shit is the word I think you were groping for. I knew Calico was crazy when I found out she slept with little boys."

Her kid brother protested, "Aw, sis—"

But his big sister insisted, "If that drunken drab was playing with a full deck I'd agree she'd have no motive to order *anybody* killed. I paid her off handsome after I'd warned her to leave my little brother alone. Gandy just told me on the way out here that you found out she had another man to buy her drinks and tickle her fancy. So anyone with a lick of sense would agree Calico should have been long gone and not bothering anybody by this time."

Gandy said, "She may well be. What if somebody *else*, such as that post office robber Longarm's been after all this time, had just heard about you kids and that dirty old woman and decided to get cute with us all? It ain't as if everyone in Cairo wasn't aware of what had been going on. At the moment the boys around the Fremont are making book on what's liable to happen once old Hernan Ramos finds out about his daughter, Conchita, and Buddy, here. So why couldn't Happy Jack or that mysterious and doubtless retired belly dancer he said he meant to meet in Cairo be behind at least some of this razzle dazzle? Who but an outlaw overloaded with swag might want to flash hundred dollar notes he'd have a tough time cashing anywheres? Anyone can buy purple ink and scented stationery. Any gal who danced with her belly hanging out should be able to manage a womanly hand. I know it sounds wild, but Happy Jack Henderson is supposed to be wild and you have to admit that whoever may be behind all this confusion, it's confusing as all get-out!"

Longarm strode over to his tethered livery nag as he mulled that over. They had the buckboard in motion as he mounted up and fell in behind it with old Gandy and allowed Tex and her kid brother to ride up ahead with their dearly departed Uncle Peter.

When Gandy repeated his convoluted notions about owlhoot riders hiding out with retired belly dancers, Longarm quietly replied, "They say the only belly dancing gal anyone recalls from out this way was named Kathleen Maguire. Last seen sick and dying whilst headed home by rail. Can you recall any Irish ladies built like a dancer getting off the train in Cairo, feeling poorly, to mayhaps up and die on you all?"

The law for Cairo Township shook his head and replied, "Ain't had any Irish folk of any description moving in recent, save for that Calico young Buddy drug up from Fallon, and I thought we were trying to *eliminate* her as a likely suspect."

Longarm said, "I reckon I have. She'd have no call to be after me if she had gone *loco en la cabeza* over a spoiled rich kid. How rich might Buddy Bishop be, by the way? I've been told the Bishops own a heap of shit besides their B Bar B."

The old-timer, who'd been there from the beginning, nodded cheerfully to confide, "Just about everything the railroad don't. Widow Bishop did well for a refugee from the Texas Reconstruction. She came out here with little more than two small kids, a handful of hired help, and the stock they were riding. Poor old Dutch, lying up ahead in that wagon bed, deserves a heap of the credit, one suspects. You always suspect some community loops and running irons when an outfit starts modest and fills out almost overnight. But they never proved Uncle John Chisholm over to New Mexico Territory really ran his Long Rail brand on other folk's cows when *he* came west from Texas after the war."

Longarm stared thoughtfully ahead at the tarp-wrapped cadaver of such a helpful family retainer as he quietly asked, "How do you feel about old grudges left over from before young Buddy got to sowing wild oats more recently?"

The local lawman pursed his lips and decided, "That ain't too likely. Any corners the Widow Bishop and her riders cut years ago when they first settled in out our way have long since been rounded over. It was Dutch Krinker, hisself, who wrangled them that beef contract with the B.I.A., and, once they had steady money coming in, invested in a heap of property in town the railroad had up for sale. The Widow Bishop, herself, died slow and dirty after a long siege with cancer and no feuds with anyone that I recall. Since Miss Tex has been the head of the family, she's built a rep as an honest young stockwoman and a decent landlady to her tenants in town. I know for a fact she'd been willing to carry tenants down on their luck and she's loaned out extra cash to merchants along Front Street having a tough time."

Longarm said, "I was wondering where a milliner went to arrange a business loan in a town too small to have its own bank. How do you feel about someone owing more they can repay stirring up trouble to distract a lender, some?"

Gandy Burgess shrugged and replied, "Might work for a time. But when Miss Tex loans money she does ask for a written I.O.U., and so even if you had her or her kid brother killed, her lawyers down in Fallon would surely demand the repayment to her estate. I think I heard they had some distant kin on their dead daddy's side, back in Texas."

Longarm decided he was grasping at straws and warned himself to hunt for sign closer in. Long-lost relatives back in Texas would have less reason to gun a federal lawman just passing by a family matter than a discarded and bought-off love toy.

Longarm let his brain chase its tail in circles until they got into town, where the odors of coal smoke and steam still hung in the noonday heat. As they all dismounted at the livery, old Gandy asked one of his deputies who'd stayed in town whether Boston Ferris had caught that recent eastbound out of town. The kid allowed Ferris must have, since he didn't seem to be around no more.

Tex Bishop caught up with Longarm in the tackroom, where he'd just racked his own saddle to dry. She was naturally packing her own light Morgan rig and, like Longarm, drew her own saddle gun from its boot once her less-tempting saddle had been stored in town for the moment.

When Longarm thoughtfully stepped over to the double-rig silver mounted roper they'd removed from that corovan barb Dutch had been shot off of, Tex asked how come he was helping himself to her ramrod's Winchester as well.

Longarm said, "Two reasons. We don't want it to go astray and it could be evidence."

He cranked the lever down to cock the hammer and throw a round in the chamber as he stared down between their feet. When nothing came out to join them Longarm said, "Empty chamber."

As he held the breech up to his mustache Tex looked puzzled and asked, "What are you getting at? Nobody packs a repeating rifle with a round in its chamber unless they like sudden noises. What are you sniffing for? Poor Dutch never got to shoot at anybody. Somebody shot at him, and killed him! Would you care to sniff at this saddle gun of mine while you're about it?"

Longarm smiled dryly and asked, "Have you fired it, recent, ma'am?"

She soberly replied, "Why don't you take a sniff and tell me?"

He shook his head and said, "I'll take your word for it, Miss Tex."

But she insisted. So he reached out to heft her Winchester one-handed and declare after one good sniff that it hadn't been fired since the last time it had been cleaned, with sperm oil, if he was any judge.

She took it back, saying, "Thank you. It's so nice to know you don't suspect me of shooting poor old Uncle Peter in the back just now!"

He asked, "Why should I think that, Miss Tex? We call considering such questions a process of eliminating. I have to go send me a heap of telegrams, now. Where might I find you and your kid brother here in town if I come up with any more eliminating?"

She said, "I can't speak for Buddy. He just won't listen to me now that he feels so manly. I reckon I'd best go on over to Fourteen Holy Martyrs and arrange for a proper funeral for poor Uncle Peter. At least, I hope he'd consider it a proper funeral. He never went to church and I suspect he was a Protestant. But we have a family plot of our own and I'm sure Mom would feel he belongs with our clan."

Longarm nodded soberly and gently warned, "You're going to have to wait until after a proper inquest, Miss Tex. But I'm sure Dutch would as soon be laid to rest amongst friends of the Irish Papist persuasion and . . . Great day in the morning and farther along we'll know more about it! As an old Protestant hymn song puts it!"

"What are you talking about?" she demanded in a puzzled voice, then added, "There was no mystery about us Bishops being Roman Catholic. Most of the old Texas land grant families had to be. Calico O'Connor is at least a lapsed Catholic and I'd be mighty surprised to discover Conchita Ramos is a hard-shelled Baptist!"

Longarm nodded, grinning like that Cheshire cat, and volunteered, "So was Kathleen Maguire, the best candidate for a recently retired Nevada belly dancer that I've been able to come up with and I'd clean forgot something I've known all along about Irish Catholic burial grounds! I asked an Irish gal in Denver about that when she asked me to escort her to a family funeral one time."

Tex Bishop thought hard, shook her head, and said, "I don't recall anyone named Kathleen Maguire buried at Fourteen Holy Martyrs. We haven't any Maguires at all in these parts!"

Longarm beamed down at her to say, "I'd be mighty surprised and downright disappointed if you did have. I

161

have to go send them wires, now. I'll be up to Sheppard's Hotel, if you'd care to talk about that belly dancer later. I have to find out where she is right now before I'll know for certain that I've figured things out at last!"

# Chapter 20

Nobody had seen Longarm for hours and another east-bound combination was due in as the shadows lengthened in Cairo late that afternoon. So Tex Bishop was concerned he might leave town before she could get him to tell her what he thought was really going on. But when she asked again at the hotel, the henna-rinsed Mabel Brookside stared across the counter at her thoughtfully and allowed Deputy Long was up in 202 and expecting her. So the younger honey blonde went on upstairs. She knew her way around Sheppard's Hotel from many a stay there of her own. When she rapped on the door of room 202 Longarm let her in and waved her to a bentwood chair near the bed he'd covered with yellow telegram forms. He was hatless in his shirt sleeves and he'd hung his holstered .44-40 over a bedpost. As she sat in the chair Tex smiled thoughtfully and said, "You *have* been busy at the telegraph office. Have you found out any more about that Happy Jack and his belly dancer here in Cairo?"

Longarm sat near the foot of the bed and commenced to gather all the yellow paper in one pile as he told her, "Happy Jack never intended to head for Cairo, Nevada. So nobody at all would have been waiting for him here. I have learned from a lawman I know in Virginia City that they did have some belly dancing at their Crystal Palace for a spell and, better yet, Happy Jack Henderson was only one of the hard-case hairpins around town at the time. I ain't been able to tie any ladies named Maguire tight to Happy Jack and his gang. But Kathleen Maguire did take sick and head on home after a spell of belly dancing over in the mining country."

The blonde from Nevada's cattle country asked, "Then you believe this gang leader who got away with all that money was lying to his followers when he said he meant to leave it in the care of a belly dancer here in Cairo?"

Longarm said, "He never told them he was meeting Kathleen Maguire or any other belly dancer here in Cairo. A court reporter took down the deathbed ravings of a shot-up outlaw phonetic. That's what you call it when you write down things the way they sound in shorthand, phonetic. When a man lies raving in his death throes you have to take care not to put down S.E.E. for S.E.A. or T.O.O. for T.W.O. Words as sound the same can have totally different meanings and it's easy to guess wrong when a suspect is making more sense."

The gal with more call for being in Cairo, Nevada, nodded in understanding and asked, "But if that outlaw was aiming to leave the money with that Irish oriental dancer somewhere *else* but here in Cairo, why did someone shoot at you from the water tower and when you were in that other room down the hall? Why did they just shoot poor Uncle Peter, mistaking him for you?"

Longarm said, "Nobody shot your ramrod by mistake, Miss Tex. Dutch Krinker was the intended target from the very beginning. All that razzle-dazzle inviting notorious hired guns to town and threatening you and your kid brother were meant as what stage magicians describe as misdirection. When I showed up like a coon hound following a false scent I was included in the shell game as more misdirection and it had me confused as all get-out! But I was never an intended victim. That shoot-out in the

Fremont hadn't been planned by anyone out to get old Dutch. But you'll have to allow it sure added to the confusion."

He leaned back across the covers on one elbow to continue, "The wild shot from the water tower was never intended to hurt anyone. When I was called to my window down the hall and got showered with busted glass from way over my head, that was just another attempt to set up the killing of Dutch Krinker so's nobody would suspect the devious doings of his one true enemy. Old Dutch was inclined to bluster, but he seems to have been a decent enough cuss, for a Texican, so I can't say I think much of the sick, twisted soul who went to so much trouble to set him up for that killing this morning!"

She moved over to sit on the bed beside him as she pleaded, "Well, for heaven's sake, get on with it! Who do you think shot poor Uncle Peter in the back this very morning?"

Longarm said, "Let's eat this apple a bite at a time, Miss Tex. A lawman can get in trouble accusing anyone of murder in the first with no more than some educated guesswork to back his charges."

She moved closer, insisting, "You surely have a pretty good idea, then, don't you?"

He nodded and said, "Oh, I'm almost dead certain, Miss Tex. But I'm still waiting on a wire from a banker down in Fallon. I fear I wired him after banking hours this afternoon, once I'd made certain that hundred-dollar note addressed to your kid brother never came from that post office robbery in Elko. The postmaster general's office wired back that there were no hundred dollar notes at all in their till in Elko when Happy Jack's gang held it up. So that told me I'd be better off looking for the source of it closer to here. I told you when you showed it to me that sending it might have been a mistake. It was meant to confuse me more about Calico O'Connor and her poor pathetic drinking pals. I *did* waste a heap of brain juice trying to figure how a barfly who couldn't pay her rent had come by a hundred dollars in paper. But when serious paper money can't be traced back to one place it can generally be traced to another, and it shouldn't be long before the firm in the county seat that everyone here in Cairo banks with wires me the proof I need to make an arrest."

"I think I hear that evening combination coming," Tex cut in as she got to her feet, as if expecting to see someone on or off. Longarm sat up straighter to say, "Boston Ferris left on that earlier one. I made sure of that before I came back here to this other room Miss Mabel was kind enough to hire me. How did you know I'd been staying in that other room down the hall, Miss Tex?"

By way of an answer the agile horsewoman stepped to the head of the bed in one long gliding step to draw Longarm's sixgun from its holster as she whirled on him, eyes blazing with hate, to hiss, "I just hate it when a man plays cat and mouse with me!"

Then she raised the muzzle to aim it right between Longarm's gunmetal gray eyes as she pulled the trigger without hesitation.

The gun never went off, of course. As she clicked the empty sixgun at him like an excited tin cricket Longarm slowly rose from the bed to ask in a weary voice, "Did you really think I'd be stupid enough to let you get betwixt me and my own loaded gun, Miss Tex? It's over. I was hoping you'd fall for that old dodge and save me gathering enough to convict you."

She wasn't listening, throwing the empty but seriously heavy Colt at his head, forcing him to duck. Tex Bishop tore out the door and was halfway down the stairs before Longarm was out in the hallway, to call after her, "Aw, don't make it a sweaty breathless chase to nowheres, Miss Tex. You need a lawyer more than you need to exercise before supper!"

But she kept going and, lest she catch that train coming in and make him wire ahead that she'd pulled another fast one on him, Longarm ran down the stairs to chase out after her.

She was already crossing Front Street, with more than one evening stroller staring thunderghasted as the two of them moved mighty sudden.

He called after her, "Give it up, Miss Tex. You ain't going nowheres!"

Then he saw the evening train was coming in even faster as the wild-eyed gal tried to cross the tracks ahead of it, probably aiming for that same culvert she and all the other kids in town had played in, growing up. Then Longarm saw to his sick dismay that she wasn't going to make it and yelled, "Don't try for it!" as she dashed on across the tracks, too late by a whisker. She was picked up and flung ahead of the slowing train, and then run over by the same when she landed limp as a busted rag doll on the tracks ahead of it!

By the time Gandy Burgess and the others had joined him by the siding the ashen-faced engineer had backed his Baldwin off what it had left of the late Theresa Bishop.

That didn't do her a lick of good. Her head was staring pensively at them from the center of the roadbed, with that honey blonde hair still pinned up as she seemed to be fixing to say something, up to her neck in railroad ballast. Her headless torso lay further along the blood-spattered ballast, missing one arm and both legs. One of her hands lay closer than her head, looking something like a stranded starfish in the fading light.

Longarm quietly asked the older lawman where her kid brother was. Gandy said, "Took the Ramos girl to a barn dance down the line, if I heard right. How come his big sister lies all along the Central Pacific right-of-way, old son?"

Longarm said, "She ran in front of yonder locomotive, because I was chasing her. I was chasing her because she just tried to shoot me with my own six-gun. She just tried to shoot me with my own six-gun because we both knew

167

I was fixing to arrest her for the murder of Dutch Krinker. How do you like it so far?"

The older lawman sighed and said, "It goes down bitter. But since somebody must have murdered her foreman, I'll accept her as the one if you'd care to elucidate some. What made you suspect she wasn't telling us the truth about that backshooting?"

Longarm said, "Eliminating. She shot him in the back, all right. They were riding single file or she reined in with some such excuse as a ladylike call to nature. Such details don't matter. Suffice it to say she only had to shoot Dutch in the back with the Winchester she'd been packing, catch your spooked cordovan long enough to put her warm gun in his saddle boot, stick his own clean and unfired Winchester in her own saddle boot, and continue with her charade. I'd started to wonder why his smelled of gunsmoke when she insisted then and there I smell her gun and see it hadn't been fired. A pal with the Denver fire department tells me they wonder about the one who turns in the first alarm whenever they suspect arson, too."

Gandy said, "I follow your drift. Why would an innocent and shook-up girl be so anxious to establish her innocence when she was the only witness to that backshooting she tore into town to report. What else did you find fishy about her story, old son?"

Longarm said, "Nothing. I circled for sign and found none. I looked in vain for spent brass. Her story was plain and simple, take it or leave it, and if she'd had no motive I'd have had no call to doubt it."

"What motive did she have?" the old-timer who'd watched the Bishop kids grow up inquired, adding, "Dutch Krinker was a mite bossy, but he meant no harm, and had she wanted to be rid of him she could have just handed him the shovel, right?"

Longarm shook his head and said, "Wrong. It ain't that easy to fire a family retainer who's raised you from a pup. Wiring hither and yon this afternoon I was able to establish, as I'd sort of suspected, that there were charges filed at state and county level, early on, accusing the Widow Bishop and her B Bar B riders of some free and easy roping and branding. Uncle Peter seems to have bullied some smaller outfits into dropping such charges in the sweet bye and bye, and then the B Bar B was big enough to play by the rules and neighborly enough to be at peace with everyone for miles. But Dutch Krinker knew where some bodies were buried, and, as we've agreed, was sort of bossy by nature. So whilst we'll never know, now, whether Miss Tex, there, ever tried to get rid of him less rudely, she found he didn't want to go gently out of her life. So, being bossy in her own right, she took advantage of her little brother's scandalous affair with a wild Irish Gypsy to make it look as if somebody was at feud with the B Bar B in general."

"An image is emerging from the mists." Gandy Burgess decided, going on to decide, "Calico O'Connor did rant and rave some when Miss Tex ran her out of town. I confess I fell in with her plans when I spied that hired gun and arrested him when his story made no sense at all because *he'd* been suckered like the rest of us!"

Doc Greenberg, their deputy coroner, came out of the gathering crowd to join them, blinking in dismay at the dismembered remains as he said, "I was just sitting down to supper when I got the word. Thanks a lot, already. I've been trying to lose weight and such a sight is just what I needed to skip dessert! As your deputy county coroner I find the cause of death, here, to be obvious. So how did the young lady get run over by a train?"

The local lawman said, "Trying to escape from this other lawman and it gets even better. Uncle Sam thinks she was the one who killed Dutch Krinker!"

Greenberg stared soberly at Longarm to say, "Thank you. All I was sure about was that he'd been shot in the back by a person or persons unknown. But why would this pretty little thing want to kill her poor old ramrod in the first place?"

Longarm didn't have to repeat himself. Gandy Burgess had been paying attention. He explained, "She was tired of being treated like a pretty little thing. She wanted to run things her own way. We all saw how bossy she could be when her kid brother took to screwing women instead of his baby fist. She and Dutch might have had words about that. We'll never know for certain, now. So why don't we gather up what's left of the bossy little thing and let this train be on its way?"

Longarm was walking away from trackside in the gathering dusk when Gandy caught up with him again, asking, "Where are you headed, now, old son?"

Longarm said, "Western Union. I have to explain why I'll be stuck here until your coroner and county clerk are satisfied with my depositions. After that I have to head on up the line to see about that post office loot Happy Jack said he meant to leave with a belly dancer he'd once admired. I'll ask him when and if I take him alive whether he knew Kathleen Maguire personal at the Crystal Palace or just took a fancy to her from afar."

The law of Cairo Township shook his head as if to clear it and then he objected, "Hold on. Your confounding me some more, old son. Where in thunder might that mysterious belly dancer be if she was never here in Cairo? And why in thunder would Happy Jack Henderson leave twelve thousand dollars with her if they weren't mighty tight pals?"

To which Longarm replied without hesitation, "She's up the line in Elko, where they robbed the post office. Happy Jack never meant to leave Elko with three to seven hundred bulksome pounds of hot money, and as to whether Kathleen Maguire was ever tight with Happy Jack or not, it hardly matters when a lady has no way of knowing she's hiding anything for you or not!"

170

# Chapter 21

Elko, Nevada, around two hundred miles by rail northeast of Cairo, saw damned few elks but might have used the name, Cairo, a tad more logical. For like the Cairo in Egypt land, it was a desert town on the banks of a real river. Albeit Nevada's Humboldt River, fed by runoff from the semi-arid Pequop Mountains, Ruby Range, and such, made for an anemic immitation of the Nile as it wandered on west to its dried-out sink around Lovelock.

Longarm got into Elko after sundown and seeing the county courthouse had shut down for the night, checked into the Winnemucca Hotel with his loaded McClellan and Winchester. He'd barely washed up for some late supper downstairs when someone knocked on his hired door. He was a tad surprised when he opened it with a weary smile. He'd sort of expected somebody else.

The ash blonde wearing a perky straw bonnet and a seersucker dress, with a carpetbag in one hand, was not a stranger to Longarm. He knew for a fact she was ash blonde all over. Her face was pretty enough for the cover of the *Police Gazette* but she wrote for the *Illustrated News* for space rates as a freelance stringer, and the last time she'd written a feature on Longarm she'd made him look sillier than the late James Butler Hickok. So Longarm didn't wave her on in. He politely but firmly declared, "I am overjoyed to see you're still breathing, Miss Lorna. But to tell the truth I have a previous engagement with another lady for this evening, no offense."

Lorna Doone, as she signed her equally dramatized news releases, stood her ground to calmly remark, "We need one another, Custis. For I know why you've come to Elko and I know my way around this clannish railroad town. Do I have to tell you how hard it can be to get folk to open up to strangers in these parts until they decided whether you might be a Mormon, a Gentile, or worse? Didn't you tangle with a bunch of old Brother Brigham's Destroying Angels not more than eighty miles from here, not long ago?"

Longarm calmly replied, "That was then and this is now. Brigham Young is no longer with us, and some pals connected with the Salt Lake Temple have assured me the main-stream Latterday Saints never cottoned to those Danite gunmen to begin with."

She went on standing there. So he added, "I ain't here to gossip with anyone I don't already know and, like I said—"

"You said sweeter things to me that week in Cheyenne," the ash blonde cut in with a sad little smile.

Longarm made a wry face and replied, "That was before I read that tall tale you wrote about me for your newspaper! I told you plain, as you were sweet-talking me in that four-poster, I had never in my life shot it out with Jesse James. The last I heard, the two of us were alive, wherever he might be, this evening and, as for me facing down Clay Allison in Denver that time, I told you Clay Allison moved up to Pueblo, not Denver, Colorado, when the army run him out of New Mexico. As for me or anybody else facing Clay Allison down, I told you right out that he was a total lunatic you'd be best advised to shoot like a mad dog or stay well clear of. Nobody ever faced Clay Allison down and nobody ever shot him. As

172

I told you, he got run over by a wagon when he fell under it, blind drunk."

She tried, "Well, he was killed in Colorado while you were riding for the Denver District Court and your more recent adventures down the line in Cairo came over the wire this morning. So I know why you got off the train here in Elko."

Longarm knew to his sorrow how the pretty little reporting gal was inclined to bluff. But his natural curiosity compelled him to ask her what she thought he was up to in Elko.

She said, "You came out here from Denver in connection with that post office robbery, right here in Elko. You followed a false trail down to Cairo. That federal want you killed in Cairo had nothing to do with the gang led by Happy Jack Henderson. So you've backtracked to the scene of *his* crime to see if you can catch him!"

Longarm quietly asked if she knew where Happy Jack might be found. When she confessed she had no idea, but added that the two of them made a great team when they put their heads together, Longarm told her he didn't want to put his head to hers any more and gently but firmly shut the door in her face.

She kicked it, hard. But when he'd put on his Stetson and sixgun to go see about that supper, she wasn't standing there. So mayhaps she was learning to take a hint, after all.

The fancy hotel near the railroad stop charged six bits a day for a single and had its own restaurant off the lobby. So Longarm was at a corner table with his back covered, enjoying a porterhouse smothered in deep-fried onion rings, when another familiar figure from the past came over bold as brass to sit down across from him, uninvited.

Longarm didn't cuss him out. He nodded across the table and said, "Evening, Boston. I sort of expected we'd meet up again, farther along. But we both know what meeting you here in Elko makes you, right?"

Boston Ferris cheerfully replied, "A bare-faced liar. But I had to say something when I got to Cairo by rail and found Jed Walters hadn't shown up yet. How was I to know those hick lawmen would find my logical little fibs so infernally suspicious? I was sort of ashamed of you when *you* bought that bullshit about mysterious letters."

Longarm said, "That was harsh, Boston. I only thought it might be best to have as few wild cards in the game as I could manage. I didn't see why such an innocent cuss wouldn't or couldn't produce the letter that might get him out of jail in Cairo. So I figured you never got one. How did you know the federal want you were tracking for the bounty got the one real recruiting letter that a gal in the market for a hired gun sent out along the owlhoot trail?"

The professional manhunter said, "I have friends along the owlhoot trail, too. A whore Jed Walters hid out with after that killing told me he'd shown her an invite to a shooting match in Cairo. He'd asked her if she thought it was a legitimate offer from an honest crook. She told me she'd told him that no bounty hunter who knew how to get in touch with him would be sending him letters when they could save the postage by just kicking in his door."

Longarm caught the eyes of his waitress and motioned her over as Ferris continued, "Thanks to her running in front of that train, we may never know how Miss Bishop got a hired gun's mailing address and, thanks to you and that .44-40 we'll just have to guess that Walters moved in slow and suspicious, riding down from Lovelock on horseback after I'd already been picked up by that foolish old liveryman!"

Longarm said, "Gandy Burgess wasn't so foolish. He solved the murder of Dutch Krinker with a little help from his friends, and as soon as Hernan Ramos guns Buddy Bishop old Gandy figures to make the arrest within forty-eight hours. Would you like something to go with your coffee, Boston?"

Ferris told their waitress he'd like a slice of cheesecake,

and as she turned away he asked in a desperately casual tone, "So, how come Happy Jack told his pals he was leaving their winnings with a belly dancer in Cairo if he never went anywheres near Cairo and you never met no belly dancers there?"

Longarm washed down some grub with his own coffee before he said, "He was being sardonical, but truthful enough. You know I can't cut you in on any recovered loot. Anything left belongs to the postmaster general. So just what might you have in mind, Boston?"

Ferris waited until the returning waitress had placed his own order in front of him and turned away before he replied, simply, "The bounty on Happy Jack, of course. He's wanted for everything but spreading the common cold, local, state, and federal. A well-to-do mining magnate in Montana has posted a private price on Happy Jack's head. Don't ever gun a mining magnate's baby boy in a saloon fight if you expect to grow old gracefully."

He dug into his cheesecake, washed some down and pronounced it tolerable before he added, "I figure if we threw in together we could both wind up content as twins with a big-titted mama. You sucking on the capture and recovery of all that loot and me sucking on more than one handsome bounty posted on the sneaky son of a bitch. How do you like my simple proposition?"

Longarm asked plain and simple, "Do you know where Henderson is?"

The bounty hunter answered easily, "Right here in Elko, just as you thought. He never left town after the robbery. I figure he already had a safe address set up to hide out in until things calmed down. He must have sent his gang on down the river because you can't hide too many strangers at the same address in a small town, or mayhaps just to give the posse somebody else to chase out of said town. I'm taking your word about him telling them the truth with a grain of salt."

Longarm said, "So am I, but like the old church song

goes, farther along we'll know more about it. How come you're being so good to me if you already know where to find Happy Jack, Boston?"

The swarthy manhunter answered simply, "I have more than one good reason to cut you in, Uncle Sam. To begin with he ain't alone, and just barging in on a wanted killer can take fifty years off one's own life. After that I have to consider the feelings of the shady lady who told me about an old chum shacked up with such a hot property. I promised her more sinister customers would never know she was the one who'd come to me for a piece of the action. I figure nobody will suspect he was betrayed by an Elko hooker if a lawman with your rep makes the headlines. All I want in the papers is mention for an assist, so's I can claim my just rewards. Do we have a deal?"

Longarm placed a silver dollar on the table, knowing that would cover their tab with a dime tip, and rose to his feet to put his hat back on as he quietly said, "We do. Is it far?"

Boston Ferris got to his own feet, saying, "Nothing's far from anything here in Elko. He's shacked up with a mulatto gal in her shanty betwixt the railroad tracks and a graveyard. If a certain railroader of the same complexion ever finds out about it, one or the other is sure to wind up in said graveyard."

Longarm led the way out to the darker street, running the bounty hunter's words through his mind again until they were striding side by side toward one end of the oil-fired street lighting of Elko. He asked the man he knew to be a liar, "How come this lady of color with a steady beau confides so much about her love life to an out-and-out hooker, here in Elko?"

Ferris replied, "You just answered that. How many respectable white women socialize for shit with either whores or a Pullman porter's true love? The hooker I talked to said her pretty mulatto chum was going out of her head with the big lonesome until Happy Jack came

176

along to cheer her up while her Pullman porter's out on the road. I don't know how much thought *she's* given to the arrangement, but I suspect Happy Jack was just looking for a place to hang his hat until the heat died down."

Longarm grimaced and said, "We'd better take him before he claims yet another victim. How far is it, now?"

Ferris pointed at a dimly visible steeple against the western sky and said, "Just past that cat-licking church. We want to swing south of it through that graveyard I told you about. There's this line of railroader's shanties along the service road beside the tracks."

Longarm had already assumed the graveyard would be Roman Catholic and Boston's remark about cat-licking churches made it safe to assume he wasn't.

They passed the dark church and dimly lit manse next door to enter the small graveyard, with most of the headstones naturally facing east toward the rising moon. Longarm scanned them in passing without seeing any names that meant anything to him. A heap of Irish railroad workers had died sort of young, building the transcontinental railroads, and enjoyed short rough careers along the tracks ever since.

As they approached a shanty set apart from its neighbors by a side garden, with lamplight gleaming from below drawn blinds, Boston Ferris murmured, "That's it. He's in there with the gal and a double-barreled Greener as well as his six-guns and a Ballard repeating rifle. What if I circled around to the back and you pounded on the front in the name of the law, sort of imperious?"

"It might work. But remember I'd like to take him alive."

Ferris nodded and said, "You want to make him tell us where he's left all that money, right?"

Longarm said, "I know where he left the money. I want to take him alive so's he can have a fair trial before we hang the son of a bitch."

Ferris allowed he'd try and circled out of sight in the

moonlight. Longarm counted a hundred Mississippis and strode over to the shanty. It would have been stupid to pound on the front door, itself. So he stood to one side, near a front corner of the frame shanty, and reached out to bang the pine siding with the barrel of his six-gun as he called out, loud and firm, "We know you're in there, Happy Jack! Come out with your hands up in the name of the law! For this is—"

Then his words were drowned out by the awesome ten-gauge roar of a double Greener, and for a moment a shaft of light beamed out through a considerable hole blown through the door panels. Then somebody doused the lamp and another door slammed open, somewhere, followed by three pistol shots in a row, out back, as a screaming woman in a nightgown tore out the front to go wailing off through the graveyard like she thought she was a banshee.

That seemed fair, seeing it was a mostly Irish Catholic graveyard.

After a long moment of silence, Longarm heard Boston Ferris calling out to him, "We got him, pard. He ran right into my line of fire, like we figured!"

Longarm strode through the dark one-room shanty by way of wide open front and back doors to find Boston Ferris standing over a shirtless cadaver in the wan moonlight.

Longarm said, soberly, "You mean like you figured and I ought to go stand in a corner for trusting such a big fibber!"

Boston Ferris replied without a trace of shame, "It was him or me. He came boiling out the back with a sixgun in each hand and where did you say he hid all that money?"

Longarm said, "Come on, I'll show you. It should be around to the graveyard and I'd like to make certain before the whole damned town tears out here to pester us about all that gunplay, you trigger-happy lying bastard."

# Chapter 22

"Over here? You expect to find all that money in this *graveyard*?" Boston Ferris demanded as Longarm led the way across the shanty's side garth and in among the moonlight grave markers. Over on the far path a side door of that church manse was spilling lamplight in a silent question as Longarm calmly replied, "I hope so. I was able to determine by wire from Cairo that the most likely bellydancer Happy Jack could have had in mind died natural aboard an eastbound train. So they took her off and planted her here in Elko some few summers ago. I figured this had to be the right graveyard when you told me it was Roman Catholic and that Happy Jack was shacked up close enough to keep an eye on his treasure trove."

He paused near a new-looking granite marker not too far from the back door Happy Jack had just run out from to his death and thumbnailed a matchhead to make sure before he said, "Here we are. Miss Kathleen Maguire from County Tyrone. It don't say she was a belly dancer. So Happy Jack must have known who she was when his mulatto gal told him they'd buried her here, unless Happy Jack asked at the county clerk's office the way I did, by wire in my case.

He shook the match out as he added, "Can't make certain without a court order to dig down a ways. But, come morning, that shouldn't be much of a problem. I doubt the money's buried half as deep as the poor dead belly dancer. Let's go over to the main road out of town to meet the local law and show them what we have over here in the shadows."

Boston Ferris said, "Hold on, what was all that shit about Cairo? We're standing over the belly dancer and hopefully the proceeds of a post office robbery miles away from Cairo, in the seat of Elko County!"

Longarm nodded and said, "A court reporter got that wrong. A dying outlaw, down the river in Battle Mountain and hence closer to Cairo Township said Happy Jack had left the swag in the keeping of a belly dancer he knew *under*, not in, the sign of Chi Rho. Here, I'll show you what he meant."

Longarm turned back to Kathleen Maguire's granite marker to light another match and hold it closer, saying, "Chi and Rho are the Greek letters standing for *The Christ* on lots of Greek and traditional Celtic grave markers. You see the monogram here, where you'd expect to see a Latin cross if they hadn't inscribed Chi Rho?"

Boston Ferris never answered as a pistol shot rang out instead, too close for comfort, and Longarm dove headfirst over the waist-high marker of Kathleen Maguire to rise from the dust on the other side with his own gun out!

The shapely figure in seersucker with a smoking derringer in one dainty fist yelled, "Don't shoot! I'm on your side!"

But Longarm kept Lorna Doone covered, anyhow, as he circled back to see Boston Ferris face down across the belly-dancer's grave with his own drawn six-gun clutched in one dead hand.

From off in the night someone was shouting, "Who's been firing all them gunshots and where might they be coming from? Answer in the name of the law, goddamn your eyes!"

Longarm called back, "Over this way. I'd be U.S. Deputy Marshal Custis Long of the Denver District Court, and I'm still working on why there's been so much shooting over this way!"

Then he turned to the pretty newspaper stringer to ask her why there'd been so much shooting over that way.

Pointing at the cadaver across the grave between them with her still-warm derringer, Lorna Doone said, "*He* was about to shoot *you* in the back! I have no idea *why!*"

Longarm stepped over the body to gently but firmly disarm her as he said, "I have. He was planning to shift my body and the blame and come back here later with a shovel. He knew where an outlaw was hiding but he needed me to show him to a hidden heap of money. How much of our conversation did you just overhear, Miss Lorna?"

She waved at a nearby crypt, looming like a marble doghouse in the moonlight, to say, "Not much. That's as far as I dared follow the two of you from your hotel. I couldn't make sense of those gunshots over by the shanty that girl just ran out of. When I spied the two of you coming back I laid low in hopes of overhearing more. So I'm confused about that conversation you had about belly dancers and Greek letters just before I saw him drawing his pistol when you turned your back on him. That's when I thought I'd better step in. Are you still mad at me, Custis?"

He holstered his unfired sixgun and took her in his arms to tell her, "I'll save my hard feelings for you until later on, when we're able to enjoy them in private. We're fixing to have heaps of company right now. So let me do the talking and, seeing I owe you, I'll give you another one of them exclusives, later on tonight, if you promise you'll get the story right for your readers, this time."

She gravely promised to be good and a couple of hours later, up in her own hotel room after they'd gotten shed of all the local lawmen and the Elko press, old Lorna was good as he remembered from that time in Cheyenne with two pillows under her trim hips and all that French perfume in her unbound ash blonde hair.

He hadn't told any of the Elko lawmen about the treasure likely buried under the body of the late Boston Ferris, seeing that twelve thousand or so would doubtless keep safer, pending an exhumation order in the morning, if nobody else knew it was there.

So it was the horny little newspaper gal who asked him, after she had come a second time, on top, whether the mulatto gal Happy Jack had been shacked up with might not know about the buried treasure just outside her back door.

Longarm asked her to roll off a minute so's he could get a smoke going for the two of them and, as Lorna did so, graceful as all get-out in the moonlight through the nearby window, Longarm told her in mock severity, "For a newspaper gal you ought to pay more attention when your elders are speaking. Didn't you hear that Elko lawman tell me they were holding her on a charge of indecent exposure if I needed her as a material witness, and didn't you hear they say they'd asked her what her white boy had been up to?"

Lorna snuggled closer atop the moonlit bedding as he lit up, asking him, "What did she say he'd been up to, Custis?"

He said, "She said she'd known he was hiding from the law but had him down as a horse thief. I know what you're thinking. The late Mister Boston Ferris was playing what he'd heard about that twelve thousand closer than I suspected to his own vest. But as you should have noticed as we were leaving both bodies in the care of Elko County, their coroner's office asked their sheriff's department to post guards out yonder until they can go over the death scene by the sunny light of day, come morning."

He took a drag on the cheroot as she snuggled even closer and told him how smart he was, adding, "By that time we'll be back out there with that court order and some shovels, right?"

He said, "I was figuring on paying the regular grave diggers to do the spadework. I'm sure the post office will be willing to help out with transporting a load too heavy for one man to carry far. But you can tag along and watch, if you've a mind to. Just don't have me beating the infamous Boston Ferris to the draw in a deadly duel with blazing sixguns if you don't want to admit it was yourself who shot the lying rascal in the back."

She reached down to fondle his limp privates as she demurely told him she wanted him to take all the credit for both outlaws, seeing he'd already told the Elko sheriff's department she didn't know beans about a federal case and they had no call to hold her for any damned inquest.

He took another drag and placed the cheroot to her softer lips as he said, "You'll be free to go off with your shorthand in search of a typewriter whilst I fill out one infernal form after another. I tried to tell you that time in Cheyenne that nobody gets to just gun a man and order drinks all around, in real life. But you newspaper folk keep shooting such bull and it cost poor old Cockeyed Jack McCall his life, in the end."

She began to stroke it hard again as she quietly asked if they were talking about the Jack McCall who'd shot Wild Bill Hickok in the Number 10 Saloon.

He said, "His name was James Butler Hickok, but you got the saloon right. Cockeyed Jack had read too many Wild West magazines and thought he could just shoot a famous gunfighter in the back and say *he* was a famous gunfighter, too. They hung him in Laramie after two trials for murder in the first. Let me put this fool smoke out if you want me to put that in you some more."

She did and they didn't talk about anything but mush for a spell.

But then, going at it dog style, the newspaper gal

183

wanted to know if that gunplay down Cairo way hadn't been fairly close to the way it was usually written up by her own kind.

He smiled down at her bare ass in the moonlight, pleased as ever by the variety womankind was blessed with by Mother Nature. For this particular gal was built nothing like anyone else he'd been dog style with in recent memory. The ash-blonde Lorna Doone was a tad taller but just as petite across the butt as little Wapzewipe had been. Her trim behind was as pale as the more ample ass of good old Mabel, and whilst neither had hourglassed to compare with good old Bonnie, Lorna's upper torso was downright lovely to look at and she sure was a tight little thing, for a gal so willing.

As ever, try as he might, he couldn't imagine her feeling any better inside as he admired himself sliding in and out of her from behind. He knew, objectively, there had to be other pussies as fine as her own. But the swell thing about changing partners was that every time a man did, he felt sure he'd never had it anywhere so fine, the first night. It usually commenced to feel like work by the end of a month in the same surroundings. That was doubtless why they called it a honeymoon. Women would never admit it, but they usually held out a month before they started nagging a man to get a steadier job or at least buy her a damned ring. So the feelings were likely mutual, and a man who moved on before a gal got to pissing and moaning at him could be said to be doing her a favor.

The one he was favoring at the moment insisted, "Custis, I asked you a question. Did you or did you not indulge in some mighty wild and wooly gunplay down the line in Cairo? From what came over the wire about that murderess getting run over by a train, it sounded as if you'd just lived through that Comanche attack on Adobe Walls!"

Longarm chuckled down at her inquisitive ass and said, "Shux, I hardly got to shoot at anybody down yonder. Miss Tex Bishop pegged more than one wild shot my

184

way, meaning me no harm until near the end when I started getting warm to what was really going on. Before I left I got a lady who sells hats down yonder to confess to a little aiding and abetting, once I convinced her I knew she hadn't been party to any serious crime and only wanted the bare facts."

Lorna murmured, "Was she pretty? Oh, do it that way some more! What did your poor milliner confess to, you brute?"

Longarm chuckled and explained, "She owed the murderous Miss Tex a heap of money. So she was willing to go along with what the younger and richer gal called a practical joke. She let Miss Tex pop out of this culvert behind her hat shop and hide under a blanket in her mannish blue denim outfit. I told her I'd wondered why her hard-drinking sister would be doing under a blanket downstairs when they had a loft bedroom right above their back door. She was anxious to tell all, once I had shown her generous pal up as a cold-blooded murderess."

Lorna bit down harder with her innards to coo, "You do have mighty convincing ways with us girls. Did you do this to the naughty Theresa Bishop before she ran in front of that train, dear?"

Longarm thrust and said, "Nope. I suspect she was too independent-natured to go along with anything a mere man might want. Once she and Dutch Krinker were both dead, others felt free to come forward about just how the poor old Widow Bishop and her tykes had materialized such a herd out of wide open space. So seeing an uppity hired hand had too much on her family to be fired, Miss Tex resolved to have him killed."

Lorna murmured, "Faster but not so deep, dear. That was why she wrote to those two hired guns, right?"

He answered, "Just one. Boston Ferris was after Jed Walters. He knew Walters had been invited to kill somebody in Cairo and tried to cover up that he was on Walter's trail by pretending to be another gunslick invited to the party. After Walters slapped leather on me, instead of Dutch Krinker, Miss Tex decided that if she wanted it done right she'd have to do it her ownself. But first she tried to muddy the waters by getting me to hunt for a dirty old woman who'd left town and a belly dancer buried here in Elko."

Lorna asked, "Why have you stopped? Don't you want to come again?"

Longarm got a better grip on her hip bones and replied, "I was losing my train of thought and you wanted me to tell you about that other gal."

He got to moving some more as he continued, "Once she figured she had us all confounded enough she simply shot Dutch Krinker as bold as brass under an open sky, swapped saddle guns with him, and all but dared us to prove it had been her. But simple eliminating made it a heap easier to figure bare-faced lying worked better than tall tales about a mysterious rifleman with no sensible motive. So I fibbed to her about a treasury note I suspected she might have drawn from her own bank. I forgot to tell her they'd wired me that they had no call to record serial numbers on fresh paper from the U.S. Treasury, and I didn't have to say one word about an empty six-gun I'd hung tempting. So we all know how things went after that and would you care to turn over and finish with me right, little darling?"

She said she would. So they did, and it sure beat all how swell bare tits bounced by moonlight or by sunlight at such times. Although those more mature as well as sunlit tits of sweet little Fran Garland hadn't bounced exactly the *same* that last lazy afternoon in Cairo.

So, kissing another gal entire in Elko, Longarm found himself sort of wondering what he might have missed by not messing with that heavy-drinking Garland sister, sleeping one off in the hat shop, downstairs.

But a man had to draw the line somewhere, and the

## Explore the exciting Old West with one of the men who made it wild!

one thing to be said for not messing with every woman he met up with was that no matter how far and wide he might wander, he'd just never be able to run out of women to mess with.